THE PRINCETTA

D1026072

THE PRINCETTA

Anne-Laure Bondoux

translated by
Anthea Bell

BLOOMSBURY

Copyright © 2004 by Anne-Laure Bondoux
Translation copyright © 2006 by Anthea Bell
First published in France as *La Princetta et le Capitaine* in 2004 by Hachette Livre
Published by Bloomsbury U.S.A. Children's Books in 2006
Paperback edition published in 2007

All rights reserved. No part of this book may be used or reproduced
in any manner whatsoever without written permission from the publisher,
except in the case of brief quotations embodied in critical articles or reviews.

Published by Bloomsbury U.S.A. Children's Books
175 Fifth Avenue, New York, New York 10010

The Library of Congress has cataloged the hardcover edition as follows:
Bondoux, Anne-Laure.
[Princetta et le Capitaine. English]
The Princetta / by Anne-Laure Bondoux ;
translated from the French by Anthea Bell.—1st U.S. ed.
p.   cm.
Summary: Rebelling against the rigid constraints of her life as Princetta of Galnicia, fifteen-
year-old Malva escapes with her maid Philomena and together they embark on a perilous
and adventurous journey that will change the course of their lives forever.
ISBN-13: 978-1-58234-924-4 • ISBN-10: 1-58234-924-X (hardcover)
[1. Princesses—Fiction. 2. Adventure and adventurers—Fiction. 3. Voyages and travel—Fiction.
4. Coming of age—Fiction. 5. Parent and child—Fiction.] I. Bell, Anthea. II. Title.
PZ7.B63696 Pr 2006   [Fic]—dc22   2005031581

ISBN-13: 978-1-59990-098-8 • ISBN-10: 1-59990-098-X (paperback)

Typeset by Hewer Text Ltd, Edinburgh
Printed in the U.S.A. by Quebecor World Fairfield
2 4 6 8 10 9 7 5 3

All papers used by Bloomsbury U.S.A. are natural, recyclable products
made from wood grown in well-managed forests. The manufacturing processes
conform to the environmental regulations of the country of origin.

CONTENTS

Part One: Leaving

Part Two: Wandering

Part Three: Coming Home

"Who would be insane enough to die without at least exploring his prison first?"

—Marguerite Yourcenar, *Zeno of Bruges*

To my father, His Alteza
the Coronador of Galnicia

A few months ago you summoned me to the Council Chamber. You asked me to take my place at the table with your ministers. In the circumstances, I thought you were going to do me the honour of including me in your discussions on the great questions involved in governing the country. I thought you wanted to initiate me into the exercise of power. My father realises that I've grown up, I said to myself. Now that I'm fifteen he thinks I'm as able to give an opinion as any of those grave statesmen. I was anxious, but flattered. At last you were taking me seriously!

I was wrong.

Much to my surprise, my mother the Coronada entered the Chamber, bringing you a large file full of notebooks and papers. I turned pale when I realised what they were.

On your orders my mother had searched my room. She had put everything I'd been writing for years in that file: my personal diary, my secrets, my dreams, my poems, my stories.

My soul was there on the table. In front of you. In front of all the Council members.

You opened the file. Your lips wore an odd kind of smile. You rose to your feet and, without so much as glancing at me, you began reading my notebooks out loud.

At first your ministers remained silent. Attentive. They didn't understand the point of what you were doing, but I realised at once.

As you read, derisive laughter escaped you several times. You stumbled over certain words on purpose, you emphasised any awkwardness. You did it so well that after a while the ministers began laughing too.

There I was at your mercy, all alone, crushed. And you thought it was so funny that you began gesticulating and pulling faces to show how ridiculous my writings were. I clenched my teeth so hard to keep myself from howling out loud that my jaws hurt for several days afterwards.

Then you abruptly closed the file, and your face grew stern again. "That's enough joking!" you said, and added, turning to the assembled company, "Gentlemen, you may be wondering to whom we owe these imperishable masterpieces. Their author is among us. Pray congratulate . . . our Princetta."

The ministers turned to look at me in surprise, their eyes reddened by tears of laughter. Some of them coughed, others were still having difficulty in containing their mirth. One of them—I think it was the Minister of Agriculture—had actually dribbled on his lace collar.

You told me to rise to my feet, and you said, "Time to make an end of such childishness, Princetta. You are the sole heir to the throne of Galnicia. Very soon you will be the country's official representative. Galnicia does not need such tall tales as these."

You handed me the file and told me to throw it on the fire.

I took a few steps towards the hearth. As I did so, I looked at the Galnician flag hanging on the wall, with its bands of yellow and green and the two arrows passing through them, and I cursed all that it represented.

I knelt down. The flames licked my hands as I let go of my notebooks. I felt them burn me to the core. I rose again, and you looked satisfied.

It was then I came to the decision that I had been putting off making for weeks.

I left the Council Chamber under the scornful gaze of your ministers and my mother, but I didn't mind that any more.

And so, "dear Father," this is how things stand.

You are a good Coronador; all the Galnicians think so, and they are right. You rule fairly and justly. Tranquillity and Harmony guide your actions. But as a father you're the very opposite.

Do as you like with this letter: burn it like the rest of my writings if it gives you any pleasure. I only hope that remorse will keep you awake at night.

I'm claiming my freedom. What a beautiful word! You'll have plenty of time to think about it now.

Malva

PART ONE

Leaving

1

A Hedgehog Haircut

To the north, the walls of the Citadel dropped straight to a sheer precipice. Perched there on its rock, it looked like a watchful bird of prey, unfolding its towers and wings above the valley and casting its imposing shadow on the calm waters of the River Gdavir. Once upon a time, invading forces from Dunbraven and the kingdom of Norj had been smashed to pieces against those walls; warriors and their mounts alike had perished here, and for months afterwards the Gdavir had washed helmets, armour and the bodies of men and animals downstream.

To the south, however, the Citadel looked very different. Its broad facades with their innumerable windows embraced a series of gently sloping terraces. Almond, olive and lemon trees grew there in neat rows, standing deep in lush grass. Basins of water adorned with blue and green mosaics had been sunk among them, to cool people strolling along and to attract birds. Recently the Coronador had become passionately interested in exotic plants, so one terrace had been turned into a paddy field and another into a palm grove. Here and there huge hedges of bamboo swayed in the light breeze of the coming summer.

It was here, in the Citadel, that the heart of Galnicia beat. For many years, far from the noise of conflict, the Coronador had governed according to the precepts of Tranquillity and Harmony, the two principal goddesses worshipped by his people. Galnicia was prosperous, the Galnicians lived happy lives, and yet . . . that evening, no one suspected that the country was enjoying its last hours of peace and freedom from worry.

Malva had finally managed to escape her mother's eagle eye.

Even ordinarily that wasn't easy to do, but today she had thought she never would. Besides the hours wasted with her dressmaker and her dancing master, an interminable session prostrated before the Altar of the Divinities had been inflicted on her. The Coronada had made her lie on the cold tiles and recite the incantations over fifty times. Malva was used to the constraints of the protocol that ruled her life as a Princetta, but today she had difficulty hiding her impatience. She clenched her fists, telling herself over and over again that soon all this would be just a bad memory.

At last, as evening fell, the Coronada was called away by other duties. She was too busy to give any orders, and didn't see Malva slip out of the Hall of Delicacies, where a whole army of domestic staff was completing the preparations for the next day's festivities.

Discreet as a shadow, the Princetta hurried towards the South Wing. She passed the kitchens and then went upstairs to the ballroom, where a dozen silent maids, skirts spread around them, were kneeling to polish the floor. In the corridors, on the stairs, up in the galleries she passed bevies of menservants handling pulleys to lower the chandeliers, replacing candles and beating carpets. None of them paid her any attention.

Outside, the gardeners were just finishing clipping the hedges, and were hanging lanterns in the branches of olive trees. As she passed an open window, Malva heard the fountains begin to play in a large basin of water, and further off, in a bandstand, musicians were rehearsing serenades. Their notes floated into the warm evening air, mingling with the scent of jasmine.

Malva felt the Citadel, and all Galnicia beyond the walls, tingling with joyous excitement. She herself was the central figure of the coming festivities, yet she didn't feel in the least cheerful. To tell the truth, her head was full of very different plans.

When she finally reached her alcove bedroom in the South Wing, she breathed a sigh of relief. A tall, thin girl was standing in the middle of the room, hands clasped over her apron. It was her chambermaid Philomena, waiting for her as they had arranged.

Without a word Malva bolted the door and sat down at the long mirror in its mother-of-pearl frame. She took the pins out of her hair, then picked up a pair of scissors and held them out to Philomena.

"Quick!" she breathed. "There's no time to lose. Night will soon fall, and the Archont is expecting us."

Philomena stood behind her without moving. Her bony face looked even paler than usual.

"I . . . I don't understand," she faltered.

Malva thrust the scissors into her hands impatiently. "Yes, you do! You understand perfectly well! Hurry up!"

Philomena had been in the Princetta's service for years. She had known Malva as a baby when she herself was a very young girl. The Princetta had always trusted her like a sister. Philomena had always been devoted to her mistress. But there were certain things that her beliefs forbade her to do, such as violating the principles of Harmony.

"Oh no, I can't!" she moaned at last. "Ask me to do anything you like, but not that!"

The mirror reflected both their faces. The chambermaid looked sickly next to Malva, who at fifteen still had the rounded softness of childhood.

"For pity's sake, Philomena, do as I say. The Archont told us that—"

"*This* isn't what we arranged!" the chambermaid interrupted, throwing the scissors down on the dressing table as if they were something evil and crossing her arms over her thin chest.

From Philomena's stubborn expression, Malva could easily see that she wasn't going to get her to change her mind.

"Oh, you're being ridiculous," sighed the Princetta in vexation. "You take mad risks for weeks without batting an eyelash, and now that it comes to just cutting my hair . . ."

Philomena shook her head vigorously. There was no *just* about it. In these last few weeks, to be sure, she had indeed agreed to everything. Malva had asked her to lie, and she had lied. If she had asked her to cheat and steal she would have done it. Philomena was ready to die for Malva, but wielding those scissors was simply beyond her.

"I've combed your hair so often since you were born," she recalled. "I've used so many ointments to untangle it, to make it smooth and supple . . . oh, you've always been so proud of your hair!"

"No, my mother has always been so proud of it," the Princetta corrected her.

"But what about later?" cried the agitated Philomena. "You don't have to cut your hair! You could always . . ."

She took Malva's hair in both hands, wound it into a coil at the nape of her neck and held it up on top of her head. Malva looked at herself in the glass. In the golden candlelight she looked as if she were crowned by a roll of silk. She remembered how a painter had painted her portrait the year before, for her fourteenth birthday. To render the colour of her hair faithfully, he had sent for a certain black ink made by mages in the distant Orniant Empire. "Essence of the night," he had said reverently as he applied his brush to the canvas. The portrait became famous throughout Galnicia and had become a symbol: the Princetta's hair perfectly represented the ideal of proud Galnician beauty.

"No one will notice under the hood of your disguise," Philomena tried again, in what she hoped was a persuasive tone.

With a brusque movement, Malva shook herself free. Seizing the scissors, she took hold of a lock of her hair and cut it off without hesitation.

The lock was left there in her hand, and then unfolded like the petals of a flower that has just been picked. Philomena stifled a sob. One by one, handfuls of hair fell at Malva's feet. She went on cutting and cutting at random, while a macabre kind of jubilation lit up her amber eyes. Whole tufts of black hair got caught in the folds of her collar and slid down between her shoulder blades, making her back itch.

When Malva finally put down the scissors, the mirror showed her a pathetic girl with a hedgehog haircut. She looked so odd and ridiculous that she started laughing.

"Galnicia can just do without its pretty doll!" she exclaimed.

At that moment she wanted to run to the far end of the Citadel and show herself to everyone, particularly her mother. She could already imagine the Coronada's horrified howl. "Malva! By Holy Harmony, what have you done?" But of course she couldn't afford such an act of provocation. It would spoil everything.

"Now go and get the disguise," she told Philomena.

Despite her feelings, the chambermaid obeyed. Malva watched her open the hidden door at the far end of the alcove and disappear into the secret passage. She felt confident. They had rehearsed their moves so often these last few weeks! And there was the Archont too; thanks to him, everything would be all right.

As soon as she was alone, Malva took the letter she had written to her father out of the folds of her dress. She spread the creased paper out in front of her on the dressing table. *To my father, His Alteza the Coronador of Galnicia.* She reread the opening, and suddenly felt alarmed. How could she make sure that this farewell letter didn't fall into her father's hands at once? Malva couldn't think of anyone to whom she could entrust it. Perhaps the Archont might have some idea. Meanwhile, she slipped it behind the mirror.

Her eyes fell on her reflection again. For the first time, Malva noticed the peculiar shape of her ears, usually hidden by her hair. Now they stuck out on each side of her face like two grotesque pennants.

Even if I fail, she thought, gurgling with laughter, who'd want to marry a jug-eared hedgehog? No one!

In her mind's eye she saw all the next day's many guests file past: the entire Galnician nobility entering the Sanctuary, the

Dons with their bull-necks squeezed into stiff collars, the Donias with their tulle hats, their curtseys, their simpering smiles . . . She imagined her mother and father, one on each side of her like guard dogs, facing the Divinities. *"The Coronador and Coronada of Galnicia are giving their only daughter in marriage! What a joyful day! Long life to this happy union!"*

Malva stifled a cry. She clenched her fists and pressed them firmly to her breast.

"Take a deep breath," she told herself out loud. "None of that is going to happen. You won't wear the Ritual dress and the crown of shells, you won't make the sacred offerings. You're not going to marry anyone."

It had all begun some months earlier during the Rite of Tranquillity. The Archont had dropped a remark inadvertently, and the truth had burst in on her. Malva could still hear his voice ringing in her ears.

"You must prepare for your wedding night, Princetta."

Malva had given a start of surprise.

"What?" said the Archont, amazed. "Hasn't your mother told you?"

No. The Coronada had not seen fit to tell her that plans had been made for her marriage. As for the Coronador, he never wasted time talking to his daughter. As far as he was concerned she was nothing but a bargaining counter, a commodity to be exchanged for political alliances.

In her state of shock, Malva had fallen into a towering rage. And in the middle of the Rite of Tranquillity, too! What blasphemy! Fortunately the Archont was a clever man, respected by one and all, and devoted to the Princetta ever since the Coronador had put him in charge of her education. He had

13

given some kind of explanation to the worshippers gathered together in the Sanctuary, and everyone had resumed worship. But Malva's own anger had not been extinguished.

Over the next few days the Archont had paid frequent visits to her. He hoped to make her see reason.

"All Princettas of your dynasty have married young," he said. "Your mother herself was only thirteen, and she didn't die of it. I really cannot understand your objections."

"But you know," wept Malva, "you know perfectly well what marriage will mean to me! I shall have to give up the only pleasures I've ever been allowed. I won't be able to study any more, or read, or say what I want, or go out without an escort!'

The Archont heaved an exasperated sigh. "I do know, Princetta. But you have no choice."

Malva was choking with rage. How could the Archont give in so quickly?

"When you've taught me so much!" she told him. "It's thanks to you that I discovered the joys of reading, writing, making up stories, thinking. You even gave me my longing to travel and a taste for freedom!"

The Archont smiled sadly. "I am only a humble tutor. It was not I who taught you all those things, but the authors of the books you read. And books are not the same as life, Princetta. You must give up your childish dreams. You must do your duty."

Malva felt betrayed and abandoned.

"Trust your mother," the Archont told her gently. "I am sure she has chosen you a good husband. The Prince of Andemark is only thirty-three, and they say he's an excellent dancer."

Malva couldn't have cared less about the Prince of Andemark and his dancing steps. Every time she closed her eyes she saw herself shut up in a room waiting for the wedding night, and dreadful panic churned in her stomach.

Once, when she was very small, she had watched the Parade of Gifts: envoys from all over the Known World had passed through the Citadel courtyard in procession. One of them had a huge reptile on a leash. "A female allicaitor that I caught in the Lands of Aremica," he announced. Then he produced a cage with a terrified hare crouching inside. The envoy had given the hare to the Coronador, saying, "Throw it in the air and watch!" The Coronador had thrown the poor creature. With a snap of its teeth, the monstrous reptile had swallowed its prey.

Alive.

While the nobility applauded.

Malva felt she was in exactly the same situation: they wanted to throw her to a stranger who would crunch her up in an instant.

In the end the Archont finally realised that she was prepared to do anything to avoid such a fate. One evening he admitted that he sympathised with her.

"You're so young, so beautiful . . . and so gifted. You've always had such an independent nature! I can see why you don't want to spend your life as a puppet on the arm of a man who's too old for you."

Malva had raised her amber eyes to him, brimming with tears. "Talk to my mother! Talk to my father!" she begged. "Ask them to call this marriage off!"

The Archont had shaken his head. His powers were great, but not great enough for that. Galnicia needed this alliance with Andemark, and the Coronador wasn't going to change his mind.

"Your father entrusted your education to me, but otherwise I'm powerless."

"Then what can I do?" cried Malva in despair.

"I don't know," the Archont replied. "But be sure that whatever you decide, you can count on my help."

For some time Malva had thought the question over from every angle. At last it seemed to her that the only solution would be flight. It was certainly the only way she could escape this marriage, but she couldn't bring herself to make the final decision. Paralysed by fear, she kept putting it off until the next day.

Then came the day when the Coronador summoned Malva to the Council Chamber and made her burn her notebooks. That ultimate humiliation had suddenly swept aside her fears and scruples. As soon as she was out of the Chamber she had gone to find Philomena to tell her what she was going to do.

"Very well," Philomena had murmured at once. "In that case I'm going with you."

And so the two of them, with the Archont, had planned their escape in meticulous detail.

Malva swung the mirror away, because her reflection was beginning to upset her. As she did so the letter slipped down behind the dressing table, but she didn't notice. She rose and went to the window to pull back the curtains.

The moon had not yet risen. There was still a fine ribbon of clear twilit sky on the horizon beyond the orchards. Towards the east stood rolling hills, dipping to valleys here and there as the River Gdavir meandered on its way. I may never come back, Malva thought. I may never taste the fruits of that orchard or see summer in Galnicia again. She felt a lump in her throat, but quickly swallowed; it was much too soon to start feeling homesick.

At that moment Philomena came back through the hidden

door. Without a word she put down the bundle containing the disguise: cotton underwear, a coarsely woven skirt, a beige top with simple sleeves, a plain bonnet. Over it Malva threw a woollen cape that Philomena had stolen from a peasant woman at the cattle fair. The worn, shabby outfit would help her to pass unnoticed. The cape had a hood which came down over her eyes when she lowered her head.

"What do I look like?" asked Malva.

"A girl of no importance," said Philomena, after solemnly inspecting her.

The Princetta smiled. From now on Malva, sole heir to the throne of Galnicia, was a girl of no importance.

Philomena collected her royal garments, wrapped them around Malva's locks of hair, and put everything into the bundle that she was carrying under her arm. It contained all their worldly goods: a change of clothing, a loaf of bread, some olives, a fair sum of money in gold pieces given to them by the Archont, and new notebooks. Malva was planning to write all her adventures in them.

"Come on," said Malva, making for the entrance to the secret passage.

Philomena followed, closing the door behind her. As darkness enveloped them, Malva suddenly realised that this time it wasn't just a rehearsal.

2

An Urgent Summons

The first houses in the Lower Town stood close to the surrounding wall that protected the gardens of the Citadel. They were tall, narrow, whitewashed buildings crowded close together. During the day, washing was spread out to dry on the flat stone roofs. Every evening, when the last rays of the sun shone over the horizon, women left their kitchens and went up to bring in the sheets and clothes that had been baking in the warmth. At that time of day they looked like a shadowy army moving on the rooftops.

Ever since he came to live in the Lower Town, Orpheus had been fascinated by the washerwomen. Leaning on his elbows at his bedroom window, he listened to their laughter, their songs, their chirruping conversation. Sometimes arguments broke out. Insults flew from roof to roof, echoing down the empty alleyways. Sometimes the women lingered on the rooftops for a little while, motionless and mute, looking down from this vantage point on the Coronador's fountains and bamboo hedges.

This evening Orpheus noticed that they had eyes only for the Citadel. No arguing, no songs; Orpheus heard only their exclamations of wonder.

"Lanterns!" said one woman. "Aren't they beautiful?"

"The fountains have been turned on," said another.

"Listen!" cried a third. "That sounds like music already!"

"Oh, do you think the ball has begun?" asked the youngest woman.

"Don't be so silly!" replied the eldest. "This is just a rehearsal. The wedding is tomorrow."

"I'd love to be invited!" sighed the first speaker.

"We can watch it all from up here," her neighbour consoled her.

"I do hope we'll see the Princetta!" the youngest woman sighed again. "She's so beautiful, so harmonious . . ."

Orpheus couldn't see the gardens from his own window, but the washerwomen's gossip told him all he needed to know about preparations for the wedding. And unlike them, he would be there. The following evening he'd be able to look at the fountains, the lanterns and the Princetta at his leisure.

Unless he decided to stay away . . . after all, he was only a substitute guest. It was his father Captain Hannibal McBott who had been officially invited. But when the Coronador heard that Hannibal was too unwell to go out, he had invited Orpheus instead.

"A representative of the proud McBott line of seafaring men!" said Orpheus out loud, remembering the Coronador's precise words. He shrugged his shoulders, vexed. If I'm supposed to be representing seafaring men I ought to be a sailor myself, he thought.

At that moment he heard laughter. Absorbed in his thoughts,

he had forgotten the presence of the washerwomen. They had heard him muttering, and now they were looking down at him from their rooftops.

"It's our shy young beau!" cried one of them teasingly.

"How sad he looks this evening!" commented another.

"Dear me!" said the third, giggling. "Do you think he's gone mad, talking to himself like that?"

They chuckled as they saw Orpheus blush. Before he had time to move away, the youngest boldly blew him a kiss, saying, "Come up and see us next time instead of spying on us from down there!"

Heart thudding and forehead moist, Orpheus quickly closed his window. So they'd noticed him there evening after evening, without ever giving any sign of it! They'd even called him "our shy young beau"!

He felt absolutely ridiculous.

He was always at a complete loss anyway when a woman spoke to him. No doubt it was lack of practice, because he had never lived in female company. His mother had died soon after he was born, and after that the only woman his father would tolerate in the house was Berthilde, an old maidservant who spent her time grumbling and polishing the furniture.

Orpheus had always both admired and feared the glances of girls. Their beauty cast him into dreadful confusion. However, it should have been easy to silence this bevy of gossips: he'd only have to stay cool and composed, assume a swaggering pose, and tell them that he was going to the Citadel the next day as a distinguished guest. That would have shown them who they were dealing with. Instead he was making them laugh! And that kiss! What an insult.

Feeling injured, Orpheus left his bedroom in haste and went

down to the sitting room on the ground floor of his house. It was a dark room, with its only window looking out on the other side of the road; he felt sure none of the washerwomen could see him from there.

When he went over to his armchair he saw that once again Zeph had failed to obey him. The big dog was rolled up in a ball, obviously deaf to all threats.

"Get off!" growled Orpheus. "That's my chair you're in."

The St. Bernard vaguely opened one eye.

"On your rug!" said Orpheus sternly. "Stay on your RUG!"

The animal merely opened his other eye. In the end Orpheus had to pull him off the chair by his paws before he could sit there himself.

The St. Bernard really belonged to his father, and had accompanied him on all his voyages. But when the Captain fell ill he had given the dog to Orpheus. "Zephyr's too old," Hannibal explained. "When I see him dragging his carcass about from room to room I get the impression he's imitating me. It depresses me."

Orpheus could refuse his father nothing, so he had taken the depressing dog into his own house. However, he couldn't get used to the ridiculous name of Zephyr. How could an old, semi-paralytic St. Bernard be called after a soft, balmy west wind? In private Orpheus shortened it to Zeph. Anyway, Zeph was a contrary dog.

In his heart Orpheus was torn: he liked Zeph's company, but at the same time he deeply resented him. The old St. Bernard had been a mariner himself! He had sailed all the seas of the Known World. His doggy eyes had rested on all that Orpheus dreamed of seeing: the wild countries and distant shores of the Orniant, the storms and hurricanes that rage at sea off the Lands of Aremica, the deceptive calm of the Sea of Ypree . . .

21

"You don't know your luck, you old mutt," he murmured. "The Coronador ought to have invited you to the Princetta's wedding. You'd represent the McBotts much better than me."

He sat back a little further in his armchair, mulling over his gloomy obsessions. As always at such times, he went over ancient history, in particular the day when his dreams had been shattered.

It had happened many years ago, when he was just eleven. Every minute of that day, every word spoken then, was deeply engraved on his memory.

At the time Orpheus had been a cheerful child, curious about everything and not in the least shy. He went down to the harbour to look at the boats every day. He felt in his element there, among the sailors and surrounded by that unmistakable odour of brown tobacco and wet rope. He went tirelessly from quay to quay, noting the names of the ships, their tonnage, their home ports and the names of their destinations.

That day he had met the captain of a schooner who was looking for a cabin boy. With all the dignity of his eleven years, Orpheus had fixed his clear gaze on the captain. "Hire me!" he had said. The man had looked back at him with a half-smile. Orpheus wasn't very large or sturdy, but he had studied so many technical manuals and read so many books about the sea that he ended up winning the captain over.

"Go and see your father and talk to him about it," the man had suggested. "We set sail in four days' time!"

Heart quivering with excitement, Orpheus had run along the alleys of the Lower Town, crossed the bridge over the Gdavir, and made straight as an arrow for the rising land of the Upper Town, facing the hill on which the Citadel was perched. The McBott house stood here at the foot of the Campanile.

He had opened the door and rushed into his father's study without even stopping to knock. It was at that precise moment that everything went wrong . . .

Suddenly, back in the present, Zeph started to growl, breaking into Orpheus's thoughts.

"Quiet!" he said.

But the St. Bernard bared his teeth, pricked up his ears and went on growling. Orpheus was about to poke him when he heard a knock at his front door. Zeph uttered a hoarse bark.

"Who's there?" asked Orpheus, going into the hall.

"Message for Orpheus McBott," piped a voice from outside.

Orpheus opened the door and saw a little boy standing squarely in front of him, his bare feet in the dust of the alley.

"Are you Orpheus?" asked the lad.

"What's the message?"

"A hundred galniks if you want to know."

Orpheus sighed, and searched his pockets for some loose change, which he handed the small messenger. The urchin's dirty face lit up.

"It's your father who wants you," he said in an important tone. "He's expecting you in the Upper Town this evening. It's urgent."

Orpheus frowned.

"That old lady told me to come and find you," the boy told him. "The one who always wears black and never smiles."

"Berthilde?"

"That's her. Told me she couldn't leave the Captain for a minute because he's very ill."

"Thank you," said Orpheus in melancholy tones. "Right, you can go now."

"Yes, right, I have to get home," said the lad, looking worried. "It's late. My mum and dad will scold me for being out after dark."

Orpheus raised his eyes to heaven and put his hand in his pocket again. He found two more twenty-galnik coins and threw them on the ground.

"For your trouble!" he said, closing his door once more.

He heard the urchin laugh and then race away down the alley. At the back of the room, Zeph was still growling in a low tone, but he paid the dog no attention. This urgent summons did not bode well.

3

Two Barrels of Rioro Wine

Malva and Philomena went down the secret passage, counting under their breath. It was a hundred and twenty-eight paces to the kitchens. At that point the passage branched; they had to take the left-hand fork, then count a hundred and eighty-five paces to get past the laundry, and it was another two hundred and thirty before they finally reached the end of the tunnel.

During their rehearsals Malva's legs had carried her along without faltering, but now she found it difficult to walk steadily. She was perspiring under her woollen cape.

The closer they came to the kitchens, the more distinct were the sounds of voices and the chink of china. Malva could easily imagine the cheerful bustle and excitement around tables where the silver was waiting to be polished. She had sought the servants' company so often when she was a little girl. She'd liked their wholehearted laughter and rough ways far better than the ingratiating hypocrisy of people of her own rank—much to the displeasure of the Coronada, who used to leave her shut up in front of the Altar of the Divinities for hours on end as a punishment.

"Faster!" whispered Philomena, nudging her mistress as she felt her hesitate.

Malva set off along the left-hand passage, and went on through the dark until she could feel a draught filtering in from under the last door: the one that led to the stables and the open air.

Here Philomena went ahead of her and pushed the door ajar. The smell of the horses immediately rose to their nostrils. The smell of freedom, thought Malva.

A shaft of moonlight fell through the planks of the stable roof, making the metal rings of the harness for the horses shine. At the back of a stall one horse was pawing the ground with his hoof. They could hear him snorting.

Philomena led her mistress outside, and abruptly pushed her down behind a heap of straw. "It's all right," she whispered. "The cart's there, ready to leave. And the Archont is standing guard as we expected." She took Malva's hands, looking steadily at her. "But are you sure you want to do this? You can still call the whole thing off."

The Princetta put her hood back, uncovering her hedgehog haircut. "I absolutely refuse to go through with the wedding," she said firmly.

"You'll be giving up the throne too," Philomena pointed out.

"I don't want the throne."

"You'll never live in Tranquillity and Harmony again," her maid said unsparingly.

"I know."

With every word they spoke, Philomena squeezed her mistress's hands more tightly. They had already repeated this so often in the privacy of Malva's bedroom. It was like a last prayer, or as if the two of them were swearing an oath.

"You may never see your mother again," the chambermaid murmured.

"The Coronada has never been a real mother to me."

"You may never see your father—"

"The Coronador has never been anything to me but the Coronador."

"You'll live as a stranger wherever you go."

"I'd rather a life of danger than a doll's life," Malva repeated firmly. "I'm not a pretty thing to be put on show in a shop window."

"Then . . . then we won't have any regrets."

Philomena pulled the hood up again to hide the Princetta's beautiful face. She peered cautiously over the pile of straw, and then beckoned to Malva to follow her.

The Archont turned when he heard them coming. His shaven head looked like a silver helmet in the light of the rising moon. Malva went up to him and, as usual, bowed her head to show respect.

"There's no time to stand on ceremony," the Archont whispered. "Everything's in order, but you mustn't delay."

He took the Princetta's arm and led her round to the back of the cart. Two men were sitting up on the driver's seat, reins in hand, waiting for the order to leave. The Archont had hired their services in the city, in one of the greasy taverns frequented by mercenaries. They had followed his instructions to the letter: the story was that they had been employed by a vintner to deliver the barrels of Rioro ordered for the wedding feast, and were going straight back with their cart this evening. At the back of the cart were a dozen empty barrels to be returned to the vintner's warehouse.

"Quick, get in!" the Archont urged. "I'll go with you as far as the guardhouse."

Malva started with surprise. "No further? I thought we arranged that—"

The Archont passed a hand over his head. His grey eyes looked deep into his young pupil's.

"Think, my child. I can't leave the Citadel, particularly not this evening. It would arouse suspicion at once. But never fear—the two drivers are trustworthy, and I've made sure the boat is waiting for you in the port of Carduz. You'll find Vincenzo on board, one of my most faithful friends."

Philomena was listening with some concern. "This Vincenzo," she asked, "are you sure he'll take us to Lombardaine?"

"Absolutely sure," smiled the Archont. "And to show him that you really do come from me, I'll give you this."

He took the thin cord with his Archont's medallion hanging on it from around his neck, and gave it to Malva.

"My name is engraved on the other side," he said. "With this pledge, Vincenzo would take you to the ends of the Known World."

Malva's hands were on the cart, but she couldn't bring herself to get in. She was sorry that the Archont wasn't going all the way to Carduz with them; she'd miss his reassuring presence dreadfully.

"When we're safe in Lombardaine I'll send your medallion back," she said. "Then you'll know that we've succeeded. All we have to do then is wait for news from you."

The Archont put his hand on the Princetta's shoulder. "You may count on me. I will say prayers for you during the Rite of Tranquillity. And now, hurry! It's a long way to Carduz."

Partly reassured, Philomena and Malva got into the cart, and the chambermaid raised the lid of one of the barrels.

"You first, Princetta," she said, holding her nose.

Malva hitched up her skirt and clambered over the rim. The barrel was just wide and deep enough to hold her. The aroma of Rioro wine still lingered and made her head spin, but she didn't complain. She'd have to get used to strong smells in her new life on the run.

Philomena leaned over to hand her the precious bundle, and then lowered the lid on to the barrel. For a second Malva felt as though she was imprisoned in a coffin. It was so dark, and she was so scared . . .

She heard Philomena open a second barrel and hide in it herself. There was a dull sound as she fitted the lid back into place. At a word from the Archont the cart set off down the stony path leading to the gates of the Citadel.

Preparations would be going on for much of the night in the Hall of Delicacies. With a little luck the Coronada wouldn't notice her daughter's absence before sunrise, when she was expected to begin putting on her bridal finery. How disappointed the lady's maids, the hairdressers and everyone else who pestered her would be to find that the bird had flown! It would be midday before they finished searching every nook and cranny of the Citadel. No wedding! No banquet! Nothing. As for the Prince of Andemark, the bridegroom whom Malva hated, he'd just have to find some other Princetta to marry!

Suddenly Malva thought of the farewell letter she had written. By Holy Tranquillity, she'd left it behind her dressing-table mirror! She wanted to get out of the barrel and ask the Archont to retrieve it, but at that moment the cart slowed down. The driver was stopping at the guardhouse. It was too late for her to climb out of the barrel now. Malva heard the Archont talking and joking with the sentries before bidding them goodnight, and a few moments later the driver was urging the horses on.

The cart went north across the plains on the banks of the River Gdavir. Oh well, thought Malva, it'll be a little while before anyone finds the letter behind that mirror. Jolted about in her stinking barrel, she felt she was suffocating. After what she thought was long enough, she lifted the lid so that she could breathe some fresh air.

Above her, the stars were coming out one by one in the black sky, and far away the Citadel was receding. She could see only its outlines now, and the trembling light of the lanterns hanging in the olive trees. Malva began to laugh quietly. She thought of the Coronador and the Coronada, and the look on their faces the next day. Their fury, like the expense of the wedding ceremony, would be immense!

"What's the matter with you?" whispered Philomena from the barrel next to hers.

"Nothing . . ." said the Princetta, stifling her laughter. "Come out and see how lovely it is."

Philomena lifted the lid of her own barrel. Her long, pale face emerged, but a bump in the road unbalanced her, and she hit her forehead on the rim. Malva started laughing even more.

"I don't see what's so funny," grumbled Philomena, rubbing her head.

"If you could see yourself, poor Philomena . . . oh, you'd laugh too!"

Philomena looked closely at Malva. In the dim light, with just her head showing, the barrel made it look as if she had a peculiar, round body without legs or arms. With her tousled hair, too, the Princetta was unrecognisable. All things considered, the scene really was rather comical. The chambermaid's face split into a smile.

"You're right," she said. "We're a pretty sight, the pair of us! I expect we'll reek of wine for days!"

They burst out laughing, while the two drivers, silent and impassive, drove the cart on towards the mountains. The landscape lay before them, bathed in moonlight: groups of yew trees, a few isolated stone cottages, wide expanses of wild grass. There wasn't a living soul in sight, and the road opened wide ahead of the horses, as if inviting them to gallop.

Later, Malva and Philomena shared a piece of bread and a handful of black olives.

"I don't think I've ever eaten anything so good," murmured the Princetta.

"That's because it's flavoured with freedom," replied Philomena.

It was true. In spite of the risks they had taken, Malva had never felt so light at heart. She closed her eyes. For the first time in her life she would not be sleeping in her own bed. For the first time in her life she was disobeying the Coronador, not to mention the precepts of Tranquillity and Harmony. Before falling into an uncomfortable slumber, she clutched the Archont's medallion in her hand, grateful to him for understanding her so well.

4

The Bitter Taste of Secrets

Orpheus crossed the bridge over the Gdavir River without sparing a glance for the silvery reflections of the moon on the waters, and started up a paved road that climbed straight to the Upper Town. Scents of almond and tamarisk wafted on the night air. He looked up at the Campanile on the very top of the hill. The family home of the McBotts stood at the foot of its tower. Orpheus had been born in that house.

His whole childhood had kept time with the sacred rites in the Campanile, the weddings and funerals, and the sound of the bells had been his lullaby. They were what he missed most now that he was living in the Lower Town: the chimes and the Angelus. When he was a child, he had liked to hear even the sad tolling of the death-bell. Someone's died, he used to say to himself, and his curiosity would draw him out of the house, hoping to see the coffin pass. As a child who had never known his mother, he found funerals particularly interesting.

But today he didn't want to hear a death knell. He had feared death ever since his father had fallen ill. The idea of being left without any family in the world was terrifying.

He walked fast up the steep streets to the Campanile, and when he knocked on the heavy front door of the house he felt as if the blows of Fate were echoing in his ears.

"Holy Harmony, there you are at last!" exclaimed old Berthilde, opening the door. "Quick, come in. The Captain's expecting you!"

Orpheus followed the old servant's thin figure. "How is he?"

Old Berthilde sighed and shook her head. "The doctor came again this morning. He didn't prescribe anything."

Orpheus anxiously passed through his father's study, a long room full of furniture, rugs, books and navigational instruments. On the walls hung wooden masks with strange distorted mouths; Orpheus shivered, as he used to in his childhood, when he met their eyes made of shells. The mementoes of Hannibal's voyages had always frightened him.

The next room smelled stuffy, of medicines and illness. Hannibal McBott was waiting for him, lying on a sofa near the fireplace.

"Good evening," said Orpheus softly, approaching his father.

The old man's head emerged from under his blankets. His face looked grey and his skin was as fragile as paper. His feverish eyes fixed on his son's face.

"I'm dying," he said straight out. "I'm glad you've come." A coughing fit shook the Captain's shrivelled frame. "Come closer, come closer," he gasped. "We don't have much time left."

Orpheus wanted to protest, to say that the doctor might be wrong and the Captain could yet recover his strength. However, he had never in his life contradicted his father. So he kept quiet, as usual, and merely sat down near the sofa.

"I have to talk to you," Hannibal began. "About something important. But I find it difficult to get the words to set sail from my lips—and there's a bitter taste in my mouth that won't go away . . ."

His emaciated hand tried to pick up a bottle from a tray beside him, but it was trembling too much. Orpheus uncorked the bottle and then, supporting his father's head, helped him to swallow a mouthful of brown liquid which smelled of burnt straw and honey.

"I must find the strength," Hannibal murmured. "I've waited so long. I ought not to have left it so late."

Orpheus listened, baffled. Perhaps his father's illness had clouded his mind.

"Do you remember our discussion?" Hannibal suddenly asked.

"What discussion?"

"The only real talk we ever had, just the two of us."

Orpheus frowned, realising that his father meant what they had said to each other on that terrible evening so many years ago.

"You mean *that* discussion?" he asked cautiously.

"Yes, yes. You were eleven. You burst into . . . into my study . . ."

". . . without knocking, yes, I remember," murmured Orpheus, in distress.

He could still feel the force of his father's cold anger when he had rushed unexpectedly into his father's study as he sat surrounded by his books, his instruments, his masks.

"I was so impatient," Orpheus remembered. "That captain would have taken me on board his ship . . . it was an amazing stroke of good luck! I ran back here from the harbour and then into your study without stopping to think."

Recalling these memories, the young man felt a pang. Why wouldn't his obsessions leave him alone? Only a short while ago, at home in his armchair, he had lived through the scene again.

"That's when you told me the truth," he sighed, looking sadly at his father. "But let's not talk about it any more. It's in the past, there's nothing to be done about it now. Let me tell you how your old dog is. He's slow these days, but his eyes are still bright . . . or would you like me to read to you, to take your mind off things?"

"No, no," said Hannibal irascibly. "Never mind Zephyr, and I don't want to be read to! What happened that day is more important. What exactly *did* I tell you?"

Orpheus wiped his moist palms on his trousers. "You told me about my birth," he said quietly. "I already knew it had been a difficult one, and that my mother didn't survive. But I had no idea that I'd had such a close brush with death myself."

He sighed, and laid his hand on his father's. All this old history just twisted the knife in the wound. Why bring it up again?

"I told you that the strain of it almost killed you," his father went on.

"Yes, that's what you told me," Orpheus sighed. "And the doctors gave me up for dead. But luckily for me you nursed me, you watched over me day and night . . ."

"Until you were out of danger, that was it, am I right? And then?" Hannibal persisted. "What else did I say?"

"You explained that in spite of all the care and nursing when I was a baby, I still suffered from the trauma of my birth. That part of my brain had been damaged."

Old Hannibal was shaken by a long trembling fit. "Your brain, yes, that was it," he murmured. "I wanted you to understand how serious your condition was."

His eyes full of tears, the old man sat up and propped his head against the sofa cushions. He ran his tongue over his lips like a man unable to quench his thirst.

"You didn't try to find out more," he said after a while. "You didn't ask me for any proof, any details."

Orpheus shrugged. "What could I have asked? All that mattered to me were the consequences of my illness. When you explained that I could never be a sailor . . ."

His voice broke. At the time his father had been a tall, strong man, a colossus, his face weathered by sun and sea-spray. In his company Orpheus felt weak and inferior. He would never have dared to doubt the Captain's word.

"You told me I would die if I went to sea. The pitching and tossing of a ship would open up the injury to my head again and probably kill me. That's what you told me that evening."

Orpheus saw his father's hands close on the blankets. He saw his chin tremble and his cheeks cave in.

"I remember exactly what I said," murmured the Captain. "For you the sea means death. If you board a ship you won't live more than two days."

Orpheus closed his eyes. For years, those words had been ringing in his ears, making him suffer.

Hannibal reached out for the bottle of brown liquid, and Orpheus gave him another mouthful. When he touched his father's shoulders he felt the skin burning with fever.

"Look at me," said the old man once he was lying down again. "Look straight at me, Orpheus."

He took a deep breath.

"It wasn't true," he said. "I lied to you. You didn't suffer any trauma at birth, you've never been ill. I made it all up."

For a moment Orpheus thought that his poor father was

delirous, losing his mind. He glanced at the bottle. Very likely whatever it contained was making the old man hallucinate.

"You don't believe me," Hannibal said.

Orpheus sighed and smiled sadly at his father.

"He doesn't believe me!" the old man exclaimed again, on the verge of despair. "But this time it really is the truth!"

He became agitated again. He started nodding his head, trembling, making uncontrollable movements. Orpheus felt numb. He didn't know what to do or say.

"Listen!" Hannibal suddenly cried. "Go and find my shipboard logbook in my study! The big volume bound in black leather! Quick!"

Orpheus rose, and went into the study like a sleepwalker. The journal was on the bookshelf just where it had been for years. Orpheus took it out and gave it to his father, who was lying with his eyes closed, trying to get his breath back.

"The proof that I was lying is in there," Hannibal murmured. "You can check it for yourself." He opened his eyes, with difficulty. "I must tell you everything, even if it means that you hate me. I owe you an explanation before I die."

Orpheus put the journal on his knees and waited.

"I always knew you'd want to go to sea," began his father. "You have it in your blood, like all the McBotts. And above all, I knew you'd make a good sailor and a good captain. I've watched you from early childhood, Orpheus. You learn fast, you have courage and energy. And above all you want to travel. You want to put to sea, to go on voyages of discovery."

Shaken to the core, Orpheus listened. His father had never talked to him like this before, so sincerely. He had never paid him such compliments.

"I rehearsed my lies well in advance," Hannibal went on, "so that I could feed them to you when the time came. I made up the story of your injury. It didn't hold water, but I knew you'd believe me. You had no one but me in the world, and you'd always trusted me . . ." He choked and coughed. "But I abused that trust. That's why I must try to put things right before it's too late."

At that moment Orpheus heard a noise and turned round. Berthilde was standing in the doorway, holding a tray. She seemed upset. Her hands were trembling so much that the glasses on the tray clinked together.

"Berthilde," gasped old Hannibal. "*She* knows! She knows I lied!"

Orpheus looked at the maid's face. She had worked for the McBott family for more than thirty years. She was as much a part of the house as the furniture. No doubt her eyes had seen all that there was to see, and her ears had heard all that there was to hear. Even the silences.

"Tell him, Berthilde," Hannibal urged her.

"Your father is right," she said, before bowing her head. "I knew."

The old captain began again. "I had secrets, my son. They're all there in my journal. I sailed the seas of the Known World for forty years under the Galnician flag. I was a servant of the Coronador. Officially, my duties were to keep an eye on foreign ships, watch over our colonies, keep order at sea and carry cargoes of merchandise. But I wasn't satisfied with so little. Unknown to anyone, I stole, I looted. I even killed."

His voice was muted and low. He raised his eyes to his son, who was looking at him with dread.

"I was a pirate, Orpheus. A thorough-going pirate. May the bitterness of my remorse carry me away now!"

At these words Berthilde burst into sobs. A glass fell off the tray and broke on the floor.

"A pirate . . ." repeated Orpheus, staring at his father in amazement.

"I acted against my country's interests," Hannibal confirmed. "I filled my own pockets, I betrayed the Coronador's trust in me. I even killed people who threatened to reveal the truth. You'll read it all in my journal."

He paused, tired out. Orpheus felt the leather-bound volume weigh on his knees like a block of granite. These revelations were so crazy!

"If you had gone aboard a sea-going vessel," Hannibal went on, his voice almost calm now, "you would have discovered my secret. Sailors would have talked. Or worse, I imagined an encounter between the two of us one day, far out at sea . . . What would I have done? Would I have given orders to fire on the ship on which my own son was sailing? I didn't want such a situation. I had to find some way of preventing you from becoming a sailor. That's the truth, Orpheus," he added. "You will hate me now, but at least you're free of the lie in which you were imprisoned. You can go to sea now if you like, because I know . . . oh yes, I know you will be a good sailor." Hannibal's grey head fell heavily to one side. His chest rose and fell with difficulty.

Orpheus turned to Berthilde, who was still weeping where she stood at the end of the room. The fire was slowly dying on the hearth. He rose, his father's journal under his arm. As he moved away from the sofa, the bells of the Campanile chimed midnight. He was so stunned that he felt empty.

"Look after my father," was all he said to Berthilde as he passed her. "And send me word when he is dead."

That was all he could do: leave his childhood home. Go away with the secret. Let his father die without any more words.

Outside the air was fresher. The empty streets seemed transfixed in silence. Orpheus went home without seeing anything. Nothing made sense anymore. He didn't even know who he was.

5

The Estafador

Malva emerged from sleep when she heard the cries of the seagulls. Eyes puffy with sleep, she carefully lifted the lid of her barrel. Dawn was setting the sky and the sea on fire. The little seaport of Carduz lay before her. When she saw the ships at anchor her heart beat faster, but she had no time to wonder what to do next. One of the drivers had just jumped down into the cart, his heavy brows drawn together.

"You stay hidden," he told her. "We'll get you on board all right." And with an abrupt movement he lowered the lid of the barrel and fixed the iron hoop around it.

Soon after that Malva heard voices, and then she felt herself being moved. When the barrel tipped over, she had to bite her lip to keep from crying out in panic. Other voices called out more orders. Now that she was properly awake, the Princetta felt stiffness and cramping in her legs, and her feet had pins and needles. What would the sailors think if they saw a girl emerge from a barrel? She had to wait. She mustn't speak, she mustn't move.

The barrel suddenly rocked, fell over on its side and began rolling. Inside, Malva was tossed around and around until she lost her breath. At one moment cracking sounds made her fear that the hoops of the barrel were breaking, but in the end the barrel came to rest intact.

"What's it got in it that's so heavy?" a man's voice gasped.

"Pork—a whole pig, if you ask me!" a second voice replied.

"Right, let's go and get the other one!"

Malva heard steps retreating. Pork! In spite of her weariness and the aches and pains in her back, she managed to smile. A Princetta disguised as a barrel of pork—one didn't see that every day!

She waited in the darkness and heat, half-dazed. At last she heard the men come back, pushing another barrel ahead of them. That must be the one with Philomena inside it.

"At least we won't go short of meat," said one of the men, catching his breath.

"Pork's pretty good with Rioro wine," said the other.

Then silence fell again. Malva heard only voices and footsteps overhead now and then. If she strained to hear she could make out the lapping of water and metallic creaking sounds, as if someone were operating rusty pulleys. She must be on board Vincenzo's ship.

It was too late to turn back now, whatever happened. The two drivers had left with their cart, and back in the Citadel the rumour of her disappearance must be racing through the corridors like the wind. Malva felt a lump in her throat. It wasn't remorse that she felt, far from it, but the fear of a future full of uncertainty. Philomena had family in Lombardaine, and they were hoping that her distant cousins there would take them in. But would Philomena's cousins understand? Would they agree to help them? And then what? How long would their exile last?

Suddenly she heard someone whispering close to her. She stiffened in her cramped hiding-place, short of breath. Then someone knocked on the barrel.

"Are you in there?" asked a man's voice. "I'm Vincenzo, captain of this ship. Are you all right?"

"Yes," said Malva timidly.

A crowbar levered the lid off the barrel. When the Princetta looked up she saw a dark face bending over her.

"Your trials are over," said the man gently. "You can come out."

With some difficulty, Malva managed to lift herself out of the barrel. Every muscle in her body made her face distort with pain as she got to her feet, and when she was finally standing she felt giddy. Vincenzo had to steady her by grasping her shoulder. His eyes immediately fell on the Archont's medallion, which Malva was wearing round her neck.

"I see your protector thought of everything," he smiled. "Never fear—we'll be landing in Lombardaine in six or seven days' time. My men won't talk. Anyway, they don't know who you are. So far as they're concerned you're just an ordinary passenger."

"What about my chambermaid?" asked Malva anxiously.

Vincenzo raised the lid of the second barrel. "Is that her?" he asked.

Leaning over the barrel, the Princetta saw Philomena lying motionless at the bottom of the barrel.

"She's fainted!" cried Malva in panic. "Quick, get her out! She needs fresh air!"

Vincenzo placed a knowing finger on his lips and shook his head. "Listen!" he murmured.

Malva frowned. Sure enough, Philomena's breathing seemed to be peaceful and regular. A gentle snore could be heard at regular intervals . . . she was fast asleep.

"Let's leave her there for the moment, shall we?" Vincenzo suggested. "Come up on deck with me. You need to get some colour back into your cheeks."

Malva picked up her bundle and followed the Captain up the ladder through the central hatch.

Outside, everything was bathed in sunlight. Malva blinked, dazzled, and then gradually made out shapes in the distance. The coast was already retreating beyond the bulwarks. She turned round. The sails were hoisted, swelling in the breeze like the cheeks of a giant about to play the horn.

"Welcome on board the *Estafador*!" said Vincenzo.

In daylight the Captain's face was still as dark as down in the hold, but his eyes, green as a cat's, gave his sombre face a mischievous look. Just like the Archont, he inspired respect and confidence, and Malva immediately felt safe with him.

She went to the handrail of the poop deck and leaned over. Sea-spray was foaming along the ship's side. She breathed in deeply, raising her face to the wind in delight. To think she was here out at sea, sailing towards the unknown, and not in the Sanctuary in the middle of a crowd of guests dressed in their finest clothes! It was extraordinary! She couldn't get over it—she had dared to escape, she'd dared to act on her own, ignoring both propriety and the precepts of Tranquillity and Harmony!

Opening her bundle, she took out the dress she had worn the night before, in which Philomena had wrapped her locks of hair.

She never wanted to wear that dress again. Never! With a sudden defiant gesture she threw it into the sea.

"Good riddance!" she called, laughing.

The dress hovered above the waves for a moment as her locks of hair fell and scattered in the ship's wake, and then settled on the water like an elegant bird. Malva watched it drift away. She smiled. It was over now. Everything that made her a submissive Princetta would be drowned in the waves. All she had to do now was live her own life! An extraordinary sense of intoxication made her head spin, and she lost her balance.

Vincenzo hurried to catch her and took her gently by the arm. "Come along, Princetta, not so impatient! You'll be leaving the *Estafador* soon enough."

6

Carabins and Musketoons

The Lower Town was in turmoil. In every alleyway, every workshop, every house the talk was of nothing but the Princetta's disappearance. Early that morning the rumour had made its way down the terraced gardens, crossed the Citadel's surrounding wall, and spread through the whole city like a lava flow. Now nothing could contain the clamour rising everywhere.

"What a terrible thing!" wailed the young women.

"Our Princetta must be found!" cried the men.

"It's a conspiracy," suggested the more suspicious among the Galnicians.

"Or some kind of practical joke?" wondered the doubters.

While servants searched the Citadel, the Coronador had sent his guards to look for his daughter. Armed troops patrolled the streets and bridges, combing the city right down to the harbour.

Only Orpheus ignored the general hubbub. Nothing, not even an earthquake, could have taken his mind off his personal cataclysm just then.

He had been prostrate in his armchair since the previous night, unable to move, with his father's shipboard journal on his knees. He hadn't opened it yet. He didn't have the strength.

His father's astounding revelations had submerged him in a whirlpool of contradictory emotions. He felt humiliated and angry, but at the same time relieved and confused. All these feelings assailed him in no particular order, making him wonder if he might be losing his mind. How else could you react when you realised that your whole life had been built on an enormous lie?

Lying in front of the hearth, Zeph didn't move either. There were some scraps of bread on his rug. During the night, seeing that his master wasn't taking any notice of him, he had gone to the kitchen to look for something to eat. Now, replete and drooling slightly, he was sound asleep.

Suddenly there was a knock at the door.

Dazed, Orpheus raised his head. He wasn't very sure where he was or what the time might be. However, as the knocking came again and louder, and imperious voices ordered him to open his door, he got to his feet. The leather-bound book fell to the ground with a thud.

He found soldiers standing outside his house, brandishing carabins and musketoons.

"Let us in!" said their leader. "By order of the Coronador!"

Without waiting for a reply, the soldiers entered the house, their hobnailed boots hammering on the floor. As Orpheus watched, they lifted the lids of chests, turned over the cushions in armchairs, opened all the doors and searched cupboards. They even checked that nothing was hidden under the carpet. Rudely awakened from his slumbers, the old St. Bernard showed his teeth, but as his hindquarters prevented him from charging at his attackers he merely changed position. Finally the men stuck their carabins up the chimney, and when nothing but soot came down they went upstairs.

On the first floor, the leader narrowed his eyes, looking suspicious. "That bed's neatly made up," he said. He turned to Orpheus, who was following the men from room to room, unable to make out what they were after. "Where were you last night? Looks as if you didn't sleep here."

Orpheus murmured huskily, "I must have dropped off in my chair. What exactly are you looking for?"

The soldiers exchanged suspicious glances. The whole city knew about it. Was this young man laughing at them?

"Carry on searching!" their leader ordered, pointing his musketoon at Orpheus. "I've got my eye on him!"

The others took hold of the mattress, lifted the base of the bed, emptied the wardrobe and drawers. This unceremonious search acted on Orpheus like a cold rain, bringing him back to his senses.

"I have nothing to hide!" he said indignantly. "What you're doing is against the precepts of Tranquillity and Harmony!"

"The precepts of Tranquillity and Harmony are suspended until further notice!" replied the soldiers' leader. "Until the Princetta has been found!"

Orpheus gave a start of surprise, but he didn't ask for explanations. Through all these years of peace, the soldiers' musketoons and carabins had been in disuse, mere decorations on guardroom walls. But this time there was a whiff of real gunpowder in the air.

After a while, when they had found nothing, the soldiers left, but not without threatening all kinds of reprisals if Orpheus had been hiding anything from them.

"And seeing you're so keen on the divine precepts," added their leader, "sleep in your bed tonight! A night in an armchair is anything but tranquil!"

Then he went out, laughing uproariously and leaving Orpheus in complete disarray. His house looked like the mirror image of his mind, all confused and topsy-turvy.

Now that he was fully awake, Orpheus heard the cries and lamentations out in the streets. So it was true: the Princetta had disappeared! How could such a thing have happened? When he went up to his bedroom, intending to tidy it up a bit, he saw the washerwomen gathered on their rooftops opposite. They weren't at work as usual, but standing on tiptoe, trying to see what was going on in the Citadel.

Orpheus quietly opened his window.

"They're draining the water from the fountains!" cried one of the women.

"Oh, Holy Harmony!" moaned another. "Let's hope the Princetta hasn't drowned!"

"Look, there's the Archont himself!" said the eldest washerwoman, pointing to the west facade of the palace. "He's questioning the servants."

"They're in trouble," commented another woman. "The Archont must be dreadfully anxious!"

"Look over there!" called the youngest woman. "There's some horse-drawn carriages coming!"

"That'll be the Prince of Andemark's party," confirmed a tall, thin washerwoman. "What a disaster! Oh, just think of the ceremony being called off!"

"If the Princetta isn't found we'll all be put to shame," sighed the eldest. "Dear me, I see sad times ahead."

Orpheus had heard enough. He closed his window again.

Sad times ahead. That last remark had a strange effect on him. It was as if, by some unfortunate chance, his own and his country's destiny had been thrown off balance together in a single night.

Suddenly there was more knocking on his door. Orpheus felt perspiration run down his back. Had the soldiers come back to arrest him? Did they suspect him? Everything was happening so fast that in his overheated mind, he even wondered if the truth about his father might have reached the Coronador's ears.

He ran downstairs and went to get the poker from the hearth. If the soldiers wanted to take him away they'd have to fight him first! Orpheus approached the door and flung it open abruptly, brandishing his improvised weapon.

But there was no soldier on the doorstep, only old Berthilde, waiting there transfixed, with a black scarf over her grey hair.

"Holy Tranquillity!" she cried. "Whatever are you doing?"

Orpheus quickly put down his poker and mumbled an excuse. The old servant's face was sad, and he knew at once why she had come.

"He's dead, isn't he?"

Berthilde nodded. "He died in the night," she breathed. "Only a few hours after you left."

Orpheus stood there for a moment in the fresh air with his arms dangling. He shivered, and sneezed twice. Since last night, in spite of the mild summer weather, he couldn't seem to get warm.

"What's to become of us?" wailed Berthilde, choking back her sobs.

Orpheus looked gravely at her; he had known her all his life, yet he felt as if he were seeing her for the first time. At that moment he realised that there was no one left for him to rely on.

He had never made friends, his father was dead, and now the lie had created a great gulf between him and Berthilde.

"I had a word with the Holy Diafron," the old woman told him. "Nothing's certain now, what with the incidents in the Citadel—the Coronador's forbidden all ritual ceremonies. But I managed to arrange for the funeral to be held all the same. It won't be for a few days, not until things have calmed down."

Orpheus nodded. With the precepts of Tranquillity and Harmony suspended, the whole organisation of the country was upside down.

"What about everything else, though?" Berthilde persisted. "What's to be done with the house? And the furniture, the books, the momentoes? Of course your father has left you everything."

"I don't want it," Orpheus calmly replied.

"But . . . but there's his fortune. It's a large one. Who's going to deal with it?"

"Do what you think best with it," said Orpheus. "Keep it all if you like."

Poor Berthilde had difficulty in keeping back her tears, but she did not reproach him. "You'll come to the graveyard?" was all she asked.

"Tell me when it is and I'll be there," said Orpheus. "Leave me now."

He sneezed again and then closed his door, leaving the old woman to return to the Upper Town in her grief.

7

Old Bulo's Story

Even after a few days Philomena couldn't get used to the pitching and tossing of the ship. She insisted on staying in her cabin, suffering from a bad case of seasickness. Malva, on the other hand, felt perfectly at home on the *Estafador*. She had exchanged her skirts for a pair of sailor's trousers and a canvas jacket. Thus clad, and with her short hair, she hardly looked like a girl any more, and the crew amused themselves by calling her their cabin boy. Delighted, she spent her time running from the fo'c'sle to the poop, watching the way the men handled the sails and demanding to be taught all about navigation.

The education that the Archont gave her had consisted mainly of lessons in mathematics, botany, legends, the geography of the world and the history of the Galnician dynasties. He had never taught her anything about the details of a ship's rigging. She wrote their new, poetic names down in her notebook with great delight: strops, pendants, shackles, halyards, sheets . . . sometimes the sailors let her climb into the sails, sometimes Vincenzo showed her how to find the ship's position with the sextant. Malva was in seventh heaven. At the end of the day, when she went below decks to see Philomena, pale and lying on her bunk, Malva was full of the pleasures of the voyage.

"Sailing is so intoxicating! One of these days I'm going to write a history of sailors and the sea. If you'd only come out of your burrow I could teach you the names of the sails. You'd have fun!"

Philomena snuggled further down into her pillows, a hand over her mouth to keep nausea at bay. But one evening, when she didn't feel quite so ill, she was finally persuaded by the Princetta to leave her berth.

"Come on!" said Malva. "Let's go up and join the crew. The cook's grilling sardines, and you need to eat something. Look how thin you are! What will your cousins in Lombardaine say when they see you? They'll think the Galnicians don't know how to feed themselves!"

Tottering, Philomena let Malva guide her up the steps through the hatch. They came out on deck just as the sun was sinking. The Sea of Ypree was covered with whitecaps, and the crests of the waves were crowned with rosy foam as far as the eye could see.

"Vincenzo says we'll be landing in Lombardaine tomorrow evening," whispered Malva. "So you're just in time to see the show."

Philomena smiled at the Princetta. She had never seen her mistress so merry, lively and light-hearted. The sailors had gathered in the middle of the deck to eat and drink. There was a smell of grilling in the air. The sardines of the Sea of Ypree might not be as good as Galnician herrings, but all the same Philomena suddenly felt hungry.

"Let's join them," Malva encouraged her. "You wait and see—when they've been drinking they sing and tell amazing stories!"

The chambermaid sat down beside the Princetta. The crew of the *Estafador* numbered about twenty men, whose coarse language, loud laughter and lined faces marked with old scars, didn't seem to bother Malva in the least. As for the sailors themselves, they thought it very amusing to see her burning her fingers as she ate her sardines, and the atmosphere was so good-humoured that Philomena finally relaxed. She even accepted a goblet of Rioro, and then a second and a third. Roses came into her cheeks.

"To Lombardaine! And long live Philomena!" cried the sailors, raising their bottles to their lips.

"To Lombardaine!" the chambermaid replied.

When only the sardine bones were left, one of the sailors picked up his mandolin and began plucking the strings.

"That's Silvio," Malva whispered into Philomena's ear. "He sings the lamento so well you might think you were in Lombardaine already."

The first stars appeared in the pale mauve sky. Silvio's musical voice soon silenced any talk, and the sailors took up his songs in chorus. Vincenzo quietly joined the group. Philomena thought he looked a little odd, and leaned over to Malva to say so, but the Princetta reassured her.

"Vincenzo works late every evening. He's shown me how to find a position by the stars. He feels responsible for us all—that's why he looks so tense." And she added, "Don't forget that I wear the Archont's medallion. That will protect us from all misfortunes!"

Philomena sighed, and gradually gave herself up to enjoying the sailors' songs, while Malva happily clapped her hands in time. Later, when Silvio put his mandolin away, she jumped to her feet.

"Philomena hasn't heard any of the stories you told me," she said. "If we're parting tomorrow, do tell her one of them!"

Bulo, the oldest of the sailors, rose to his feet. He had kept silent on the other evenings, merely making comments on his companions' tales.

"Then it's my turn to tell the ladies about my long seafaring experience," he said. And standing on deck under the stars, with a bottle of Rioro in his hand, he began the tale of one of his voyages.

"It's a long time ago," he began in a quavering voice. "Ah, in those days I was young, and I didn't fear the unknown. I went aboard the *Fabula*, a schooner chartered by a Polvakian ship-owner."

Malva was already captivated. She leaned her chin on her clasped hands and didn't move.

"We set off eastward for the Highlands of Frigia," old Bulo went on. "But as we were approaching the Frigian coast, a terrible storm broke over the *Fabula*. It rained so hard that the raindrops made holes in the deck! There was thunder and lightning. By all the gods, the lightning was so bright that some of my comrades were blinded! And as for the swell . . ."

He paused to get his breath and to toss back some Rioro.

"Oh, shipmates, I never saw such a raging sea," he murmured, his eyes widening as if he saw the scene again and was overcome by fear once more.

Leaning casually against Philomena's shoulder, Malva felt an enjoyable shiver run down her spine. These tales of storm and tempest reminded her of the stories the Archont had told her. She loved them.

"So did the schooner sink?" she asked.

Old Bulo turned towards her, his sparse hair standing up on his wrinkled head. "No, no," he said in mysterious tones. "If we'd sunk, would I be here to tell the tale?"

"I was thinking you were the sole survivor of the shipwreck," murmured Malva. "It's so exciting!"

Bulo shook his bristly head. "If you'd seen the reefs off the coast of the Highlands of Frigia, you'd know there was no surviving them at all."

"That's true," put in Vincenzo, emerging from his reserved silence. "Those reefs are at least as fearsome as the reefs along the frontier between Lombardaine and Sperta."

The other sailors solemnly nodded their agreement.

"What a pity we can't see those reefs close up," exclaimed Malva. "I'd love to know the thrill of fear!"

Philomena nudged her, and gave her a look to keep her quiet. Speaking of shipwreck while on board a ship was tempting fate. Vincenzo moved his face close to the little brazier on which the sardines had been cooked. He lit a cigar from the glowing coals, and disquieting glints played over his black face for a moment.

"I wouldn't wish you to make the acquaintance of such reefs," he murmured, his green cat's eyes looking straight at Malva. "You'd be torn to shreds."

"That's enough!" cried Philomena. "You're frightening us with your stories!"

"Not at all," Malva disagreed. "I want to hear the rest!"

Old Bulo took another gulp of wine. His voice slowly made its way through the deep shadows that had engulfed the deck.

"Well, the storm didn't send us to the bottom, but it blew us off course. For days on end the wind howled through the sails, until the sails themselves were in rags. Many of the men died.

We were driven east, always east, and there was nothing we could do. Hunger left its mark on our faces and fear clutched at our hearts. At last, one fine morning, the wind fell, and the stem of the *Fabula* ran ashore on sand. We'd been beached."

"So where were you?" asked Malva, her eyes shining.

"Ah, that's it, young lady! We didn't know. We had come to a country unknown to any map!"

There was a sudden murmur from the sailors, and Silvio burst out laughing.

"That old rogue Bulo, it's always the same. High time he left off talking about that old imaginary country of his!"

The others started laughing. But Bulo didn't seem inclined to leave it at that.

"You mark my words," he went on, "that country exists. I've been there and I know! And I swear on the heads of my ancestors that if I could only find the way back to it, that's where I'd like to end my days! Because—"

"Oh, stop your nonsense!" Silvio interrupted him again. "That's just an old yarn. You've lost your marbles, Bulo!"

Malva looked at the old drunk and the other laughing sailors, trying to guess who was telling the truth. Philomena was trembling impatiently.

"It's very late," she suddenly said. "I think we should go and get some rest. In Lombardaine tomorrow—"

"Oh no!" Malva begged her. "Do let Bulo finish!"

Vincenzo ground out his cigar. Sparks flew into the black night.

"Yes, let's hear the end of it," he decided. "And after that we'll all get some sleep, for there's certainly a long day ahead."

Thus encouraged, the old man finished his story. Malva listened with bated breath.

"We called that country Elgolia, young lady. And as I was saying, that's where I'd like to end my days. The climate is hot and dry, but the earth is fertile all year round, for hundreds of rivers flow through its plains. The sky is full of red birds, the trees groan under the weight of their fruit, and the folk of that land don't know the meaning of poverty. There's a lake of warm, bubbling water in the heart of a forest, called Lake Barath-Thor, and those who bathe in it come out ten years younger! And on top of Mount Ur-Tha grows a tree a thousand years old. Sit on its highest branch, and by some kind of magic you can see right to the other end of the Known World. So you can always find out how the people you left at home are doing, in Galnicia or wherever you lived. Last but not least, there's a wonderful bay, the Bay of Dao-Boa. A sweet wind blows gently there, and you have only to breathe that air to feel blissfully happy."

Old Bulo sighed nostalgically. He poured a final draught of Rioro down his throat and threw the empty bottle overboard.

"I'm not crazy," he muttered. "Elgolia exists somewhere, far to the east, at the outer bounds of the Known World."

"What I don't see," said Silvio derisively, "is why you didn't stay in that Elgolia of yours, if you were so happy there!"

Bulo suddenly hid his face in his hands, overcome by profound sadness.

"You have to deserve Elgolia!" he sobbed. "And I turned out unworthy of it! To my great grief I was driven away. It was my fault, all my fault! If only I could put things right!"

He fell to his knees on the deck. Philomena jumped nervously. The man seemed both sincere—and very drunk. What impression was this scene going to make on young Malva's mind? She drew Malva away by the hand, hoping to persuade her to go back down to their cabin, but the Princetta wriggled out of her grasp and knelt down beside the old sailor.

"What happened?" she asked very gently.

"I was greedy!" snivelled Bulo. "I tried to take the Vuth-Nathor away with me, and I ruined everything!" He seized the Princetta's wrists. "If you ever go there, be on your guard! Don't let the brightness of the Vuth-Nathor tempt you."

land in   "What are you talking about?" breathed the fascinated Malva.

"The Vuth-Nathor, the Vuth-Nathor," stammered the sailor, exhausted. And suddenly he collapsed on the deck. Malva let out a cry.

"Well, I think the joke's over now," observed Vincenzo. He snapped his fingers, and all the sailors rose to their feet. Philomena plucked at Malva's sleeve.

"Leave him to sleep it off. You can see he's dead drunk—he doesn't know what he's saying any more."

Malva shook old Bulo once again. "What is the Vuth-Nathor?" she persisted.

But the man was unconscious, lying there full length, as if merely saying that strange name had felled him.

Disappointed, Malva followed Philomena. As they were starting down the steps to the cabins, Vincenzo caught up with them. He leaned forward, his dark face close to them.

"Sleep well," he told them. "Tomorrow is the great day." He brushed the Archont's medallion with his fingertips. Malva never took it off. "Tomorrow, Princetta, you will discover how well your protector has fixed everything."

"We'll soon be landing in Lombardaine, won't we?" Philomena wanted reassurance.

*   *   *

That night Malva slept soundly. She dreamed of Elgolia, Lake Barath-Thor, the thousand-year-old tree growing on top of Mount Ur-Tha, and the Bay of Dao-Boa. But the next morning a terrifying noise woke her abruptly from her dreams. She sat up in her bunk with a start.

Philomena was snoring beside her. Malva felt anxious and nudged her, but however hard she shook her, Philomena stayed fast asleep. There was a second crash. Malva put her hands over her ears: it was as if the ship were screaming with pain.

She raced out of the cabin and went on deck. She stopped, staring: the *Estafador* was making straight for a line of rocks, their skeletal white heads sticking up above the water. The sea was bristling with them, and the crashing noise she had heard was the sound of the ship's bows already scraping on the rocks in the shallows.

Malva felt like screaming, but she didn't have the strength. She stayed there on deck, spellbound by the sight of the waves breaking on the reefs. The bows of the ship were close to disaster, yet nothing suggested that she was about to turn!

The Princetta raised her head. Above the horizon, the sky was cloudless. The mainsail, mizzen, foresail, forestaysail and jib topsail were all hoisted, but there didn't seem to be anyone in charge of them. The deck was deserted—there was no sign of the crew.

"Vincenzo?" she managed to call. She went to the poop deck. It was then she realised that the two lifeboats which usually rested in solid oak cradles amidships were gone too.

"Vincenzo!" she cried, louder this time.

The only answer came from the wind in the rigging, and the

vast backwash of the waves on the jagged rocks further away. Malva felt as if a gulf were opening up beneath her feet. She let out a terrified yell.

"Philomena! Philomena!" she shouted, racing back down to the cabins at desperate speed. "They've abandoned us! We're going aground on the reefs! Philomena!"

Malva ran into the cabin, took hold of her chambermaid and shook her with all her might.

"Wake up!" she yelled. "We're sinking!"

Philomena opened one dull eye. Its pupil seemed extraordinarily dilated.

"They drugged you!" Malva suddenly understood. "The traitors! They put poison in your wine!"

Tugging at her chambermaid's arms, she managed to haul her out of her bunk. The shock of falling on the floor seemed to bring Philomena back to her senses.

"What are you doing up at this hour?" she asked in a thick voice.

Malva took Philomena's face in her hands. "We must get off this ship, Philomena, do you hear? If we don't we have no chance!"

"Get off . . . the ship?" repeated the young woman. "But I . . . I don't want to . . . I can't swim!"

Malva slapped her twice, briskly. "Wake up! We're going to die!"

This time the mist veiling Philomena's eyes abruptly cleared. A spasm shook her chest. She crawled to the back of the cabin, turned and vomited on the floor. When she had finished she got to her feet, staggering.

"Hurry, hurry!" Malva urged. "Follow me!"

Still groggy, Philomena set off after her mistress. The

Estafador was grinding and creaking now, on the point of breaking up. When they came out on deck the rocks were alarmingly close.

"Help me!" Malva ordered. "We can float on this!"

She was trying to lift the open-work wooden grating that covered the central hatch. Philomena lent her a hand, and between them they managed to free the panel of wood. They started the same operation on another hatch cover.

"And now we must jump!" said Malva, making for the stern of the ship. Where they stood they were at least ten metres above the waves. The water was boiling against the hull. Pale as death, Philomena clutched her panel of wood to her breast.

"I can't," she murmured.

"You can!" Malva told her.

At that moment the prow of the *Estafador* hit the first reef head on. The wood shattered with a dry cracking sound, and the whole vessel started breaking up.

"Now!" cried Malva, and grabbing Philomena's dress in her free hand, she flung herself into the void.

They fell heavily into the tumultuous waves. The cold seized them, and they swallowed water several times. Then, clutching their panels of wood, they kicked to get away from the ship and the rocks.

Their clothes were clinging to them, sticky as seaweed, making movement difficult. But fear gave them strength. By encouraging each other, they managed to get out of the most dangerous area where the currents would inevitably have washed them against the rocks.

When Malva thought she was far enough away she turned to look at the ship. The *Estafador* was taking in water everywhere. A great gash had opened up the hull from the rail to the hawse holes. The sails were sagging, the bowsprit was hanging inert from the end of the stays.

"What happened?" asked the frightened Philomena. Contact with cold water had brought her back to her senses.

"Vincenzo tried to kill us," Malva replied. "He and his men left the ship while we were asleep. They must be far away by now."

The two girls were having a hard time fighting against the waves. Their fingers kept slipping on their improvised life-rafts, while the salt water got into their mouths and noses and stung their eyes.

"We're going to die," said Malva after a while, shaking. "I can't see land. No one will come to our rescue."

Philomena, though she was short of breath, kicked out and brought her raft up to the Princetta's. "You made me jump," she said. "Now I'm going to make sure you survive."

For two long hours they encouraged each other to keep going. Philomena thought it would be best to follow the direction of the rolling waves.

"Suppose there are counter-currents?" said Malva, feeling discouraged.

"Don't think about that," Philomena replied. "Keep swimming."

The sun rose in the sky, baking their salt-caked faces. Their throats were dry with thirst. Exhausted, they took turns singing to keep themselves awake. Then they fell silent, overcome by thirst and weariness.

Suddenly, just as she was falling asleep, Malva felt something gliding past her legs. She flinched.

"Philomena—did you feel that?"

"What?" asked the chambermaid, waking with a start. She had collapsed on her raft, and had nearly fallen asleep.

"I could feel someth—"

Malva had no time to finish her sentence. She let out a shrill scream, and her face twisted in pain.

"Malva!" cried Philomena, kicking out vigorously to get closer.

"My leg!" wailed the Princetta.

Philomena let go of her panel of wood and grabbed Malva's. She tried to haul her mistress up on it, while Malva groaned in pain.

"Something bit me!" she wept. "My leg . . . oh, my leg . . ."

Philomena was breathing hard. She almost slipped and lost hold of the raft, but she recovered just in time and finally got Malva up and lying across the wooden panel. Blood was turning the water red around her right calf. Philomena's stomach heaved.

"What happened to me?" cried Malva in panic. "I can't feel my leg!"

"You're leg's there all right," Philomena told her. "You're bleeding. It's nothing much—don't move. A rock must have scraped it . . . only a rock."

As she uttered these reassuring words she stared in terror at the Princetta's leg: a deep wound in the shape of a pair of jaws, with the marks of two rows of teeth.

Philomena put her hand on Malva's forehead, stroking it. "It's nothing," she murmured. "You bumped into a rock. I'll look after you, little Princetta. Don't worry, I'll look after you."

A lump in her throat, Philomena summoned up the strength to sing the lullabies she used to sing to Malva as a child, when she was afraid of the dark. She sang on for a long time, always expecting to see the head of the monstrous creature that had bitten her mistress emerge from the water at any moment. She still sang on, thinking that they were about to die like this together, lost in the middle of the sea.

Malva had fainted.

The sun was beating down so hard on the surface of the water that Philomena couldn't open her eyes any more. So she didn't see the shape of a boat in the distance—a boat coming towards them. Just as she felt she was about to breathe her last, two hands took hold of her and pulled her out of the water.

8

Funeral of a Traitor

Within a few days the weather had changed. First the sun gave way to a sky of gloomy and uniform grey, then the wind rose. But instead of chasing the clouds away, the wind had driven them together, piling them up above the country as if they were collecting at the bottom of a bowl, and it began to rain. Rain was unusual in Galnicia at this time of year. Soon superstitious voices were raised, claiming that the unsettled weather predicted more catastrophes to come. Fortune tellers arrived from the neighbouring countries of Armunia and Tildesia, drove their caravans into squares and avenues, and began spinning their tales: fifty galniks to tell your future for the next six months, a hundred to know everything about the years to come, two hundred if you wanted to postpone the fateful hour of your death. Long queues of anxious Galnicians lined up outside the caravans, and no one paid any attention to anyone who tried denouncing these charlatans.

In the Lower Town, some women wore scarves coated with

beeswax over their heads to protect them from misfortune. Down in the harbour, sailors carved mysterious signs in the stone of the quays to keep evil spirits away. The craftsmen's workshops did a roaring trade in all kinds of amulets, and customers were eager to empty the shelves. Dealers selling the red stones known as *cornalinos* piled their stalls high with those good-luck charms.

Night and day, troops of soldiers marched through the town, their hobnailed boots clattering on the paving stones. The Coronador was sure that the Princetta had been abducted, since he could see no other explanation for her sudden disappearance. The Archont, of course, did nothing to correct him, and encouraged him to send men to search the provinces all the way to the frontier.

People were beginning to murmur the names of brigands and to suggest conspiracies instigated by this or that foreign country. Ambassadors were sent to Dunbraven, to the kingdom of Norj, even as far afield as Polvakia. The Coronada spent her days saying her prayers before the Altar of the Divinities. The Coronador was beside himself. He trusted only one man to find the Princetta: the Archont.

It was in this tense situation that soldiers returned to the Citadel with the dress that Malva had been wearing on the evening when she disappeared. They had found it near the port of Carduz, washed up on a beach among the seaweed. Some locks of black hair were still caught in its lace collar.

The Coronador and the Coronada felt stunned as they looked at this relic. They examined it, they touched it. For a moment they refused to admit the truth . . . yet did this dress not prove that the Princetta had been drowned?

"Drowned?" murmured the Coronada in an expressionless voice.

"Drowned?" repeated the Coronador in the same tone.

The Archont discreetly signed to the soldiers to take off their helmets and lower the mouths of their musketoons. Then, with velvet tread, he approached the royal couple.

"We shall long mourn our beloved Princetta," he murmured. "Galnicia has lost a lady of great distinction."

The rules of protocol that had weighed so heavily on the relationship between Malva and her parents were now shattered. For the first time in their lives, the Coronador and the Coronada let their feelings overwhelm them. They were prostrated by grief.

Horribly embarrassed, the soldiers left. No sooner were they out of the Citadel than the news was flying all around town: the Princetta, sole heir to the throne of Galnicia, was lost forever in the waters of the Maltic Ocean.

A leaden silence enveloped the Citadel for several days. The Coronador had shut himself up in his own rooms, and the Coronada would not leave Malva's. Neither of them wished to see anyone except the Archont, the only man authorised to visit them, as more or less a member of the family. He could be seen pacing the silent corridors and galleries with a frown on his brow, carrying steaming bowls of concoctions to cure headaches, and watching everything like a hawk.

Baffled by the situation, the servants, the soldiers, the Holy Diafrons and the ministers began applying to the Archont directly for instructions as a last resort. At first he promised to take their questions to the Coronador and bring back the answers. But as the Coronador was no longer capable of anything the Archont had to act in his name. He therefore issued his first edicts:

Edict 1—Galnicia was entering a period of mourning of uncertain duration. The frontiers of the country were closed.

Edict 2—The precepts of Tranquillity and Harmony were suspended until further notice. No more marriages or funerals could be celebrated, since Malva had not been able to marry and, in the absence of a body, could not be buried either.

Edict 3—The only authorised ceremonies were those held to preserve the memory of the Princetta.

The Archont had the portrait painted of Malva on her fourteenth birthday hung in the Hall of Delicacies at the heart of the Citadel, with the dress that had been found in the sea beside it. All Galnicians were invited to come and leave votive offerings there.

This had all happened very quickly. In less than two weeks the country, which had seemed so firmly established and so serene, had been rocked to its foundations. It was as if, when she fled, Malva had taken with her the pillar on which the whole of Galnicia rested.

While the first edicts were being put up on the town walls, old Captain Hannibal's body was slowly decomposing in the McBott house. It gave off a dreadful smell. Plucking up all her courage, Berthilde opened the chest in which her master had left his fortune.

She knew that no law could resist the allure of gold. She took out a green velvet purse and went to see the Holy Diafron.

Night was falling when Orpheus heard a knock on his door. He hadn't spoken to anyone since the morning when Berthilde brought him news of his father's death. The rain put him in a bad temper; he hadn't ventured out of doors. He hadn't even gone up to spy on the washerwomen from his bedroom window, guessing only too accurately that news from the outside world would do nothing to improve his mood. He had spent his time dwelling on his grievances, and wondering what he was going to do with the rest of his life now that he knew he was perfectly healthy.

He approached the door with suspicion. After a moment's hesitation he opened it, to find himself face to face with the lad who had already brought him a message once before. The poor boy was shivering with cold in his wet rags, but he had the same mischievous look in his eyes.

"Still Orpheus, are you?" the boy asked.

Orpheus sneezed, hunched his shoulders, and replied, "Does the message still cost a hundred galniks?"

"No," said the boy, "it's two hundred now. All the merchants are putting up their prices. Me too."

Orpheus sighed, and searched his pockets for coins to pay the little messenger.

"It's from the old lady who sent me before," the boy explained. "She wants me to say it's this evening at eleven."

Orpheus frowned. "Rather an enigmatic message. Didn't she say anything else?"

"No," said the boy. "And if you ask me, hanging around in graveyards is not a good idea at the moment . . . don't you know it's forbidden?"

Orpheus easily understood what he was getting at. He added another hundred galniks. "I hope that this will buy me your silence."

A little colour came back into the boy's cheeks as he closed his dirty paw on the money. "I'll be silent as the grave!" he said confidently. And with these words he turned on his heel and disappeared round the corner of the next alley.

Orpheus sneezed again, and made haste to get back into his sitting room. Hanging on the wall in front of him was the map of the Known World drawn up by the Geographical Institute of Galnicia. He had bought this valuable reproduction five years ago when he decided to set up house on his own. He often stood in front of it looking at the lands and seas whose names made him dream: the Lands of Aremica, the Orniant Empire, the Ochre Sea, the Sea of Ypree, Gurkistan, the Maltic Ocean . . . the whole of the Known World lay there before Orpheus, from east to west, strung out all along the Great Latitude. Galnicia, at its centre, had always seemed ridiculously small to him. Today, that impression weighed on him more than ever.

"I can't go on living here," he said out loud.

The old St. Bernard growled.

"Something you want to say, Zeph?" enquired Orpheus ungraciously.

The dog pricked up one ear and then let it drop again.

"You'd like to leave, yes, of course!" sighed Orpheus. "Nothing surprising about that, but how about me?"

It was the only hope he had left—but how *could* he leave Galnicia at the moment? The fleet was requisitioned until further notice, all the borders were closed. The mourning imposed on the Galnicians by order of the Archont prevented any travelling.

Time was getting on. Night was falling in the alleyways, fine raindrops lashed the windows, but Orpheus would have to go out.

He went up to his room and sat in front of the mirror. A two-day beard covered his cheeks, and the pallor of his skin emphasised the brightness of his blue eyes. Every time he looked at his reflection Orpheus was surprised to find that he had grown to be a man. In his heart he still felt like a child. It was as if he had never really lived except in a dream.

He put on black clothes and gloves, placed a hat on his head, and then went back down to the sitting room. Before leaving he slipped the Captain's journal under his rain cape. He hadn't been able to bring himself to read it. What was the point? From now on the name of the McBotts was soiled with shame, and Orpheus needed no further details.

He was going to close the front door when Zeph let out another growl. The old dog had risen to his feet and was padding into the hall, his tail hanging.

"What do you want?" asked Orpheus, taken aback.

The St. Bernard raised his moist eyes to his master. The look in them left no doubt of the answer: he wanted to come too.

Orpheus heaved a sigh of exasperation. The old dog would lie flat on the floor for days on end, hardly moving, and now he wanted to go for a walk to a graveyard in the middle of the night, in this foul weather!

At last Orpheus shrugged his shoulders and let Zeph out. He had long ago given up trying to work out what went on in the dog's head.

The city was shivering beneath a moonless sky. Not a lighted candle behind its windows, not a gas lamp burning in the carriage entrances; all was shadows and sadness. Shoulders hunched, Orpheus went along the streets, avoiding the puddles and the ruts dug by cartwheels. In only a few days the whole country had turned fluid and muddy. Galnicia was taking water on board, and Orpheus himself, wet and unhappy, had taken a dislike to Galnicia.

He saw a faint light on the outskirts of the graveyard and told the dog to hurry up, but Zeph kept trailing behind, sniffing the ground or stopping to get his breath back, sitting on his stiff old hindquarters with a sanctimonious look.

Berthilde was waiting at the railings outside the graveyard, with four men who had agreed to be gravediggers in return for a purse of gold, and the Holy Diafron, who was clutching a dog-eared old prayer book to his chest. They all greeted Orpheus in silence, with a mere nod of the head. A venture of this kind made everyone nervous.

Holding two gas lamps, Berthilde went to the front of the procession, while the four men picked up the Captain's coffin. The Diafron approached Orpheus and put a consoling arm round his shoulders.

"We shall miss your father," he murmured. "He was a good, patriotic man, one of the Coronador's most faithful servants. He deserves a funeral with full pomp and ceremony, but today . . ."

Orpheus forced himself to smile. Yes, in other times the funeral of Captain Hannibal McBott would certainly have taken place in broad daylight, before everyone's eyes, and no doubt a crowd of curious onlookers would have made their way to the Sanctuary to watch the ceremony. But knowing what he now knew, Orpheus thought that his father was getting only what he deserved: a clandestine burial. Wasn't that how traitors ended their days?

They entered the graveyard, followed at a distance by Zeph, who was panting like an elderly asthmatic. The caretaker of the graveyard was waiting hidden behind the trunk of an almond tree. A hole the size of the dead man had been dug at its foot. The stone on the grave next to it bore the name of Merixel McBott, Orpheus's mother. It was cracked here and there, and overgrown with moss. Orpheus hadn't been here to pay his respects for a long time. Merixel had always been a stranger to him, a distant image. He had never known what the word "mother" meant.

"Quick, quick!" begged the caretaker when Berthilde was close enough to hear him. "The patrol could turn up any moment."

The maidservant gave him a purse of gold to buy his silence, and then put her gas lamps down beside the hole. The four bearers lowered the coffin into it under Orpheus's fixed gaze. When the wooden casket touched the bottom of the hole with a dull sound, the Holy Diafron came forward, picked up one of the lamps and opened his prayer book.

"Divinities of the World Beyond," he began, "tonight we entrust to you the soul of our beloved Hannibal . . ."

A north wind had risen. The Diafron was having difficulty making himself heard. Orpheus, head bent, couldn't concentrate on the words. There were too many contradictory thoughts and inadmissible feelings in his heart and mind. Now and then he glanced at his dog. Zeph was scraping at the earth near the other graves.

". . . open your arms to the Captain who commanded his ship courageously all his life, facing storms and tempests while bringing up his son," the Holy Diafron went on.

Orpheus saw that Berthilde was crying, and the caretaker of the graveyard had picked up his spade, impatient to get the hole filled in. The Diafron finally finished reading his address. He turned to Orpheus.

"Anything you'd like to add?"

Orpheus took a step forward and looked down at the lid of the coffin. He took the volume bound in black leather out from the folds of his cape, and held it above the grave.

The Captain's journal fell heavily on the coffin.

"Is that all?" the Diafron asked.

Orpheus nodded. The four men and the caretaker of the

graveyard immediately set about filling in the grave. The Diafron went over to whisper a few words in Berthilde's ear. Orpheus guessed that she was giving him a purse of gold too. Prices were certainly high these days.

When the earth was well packed down on the grave, Orpheus turned up his collar and prepared to leave, but Berthilde took his arm, detaining him.

"I'll come and leave offerings from tomorrow onwards," she said. "I'll see to everything here . . . but what about you? What will you do?"

"Leave this place," said Orpheus. "As soon as I get the chance."

"I understand," murmured the old woman. "Will you come to say goodbye before you go?"

Orpheus shook his head.

"Well then," said Berthilde, "I'll bid you farewell now."

She tried to kiss Orpheus on the cheek, but he escaped from her embrace. He left the graveyard with the old St. Bernard at his heels, and did not turn back.

9

The Goat's Hair Potion

Malva was lying on a straw mattress, and had not yet come round. She was running a high temperature, and her forehead was covered with sour sweat that trickled down her neck and soaked the collar of her jacket. Sometimes she lay there without moving, her eyes closed, sometimes she flung herself about as hallucinations blurred her mind.

"Elgolia . . . Elgolia," she kept repeating. "The Vuth-Nathor . . . Dao-Boa . . ."

Philomena held her hand, sponged her forehead, made her drink as often as possible, and bathed the nasty wound in her leg. Unfortunately her nursing was doing no good. The Princetta seemed to have drifted away into another world, and Philomena despaired of bringing her back to reality.

Every morning, the fisherman and his two sons left the cottage and put out to sea to haul in their nets. It was while fishing that they had rescued Philomena and Malva from drowning. They spoke neither Galnician nor the language of

76

Lombardaine, but a strange language full of accentuated vowels and sharp consonants. Communicating through gestures, Philomena had finally worked out that they were in Sperta, much further east than she had expected. If Malva ever got better, they would have to retrace their steps to reach Lombardaine, but at the moment such an expedition seemed a very uncertain prospect.

The fisherfolk's cottage was isolated, standing on a white cliff above the sea. A winding path led down to a cove with a stony beach, another climbed hillsides covered with short grass where scrawny goats grazed. That was all.

When she was not with Malva, Philomena helped with the cooking and washing and tended the goats. The bundle containing the Archont's gold pieces, their spare clothes and Malva's notebooks had gone down with the *Estafador*. They were destitute now, but poverty held no fears for the chambermaid. She worked hard, never flagging, so as not to be too much of a burden on their hosts.

Every evening the fisherman's wife sacrificed several fish to making poultices for Malva's injury. Philomena thought she understood the woman's logic: since Malva had been injured by a sea creature, she must be treated with sea creatures too. Anchovies, bream, scorpion fish and cod, reduced to a pulp, were applied to Malva's leg.

"*Akanaiké!*" the fisherman's wife said as she put the poultice on.

Philomena repeated the strange word like a magic spell, hoping that the fish would take effect.

But at the end of two weeks, when the Princetta was still delirious and was becoming alarmingly weak, the younger son of the family took his stick and an empty wheelbarrow and left the house.

"Thera," the fisherman's wife explained to Philomena. She made vague gestures, indicating the way her son had gone.

"You mean he's gone to Thera?" asked Philomena. "Is it the name of a town? And what's the wheelbarrow for? Is he going to look for other medicines?"

"Thera, Thera," the woman repeated in encouraging tones.

Her younger son came home next day, wheeling the barrow in front of him along the steep paths and making his way carefully down to the cottage. Philomena saw a black shape which looked like a heap of fabric in the barrow. But as the young man came closer she saw that she was wrong: it was not fabric. There was someone sitting in the wheelbarrow.

"Thera," said the fisherman's wife, placing a kindly hand on Philomena's arm.

So Thera was not a place, but a very old woman, so old and tired that she could no longer walk. Her lined face, yellow as a lemon, was buried under a mass of dark scarves.

The fisherman's son took her into the house and showed her where Malva was lying. With his father's help, he carried the old woman over to the sick girl, and then unloaded all kinds of implements from the barrow: phials, large jars, pincers, ladles, oilcans and retorts were soon piled on the packed earth floor.

Philomena timidly went over, intrigued by the old woman's presence. For several long moments Thera did not move, and her eyes remained closed. She had placed her sallow, spotted hand on Malva's forehead. Only her wheezing breath broke the silence that had fallen on the cottage, and Philomena wondered if the old lady had simply gone to sleep.

But suddenly she opened her eyes. "*Pneuma*," she said, in a croaking voice.

She began rummaging around in her pile of implements, and

picked up an earthenware pot into which she poured the contents of one of her phials. Philomena narrowed her eyes to see better. The liquid looked viscous, like oil. The old woman added a few drops of something black, a bag of herbs, some red powder, and a few white particles of what looked to Philomena like goat's hairs.

Meanwhile the fisherman's wife had lit a fire under a cauldron to boil water. Old Thera handed her the pot containing the mixture, and the woman mixed it all together above the hot water.

A revolting smell immediately filled the room. Philomena coughed and grimaced, but she never took her eyes off the old woman. When Thera put the concoction to Malva's lips, Philomena flinched slightly with disgust.

"*Pneuma, atman, psuché, nephech,*" chanted Thera as the liquid flowed into the Princetta's mouth.

Then she packed up her equipment, and the fisherman's son conscientiously put it back in the barrow. Malva had not moved since the old woman entered the cottage. She was breathing quietly with her arms lying beside her body.

Thera put her left hand under her scarves and brought out a little carved wooden figure of a fish, which she placed on the ground. She reached for another bag of herbs with her left hand, sprinkled them over the little figure, and then signed to the fisherman's wife to put a glowing coal to them. As they burned, the herbs gave off a dense, aromatic smoke.

"*Keryke asclepios hebé,*" the old woman murmured as she dispersed the smoke with her twisted hands.

Then she closed her eyes and waited to be put back in the wheelbarrow. Without another word, the fisherman's son carried the mysterious guest out of the house, and they went away again up the steep paths, leaving Philomena stunned and puzzled.

A few hours later Malva opened her eyes. Her forehead was dry and there was a little colour in her cheeks.

"I'm thirsty," she said.

Within three days scar tissue had formed over the Princetta's injury. She recovered her spirits, and it was a pleasure to see her hearty appetite. Philomena couldn't stop weeping and expressing her gratitude to the old Spertan healer who had saved the Princetta's life. It was a miracle.

"I remember it all," said Malva. "Our last evening on board the *Estafador*, those grilled sardines, the songs, Bulo's story . . . and then the reefs, Vincenzo's disappearance, our struggle against drowning."

She looked up at the ceiling for some time, lost in thought, brows drawn together. Then her fingers went to her neck and lingered on the Archont's medallion. Philomena made haste to talk about something else, fearing that gloomy thoughts might be bad for the Princetta's health.

"When you can walk I shall take you to Lombardaine," she said. "It's not so far to go, you'll see. The fisherman and his wife will find us a mule. Then you can ride it and I'll lead you there."

Malva smiled, but she went on gazing at the ceiling as if her future were written on it, and Philomena began to fear that her mistress might have some strange fancy in mind. She was so young; so impressionable. She had read so many fantastic tales with the Archont! Philomena only hoped that all these disasters hadn't clouded her reason.

One morning Malva was able to get up at last. Clinging to Philomena's arm, she slowly walked across the room. Her right leg was weak, but she made it to the door. Sunlight was flooding the hills, falling on the chalk cliffs and making the surface of the sea so bright that it dazzled the eyes. A little way from the cottage the fisherman's wife was spreading out her washing on a flat rock. When she saw Malva on her feet she just smiled and gave a friendly little wave.

"So here we are in Sperta," murmured Malva, with a note of surprise in her voice.

All her geography lessons with the Archont came back to her. In her mind's eye she saw the map of the countries of the Known World, hanging from the Great Latitude like sheets from a washing line: Galnicia, Lombardaine, Monteplano east of Polvakia, and then Sperta. And there, still further to the east, the mountains of Gurkistan that bordered the vast expanses of the Great Azizian Steppes.

"Lombardaine is over there," said Philomena, pointing east. "Four or five days' journey on foot."

Malva did not even turn her head. "We're not going to Lombardaine," she said brusquely.

Philomena gave a start of surprise.

"You see, I've been thinking," Malva went on in a firm voice. "Why would Vincenzo have abandoned us on board the *Estafador*? He had nothing to gain by it . . . unless someone had paid him to do it." Her hand went to the medallion hanging round her neck. "And only one person could have ordered Vincenzo to kill us. It's hard for me to say so, but the Archont betrayed us."

Philomena leaned against the door frame, her legs suddenly feeling weak. Such thoughts had certainly crossed her own mind more than once, but she hadn't felt like pursuing them. All that mattered was for Malva to live. The rest of it seemed so complicated, so alarming that she had done all she could to put off the moment of discussing it.

"I trusted the Archont for ten years. I trusted him like a father," Malva murmured. "I thought he understood me. I even thought he loved me . . ."

She stifled a sob, and then laughed bitterly. She owed the Archont so many happy moments! She had thought he was sincere, but no. Her jaw hardened, and she suddenly cried angrily, "And now I hate him! The Archont used my rebellious feelings for his own ends! I even wonder whether he read me all those books just to make me discontented with the life I could expect in Galnicia . . . It was he who encouraged me to write, to make up stories, to believe in all the fabulous legends. What was he doing? He knew perfectly well that the Coronador would never allow such fancies! He knew perfectly well that my parents were going to marry me off, yet he never warned me!"

A host of memories flooded into her mind. She sadly revisited the scenes of her childhood, when the Archont used to take her on his knee to tell her stories of adventure. He had filled her imagination with so many legends that everything else seemed dull and uninteresting. How often he had praised those heroes of the past who set out to accomplish their great tasks without a thought for what they left behind!

Malva took Philomena's arm. "Am I mad?" she asked. "Do you think the Archont offered to be my teacher simply to remove me from the throne? Do you think he could have manipulated me patiently for ten years before finally reaping the fruits of his labours?"

Such a chain of thought made Philomena feel quite dizzy, and she cast her mistress a desperate glance. Malva's nostrils were quivering, and her mouth was twisted with rage.

"Well, it doesn't really matter whether I'm right or not. I won't be a tool in anyone's hands any more. I'm not a doll to be married off or an heiress to be got out of the way. I want to live my own life, that's all."

Distraught, Philomena looked at her. Malvas thin face suddenly seemed so hard. And she spoke with such determination!

"But . . . but why not go to Lombardaine? My cousins will hide us," she stammered. "They're very—"

"The Archont is far more powerful than you seem to think," Malva interrupted her. "If we go to Lombardaine I'm sure he'll find out that we're still alive some day. Then nothing will be easier for him than to send more mercenaries like Vincenzo to kill us."

Philomena shivered. Everything she feared was happening! But how could she struggle with the determination of a Princetta who had been so humiliated and deceived?

"Holy Tranquillity!" she wailed. "Why did all this happen? What's to become of us?"

Malva took her hand. Her amber eyes gazed into Philomena's.

"I don't want any more part in my country's destiny, Philomena. If the Archont wants to overthrow the Coronador and seize power, there's nothing I can do about it now. Everyone must think I'm dead. I'm free to go anywhere I please."

"Free?" repeated Philomena faintly. "But to go where?"

She immediately regretted asking this question, because she knew the answer in advance and it terrified her.

"Are you still like a sister to me?" asked Malva.

How often had the two of them sworn vows of friendship to each other? They had sworn to stay together all their lives. To share their joys and sorrows, their secrets and their hopes.

Philomena loved Malva more than anyone in the world. How could that bond be broken now, when they were together in their hour of need? It was impossible.

"I'm like a sister to you," Philomena replied. "I'll go wherever you go."

A smile lit up Malva's face. She looked up at the cliffs and far, far away, as if trying to see beyond the horizon.

"I've survived shipwreck and the attack of that sea creature," she said. "Nothing can frighten me now."

She let go of Philomena's hand, turned and hobbled over to her mattress, where she lay down, sighing with pleasure, and massaged her leg before adding, "That's decided, then. We'll set off for Elgolia as soon as possible."

10

Edicts and More Edicts

Orpheus went down to the harbour for the fourth time that week. He had shut Zeph into the sitting room, and as he turned the corner of the third alleyway he could still hear the faint sound of reproachful barking. That idiot of a dog was wreaking havoc with his nerves. Whatever Orpheus did, Zeph was never satisfied: out of doors he growled and snuffled at the skirts of women passing by, indoors he barked. The neighbours would soon be complaining—indeed, they had already become less easy going. Only the day before a woman had pinned a copy of the Archont's thirty-eighth edict on Orpheus's door. It was the one banning all forms of loud noise.

"The thirty-eighth edict!" sighed Orpheus, shaking his head sadly.

Since the country went into mourning, the Archont had been issuing more and more edicts. No one could be sure if he was acting on the Coronador's orders, for the Coronador himself had not been seen in public since the terrible day the

Princetta's dress was brought to him. The bans on weddings and funerals were followed by edicts forbidding theatrical performances, the sale of newspapers and flowers, the teaching of arts and sciences, walking out of doors after dark, swimming, kissing and singing in public, even taking a siesta under the trees.

To ensure that these edicts were observed, troops of armed soldiers patrolled the Lower Town, their hobnailed boots ringing on the paving stones at all hours of the day and night. The schools closed, travelling peddlers left town, musicians played under the bridges in muted tones, mothers were afraid to let their children play in the street, women stopped using cosmetics, and men deserted the terraces outside taverns. People didn't even dare to do what *was* still allowed, for fear it might be forbidden tomorrow.

"What a dismal scene!" sighed Orpheus as he set out along the avenue that ran beside the river.

Further on, after passing a series of windy and almost deserted squares, the Gdavir grew wider and branched into a delta before it flowed out into the Maltic Ocean. Here was the port with its harbour, a little way from the city and lying under the layer of cloud that seemed to have settled permanently over Galnicia.

As he arrived on the quayside Orpheus took a deep breath. At least that hadn't changed: the sea air still smelled of salt and adventure! He sneezed, but smiled all the same and made for the Maritime Institute with a determined tread. He had been going there for weeks to consult works on navigation and polish up his knowledge of the subject. He would spend hours with his nose in a book, and then go to sit for a little while in the front hall, hoping to meet the captains of vessels that had just cast anchor in the harbour. If he hung around there, Orpheus thought, he might finally hear of a ship on the point of sailing. Then he would only have to seize his chance, and with luck he'd be free of Galnicia and its oppressive atmosphere!

But when he had climbed the few steps leading to the entrance of the Institute, he found the doors closed. He strained his ears. Yes, he could hear voices and other sounds clearly inside. This was a strange time of day for the Institute to be closed. What did it mean?

Stepping back, Orpheus looked at the pediment of the building. It usually flew the green and yellow Galnician flag, but today the flag had been lowered.

"Strange," murmured Orpheus to himself as he went up to the doorway.

He waited in the draughty air, taking care to put up his coat collar so as not to catch cold, but all the same his throat began to feel sore. He sneezed another three or four times. When he raised his head he saw that he was no longer the only one waiting for the doors to open: two other men were pacing up and down at the bottom of the steps. One of them struck Orpheus as familiar. He was a small, thin man, nervous and frowning, who could hardly pass unnoticed because of his mop of bright red hair. Orpheus had seen him in the reading room and front hall of the Institute. He didn't look like a sailor, but if he frequented this place so often he surely had some interest in the sea.

Orpheus was busy wondering about the redheaded man when the doors of the Institute were flung open, and a troop of soldiers marched briskly out. Behind them voices rose in protest. Then Orpheus saw a man with a shaven head and grey eyes between the two columns of soldiers. He was walking fast, shoulders straight, the high collar of his ceremonial coat fitting closely around his neck. Much impressed, Orpheus moved aside to let him pass with the troop of soldiers around him, and then watched while they moved away along the quaysides.

"The Archont," murmured Orpheus. "The Archont in person!"

Once his surprise had passed, he turned back to the Maritime Institute, determined to get in this time. But the doors were closed again.

"This is too much!" the little redhead exclaimed, climbing the flight of steps. "Who do they think they are in there, slamming the doors in our face like that! You'd think we weren't good enough for them!"

Orpheus pounded on the heavy wooden panels with his fist. Once, twice, three times, harder and harder as the little man encouraged him to carry on.

"The Institute is closed!" a voice on the other side of the door replied at last.

"When is it going to open?" shouted Orpheus.

"You don't understand!" the voice yelled back. "It's closed! Closed for good, by order of the Archont!"

It took Orpheus's breath away. How could such a place as the Institute be closed? There was no sense in it!

"Here!" said the voice again. "Take a look. This is the edict!"

Looking down, Orpheus saw a piece of paper being slipped under the door. He picked it up. According to the terms of this forty-third edict, there was to be no more access to the Institute's public rooms, its books were to be locked away and seals set on the cupboards, its maps and charts and navigational instruments confiscated . . .

"What a bunch of cowards!" shouted the redhead, kicking the door several times. Then he marched off, uttering several nasty remarks about scholars, scientists and a set of incompetent idiots whom he appeared to know well.

Orpheus stood there transfixed, his fingers clutching the piece of paper. The wind ruffled the skirts of his coat and he shivered feverishly. He felt as if his last hope of leaving Galnicia had vanished with the issuing of this edict.

11

An Ambush in the Steppes

Eastwards. Eastwards all the time.

Malva and Philomena had been walking in the direction of the rising sun for twenty-eight days. They had crossed arid plains, passed villages and fields, forded tumultuous rivers, made their way through the dark forests on the frontier of Monteplano, and now they were approaching the mountains of Gurkistan. They took turns resting on the back of the mule that the Spertan fisherfolk had given them, but every step was painful. When their feet weren't bleeding their backs ached, their eyes streamed under the constant assault of wind and sun, and their stomachs were crying out for food. They had finished their meagre provisions long ago. While they were still in inhabited country-side they had managed to beg a little bread and soup, and had even stolen cabbages from kitchen gardens . . . but now they were coming to deserts where not a soul lived.

Before nightfall they would look for somewhere to shelter. If they were lucky, it might be an abandoned shepherd's hut, but more often it was a dip among some rocks, a tree with low branches, or just a ditch at the roadside. They slept there, stunned by exhaustion. The wild berries, chestnuts and mushrooms they found, and the mice they sometimes caught for dinner, were never enough to satisfy their hunger. At night they dreamed of the banquets of the luxurious days when they still lived in the Citadel.

Malva was awakened by the same pain every morning: violent cramps in her right leg going all the way up to the small of her back. The first time it happened she had screamed horribly, so loud that Philomena awoke with a start.

Then she had got used to her affliction. She had found out how to relieve it: stretching her leg while holding on to her foot, then letting go and standing up as quickly as possible to take a few steps, limping at first, then more easily. Finally she had to drink several mouthfuls of a bad-tasting medicine that the fisherman's wife had brewed her, and which she kept in a goatskin bag. At last the cramp would fade, and it was such a relief that she suddenly felt very well.

"Time to get up, lazybones!" she told her chambermaid. "The sun's rising, and Elgolia lies ahead!"

Philomena muttered. She had sworn to accompany her mistress to the end, but by all the divinities of the Known World, her oath was costing her dear! Some mornings, if she'd had the choice, she would have stayed where she was, lying on the ground, waiting to be eaten by a wild beast or baked by the sun. She would rather have died than set off again for the wretched country that Malva kept talking about.

"We'll get there," Malva said encouragingly, her eyes gazing eastwards.

"Yes, well, we're bound to get *somewhere*," grumbled

Philomena. "Elgolia or no Elgolia, the world has to have some kind of end!"

"Do you realise," said the Princetta happily, "we'll be the first Galnicians ever to set foot on Elgolia? No one else has ever gone so far!"

Malva was already dreaming of the pages she would fill when she wrote down all her adventures. She had lost her notebooks in the shipwreck, but her memory would be enough.

"Help me to think of a good title," she said. "What about *Journey into the Unknown*? Or *Two Girl Adventurers in Elgolia*?"

Philomena looked sideways at her. She could only very vaguely understand her mistress's enthusiasm. So many dangers could confront them! So many traps could open at their feet. True, they hadn't met many people in twenty-eight days of walking: some suspicious peasants, a few vagabonds who had offered to let the girls join them, merchants who had tried to sell them jewels. Every time they had hastened to leave such company behind. But over there in those forbidding mountains, who knew what kind of men or monsters they meet?

"What a typical Galnician you are!" Malva laughed, seeing Philomena's frightened look. "Why do you have to see enemies everywhere? I'd rather think the Known World is full of such kind and generous people as the Spertan fisherman and his family!" And she added mischievously, "Anyway, we're so poor that we have nothing to lose!"

She put her hand to the Archont's medallion, which she still wore around her neck, "to remind me of his villainy," she told herself.

"This is all anyone could steal from me. But what's a traitor's medallion worth?"

*   *   *

A week later, when they reached the first snow-covered pass in the high mountain ranges of Gurkistan, they saw plumes of smoke in the distance.

"Perhaps there's a village there?" Malva suggested.

She was shivering with cold, hunched on the mule, whose hooves sank into the soft snow. Her lips were tinged purple. Beside her, Philomena was struggling forward, gasping for breath. They must be on their guard, but what option did they have? They had to get over the pass before nightfall and reach the milder temperatures of the valley. As for going back, that was out of the question.

As they gradually approached the black smoke, they realised that there was no village there. Something was burning, but it wasn't a campfire or even an ordinary bonfire. Black forms lay all around: shattered carts, barrels, gutted crates. Silent and chilled, Philomena and Malva moved on. There was an acrid smell in the icy air. When they were close to the fire they froze. Burning there before their eyes they saw . . .

"A horse?" said Malva, hesitantly.

"No," moaned Philomena, feeling her stomach heave. "Horses. Lots of horses . . ."

And at that moment figures emerged from all directions, like shadows coming from the Sea of the Dead. There were about twenty of them, mounted on huge animals that were half-bull, half-deer, with steaming nostrils. Seeing them, Malva and Philomena turned pale and clung to one another.

In spite of the cold, the mounted men wore plain tunics open wide to show their hairy chests. Their faces were hidden by black hoods that made them look like ghosts. What terrified Malva most, however, was the sight of the necklaces hanging around their throats: leather thongs with rows of human teeth strung on them.

Philomena suddenly fell on her knees in the snow. She wept and sobbed, begging these spectral warriors not to kill them. They did not react, but their circle was perceptibly closing in on the two travellers.

Malva dismounted from the mule. Her legs and arms and the muscles of her face were numb with cold. She joined Philomena on the ground and began weeping too.

This is the end, she thought with infinite sadness. We shall die here and never see Elgolia.

She felt warm, moist breath on the back of her neck. Looking up, she saw that one of those monstrous beasts was snuffling at it. Its slimy nostrils were touching her skin! Without stopping to think, Malva tapped its flat muzzle smartly.

"Go away!" she shouted.

The animal gave a low growl and rapidly straightened up, almost throwing its rider. Then sudden panic seemed to overcome the whole troop. The masked warriors uttered cries as they brandished metal weapons in their hands: crescent-shaped axes with shining blades.

At first Malva thought her gesture had aroused the warriors' wrath, but suddenly she saw another army of men on horseback making straight for them. They would distract the warriors' attention! This was their chance! She tugged Philomena's sleeve hard.

"Come on!"

They ran, stumbled, then crawled through the snow to take shelter behind an overturned cart. From this vantage point, they watched the fight between the hooded warriors and the army of horsemen. The horsemen greatly outnumbered their opponents.

They fought valiantly with swords and whips, and seemed to be obeying the orders of a single leader, a strong young man wearing a fur cap and standing erect on his horse's back. Arms raised above his head, he was commanding his troops with astonishing elegance of movement.

"My goodness," Philomena murmured. "I've never seen anyone so agile!"

Watching this exceptionally skilful horseman, she almost forgot her fears. It was as if pure beauty had visited the battlefield: swords clashed, the crescent-shaped axes shone, whips cracked, and the hooves of the animals pounded the snow, as if it were some kind of extraordinary ballet. Malva did not seem moved by the spectacle. She couldn't take her eyes off the strings of teeth hanging around the necks of the hooded warriors, and the sight chilled her to the bone.

Soon, however, the warriors began to falter. Some were wounded, others disarmed, and they turned to flee westward, uttering furious cries and digging their heels into the bellies of their bull-deer mounts.

When they were far enough away and silence fell over the mountains again, the leader of the horsemen jumped down and knelt beside the fire. He threw handfuls of snow on the blackened skeletons, reciting incomprehensible words. His guttural voice rose from the depths of his throat, and he swayed back and forth as he took in the terrible sight of the charred horses. The other horsemen remained motionless around him, their eyes fixed on the scene, while the plumes of black smoke dispersed in the sky.

At last the man straightened up, and walked towards the cart with a confident step. When he saw the two girls huddled in it, shivering, he bowed to them and threw his whip on the snow as a sign of peace.

Without realising it, Malva and Philomena had just been rescued by the Baighur people, and the man now smiling at them was none other than Uzmir, their Supreme Khansha.

A new life began for Malva and Philomena. Uzmir had taken them under his protection, and they only had to follow the movement of the tribe, always going eastward.

The Baighurs were nomads and hunters. They had moved over the Azizian Steppes in their long caravans since time immemorial, following the rhythm of the seasons and the oryak migrations, eating their meat and using what was left to barter with merchants. The animals' skins, bones and long hair were all transformed by the clever hands of the Baighur women. They made harpoons, rugs, cords, oil and lucky amulets which were in great demand among the people of distant cities. In exchange for all this, the Baighurs got horses. Their horses were their only real wealth. Without horses they could not track down the oryaks. Without horses they could not move the carts carrying their children and old people. Without horses, the Baighurs had no hope of surviving in these vast and icy steppes.

As Malva and Philomena gradually came to understand all this, they knew why Uzmir had seemed so sad as he gazed at the fire consuming the dead horses on the day when they first met. And they realised, too, that the only enemies of the Baighurs were those warriors in black hoods who had attacked them: the Amoyeds.

The name alone sent shivers down Malva's back. And the further east the caravan moved, the more grateful she was to the Divinities of the Known World for sending Uzmir to cross her path. If not for him, the Amoyeds wouldn't have hesitated to kill her, pull out her teeth and add them to the other gruesome trophies hanging round their necks.

Days and weeks passed.

Malva's fears were calmed as the caravan went across the steppes. Uzmir had given her and Philomena jackets and boots of oryak skin so that they could bear the extreme temperatures. The Princetta's hair had grown again, and she wound a length of woollen cloth around her head like a turban to protect and hide it. She rode through the wind and the silent steppes all day, buoyed up by her growing hope of reaching Elgolia soon. Philomena had stopped complaining. She seemed to have been won over by the kindness and hospitality of the Baighurs.

In the evenings, exhausted, Malva would join the women to help prepare a meal and to plait cords of oryak hair. The Baighur women taught her to chew paghul, strange seeds that seemed to have many virtues, including strengthening the teeth and making it easier to digest oryak meat, but the paghul had no flavour of its own.

"What about a cramp?" Malva asked her companions. "Are the seeds any good for a cramp?"

Of course no one understood her question, and the women just smiled and nodded. So Malva helped herself to a few more paghul seeds, thinking that they could hardly do any harm.

As they worked some of the women smoked the chibuk, a kind of long-stemmed pipe, but they did not offer Malva one. They indicated that she was too young; according to their traditions, she must wait to be married before she could own a chibuk. Malva smiled, and tried to explain that in her own country her parents had wanted to marry her off in spite of her youth. The women opened their eyes wide with surprise: they evidently thought the Galnicians must be real barbarians!

Philomena did not join in these working parties; she refused to chew paghul, and kept finding excuses to be somewhere else. Malva watched her surreptitiously, and saw that she was always going about with the men, with Uzmir beside her.

"He's teaching me his language," Philomena explained, rejoining Malva.

"Yes, of course!"

"It's true!" said the chambermaid, taking offence. "I'm learning fast and Uzmir is very pleased with me, if you really want to know."

"I don't doubt it for a moment!" replied Malva with a mischievous smile. "A heart in love learns easily!"

Philomena shrugged, but Malva knew she had guessed correctly. Her chambermaid had fallen for the charms of the Supreme Khansha the moment she set eyes on him standing on horseback, leading his men into battle against the Amoyeds.

"I've heard something very interesting," Philomena said one evening, creating a diversion. "About Elgolia."

Malva stopped plaiting cords. "Did Uzmir talk to you about Elgolia?"

"I mentioned it to him myself: I said we were going there. According to him, it may really exist, but it's far beyond the horizon. Certain travellers have described it, but no Baighur has ever been so far."

"I was sure of it!" cried the delighted Princetta. "How many days will it take us to get there?"

"Who knows?" sighed Philomena. "For now we're going the right way and we're in good company. Don't be so impatient."

Malva nodded, guessing how difficult it would be for Philomena to leave her handsome horseman when the time came.

"Uzmir told me about the Amoyeds too," Philomena went on, in a lower voice. "If I understood him correctly, those brutes carry out commissions for people who will pay them. They steal and loot, and they often abduct women and children to be sold to some emperor whose name I've forgotten. They kill the Baighurs' horses to weaken the tribe, but Uzmir opposes them bravely."

"Uzmir is a great chief," admitted Malva.

"He's the Supreme Khansha," said Philomena, admiration evident in her voice. "And he's even promised to teach me to ride standing on horseback!"

Malva laughed. "Well, while you're waiting for a chance to break your bones, you might lend me a hand plaiting these cords!"

One morning, when Philomena was still asleep and Malva was walking round in their tent to soothe the cramp in her leg, Uzmir came in. Malva looked at him in astonishment. Until now the Khansha had been the soul of courtesy, and she knew he would never have intruded on their privacy except for some urgent reason. There was indeed an expression of deep anxiety on his face.

"What is it?" asked Malva, still pacing round the tent to make sure the cramp didn't come back.

With a nod of the head, Uzmir indicated Philomena, snuggled into her blankets. He needed an interpreter.

Malva shook her companion, who woke with a start and blushed when she saw Uzmir standing there. They exchanged a few words in that guttural language which Malva didn't understand at all, and Philomena turned very pale. When Uzmir had left, she leaped out of her blankets.

"Quick!" she cried. "Pack up your things! We're striking camp! Some of the horses were stolen overnight."

Malva felt her heart beat faster. She hastily put on her turban.

"The thieves left tracks," Philomena went on, her breath coming short.

Malva bit her lip. "Tracks of what?" she asked in an expressionless voice.

"Hoof-prints of enlils, those bull-deer animals. The caravan is leaving at once. We're going to turn back westward."

"Westward?"

Malva almost cried out aloud with the combined shock of fear and dismay. Philomena turned to her, hands on her hips. "It's a matter of life and death, Malva. If the Amoyeds have found us again they're not going to let us beat them so easily this time." And then, to soothe Malva, Philomena took her in her arms. "We have to trust Uzmir. He saved us once, he'll save us again! And as soon as the danger's over we'll set off for Elgolia again, I promise you."

Feeling stunned, Malva gathered her things together, put on her oryak-skin jacket and boots, and then stepped out into the early morning air with Philomena. At once the icy cold paralysed them.

The steppes stretched before them as far as the eye could see, flat and still, while a weak sun tried to rise above the horizon in the east. Malva cast a bitter glance in that direction. The promise of Elgolia was retreating, and with it a little of the hope that helped her to rise above the ordeals of the harsh nomadic life: the biting cold, the monotony of the high plateaux, the shattering exhaustion. She sighed. The great Azizian Steppes set a boundless, hostile barrier between her and the country of Elgolia. Would she have the strength to face all this again if she had to turn her back on her dream now?

While Philomena strapped their blankets under her horse's belly, Uzmir came to offer Malva a cup of grey tea and a few paghul cakes. Then he turned to their tent, and took it down with the help of two other men.

"Those horrible cakes again!" wailed Philomena, when Malva handed her a share. "No thank you!"

Malva put the cakes in the pocket of the jacket she still wore under her oryak-skin coat. She usually laughed at Philomena and her taste for luxury. "I'm the Princetta!" she used to point out. "I'm the one who ought to be complaining!" But this morning she made no comment. The atmosphere weighing on the camp was heavy with anxiety, and no one felt like laughing.

The women and children had gathered around the carts after piling them high with blankets, tentpegs, battered copper cauldrons, cooking utensils and chibuks. Malva saw at once that they were going to miss the stolen horses badly. Some of the old people were preparing to walk, even though they could hardly keep on their feet. She went to find Uzmir to indicate that she could walk herself. But Uzmir shook his head and pointed to her right leg. Malva was surprised. How did he know about her injury?

"I told him all about it," admitted Philomena, seeing her look so taken aback.

"What do you mean, *all about it*?"

"Well . . . our shipwreck, that creature whose name we don't know that bit you, the wise woman in Sperta . . ."

Malva was annoyed. "What else? Did you tell him about our flight from Galnicia too, and the wedding I missed? We swore to keep all that a secret!"

Philomena blushed slightly, but the Princetta had no time to scold any more. The tents had all been taken down, the horses were pawing the ground, and there was a sense of urgency in the air.

Malva resigned herself to mounting her horse, and the caravan immediately set off. The men led, the old people and children were in the middle, and the women brought up the rear.

As the sun rose, a cold, unpleasant wind began to blow, sweeping over the short grass and stinging the riders' lips. Malva hunched her head down between her shoulders and bent her back under its icy gusts. Philomena was walking beside her, holding the bridle of the horse Malva was riding. There was a smell of fear and disaster in the air; none of the horsemen said a word.

After an hour, Malva began to feel the silence was oppressive. She needed to talk to drive her fears away. "What will be the first thing you do once we get there?" she abruptly asked Philomena.

The chambermaid looked up, frowning. "Oh, Malva, you've asked me that a hundred times already!"

"Tell me again!"

Philomena heaved a sigh of resignation. "There," of course, meant Elgolia. "I'll look for that lake the sailor talked about," she said obligingly. "The bubbling lake of warm water."

"Lake Barath-Thor," said Malva, feeling a little more cheerful.

"Yes, that's the one. I shall plunge into it and stay there for hours doing nothing at all, bathing my frozen feet and my poor tired back. And if I get ten years younger too, as the sailor said, well, why not?"

"I won't bathe in it!" Malva laughed. "I'd risk ending up a little girl again!"

Philomena nodded.

"Well?" said Malva. "Ask me what *I* shall do first!"

Philomena tightened her lips. These questions troubled her, but she always ended up doing as her mistress wanted. "Well, what will you do, then?"

"I'll climb the thousand-year-old tree growing on top of Mount Ur-Tha," replied Malva delightedly. "With a little luck I'll be able to see all the way to Galnicia."

"If you do that you might want to go home," Philomena teased.

"Not me! When I'm at the top of that tree I'll put out my tongue at Galnicia, the Archont, the Coronada and the Coronador. Then I'll come straight down again and build a house beside the sea, in that bay where a sweet wind blows. The Bay of Dao-Boa. I'll live there for ever and write the story of our adventures!"

In her imagination, the Princetta had drawn a map of the entire geography of Elgolia, using the descriptions and names mentioned by old Bulo. She could see herself in the Bay of Dao-Boa, chopping wood, nailing planks together, building the framework of her future home.

"It won't be a big place, Philomena. There won't be any towers, any Hall of Delicacies, any fountains like the ones in the Citadel. But it will be my house. The house I built with my own hands."

Philomena wasn't really listening. She knew these dreams by heart, and if the truth were told, she didn't really believe in the existence of Elgolia. Galnician girls have their feet planted firmly on the ground and believe only what they can see. Malva was exactly the opposite: she needed to believe in what she couldn't see.

The caravan was making slow progress. Malva looked up at the sky, and saw that the sun would soon be halfway through its daily course. She pulled at her horse's bridle to make it stop.

"Your turn to ride," she told Philomena, jumping down.

The chambermaid didn't have to be asked twice, and Malva began walking, limping slightly. Her feet were numb and her fingertips frozen. In front of her, the children in the carts had fallen asleep on their mothers' knees. Further ahead, she saw the sturdy shapes of the men riding beside Uzmir. It all seemed like any other day, and there was nothing threatening on the horizon.

"Uzmir may have been wrong," suggested Malva, as they went up a small rise in the ground where thornbushes grew. "Perhaps the horse-thieves weren't Amoyeds after all . . ."

She had hardly spoken these words when cries arose at the head of the caravan. The men had temporarily disappeared into a dip in the ground below. Malva and Philomena couldn't see them, but the wind carried alarming sounds back to them.

The carts stopped, and the horses pricked their ears nervously. Women stood in their stirrups, straining to see. Through the howling gusts of wind, Malva thought she heard the clash of weapons and the sound of men riding in haste.

Suddenly one of the women kicked her horse's flanks, dropped the reins, and set off to scout ahead. Philomena and Malva exchanged glances, but not a word passed their lips. Their mouths suddenly felt dry. Soon afterwards the woman came back at a gallop, shouting.

"Amoyeds! Amoy—"

Her cry was immediately stifled in her throat, and she collapsed over her horse's mane: a crescent-shaped axe had just landed between her shoulderblades.

Malva felt the blood in her veins turn to ice. Instantly, panic seized the caravan. Horses reared, women rode away at the gallop, carts overturned with a crash.

"Take the horse!" Philomena ordered. She scrambled off its

back and pushed Malva towards it instead. The Princetta was petrified. Her legs would no longer obey her.

"Quick!" shouted Philomena. "Get up on that horse and save yourself!"

"What about you?" said Malva, distraught.

Philomena stared at her, eyes wide with fear. "Never mind about me. Get up on the horse, I tell you!"

Without knowing quite how, Malva suddenly found herself on the horse's back. At the front of the column riders appeared, brandishing their silvery weapons. They wore the black hoods of Amoyed warriors.

All around was chaos. The children were crying and running this way and that, dishevelled women were trying to escape, pricking their legs on the thorny bushes. Philomena tugged at the horse's bridle and then hit its croup.

"I'll find you later!" she called to Malva. "I must go and help Uzmir!"

Malva turned just in time to see Philomena running and leaping over the wrecked carts. She was making straight for the Amoyeds! Malva wanted to call to her, to beg her to stay, but her terrified mind was floating in a kind of fog. The horse was galloping on, away from the battlefield. Behind Malva, other horses were pounding the earth with their hooves, trampling on tents now left in rags, abandoned utensils, crates of food that had broken open.

Suddenly the horse shied. Malva's leg collided with another horse's flank, and she felt a terrible burning sensation on her skin. The next moment blood was flowing from her old wound. It had just reopened under the impact.

The effect was electrifying. The fog in her mind cleared instantly, and she recovered her spirits. "Philomena!" she yelled, suddenly realising that they had been separated for the first time since the beginning of their journey.

She seized the reins and pulled with all her might. The horse almost reared and Malva lost her turban, but she managed to keep her balance. When she finally turned, what she saw stunned her. The caravan was only a shapeless heap: men, horses, carts all jumbled up together, a scene of confusion from which the steel of swords and the shining blades of axes flashed out now and then. Cries rose to the sky. The ground was nothing but mud and blood.

"Come on!" Malva shouted to her horse. She forced it forward with all her might. The pain in her leg made her breath come short, but she had to find Philomena. Without Philomena, she was lost. Nothing seemed possible without her!

As she came closer, arrows whistled past her ears. She flattened herself on her horse's neck as best she could. "Philomena!" she shouted again.

Suddenly the horse stumbled over a wrecked cart. Malva felt it falter. Whinnying, it threw her to the ground, but her foot caught in the stirrup, and she was dragged through the dust for a few moments, until her horse rolled over in the midst of the chaos. Malva uttered a cry of pain and distress.

The last thing she saw was the moist muzzle of an enlil bending over her, and a row of human teeth dangling from a leather thong.

12

Philomena's Decision

The noise of fighting had died away, and cries had given way to groans and weeping. The little rise covered with thornbushes looked as if it had been ploughed up. But neither wheat nor barley had been sown there. Only the dead and wounded lay in the deep furrows, their weapons broken, their oryak-skin coats torn.

The Amoyeds had ridden away, abandoning those Baighurs who were still alive to their fate. Not a single horse was left on its feet. And over in the dip in the ground, a man was on his knees in front of a new bonfire, with his face in his hands: Uzmir the Supreme Khansha, weeping and chanting over the disaster.

Philomena came back to her senses when she heard those strange sounds. She had fallen down the slope, rolled into the thorns, and hit her head against a stone before fainting.

"Uzmir . . ." she murmured, trying to get up. "Holy Tranquillity—he's alive!"

Although it cost her an enormous effort, she managed to

stand up. And then, seeing the dead all around her, she took in the magnitude of the catastrophe. Her head was spinning, and her blood suddenly drained towards her heart.

"Malva," she said. "Where's Malva?"

She climbed the slope, ignoring the thorns that dug into her knees and the palms of her hands when she fell. Once at the top, she saw the upturned carts, the trampled crates and chibuks, the tents torn to shreds, and had a dreadful realization.

"Malva!" she shouted.

Her voice was carried away by the gusts of wind from the steppes. In the midst of the chaos, a Baighur woman and her little girl were wandering about in tears, disorientated, their faces smeared with mud. Philomena went over to them. In the Baighur language, she asked if they had seen Malva.

The dazed woman shook her head, but the little girl clinging to her skirt pointed to the way the Amoyeds had gone. She told Philomena that she had seen one of the warriors carry the Princetta away on his enlil.

"Are you sure?" breathed Philomena, on the verge of fainting.

The little girl nodded, and searched her pocket. She brought out the Archont's medallion, which she had just picked up from the wreckage. Her mother looked despairingly at Philomena. Everyone who travelled the steppes knew that the Amoyeds sold young girls to the Emperor of Cispazia.

"Cispazia . . ." Philomena said. "Malva . . . sold!"

She took the medallion and burst into tears.

"By all the Divinities of the Known World!" she cried. "If anything happens to my Princetta, may the Archont die on the spot!"

She collapsed in the mud. All the hard times they had known

together went through her mind. The Archont's medallion burned like a hot coal in her hand. A momento of his villainy, Malva had called it. Philomena raised her eyes to the vast sky of the steppes. Who in the world could help her save Malva now? It would take an army to snatch her from the hands of the Amoyeds or this Emperor. The Baighurs were decimated. Where could Philomena turn?

She pounded the ground with her fist. If only the Coronador and the Coronada had felt a little compassion for their daughter! If only they hadn't been so cruel, so set in their ways! If they'd listened to their child none of this would have happened!

Philomena sobbed for some time. She thought that back in Galnicia, everyone must believe them dead. She imagined the country plunged, as it surely was, into mourning. The Galnician people had always loved Malva. They would be lamenting the loss of their Princetta. In the face of this tragedy, perhaps the Coronador was beginning to realise that he had done the wrong thing? Perhaps he felt remorseful? Perhaps, after all, he'd be glad and relieved to know that Malva was alive? Suppose he knew how the Archont had worked on his young pupil's mind until she made her rash bid to escape?

Perhaps, yes . . . and anyway, what other choice did she, Philomena, have?

"Holy Harmony!" she murmured. "Forgive me, Malva . . . forgive me, my sister."

Before she lost consciousness again, she knew exactly what she must do.

13

The Mysterious Messenger

Orpheus was awakened by a ray of sunlight tickling his nose, and voices coming in from outside. Surprised, he opened his eyes. He saw a scrap of blue sky through his bedroom window, and smiled with pleasure. It was months since he had seen the sun!

He went to open his window, and saw an extraordinary sight outside: the washerwomen were back. Taking advantage of the good weather, they were spreading their sheets and tablecloths on the rooftops opposite. Their voices answered each other in the old familiar way, rising in the fragrant morning air.

"It must be wrong!" said one woman. "Just a rumour, that's all it is!"

"Not at all!" said the eldest washerwoman huffily. "I heard it from my sister. She's a cook in the Citadel, and if you call her a liar again I'm denouncing you to the patrol!"

The first woman raised her fist threateningly. "And what, may I ask, would you be denouncing me for?"

"For infringing the sixty-fourth edict, that's what!" retorted the other woman, pouting. "I heard you the other day! You were singing in your kitchen!"

Under the amused eyes of Orpheus, the other women soon joined in the argument. Some of them ventured to say in an undertone that the Archont's edicts were unjust, and anyone had the right to sing in her kitchen, while other, more timid souls said that the law was the law.

But they stopped squabbling when the youngest cried, "Oh, do look! There's our shy friend at his window!"

Orpheus started in alarm. He'd been caught at it again. But this time he made himself stand his ground. He wasn't going to be humiliated by these washerwomen again! And anyway, the air was so mild this morning. He felt himself reviving a little, like a bear coming out of hibernation.

"Good morning!" he called to them.

"Well, fancy that! He has a voice!" mocked the first washerwoman.

"And blue eyes . . . very, very blue," the youngest added.

Orpheus blushed slightly but decided to keep cool. "What rumour were you talking about?" he asked.

The oldest washerwoman came to lean against the parapet of her rooftop. "You know, Master Shrinking Violet, eavesdropping on other people's conversations is not very polite!" she teased him. "But if you really want to know, it seems that a horseman arrived at the Citadel yesterday evening. My sister saw him. He's a very strange fellow, with slanting eyes and dark skin, and he doesn't speak our language, but he was bringing the Coronador a letter. That's what I was just telling my neighbours."

The youngest washerwoman put her laundry basket down and came to lean on the parapet too. "According to her it's a letter from the Princetta's chambermaid. You remember her—

the chambermaid who disappeared at the same time as the Princetta herself."

"I see," said Orpheus, more and more interested. "So this chambermaid isn't dead after all?"

"Well, no," replied the oldest washerwoman. "And if she's not dead, and if she wrote to the Coronador, I think all sorts of things may happen!"

"Where did the horseman come from?" Orpheus asked.

"A country very far away," the woman told him in hushed tones. "Beyond the mountains of Gurkistan. My sister told me he'd covered the distance on horseback in less than ten days!"

"That's impossible!" put in one of the other washerwomen. "No horse and no rider could have done it in that time!"

"Oh yes, they could!" replied the oldest. "So are you saying that my sister's a liar again?"

The argument broke out with renewed force, but Orpheus had heard enough. With a friendly little wave to the young washerwoman, he closed his window before hurrying into the sitting room. He found Zeph occupying his armchair again, but he didn't get angry.

"Zephyr, you're not a St. Bernard at all, you're an obstinate old mule!" he said. The dog pricked up his ears and opened his large, moist eyes. "It's all right," smiled Orpheus, "don't look so surprised. I'm not scolding you! You can even stay in my chair, because I have to go out."

He quickly dressed. If what the washerwoman said was true, surely the Coronador would be taking some action over this chambermaid. Perhaps he might mount an expedition, and he'd be needing brave men.

"In which case I'll be one of them!" Orpheus told his reflection in the mirror out loud.

A thrill of excitement ran down his spine. He absolutely had to know the identity of the mysterious horseman and the contents of the letter he had brought. He must know before anyone else, so that he could be the first to offer the Coronador his services. Orpheus tapped his foot impatiently: if his chance had finally come, he mustn't let it get away!

He left his house and decided to climb up to the Old Town. The sun broke through the clouds at intervals, and a little breeze had swept up the refuse piled in the doorways of buildings. As he went from street to street, Orpheus met more passers-by than he usually saw these days. Women were coming out like flowers in spring, when it should have felt like autumn. But no: a sight of the sun at long last made November seem like April.

Further away, Orpheus saw a gang of ragged boys throwing stones at stray cats. They were laughing, running and jumping, in defiance of edict thirty-one. Orpheus went over to them. He thought he recognised the bright lad who had knocked on his door twice.

"Hey!" he called. "Remember me?"

The urchin broke off his game and came over to plant himself in front of Orpheus. "You're McBott, aren't you? Of course I remember you. And all those galniks I earned from you! Thanks to you I had a fortune-teller read the cards for me."

"A good way to spend your money, I'm sure!" said Orpheus sarcastically. "I hope she at least predicted all kinds of marvels."

"You bet!" replied the boy. "You've no idea what a wonderful future awaits me! I bought some soldier's boots too. Look at these!"

He proudly displayed the boots he was wearing. They were hobnailed, and slightly too big for him.

"These make me boss of my gang!" he said, puffing out his chest. "All the others go barefoot!"

"Your parents must be proud of you, I'm sure," exclaimed Orpheus.

"Parents? What parents?"

"Why, the first time you came to my house, you said they'd be worried to think you were out alone at night," Orpheus recalled, frowning.

The lad shrugged his shoulders. "Did I say so? I must have made a mistake. I'm an orphan!"

Amused by the boy's clever tricks, Orpheus started to laugh. "What's your name?" he asked.

"It used to be Diego, but since I got these hobnailed boots everyone calls me Hob."

"Well, Hob, how would you like to earn a few more galniks?"

The urchin narrowed his eyes with a wily look. "How many?"

"Er . . . at least three hundred," said Orpheus in an undertone.

The boy's eyes shone. "What do I have to do?"

Orpheus pointed to the Citadel on top of its cliff. "I want you to get yourself in there," he said.

Hob raised his eyebrows and wrinkled his nose.

"Yes, I know it won't be easy, but you look like a bright lad to me. And when you get inside I'd like you to keep your ears open. It seems a stranger arrived last night with an important message. If you can tell me what the message is, I'll give you—let's say four hundred galniks!"

Hob cast a bold glance at the walls around the Citadel. He nodded, accepting Orpheus's offer.

"And we'll meet this evening under the Gdavir bridge!" called Orpheus as he scurried off.

"I'll be there!" said Hob.

* * *

Orpheus spent the day out and about. Whenever he heard Galnicians in conversation, he stopped to listen, and found out that the rumour was spreading. Only the arrival of a stranger on horseback had been mentioned that morning, but as the day wore on a wealth of detail accumulated.

"Seems he's an Emperor," said some. "He comes from a country with no name where they breed flying horses! He travelled here through the air, that's for sure!"

"Seems he's bringing the Coronador gold," added others, "because he wants to marry a Galnician girl."

"What Galnician girl?"

"No one knows."

By the end of the day the city was buzzing with the wildest of rumours. People stayed out of doors gathering under the trees, talking, sometimes laughing, and all this in defiance of the Archont's many edicts. It was said that the patrols were suspended, and not a soldier had left the Citadel. It was even said that the Archont had disappeared.

When Orpheus met Hob under the bridge, the boy was red in the face, breathless, and very dirty.

"Well?" asked Orpheus. "Did you get inside the Citadel?"

"Yes, through the gardens—I almost drowned myself falling into one of those fountains too. It was full of mud and toads. Yuk!"

"You've earned your wages," smiled Orpheus. "But tell me what you found out first."

Hob cast a few glances around to make sure that no one was listening, and then launched into his story. "I saw the stranger," he said. "He's called Ugmir or something like that. He's very strong and he wears really strange clothes—a hat made of animal fur. And it was Philomena, the Princetta's chambermaid, who asked him to come to the Citadel."

"*Why* did he come, though?" Orpheus prompted the boy.

Hob clicked his tongue and held out his hand. "The rest of the story will cost you another hundred galniks."

Orpheus sighed, and handed him the coins.

"The stranger came to deliver a message. He insisted on giving it to the Coronador in person. It seems the Archont fell into a towering rage because the stranger wouldn't let him see what was in the letter. But I heard it all from one of the Coronada's maids. Philomena wrote to say the Princetta isn't dead. She wasn't drowned off the port of Carduz after all!"

"But . . . but then where is she?" stammered Orpheus.

"Another hundred galniks to find out the answer," announced Hob, crossing his arms.

Orpheus paid up.

"The Princetta's been kidnapped by warriors called . . . wait a minute, called Amids, I think. They're planning to sell her to some kind of emperor in the Orniant."

"*Sell* her?" choked Orpheus.

"I'm only telling you what I heard," said Hob apologetically. "This emperor has a hornbeam and he keeps girls prisoner in it."

Baffled, Orpheus scratched his head. "Oh, a harem!" he said. "That's the word, I believe."

Hob shrugged his shoulders. As far as he was concerned, none of these exotic words made much sense.

"But the most interesting thing of all," he said, "is that the stranger brought something else with him too. In a locked box. Something really, *really* surprising."

Resigned to his fate, Orpheus paid the two hundred galniks it would cost to hear the rest.

"The Archont's medallion!" cried Hob triumphantly. "When the Coronador opened the box, they say the Archont turned white as a sheet! In her letter the chambermaid accused him of sending the Princetta to her death. The Coronador asked for an explanation, but the Archont ran out of His Alteza's apartments. Some of the servants saw him riding away from the Citadel at a gallop. And no one knows where he is now!"

Orpheus was astounded. These revelations went far beyond his wildest imaginings that day. He couldn't explain the link between the Archont and the stranger, but there was something very peculiar about it. One thing was certain: Galnicia would be roused from its apathy at last. There could be no doubt that the Archont's rule of terror was over!

Looking at Hob, he put a hand on his shoulder. "Thanks!" he said. "You're a good lad."

"I even managed to steal this," said the boy, laughing, as he took a small bag of cured skin out of his pocket.

"What is it?" asked Orpheus.

"A present the stranger brought for the Coronada. I pinched it from one of the cooks. Here, try it. You chew them."

He trickled a few seeds into the palm of Orpheus's hand. Orpheus put them in his mouth. They tasted like nothing he knew. In fact they didn't taste of anything much, yet chewing them was pleasant.

"I'm going to plant these on the banks of the Gdavir," Hob told him. "You think they might grow?"

"It's possible," said Orpheus, thoughtfully.

Whether they did or not, those strange seeds had a flavour of adventure and travel.

14

The Daughter of Balmun

The Amoyeds had tied Malva up, then they blindfolded her before throwing her into the back of a cart. For an endlessly long time she was jolted around, so scared that she couldn't even weep or cry out. The wound in her leg hurt. She was hungry, but she couldn't even get hold of the paghul cakes in her pocket. She tried to reassure herself by repeating all the new words she'd learned since her flight from the Citadel. She occupied her mind by combining them in different ways to make satisfying curses, but most of the time her thoughts were in confusion. All that was left to her was fear. Dreadful, stomach-churning fear.

From time to time she heard shouting outside, laughter, muttering, sometimes terrifying howls. Did the Amoyeds speak a language full of growls, whistles and barking? Were they really human, or hybrid creatures like their dreadful mounts the enlils? Were they half-man, half-beast?

As she was brooding over these dark thoughts, the jolting of the cart suddenly stopped. She thought she heard a call, but the next moment there was silence. This was the first time the convoy had stopped. The first time such a silence had fallen.

Malva took her chance to change position and try to relieve her aching muscles. There were some sacks to her right. She moved her bottom over the floor of the cart, which was full of splinters, and fell against the sacks, her cheek against their well-stuffed contents. At that moment another cry, closer than the first, broke the silence. She thought it said *Mirgai!*

Then nothing happened for some time. Even the enlils were quiet. Malva fell into a kind of half-sleep. In her dreams she saw Philomena running towards her with blood all over her face. She saw her stumble and fall lifeless to the ground. Malva tried calling out to her, but suddenly two hands came down on her shoulders and she awoke.

Malva uttered a sharp cry of pain, while a powerful smell of sweat made her stomach heave. An Amoyed! One of the Amoyeds had climbed into the cart and was shaking her to wake her up. He barked out a few words and then, without warning, tore the blindfold off Malva's eyes.

A blinding light cut her breath short. The Amoyed didn't give her time to work out what was happening, but dragged her unceremoniously out of the cart, picked her up, and then pushed her ahead of him to make her walk. The Princetta's feet were on the ground, but she couldn't take a step; her legs were much too weak to carry her. She collapsed on the grass.

"Temir-Gai!" A new cry rang in her ears. The Amoyed immediately called something back and made her get up, seizing her arm. He held her like that, staggering and frightened, while more cries were heard on all sides. *"Temir-Gai, Temir-Gai!"*

Gradually Malva's eyes adjusted to the bright daylight. Standing beside her guard, aching all over, she saw a striking scene:

she was in a huge enclosure like a courtyard, surrounded by wooden walls as tall as cliffs. She saw watchmen stationed on the battlements on top of the walls. It was their cries she had heard just now.

Thousands of warriors had gathered in this arena-like enclosure, and were pacing up and down on the dry grass. Most of them were Amoyeds with masked faces, but there were other barbarians riding animals with woolly coats and bearing black and red banners. Malva saw that there were young girls, bound and trembling like herself, in the middle of each group. Her breath quickened. Where had all these girls come from?

She turned her head. Quite close to her, standing next to another cart, she saw a small, fair-haired girl with blue eyes the shape of pearls. She wore a simple cotton shift, and her feet were bare. Their eyes met.

"Lei!" said the girl. Was that her name?

"Malva!" the Princetta replied.

The girl gave a shy smile, but the Amoyed standing next to her hit her roughly on the head. Malva looked away. Better not to anger these brutes.

Another cry rang out, and the crowd immediately moved aside. A gate opened in the wall at the back of the enclosure. *"Temir-Gai!"* murmured the Amoyed who was holding Malva's arm.

A column of armed men marched in through the gate. They were lined up three by three, in shimmering robes, with golden turbans on their heads. An extraordinary animal walked in the middle of the column. It was like a moving mountain: as tall as three men, as broad as six, with an oblong head on the end of its massive neck. Two pairs of silver horns grew above its eyes, and its legs were as thick as pillars. Malva had never seen such a creature before. The impression of sheer power that it gave left her breathless.

"Celestial-charioteer," a voice behind her suddenly whispered. "Mythical creature of Orniant Empire."

Malva jumped. The little blonde girl called Lei had joined her and was touching her shoulder. On her right, her guard was watching the arrival of the soldiers, fascinated.

"You speak my language?" asked Malva quietly.

"I speak all languages," replied the girl in a low voice, "for I am daughter of kingdom of Balmun. Look: Temir-Gai, only emperor to possess celestial-charioteer. Means vast power for him. Emperor like a god now."

Malva saw a shape sitting on the back of the beast with the silver horns. The emperor was there, hidden under a canopy, and obviously the barbarians had gathered inside these wooden walls to welcome him.

"We presents," Lei went on explaining quietly. "Presents for Temir-Gai."

Malva shivered, but she had no time to ask her companion more. Another shout rose in the arena. The emperor Temir-Gai had come out from under the canopy and, standing on the back of the celestial-charioteer, had just unveiled his face. Total silence followed the shouts. The Amoyed holding Malva relaxed his grip and bowed his head. All the faces around her wore an expression of respectful fear.

"You frightened?" Lei murmured in her ear.

Malva nodded.

"Me, I angry. The Amoyeds and the emperor . . ." Lei spat on the ground to show her scorn for them. Then she turned her blue eyes on Malva and smiled.

"We stay together, you and me. Stronger together. Promise?"

This unexpected meeting with the girl heartened the Princetta. Not only did Lei speak Galnician, she seemed to have a spirited nature which was very comforting. Malva smiled back.

"Promise," she murmured.

She had hardly uttered the word before her guard's hand closed round her arm again. The momentary respite was over. He pushed her ahead of him, and Lei was made to walk forward at the same time. The barbarians were propelling their prisoners towards the emperor.

Presents, thought Malva. We're presents. Terror made her mute. Limping and gasping with pain, she walked as well as she could, with Lei beside her. Lei kept her head raised and looked at the emperor without trembling. Malva had never heard of the kingdom of Balmun. Perhaps they bred women warriors there, fearless girls prepared to face any peril? Whether that was so or not, Lei showed extraordinary self-possession.

When they were only a little way from the celestial-charioteer, and despite the fear in the pit of her stomach, Malva couldn't help marvelling at that improbable creature. At close quarters, it seemed even vaster and more majestic. The emperor had disappeared under the canopy again, but she thought she caught an eye looking through a slit in its fabric. He was watching them, her and Lei—or no, it was Malva he was watching!

"Your leg," Lei whispered. "Not limp! If you limp, emperor reject you."

"I can't help it. I was injured, I—"

"If Temir-Gai reject you, Amoyeds kill you."

Terrified, Malva clenched her teeth and, despite terrible pain, took the last few steps without limping. At last the emperor took his eyes off her. He turned his head, rose to his feet on his mount, and uttered a hoarse cry. At his command, his turbaned soldiers led the prisoners out of the arena.

"Go on, go on," Lei encouraged her. "When we in harem, I make your leg better."

"A harem?" Malva made a face.

"Harem of Temir-Gai here in Cispazia. Very famous through whole Orniant Empire! They say he dream of having ten thousand girls for his pleasure." Lei smiled. "My sister went same way as us. But she escape! Came back to Balmun three moons ago. I do the same, and you too, Malva! You come with me!"

How many of them had gone through the gate behind the Emperor's soldiers? Forty? Fifty? Some of the girls were weeping silently, others looked pale as death. Only Lei retained her dignity. Seeing her so proud and so full of life, Malva felt a little hope rise within her again.

She had lost her liberty, she had lost Philomena and the protection of Uzmir, and no doubt she had many humiliations still ahead, but she wasn't alone any more. Those few words exchanged in their desperate situation had been enough to forge a friendship between her and the daughter of Balmun.

15

Bound for the Orniant

At dawn Orpheus double-locked the door of his house, put his bunch of keys at the bottom of his canvas bag, and threw the bag over his shoulder. It contained warm clothes, a rainproof cape, handkerchiefs, several treatises on navigation, a logbook, a naval chart and a compass. That was all he'd be needing now. Old Zeph, sensing that something unusual was going on, paced around his master, keeping an eye on every move he made, as if he had guessed that this was not their usual morning walk.

Within the last few days events had come thick and fast. As soon as he had understood the message brought by Uzmir, the Coronador had emerged from his state of despondency. Leaving the Citadel with those councillors who were still faithful to him, he had gone into the city to tell the Galnicians in person that he was taking over the government of the country again. He had rescinded the Archont's edicts one by one, putting an end to national mourning, reopening the frontiers and reinstating the right to hold services of worship to Tranquillity and Harmony, before sending official criers out to all the provinces to announce that the Princetta was not dead. Moreover, there would be a reward for anyone who gave information leading to the arrest of the Archont. Philomena's letter had hit the right target: the Archont stood accused of plotting against the Princetta's life, with the aim of usurping power for himself.

These revelations caused a great stir among the common people: so it was all that man's fault! He was blamed for everything now: the rain, their sorrow, fear, hunger, cold and despair. In no time at all the Archont was the national villain of Galnicia. Hunts were organised in the hope of finding him, caricatures were circulated, people even wrote mocking songs to exorcise the terror he had so cleverly orchestrated.

And another piece of news spread very fast: the Coronador was calling for volunteers to go on an expedition to Cispazia, the distant land where Malva was held prisoner. Orpheus had wasted no time in preparing. The chance he had hoped for so much was here at last!

So he set out with gusto on the road to the Citadel that morning, striding along and forgetting about his dog, who was trying to follow him through the city streets with his tongue hanging out. There was a nip in the air, the sky was azure blue, and something new and electric in the atmosphere made his heart beat fast.

The doors of the Hall of Delicacies were still shut when he arrived. Several dozen men were already waiting for an audience with the Coronador, standing in the morning mists and stamping their feet to keep warm. Guards stood outside the doors on sentry duty, armed with musketoons.

Orpheus elbowed his way through the crowd, taking a good look at everyone present as he passed. He couldn't help seeing a rival in each of them, for obviously the Coronador would choose only the very best for this mission. One man in particular attracted all eyes: a huge figure with enormous hands and shoulders as wide as a doorway. He towered above the rest, and there was something disturbing about his angular face. Passing close to him, Orpheus felt ridiculous. For years he had avoided exercise because of his supposed illness, and now he regretted not having more muscle to show. Yet again, his father's lies looked like damaging his chances of going on the expedition! How often recently had he felt like going to the cemetery and kicking Hannibal's brand-new tombstone!

"Whose dirty mutt is this?" an angry voice suddenly shouted.

Startled out of his thoughts, Orpheus suddenly realised that he had lost Zeph. He went towards the place where a group had gathered, and saw the St Bernard lying full length on someone's kit-bag with a roast chicken in his mouth. Red with embarrassment, Orpheus approached the man who had uttered that angry cry.

"I'm terribly sorry," he said. "He's a very old dog . . . he—"

"He stole my chicken!" shouted the man.

Orpheus recognised him at once. He was the nervous, active little man he had met so often at the Maritime Institute. His shock of red hair was even more striking than usual this morning; anyone would have thought he was an elf escaped from the moors of Dunbraven.

"I'll gut that animal!" he was shouting. "I'll wring his neck, I'll make mincemeat of him!"

Orpheus bent down and tried to recover the chicken, but Zeph had his teeth so firmly clamped on it that all he could save was a drumstick.

"Too late!" snapped the elf furiously. "By Holy Tranquillity, that wretched dog should be spit-roasted himself!"

"I'll pay for the chicken," Orpheus ventured.

"You can keep your galniks!" said the man indignantly, thrusting out his chest. "How many hours do you think I spent cooking that wonderful fowl? It was going to be a present for the Coronador! Chicken marinated with spices and wild onions! I alone know the secret recipe! Such a chicken is priceless in these times of famine!"

The man cast a mournful glance at his mangled masterpiece. Suddenly his voice broke. "And now," he wailed, "how am I to show the Coronador that I'm the best cook in all Galnicia, indispensable to the success of the expedition? There's nothing like good food to keep up the sailors' morale!"

Orpheus swallowed with difficulty. Voices were raised around them, either shocked or amused by this little hitch.

"If you're such a good cook," remarked one fellow, "why not invent a dog-slobber sauce?"

That brought laughter, but the little redhead didn't join in. He gave Orpheus a nasty look, muttering, "I don't know who you are, but I'm sure I've seen you somewhere before. I'll remember, you can be sure of that! If the Coronador doesn't engage me I'll be rev—"

He was interrupted by the opening of the doors, and the booming voice of a guard announcing that the audience was about to begin.

Orpheus felt his heart leap as he and the others entered the Hall of Delicacies. Much to his relief Zeph didn't try following him, but stayed outside on his own, guarding his chicken.

The procedure was swift and rigorous: the Coronador talked to each applicant, then the doctor from the Maritime Institute

127

examined all who seemed likely candidates. Finally the luckiest of them disappeared into the next room to swear an oath. Down in the harbour, two frigates were waiting for the fortunate elect who would make up their crews.

When his turn came, Orpheus stepped forward and knelt on one knee.

"Your name?" asked the Coronador.

"Orpheus McBott, your Alteza."

"McBott?" repeated the Coronador thoughtfully. "Are you by any chance Hannibal's son?"

There was a lump in Orpheus's throat. "Yes, your Alteza."

"Good!" said the Coronador, pleased. "No doubt you're a fine sailor! How is your father?"

"He's dead, your Alteza."

The Coronador seemed genuinely sorry to hear it. He offered Orpheus his condolences, and then signed to the doctor.

"Am I being taken on?" asked Orpheus in amazement.

"Your name speaks for you!" said the Coronador. "You'll be quartermaster. The McBotts have always served Galnicia with unselfish courage!"

This remark hurt Orpheus so much that he almost confessed the truth about his father. He wanted to be engaged on his own merits, not just because of his name! But how could he prove his worth? Books and fine speeches wouldn't carry any weight. If the Coronador learned that he had never set foot on a ship, he might change his mind.

So with a heavy heart Orpheus rose, thanked the Coronador humbly, and turned to the doctor, while the next applicant knelt before the throne.

"Any problems with your eyesight?" enquired the doctor, writing Orpheus's name down in a large book.

Orpheus shook his head, and the doctor ticked a box with his pen.

"Hearing?"

"Excellent."

"Is your blood a good healthy red? Does it flow freely?"

"I don't know. I never cut myself."

"Not even when you're shaving? Well, you're a skilful man!" said the doctor, laughing, as he ticked another box. "What about the rest of your anatomy? Head, heart, liver, lungs?"

Orpheus thought of the illness from which he had believed he suffered for so long. He turned pale, but said, "I tend to get colds and sneezing fits, that's all."

"Any seasickness?" asked the doctor.

This time Orpheus felt himself reddening. How could he answer that question without admitting his lack of seafaring experience? But the doctor, seeing his embarrassment, began laughing again.

"Don't worry, the best sailors sometimes have sensitive stomachs. It's no bar to going to sea!" He pointed to the entrance to the next room before adding, "Galnicia counts on you to bring the Princetta home. Good luck."

Orpheus went into the antechamber of the Hall of Delicacies. It was a dimly lit room with a low ceiling, and a window facing north. A thick carpet on the floor absorbed all sounds, and everyone who entered instinctively walked on tiptoe as if to avoid waking a sleeper. The Altar of the Divinities stood in the middle of the antechamber: a wooden pedestal on which the statues of the goddesses Tranquillity and Harmony were placed. The air was cold and damp. Orpheus could tell that the room had been closed for many long months in accordance with the Archont's various edicts.

The Venerable Monje, an old man with a body as dry and twisted as an ancient olive tree, laid his gnarled hand on Orpheus's shoulder. "Approach the altar," he told him.

Orpheus obeyed. From their wooden pedestal, Tranquillity and Harmony seemed to look down kindly on him.

The Venerable Monje picked up a goblet carved from stone and handed it to Orpheus.

"Drink a little of this," he said.

The goblet contained pure mountain water, cool with a slight peaty flavour. Orpheus drank a small mouthful with pleasure.

"Now repeat your oath after me," said the Monje. " 'I swear on my honour to serve my country and the Divinities. I swear to suffer and face a thousand trials steadfastly.' "

His throat tight with emotion, Orpheus repeated the oath. His ancestors before him had sworn these solemn words in this very place, from generation to generation. Until his father had broken the oath he took . . .

"Tranquillity and Harmony hear your oath," the Monje went on. "Now drink it all!"

He gave Orpheus the goblet again. When he raised it to his lips this time he sensed that the water was not the same: no longer pure and peaty, it had become very bitter. All the same, he swallowed it in a single draught, with a tingling that went right through his body. The Venerable Monje concluded the ceremony with these words:

"May this water, now bitter to the taste, defile your mouth for ever if the day comes when you break the word you have just given. Now go."

Greatly impressed, Orpheus left the antechamber.

*   *   *

Two days later, carrying his kit-bag and accompanied by Zeph, Orpheus crossed the gangplank leading to the deck of the *Errabunda*, the ship to which he had been appointed as quartermaster. He felt both happy and scared. Suppose my father was still lying to me? he thought. Suppose I really do die after two days at sea? Feeling dizzy, he had to grab the rail to keep himself from falling into the waters of the harbour.

"Want any help, Don McBott?" a piping voice suddenly enquired.

Leaning over the rail, Orpheus saw Hob encamped at the foot of the gangplank, looking at him with amusement. He wore new trousers, he still had his military hobnailed boots on, and a merry sparkle danced in his eyes.

"Carry your bag for fifty galniks?"

"Only fifty? Your kind heart will be the ruin of you, Hob!" replied Orpheus. "What are you doing here?"

The lad crossed his arms. "I wanted to see the heroes leave! Let me help you and I'll give you some very interesting information."

Orpheus hesitated. This urchin was perfectly capable of bamboozling him, but he liked the lad's nerve. He put his bag down in the middle of the gangplank, and with two agile leaps Hob was beside him. Zeph began growling as he sniffed the newcomer's feet.

"Is that your dog?" asked Hob. "Is he going too?"

"Zeph's had plenty of sea-going experience," said Orpheus. "He's crossed the Maltic Ocean, the Sea of Ypree, and he's even sailed to the Ochre Sea and the coasts of the Orniant."

Hob looked impressed, and hunkered down in front of the St. Bernard. "So you're the one who will rescue our Princetta?" he murmured, ruffling the fur on the dog's chest. "I can see Galnicia's in good paws!"

"I didn't have the heart to leave him behind," said Orpheus defensively. "He's old. By the time I'd gone to Cispazia and back he could be dead. He might as well come with me."

Hob rose and picked up the bag. "It's very heavy," he pointed out. "I think I'll need help."

The boy whistled. On the quayside, Orpheus saw another boy emerge from behind a pile of barrels where he had been hiding.

"By . . . by all that's holy!" Orpheus stammered.

The second boy was as like Hob as two peas in a pod! The same clear eyes, the same quick movements, the same dirty face, the same tousled hair.

"We'll offer you a bargain!" said the second boy. "Fifty galniks between my brother and me."

Twins, thought Orpheus, with a certain sense of relief. For several seconds, he had thought he was hallucinating. He smiled. "It's a deal. Bring the bag up here. But get a move on. We'll be setting sail soon."

In a twinkling of an eye, the twins had carried the kit-bag up the gangplank. They raced across the deck of the *Errabunda*.

"Hey, wait! What about that interesting information?" Orpheus shouted after them.

But the two boys had already disappeared down the first open hatch. Orpheus sighed. His dizziness was slowly passing. All around him the sailors were busy, climbing ladders, working pulleys, winding up the sheets. The quay was teeming with porters and curious onlookers. To the sound of much shouting, the holds of the *Errabunda* were being loaded up with barrels of water, Rioro wine and crates of pickled herrings, as well as fifty live chickens, twenty goats, ten sheep and four bullocks.

Orpheus caught sight of a flamboyant redhead on the poop: the ship's cook supervising the stores being taken aboard.

"Well, Zeph," murmured Orpheus, "I think we already have an enemy on board. You'd better make sure you don't show your face in his galley!"

Orpheus also noticed the presence of the giant with the sombre face whom he had seen on recruiting day at the Citadel. With unusual dexterity, he was carrying crates over the gang-plank of the *Errabunda*'s sister ship. The holds of the *Mary-Belle* were given over to arms and armour: stocks of gunpowder, carabins and musketoons, arbapults and a great many arrows. All these weapons were being taken in the expectation of battles against the armies of Temir-Gai, the formidable emperor of Cispazia.

According to the calculations of the official map-makers, the expedition could reach its destination in less than two months, for favourable winds blew when ships sailed that way. Coming back, they would probably have to take new sea routes and sail to the limits of the Known World. The venture had its risks, so the Coronador had insisted that a surgeon be taken on board the *Mary-Belle* and a Holy Diafron on board the *Errabunda*.

Orpheus looked up at the topgallant mast. The sails were quivering in the wind, and the green and yellow of the Galnician flag was already fluttering against the pure blue sky. Hadn't he always dreamed of this moment? Come along, he thought, time to move.

Followed by Zeph, Orpheus went over the deck looking for the twins. It was some time since they had disappeared. Suppose the rascals had made off with his things? They had a crafty look! Worried, he went down the ladders leading between decks. Several of the sailors were waiting beneath the low ceiling for the moment of departure. Orpheus questioned them, but none of them had seen the twins.

How stupid of me, thought Orpheus crossly. Those two urchins have robbed me, that's what! They'll sell my clothes, my books, my compass—and they're sure to get more than fifty galniks!

As he was fulminating to himself, he suddenly saw his kit-bag lying in a corner with all the others. He opened it. Everything was still there. Disturbed, he looked for the brothers among the sailors again, but without success. When he climbed back on deck, he had to admit that they were no longer on board.

"That's funny," he murmured. "It's not like Hob to go off without being paid."

But there was no time to search for an explanation now. Orpheus shrugged and went to look for the Captain and report for duty now that the anchor was being raised.

A few moments later the *Errabunda* and the *Mary-Belle* were leaving harbour to the cheers of the crowd. Feeling nervous, but with his mind full of all the navigational knowledge he had stored up, Orpheus supervised the hoisting of the sails without making any mistakes. The mizzen topgallant went up, then the fore topgallant, then the fore topsail. At last, standing on the fo'c'sle, he watched the Citadel and the shores of Galnicia move away, while Zeph, sprawled on deck, was taking his first siesta of the voyage.

A great peal of bells rang out from the Campanile on the highest point of the Upper Town, saluting the sailors as they left. Orpheus even saw the white walls of the McBott house in a ray of sunlight. As he watched it dwindle in the distance he swore to himself that if he survived this expedition, he would restore the glory to the name that he had inherited and that his father had besmirched.

PART TWO

Wandering

16

The Baths of Purity

When the gong sounded for the fifth time, all the girls had to be ready and waiting. Malva and Lei had soon found out what ready and waiting meant. Dressed in their red sarimonos, hands crossed on their breasts, their feet bare, they joined the long line of women captives as they all made for the Baths of Purity in silence. None of them must speak or smile or sigh. Only the soft sound of their bare feet on the white sand of the cloisters was to be heard.

At this early hour of the morning even the birds were still quiet. Wisps of mist drifted past the carved wooden columns, and only an occasional frog in the distance dared disturb the imperial silence.

Lei always positioned herself just behind Malva. As soon as the Princetta began to limp she managed to slow the pace slightly so that her friend's handicap would pass unnoticed. For Malva, the fifth stroke of the gong meant the beginning of an interminable period of suffering every morning. Not only was it a long walk to the Baths of Purity, after that they had to face the Immersion ceremony.

The Emperor Temir-Gaï had built a vast city on the heights of his capital city of Cispazan. Every building, every door and every column had been carved from the wood of the mesua tree, also called the iron tree. The city's skyline bristled with terraced towers capped with bell-shaped roofs. Watchmen mounted guard in every one of them.

Malva walked with her head down, trying not to put too much weight on her right leg. The procession soon came out into the mandapa, a strange hall open to the sky, where rows of pillars adorned with scrolls and encrusted with hundred of gemstones reflected the light like a mirror. When the first rays of the sun fell on the pillars of the mandapa, it was the hour of Immersion.

The girls separated and stood in little groups in front of the pillars as the chief preunuch had taught them. None of them risked disobeying his orders, or indeed those of any other preunuch. They all knew what punishment they could expect: the Cage of Torments.

On the day of her arrival, Malva had heard desperate cries and pleas for mercy. They came from a place in the city that the girls called "the slaughterhouse." She had gone there during her rest period to find out who was crying aloud and calling like that. Her heart missed a beat when she saw what the slaughterhouse actually was. Cages of mesua wood stood on a vast platform, exposed to the sun and the wind. Outside them, a mechanism of interlocking wheels allowed the top of the cages to be lowered, and the sides to be moved apart, or brought closer together. And there were girls inside the cages, some of them so tightly compressed between the bars that they were weeping and screaming. The more they screamed, the tighter the preunuchs turned the vice that was slowly crushing them. The same torture was inflicted on all who disobeyed Temir-Gai or failed to satisfy him.

At last sunlight flooded the mandapa. The preunuchs immediately emerged from the recesses where they had been concealed and raised their clear voices in honour of the new day.

To the sound of that crystalline song, the girls moved towards the Baths of Purity: a series of artificial pools in which the harem inmates bathed at certain times of day. The largest, full of seawater, was covered with lotus flowers. It was in this pool that the Immersion took place. Malva felt her pulse quicken again. She feared this moment so much that the pain grew worse every day, but what could she do? She must obey or be condemned to the Cage.

She stopped on the rim of the pool. Beside her, Lei was looking at its grey surface. At a change of tone in the preunuchs' singing, all the girls stepped into the water.

Malva took a deep breath and then held it. The salt water was already stinging her injured leg like thousands of needles driven into her skin.

"Swim," Lei murmured. "Don't make a sound."

Gritting her teeth, the Princetta began swimming, and all the girls around her made their way to the centre of the pool through the lotus flowers. The emperor Temir-Gai had appeared on the opposite bank in his silver robe, which had sleeves so long that they fell to his feet. He was watching the Immersion with a host of preunuchs beside him.

Every time she stretched her leg Malva felt her wound burning. It was almost unbearable, but she reached the middle of the pool somehow, casting Lei a glance of great distress. Any moment now the gong would sound for the sixth time. Then they must dive under water and stay there as long as possible. If they didn't . . .

The gong was struck. Malva opened her mouth, filled her lungs, and dived at the same time as all the others. The rules were very simple: the first to come up again was chosen by Temir-Gai to spend the next night with him. Every time she went down into the cold waters of the pool, Malva tried to imagine what that night would be like, and it gave her the strength she needed to stay below the surface. Except that after a while she was so short of breath that she couldn't stay down any longer.

This morning, when she came up again, she saw that she had been saved once again; another girl had been chosen.

"It's all right, Malva," Lei smiled as she came up too. "We have another day left."

Malva sighed at her, but she knew it was only a reprieve. Who knew—tomorrow, or the day after, the pain in her leg might prevent her from swimming at all, and then . . .

While the preunuchs were fishing out the unfortunate girl, the other prisoners moved quickly back to the bank. Malva cast a glance at that day's victim: a small girl with pale brown skin and curly hair, probably from the Mahara Desert. She was struggling and begging the emperor to spare her, but in vain. Everyone in the harem knew that no girls ever came back from Temir-Gai's chamber.

"Last night I find galeod larvae at last," Lei suddenly told her in a low voice. "Final ingredient missing to make medicine. You see—I heal leg tonight."

Full of hope, Malva looked hard at her friend. Since they had been held captive she had lived only for that magic medicine. Lei had been patiently collecting its ingredients, but it had taken her a long time to find the larvae of those nocturnal spiders.

"I do hope your medicine works," sighed Malva, reaching the bank of the pool at last.

"Is sure to!" Lei happily replied. "Is Balmun knowledge, remember!" And in her dripping sarimono she gave Malva her hand. "So soon as wound healed, you and me escape harem," she whispered. "Like my sister before us. Trust me."

Malva lay down in the grass, exhausted. The sun was climbing in the sky now, and all the girls dispersed among the columns to rest and talk. The Emperor Temir-Gai had disappeared with his prisoner, and the rest of the day would pass without too much anxiety—until the gong sounded tomorrow, and the cruel little game of the Immersion began again.

Yes, I trust you, daughter of Balmun, thought Malva. And once we're out of here I'll go and find Philomena, wherever she is, and take her to Elgolia. There'll be no Coronador there, no Archont, no Vincenzo, no sea monster, no Amoyeds, no Emperor, no harem and no torture.

Ever since she left the Citadel Malva had been adding more names to the list of dreadful people and things she never wanted to suffer from again. She was coming to realise that the Known World very rarely obeyed the precepts of Tranquillity and Harmony.

17

Midnight Feast

Our 69th day at sea, wrote Orpheus in his logbook. *I'm not dead yet. The sea is calm and there's a favourable wind. While I was on watch I saw birds like our seagulls, and larger shoals of fish than usual. Yesterday our cook—who's an excellent fisherman too—took advantage of a moment of calm to dive into the sea with a harpoon. He brought back some big breamacudas with silvery scales, which he says are typical of the Ochre Sea. There's no doubt about it: we're approaching Cispazia.*

He closed the logbook thoughtfully. In the silence of his cabin the candle cast moving shadows on the wooden walls. Zeph was asleep. This was the calmest hour of the night, a little before dawn, when only the hull of the ship creaking and the snores of the sleeping sailors could be heard. It was the perfect time to go about his business in secret.

Orpheus blew out his candle, rose from his chair, slowly opened the cabin door and made for the galley on tiptoe. Except for the two men on deck who had just taken over after his watch, no one would find him taking provisions on the sly.

Having made his way secretly into the galley for so many nights running, Orpheus had come to know the ways of the cook, Finopico. There was a shelf full of books and treatises behind the cast-iron stove. They were not cookbooks, but scientific works about fish. The cook was obviously passionately interested in the species populating the deep waters of all the known seas. But what interested Orpheus was the stores behind them: fruit pastes, blueberry fritters, marzipan cakes. He could always find a jar of herrings or spiced anchovies on other shelves. Of course Finopico noticed the food disappearing, but he dared not complain to the Captain, for these delicacies ought not to have been on board at all. The only problem was that the little redhead's suspicions fell on Zeph, and he kicked at the poor St. Bernard in the ribs whenever the dog put his nose out of the cabin.

Oh well, thought Orpheus, filling his pockets with sweetmeats. Zeph is pretty tough. He reassured himself as best he could, easing his conscience by reflecting that it was all in a good cause.

He came out of the galley and went stealthily down to the hold, where he groped his way past the stacks of barrels, the salt-corroded mooring ropes and the sacks of flour.

"It's me!" he whispered into the dark.

Soon he heard movement behind the sacks.

"What have you brought us?" asked a voice.

"Fruit paste, I hope!" added another.

"Everything you need," replied Orpheus, sitting down on a crossbeam. He took a candle end out of his pocket and lit the wick. Two dirty but hungrily beaming little faces emerged from the darkness.

"Herrings first!" said Hob, seizing the jar.

"Fruit paste for me!" exclaimed Peppe.

Orpheus watched the twins attack their feast with amusement.

"One meal a day doesn't go far," commented Peppe, licking his fingers, "but it tastes good all the same."

"I can't come down and see you in the daytime," said Orpheus apologetically. "You know it's too risky. If anyone noticed you were on board—"

". . . the Captain would have us hung from the main yard by our feet, we know!" chanted the twins in chorus.

"And me too!" Orpheus pointed out. "A quartermaster who hides stowaways deserves no better. Frankly, I don't know what's kept me from throwing you overboard since the first day of our voyage. To think I was idiot enough to believe you'd gone back on land without asking for your fifty galniks!"

The two brothers nodded, still eating.

"We knew we could count on you," smiled Hob. "You're the sort who wouldn't hurt a fly!"

"We didn't hesitate for a moment, not once we knew you were going on board the *Errabunda*," Peppe continued, between mouthfuls.

"And we've sort of paid our way," said Hob. "The information we gave you was worth two berths down in the hold here, wasn't it?"

Orpheus looked doubtful. That information hadn't amounted to much: just some fortune-teller's predictions! According to the fortune-teller the Archont had taken ship for Cispazia a few days before the *Errabunda* sailed. The two boys believed firmly in what she said, but Orpheus had too rational a mind to put his faith in a fortune-teller and her cards. To ease his conscience, however, he had mentioned it to the captain, but the captain had laughed in his face. The Archont couldn't have put out to sea ahead of them, for no ship had left Galnicia for months!

"Good, is it?" asked Orpheus, to change the subject.

"A real banquet!" sighed Hob, devouring his fourth herring. "How's your dog, by the way? Is he still seasick?"

"I don't know!" laughed Orpheus. "He spends all his time asleep—and there was I thinking he was such a good sailor!"

"When do we arrive in Cispazia?" enquired Peppe.

"Tomorrow, with a favouring wind."

"And then what? You're going to save the Princetta, aren't you? How are you going to go about it?"

"I don't know," Orpheus admitted, "but I suppose the captain has his plans."

Hob abruptly straightened up. "I know what I'd do if I was captain of this ship. I'd send the giant to talk to Temir-Gai, and—"

"The giant?" Orpheus spluttered with laughter. "You mean Babilas?"

"That's him! The one who can lift four barrels with one hand! I saw him do it when he came down to the hold the other day. He's very, very strong!"

"He is indeed," agreed Orpheus. "I've never seen a man as strong as Babilas. But the captain can't send *him* to talk to Temir-Gai."

"Why not?"

"Because Babilas is mute," Orpheus explained. "He hasn't spoken a word for years. No one knows why not."

"Oh," said Hob, disappointed. He sat down beside his brother and pinched a marzipan cake from him.

"There'll be fighting anyway!" said Peppe. "With all the

145

cannon and the loaded musketoons aboard the *Mary-Belle*, the Cispazians will soon see who they're dealing with!"

"You bet!" Hob agreed. "And they'll give us back our Princetta like a shot!"

Orpheus smiled as he saw the eyes of these two little warmongers shine. Every night, when he came down to talk to them, he briefly forgot the cares and responsibilities weighing on him. He was certainly doing very well as quartermaster, and if he had made a few mistakes they hadn't been serious. But the crew could be sullen, and some of the old salts didn't like taking orders from him. Among themselves they called Orpheus "greenhorn." If they could play a mean trick on him they did: it might be beetles in his soup, a dead rat in his shoes, a squirt of vinegar "accidentally" sprayed in his face. Nothing really vicious, just the rough humour of seamen. All the same, Orpheus felt that he was an outsider and they misjudged him. In making him quartermaster, the Coronador had handed him something of a poisoned chalice. So these moments spent with the two boys did him good.

"Are you finally going to tell me why you were so keen to sail with the *Errabunda*?" he asked them. "Whenever I ask you turn all mysterious!"

In the course of their nights on board, the twins had told Orpheus something about their eventful if poverty-stricken life. They had been born thirteen years earlier in a distant province on the border between Galnicia and Armunia. Their parents had fallen ill and died, and the two little boys were left orphans before they were three. An old woman in the village took them in, and they had lived with her for many years, but she gave them more beatings than bread, and at the age of ten they had decided to run away.

Wandering the roads and begging for food, they had eventually reached the city, but once there they were caught and sent to an orphanage. "It was worse than a prison!" said Hob. "They made us sleep on straw mattresses full of bugs, and we had to go out begging for the monjes who looked after us. By way of thanks they whipped us and shut us up in dark cells for days on end."

Tough and resourceful, Hob and his brother had run away again. Ever since then, they had been living in the streets, their only family a gang of other urchins. Such hardships no doubt explained their wish to leave Galnicia, but Orpheus guessed there was something else too. A secret that they were keeping between them.

"We don't have any secrets," Hob assured him. "We just wanted to see something of the Known World."

"If we have to live in poverty, we might as well be free!" added Peppe. "And anyway, our future is going to be—"

Hob elbowed him in the ribs to make him shut up.

"Nobody knows the future, you fool! Don McBott has told us we shouldn't believe everything that fortune-tellers say!"

Just then Orpheus heard hurry and bustle between-decks. Day was dawning. It was time for him to go back and join the crew.

"Keep as quiet as mice," he told the two boys. "As soon as we land I'll come and get you, and then you'll be free to go where you like."

He snuffed out the candle and hastily went back up. He didn't in the least want to run into one of the sailors, still less the cook. When he was safe in his cabin he took out his china bowl, filled it with water, and splashed his face. He was short of sleep, but he couldn't lie down now. He began shaving.

As he ran the razor-blade over his cheeks, he thought of his little protégés. He was certainly getting fond of them. They had dared to do what Orpheus himself should have done at their age: they had struck out on their own without asking anyone's permission! It was for all these reasons that he took the risk of hiding them. It wasn't entirely honest, of course, and his conscience had given him trouble, but he'd have felt even worse if he had given the boys away to the Captain. And the presence of the twins didn't put the expedition in any danger; it hurt no one and nothing but the irascible cook's personal stocks of food.

Zeph moved at the end of the bunk and gave a big yawn. Then he went back to sleep.

As he put down the shaving soap, Orpheus looked at himself in the mirror. The sun and the sea-spray had weathered his skin. He almost looked like a real sailor, but these sixty-nine days of easy sailing weren't enough to make a man of him. Storms, he thought. I want storms and tempests! Shipwrecks! Battles and the sound of cannon fire!

18

In Temir-Gai's Cages

Malva and Lei woke well before the gong sounded for the first time. All around them the other girls were sleeping peacefully on their bamboo mats.

"Show it," murmured Lei.

Malva pushed back her sheet to uncover her leg. The night before, Lei had wrapped her wound in a dressing of her own making, and now it was time to see what effect it had taken.

With a delicate touch, the daughter of Balmun lifted the dressing a little way. Malva clenched her teeth and searched feverishly under her mat for one of the paghul cakes she had hidden there. She crunched one to give herself courage. Since she had been torn from Uzmir's protection she had chewed the seeds in the cakes all the time. They had the power to soothe her body and her mind.

Suddenly Lei's face brightened. "See!" she whispered.

Malva bent her leg. Incredible: the wound had almost

disappeared! There was nothing left but a long white scar where the nameless monster had dug its teeth in.

"You touch!" Lei suggested.

With a trembling hand, Malva put her fingers on the scar. She felt nothing but her fingertips. She rubbed harder. Nothing! No pain at all!

"Move it," Lei suggested again.

Malva did, with obvious delight. She kicked her leg in the air several times, and finally ventured to stand up.

"It doesn't hurt," she breathed, eyes wide with amazement. "It doesn't hurt at all! Look, Lei! I can walk! I can walk as well as ever!"

"Ssh!" whispered Lei, putting a finger to her lips. "You wake other girls."

"I can walk! I can walk!" repeated Malva, deliriously happy. "This is wonderful, Lei! You're a real magician!"

She was almost dancing now. She jumped up and down on the slatted mesua wood floor so vigorously that one of the girls eventually raised her head.

"You sleep," Lei murmured to her. "What you see just a dream."

The girl muttered, turned over and went to sleep again. But that had calmed Malva down. She sat cross-legged, her eyes riveted to her leg, marvelling.

"Thank you, thank you, Lei! You've saved me! I don't know how to—"

Here the gong suddenly sounded for the first time, cutting her short. All the girls woke with a start. They leaped to their feet, picked up their sarimonos and flung them around themselves before kneeling beside their mats.

"Quick," breathed Lei. "No one see us!"

She and Malva hurried to put on their clean sarimonos. No sooner had they knelt down than the second stroke of the gong made them tremble. With a single identical movement, all the girls picked up the ivory combs beside their mats and began arranging their hair.

Malva saw the scene with new eyes. On other mornings, concentrating entirely on her own pain, she hadn't noticed the rest of the girls. Today she was fascinated by the perfect choreography of their movements. How did anyone, even if he was emperor of Cispazia, manage to get so many people to do such things all at once? It was both very beautiful and very disturbing. And yet Malva could not help joining in the movements of the ensemble: she too combed her black hair, which had grown again and now fell to her shoulders like the wings of a crow.

The third stroke of the gong heralded the entry of the preunuchs. They advanced in single file, silent, heads bent, with the yellow headband around their foreheads showing that they were slaves. They put down a bowl of steaming mococo milk in front of each girl.

At the fourth stroke of the gong, the girls raised the bowls to their lips. The milk was creamy and fragrant, and, as usual, Malva discreetly added a paghul cake to it. But this morning she didn't have time to let the delicacy dissolve in her bowl. In her haste, she slipped the remaining cakes into the pocket of her sarimono.

At the fifth stroke of the gong the girls were ready in the cloisters, lined up in silence. When they started walking Malva felt a joy that she could hardly contain. I'm walking normally, she told herself. It's incredible! I'm not limping at all!

She was so relieved that she didn't even mind the prospect of the Immersion. The salt of the first Bath of Purity might attack her skin, but now it wouldn't sting!

As she stood on the edge of the pool she was almost smiling.

"Your face," Lei whispered. "Careful. Not smile."

Malva bit the inside of her cheeks and stepped into the water. The lotus petals were fragrant around her. She began swimming strongly and was first to reach the middle of the pool. It was only then that she noticed the man who had just appeared beside the emperor Temir-Gai.

He wore garments like those of the rich merchants who traded along the coasts of the Ochre Sea. A tall man, he towered a head above the emperor. An embroidered hat hid part of his face. All the same, Malva felt uneasy in his presence, as if she were facing someone she already knew. Standing on the bank, the emperor was murmuring confidentially into his guest's ear.

"That man," Malva breathed to Lei. "Who is he?"

The daughter of Balmun examined him from a distance and shrugged. "Not know. But two girls picked today. You take very care."

The gong was about to sound for the sixth time. Malva needed to be ready to dive, yet that man was taking up all her attention . . . Now his glance was wandering attentively over the girls waiting in the middle of the pool. Suddenly his steely eyes pierced Malva like two arrows.

Her heart missed a beat and she almost cried out when she recognised him. But the gong was struck at that very moment. Lei just had time to catch hold of Malva's hand, and all the girls dived at once.

Malva felt bad as soon as she was under the water. She hadn't taken enough air into her lungs. And that look of his, by Holy

Tranquillity, that look! She kicked her feet out as best she could, but her tight chest was crying out for air. Air, air!

When she came up from the water there was only one other head above the surface. The emperor instantly pointed to her and called out orders to his preunuchs: Malva was to be given to the emperor's guest.

Once again her eyes met the piercing glance of the man who was claiming her. And what she read in those grey eyes left her in no doubt: yes, he really was the Archont.

How had he come to this place? What claim had he on Temir-Gaï's hospitality? Malva couldn't understand it. But one thing seemed clear: he had come all this way to kill her. And he would get his chance to do it this very evening with complete impunity, in the room placed at his disposal by the emperor.

The preunuchs fished Malva out and immediately took her to one of the buildings in the main palace at the other end of the city. They shut her up in a small room with screens of lattice-work over the windows, and only a single white cushion in the middle of it.

She stayed there, alone and terrified, for much of the day. She paced up and down, refusing to sit on the white cushion or even look out of the window. Her sarimono dried on her. She was neither hungry nor thirsty. Through the ornate latticework over the windows she saw the sun pass slowly over the sky, and when it turned red two more preunuchs came into the room and signed to her to go with them. She followed them to the entrance of a much larger room with lotus petals sprinkled over its floor. Apparently she had to undergo a ritual to prepare her for the emperor's guest.

Once again the preunuchs left her alone.

Malva walked into the room. She saw a chest at the far end,

with bowls of fresh fruit and a flask of some kind of liquor on it. The food and drink were obviously meant for her, but she didn't touch them.

All the time, all the time she saw the Archont's grey eyes before her. Anger and disgust churned in her stomach. How had he picked up her trail? Why was he hounding her? Had something happened in Galnicia?

Oh, Lei, she thought sadly. If only your magic could save me again! But there was nothing the daughter of Balmun could do now, and time was inexorably passing.

A chime of bells heralded the arrival of more preunuchs. They took away the bowls of fruits and the flask, and then led Malva to a third room.

This time she had to climb down stairs and go along the city's hidden underground passages. At last the preunuchs pushed Malva into a bedroom. An enormous bed on carved wood feet stood enthroned in the middle of the room. A gallows wouldn't have made a worse impression on her. This is the end, she told herself, hearing the door close behind her. The intense fear she felt fanned the flames of her anger and revulsion. And the waiting went on and on, so long that when the door opened again Malva was nothing but a bundle of nerves.

She gave a start and spun round. The Archont was standing in the doorway of the room, wearing a green sarimono. Malva felt her chest contract. Violent spasms twisted her stomach.

"Well, Princetta," began the Archont. "You appear to be unsinkable."

He did not move, but leaned against the door frame, very sure of himself. Malva was unable to utter a word.

"You've led me a pretty dance, Princetta," continued the Archont in honeyed tones. "And you are causing me a great deal of trouble. So I decided to do the job myself rather than leave it to incompetents like Vincenzo."

With these words he untied the belt round the waist of his sarimono, ran it through his fingers and took its ends in both hands. Malva opened her mouth to scream, but controlled herself. If she was to have any chance of escaping the worst she absolutely must keep calm. She stood firm on her feet and took control of her breathing again.

"Did the Coronador send you?" she asked, hoping to gain time.

The Archont smiled unpleasantly. "No one sent me. The days when I took orders from the Coronador are over. You and I still have something in common, you see: we don't like blind obedience to the powerful men of this world."

He brandished the belt.

"Temir-Gai is sure to understand that accidents can sometimes happen . . ."

He wound the belt around his fists and pulled them sharply apart. There was a small, dry sound. Malva swallowed with difficulty.

"The whole country was literally distraught with grief on learning that you had disappeared," continued the Anchor. "I did try to inject some tranquillity and harmony into the chaos . . . but you resurfaced too soon."

Malva tried not to tremble, tried not to flinch. But every time the Archont tensed the belt between his hands she shivered. It was strange: she had been close to this man for ten years without suspecting anything, she'd even enjoyed his company! And now, facing him, she had never been so frightened in her life.

"I've waited ten years!" exclaimed the Archont, as if reading her thoughts. "It was all so well calculated. I contrived to turn you against your parents and vice versa. You were ripe for the plucking, Princetta. I had only to make it easy for you to run away . . . and didn't you think it was an excellent plan?"

"You can still seize the throne," replied Malva, never taking her eyes off the sarimono belt. "I won't stop you. You're wasting your time here. You'd do better to go back to Galnicia and finish the job there."

"I don't need any advice from you!" the Archont exploded, lashing the air with the belt.

Malva took a step back in panic.

"If it's any consolation to you before you die, the throne has slipped through my fingers once and for all. Your chambermaid got a message through to the Citadel. I was unmasked . . . and by a servant, by that . . ."

The Archont was quivering with rage, while Malva, in the grip of terror, took in this information without fully understanding it.

"And when I've finished with you," the Archont went on, "I shall deal with that girl. Wherever she is, I'll find her. I have only one thing to live for now, and that's revenge."

He took a step towards Malva. The door was still open behind him. It was now or never!

Malva charged forward with the energy of despair and managed to race through the open door. The Archont just had time to turn and see her disappearing down the long corridor.

Malva had never run so fast in her life. Her leg, healed now, allowed her to take great strides and speed along the stairs and passageways that wound beneath the imperial city.

But the Archont, reacting fast, uttered a cry of fury and set off in pursuit of her.

"You won't escape me again!" he shouted. "I shall kill you this very evening. That's what I came for!"

Malva ran faster and faster. The corridors turned, branched, flights of steps went up or down to connecting suites of rooms. She took the stairs at random, without stopping to think, terrified by the shouts of the Archont hard on her heels.

Suddenly she came to a dead end. She pressed her hands to the wall, hammered it with her fists. Nothing, no door! She turned. Looking this way and that, she finally saw an opening at floor level. She lay down and put her head into the space. It was a kind of tunnel sloping down, perhaps a sewer to get rid of rubbish or drain away dirty water. Using her elbows to help her, she clambered in. It was tight, but she had grown so thin since leaving Galnicia that she could get her whole body into it.

Just as her feet were disappearing into the tunnel she heard the Archont arrive and come to a halt in front of the blank wall. Heart thudding, Malva steadied herself against the walls of the tunnel and slid further down.

"There she is, naughty girl!" said the Archont's voice.

His words echoed down the tunnel. Twisting her neck, Malva could see the opening through which she had escaped. It was now filled by the Archont's face. He was watching her with a terrifying smile on his lips.

"She's caught herself in the trap!" he laughed. And he put his own head into the opening.

Panic-stricken, Malva climbed down with all her strength to get away from the Archont. And when she turned again, she realised that he couldn't follow her: his broad shoulders wouldn't fit into the opening! He was hammering the floor with his fists, his face distorted by hatred.

Malva wriggled along the narrow passage. The one thing she feared was coming up against a grating which would prevent her from emerging at the far end. But luckily the tunnel finally broadened out, and she found herself in a kind of dark sewer stinking of urine and decomposition.

She rolled over on the ground and managed to get up. It was so dark that she couldn't even see her feet. But straining her ears, she detected the presence of something there. She had a lump in her throat. What she could hear was the sound of breathing.

Hands stretched out in front of her, Malva groped her way forward. Suddenly she seemed to have stepped on something. It was soft. She bent down. Whatever she had just stepped was warm . . . and hairy.

A growl suddenly broke the silence. Malva jumped back and pressed herself against the wall. An animal! She had fallen into an animal's den! And the shaft along which she had come was meant to ventilate its cage!

The animal breathed noisily. Malva heard it moving, and when she felt the ground shake she realised it was getting to its feet. With her back against the wall, she tried not to breathe.

As the animal growled louder and moved restlessly, there was a sudden clink of keys and a light appeared, illuminating a corridor and the bars of the animal's cage. Attracted by the noise, a preunuch with a flaring torch had come to investigate. Malva slipped down against the wall and crouched on the ground.

Whispering a few soothing words, the preunuch raised his torch. In the orange light of its flame, Malva could finally make out the animal's massive outline. And suddenly she saw two pairs of horns shining. Her heart missed a beat. The celestial-charioteer! By Holy Harmony! She was shut up in the monster's cage!

The celestial-charioteer was so big and heavy that it had difficulty moving in the small space. However, it managed to turn round, and Malva saw its terrible oblong head lower towards her. She bit the inside of her cheek to keep herself from screaming with terror.

Meanwhile, out in the corridor, the preunuch was still waving his torch about, trying to see the back of the cage. But Malva was hidden by the celestial-charioteer's enormous body. It was snuffling at her now with slimy nostrils. She felt a long trickle of saliva drip on her left arm: no doubt about it, the charioteer was hungry!

Suddenly Malva remembered that she still had the paghul cakes in her sarimono. She slowly slipped her hand into her pocket. The cakes had been soaked with water during the Immersion, and had turned to a kind of mush, but she had no other choice. She opened the palm of her hand under the charioteer's nostrils.

For a few seconds the monster stopped growling and shifting about. It sniffed the cakes. Then it seemed to make up its mind. Malva felt its enormous tongue sweep over her hand, and soon she heard the spongy sounds of munching. She quickly felt in the bottom of her pocket and held out all that remained of the cakes under the monster's muzzle. But she was trembling so much that the paghul mush fell to the floor. The charioteer lowered its head to lick them up.

At that moment the light of the torch dazzled Malva. In lowering its head the animal had revealed her to the preunuch, and he immediately let out a harsh cry. Frozen against the side of the cage, Malva sighed with despair. This time she was trapped with no chance of escape.

A dozen preunuchs hurried into the corridor outside, armed with torches and swords. One of them opened the celestial-charioteer's cage and four others marched in. They seized Malva by the shoulders and took her out, while the monster continued to lick the ground in search of more paghul cakes.

From the cries of the preunuchs, Malva realised that she had committed a terrible crime: intruding into the den of Temir-Gai's totem animal amounted to sacrilege! Her guards dragged her roughly up and down stairs and along corridors to the chambers of the emperor who, alerted by more preunuchs, was waiting for the culprit.

The preunuchs threw Malva at his feet, and in their own language gave the emperor a brief explanation. Face on the floor, Malva felt the blood beating in her temples. She didn't understand a word they were saying, but Temir-Gai's fury was so great that she needed no translation. For a moment she thought they might simply cut off her head on the spot.

The emperor bent down, seized her by the hair and forced her to look at him. His face was blotched with red. The emperor barked out a few words, let go of Malva and strode out of his chambers.

Immediately after that, the preunuchs dragged Malva outside the building. It was a dark night, and the croaking of the frogs over by the Baths of Purity could just be heard. The preunuchs pushed Malva on from one garden to the next. She knew what fate awaited her when she saw the "slaughterhouse" with its platform and Cages of Torments.

The preunuchs opened one of the cages and thrust Malva inside. They closed and locked the door, and then one of them took hold of the handle that worked the mechanism and turned it several times. Malva saw the top of the cage come down. Sitting on the floor, she brought her knees up and laid her head on them. The top of the cage came to rest on her backbone, and she grimaced.

At that moment she heard voices as if there were a whole cavalcade coming. Malva turned her head slightly. More pre-unuchs arrived at a run, holding lanterns, and in front of them ran a girl in a simple white cotton shift. Malva's heart leaped when she recognised her: it was Lei.

"Malva!" Lei cried, sobbing. "You alive!" She knelt down beside the cage and put her hands over it. "Preunuchs come find me, must translate what you say," she said in a toneless voice. "Daughter of Balmun speak all languages, they know that."

There was more commotion in the gardens, and Temir-Gai appeared, accompanied by the Archont. Both of them climbed up on the platform. The emperor pointed to the Archont and let fly several furious remarks.

"He want to know why you disobey guest of honour? Why you escape?"

Malva felt icy sweat trickling between her shoulderblades. Vertigo blurred her vision. She was on the point of fainting.

"He wanted to kill me," she murmured.

"She's lying!" cried the Archont, before Lei was even able to interpret.

The emperor went on with his interrogation.

"He want to know what you do in celestial-charioteer's cage . . . and what you give it to eat. He think it poison."

"Paghul cakes," sobbed Malva. "It was only paghul cakes!"

Lei translated her reply into Cispazian. The emperor gave

some orders. Lei turned paler than ever. Her lips began to tremble.

"He think you poisoner! He think you liar! He condemn you to Cage of Torments. He say you die in three days—"

"And no less than she deserves," interrupted the Archont with satisfaction. He took a step forward and leaned towards Malva. "I'd rather have killed you with my own hands, but tomorrow morning I shall come to admire the effect of this cage on your bones. I want to hear them breaking one by one."

Lei was weeping, one cheek against the wooden cage. The preunuchs hauled her away, and then the emperor told everyone else to go. They all left the platform, abandoning Malva to her fate.

19

A Night in Cispazan

That same evening, the *Errabunda* and the *Mary-Belle* cast anchor in a creek sheltered from the wind. It was exactly seventy days since the crew had last set foot on land, and when the captain asked for volunteers to set out for the port of Cispazan as scouts, dozens of hands went up. Only Orpheus, who was anxious about leaving Hob and Peppe alone, kept his hands behind his back.

The captain picked a dozen of the heftiest men, and then looked at Orpheus in surprise. "I need a man with a head on his shoulders to command this expedition. Don't deny yourself, McBott. You've worked well during the crossing, you've earned the right to stretch your legs."

Orpheus felt several hostile glances resting on him. If he declined to go he'd risk being called greenhorn again . . . And so he found himself on board a dinghy seated opposite the gigantic Babilas, who was rowing and never took his eyes off Orpheus.

They came ashore on a little beach surrounded by cliffs.

Babilas raised the dinghy with one hand and hauled it up on shore with disconcerting ease. Orpheus felt very ill at ease in the company of these tough men, but he tried not to let it show, and set off with them along a path criss-crossed by tree roots. It ran on into the black night of the Orniant.

Everything here was so different from Galnicia! The plants, the smells, the sounds, even the stars in the sky were like nothing Orpheus knew. He stumbled and almost fell several times, which made him even more nervous. And in spite of the darkness, he sensed Babilas looking at him all the time.

After walking for an hour, they saw the lights of the imperial city of Cispazan. Red lanterns marked the entrance to the harbour, where strange flat-bottomed sailing ships were anchored.

"I suggest we separate," said Orpheus when they reached the first houses. "If we go in pairs we'll be less conspicuous than in a group."

The sailors turned to Babilas, who nodded his assent and placed himself beside Orpheus.

"We'll meet at the far end of the creek before first light," Orpheus added. "And be on your guard. Don't forget that we have no musketoons or carabins to help us out of trouble."

Orpheus patted the pocket of his quartermaster's jacket to make sure his knife was still there. Knives were the only weapons the captain had allowed them to take on this mission. Anything else could attract suspicion.

Each pair of men set out. Orpheus and Babilas skirted the harbour area and made for the heights of the city. Silent and watchful, they avoided going too far down the streets, and instead hid behind flowerbeds to watch the Cispazians coming and going.

"These people enjoy their night life," said Orpheus in an undertone.

A crowd of men was walking past the wooden houses with their conical roofs, by the light of red paper lanterns. The men talked in loud voices, laughed a lot, and sometimes stopped to slap their thighs. They wore embroidered jackets with long sleeves, and braided skull caps on their heads. Some were smoking long pipes, others were drinking from little silver flasks.

"I don't know what kind of alcohol it is," whispered Orpheus, "but they're all tipsy. This is our chance. A drunk doesn't get suspicious. Come on, Babilas."

Feeling more confident, he led the giant under the lanterns and down a series of identical streets. At each gateway, wooden statues of animals, their eyes encrusted with jade, seemed to stand guard. Orpheus shivered at the sight of their grinning faces; the monsters reminded him of the masks hanging from the walls in his father's study.

Babilas suddenly put his enormous hand on Orpheus's shoulder. A troop of very strange men was approaching. These new arrivals didn't laugh, didn't talk, didn't drink and didn't smoke. Instead, they marched in close formation with their heads lowered. Bright yellow ribbons were tied round their foreheads. In their midst, keeping time with them, marched several boys who did not seem to be more than eleven or twelve. These boys all had their heads shaved, except for a short lock falling over the forehead.

"Do you think those are soldiers enlisting new recruits?" Orpheus whispered to Babilas once the troop had passed.

The giant shook his head.

"All the same, let's follow them. I'd like to find out where they're taking those children."

They hurried to catch up with the strange procession, and followed it at a suitable distance along roads that widened as they went uphill. At last they came out into a huge grassy square, this time lit by green paper lanterns. The noise and confusion of the red-lantern district was left behind.

"Look at that, Babilas," whispered Orpheus.

At the far end of the square rose a huge wooden wall. A massive gate in the middle of it opened to let in the men with yellow headbands and the boys.

Orpheus and his companion approached the wall. In spite of the darkness, they could just make out other monumental buildings rising beyond it: terraced towers with bell-shaped roofs, columns, long, low structures. The whole place seemed to be entirely made of carved wood.

Orpheus and Babilas stopped at the huge gate. Now that it had been closed again, they saw that there were inscriptions carved on it.

"Can you read those?" Orpheus asked hopefully.

By way of reply, Babilas pointed to the top of the gateway. The building was dominated by the statue of a man riding a gigantic animal with silver horns.

"Just as I thought," said Orpheus. "We must be outside Temir-Gai's palace. And his harem is sure to be in there. Behind that wall."

As he lingered, looking at the statue, he saw the sky turning pale in the east. Dawn came early in these distant countries.

"Let's get back to the *Errabunda*, and fast," said Orpheus.

When they reached the creek the stars were fading one by one in the pale sky. The other men on the scouting expedition were already waiting for them in the dinghy. They quickly went down to the beach, and once they were aboard Babilas took the oars.

Orpheus heaved a sigh. He was exhausted, and nearly fell asleep on the way back to the ship when loud shouts awoke him.

"Hey!" laughed one of the sailors, looking up at the sails. "What's going on there? Looks like there's been some good monkey-hunting!"

Orpheus sat up straight in the boat and looked in the direction the sailor was pointing to. What he saw sent a chill through him: two figures were dangling from the main yard. It was Hob and Peppe, hanging from their feet and wriggling like eels as they called for help.

A rope ladder had been let down from the stern of the ship. One by one the men in the dinghy climbed up it to the deck of the *Errabunda*, but Orpheus didn't have the strength to follow them. He needed a little time to collect his wits. If the twins talked, if they gave his name, he was done for. The captain would wash his hands of him, the crew would curse him roundly, and he would never again be able to go to sea.

"Well, quartermaster?" said the captain as Orpheus finally scrambled over the ship's rail to jump down on the deck. "It seems you've had a fruitful expedition! Babilas has let me know that you found the harem!"

Unable to say a word, Orpheus nodded. The cries of Hob and Peppe left him literally speechless.

"See those two clowns we found while you were away?" added the captain. "Stowaways! They were stealing herrings from the galley, but Finopico caught them in the act."

"Oh," was all Orpheus could say in a hollow voice.

"We'll let them hang up there for a few more hours. That'll take their appetite away."

As the captain seemed to be going on to other matters, Orpheus found his voice. "Did they say how they got aboard?"

The captain shrugged. "Can't get a sensible word out of them. They've done nothing but yell ever since we caught them."

Orpheus felt enormous relief. Good boys! They hadn't confessed anything. But now, how was he to get them out of this fix?

"Tell me about the harem!" the captain ordered.

Orpheus suddenly had an inspiration. Yes, it was a brilliant idea!

"The harem . . . well, that's just it!" he cried. "Believe it or not, we could use those two lads."

"The thieves? Nothing doing!" growled the captain. "They're thin as sticks, good for nothing but feeding the fishes!"

Ideas were coming thick and fast in Orpheus's mind. The more he listened to the twins' shouts, the better his plan took shape. He gave the captain a brief account of all that he and Babilas had seen. He described the troop of men escorting the boys to the wall that surrounded the harem.

"A wall, yes, of course," muttered the captain. "So we'll have to force our way in. I'll go and count our carabins."

"Wait!" said Orpheus. "I have another suggestion to make. We could get into the harem in disguise."

"Disguise?" said the captain, surprised. "The Coronador ordered us to attack Temir-Gai. A thousand-years' war if necessary. Our gunpowder will speak for us!"

Orpheus mopped his brow. The pitiless sun of the Orniant was rising, and it was already beginning to get muggy.

"Yes, gunpowder certainly will speak for us," he said diplomatically. "But suppose we wound the Princetta?"

The captain raised an eyebrow. He obviously hadn't thought of this possibility.

"The harem buildings are made of wood," Orpheus went on. "If we fire on them with our cannons and musketoons, we risk setting fire to them."

"You have a point there," the captain admitted.

"My suggestion is, we quietly abduct the Princetta. Once she's aboard the *Errabunda* you can set fire to anything you like."

The captain rubbed his chin, looking perplexed. "And how are those two herring-thieves going to come in useful?"

Orpheus looked up at the main yard.

"Haul them down, find me some yellow fabric, and I'll show you," he said, with a small smile.

20

Rescue

"Fifty jars of herrings! Thirty-seven rations of biscuits! A kilo of olives, and I don't know what else!" cried Finopico, spitting with fury.

The cook struck his chest and shook his mop of red hair, raising his eyes to heaven, as if calling on the seabirds swooping around the *Errabunda* to bear witness.

"Those young rascals have cleaned me out!" he stormed. "And instead of punishing them we kindly make room for them on board! This is too much!"

Orpheus tried to concentrate on the arduous task in front of him, but he had difficulty containing his mirth. His idea really was a brilliant one: not only was he coming to the twins' rescue, he was also giving himself the pleasure of infuriating that nasty piece of work, the cook!

"They ought to have their hands chopped off!" shouted Finopico, going over to the barrel on which the two boys were sitting. "Chop off their hands, not their hair! That's what I say!"

"Stop shouting like that," Orpheus interrupted him. "You'll make my hand slip."

With a long barber's razor in his hand, Orpheus was just finishing shaving Peppe's head. Locks of dirty hair fell to the deck, making Zeph sneeze. For once the dog had dragged himself out of the cabin, enraging the cook even more. To Finopico's way of thinking, the St. Bernard and the two stow-aways were nothing but useless mouths, parasites, freeloaders.

Sitting beside his brother, Hob sighed as he inspected his reflection in a scrap of mirror glass.

"I look like an egg," he decided. "It's horrible. And that silly little lock over my forehead—is it really necessary?"

"Yes," said Orpheus. "It's the Cispazian fashion."

Once he had explained his plan to the captain, everything began moving faster. The crews of the two frigates were actively preparing for the mission, to take place that very evening. Divers were in training around the *Errabunda*, assessing the time it would take them to swim to the harbour, while on the deck of the *Mary-Belle*, the cannons were being polished up, gunpowder was brought out, and the carabins and musketoons were rubbed until they shone. If the first phase of the operation had been meant to take place quietly, the same could hardly be said of the second.

"And once the captain doesn't need you any more," Finopico threatened the twins, raising a vengeful finger, "I'll teach you manners!" He looked around him, and added, "The deck of the *Errabunda* badly needs sanding down and scrubbing with vinegar. You'll spend the whole of the voyage back on the job if necessary!"

At nightfall Orpheus, Babilas, the twins and two more sturdy sailors set off for Cispazan. They had put on dark tunics to avoid attracting attention, and the only arms they carried were their pocket knives.

"And remember," said Orpheus, "no one's to talk! Not a word of Galnician, understand?"

"We'll be as mute as Babilas," promised the twins, hands on their hearts.

In spite of the risks of this expedition, the brothers were excited to be going on dry land. It had been more than two months since they had been able to stretch their legs, and now, intoxicated by their adventure, they climbed the cliffs, gambolling about like goats.

Before the party entered the city, they hid behind some bushes, and the four men tied the makeshift headbands that Orpheus had made from fabric of the Galnician flag around their foreheads. Yellow, like the headbands worn by the Cispazians.

The men took Peppe and Hob in their midst, and then, striding out, they made for the tall wooden wall. The twins docilely lowered their shaven heads. They were acting their parts to perfection. As on the previous evening, the people out in the streets were staggering around and laughing as they went from tavern to tavern in the red light of the lanterns.

We pass muster so far, thought Orpheus. Let's hope it lasts . . .

When they reached the huge grassy space in front of the wall, they hesitated for a moment. Another group had got there just ahead of them—also consisting of men with headbands and boys with shaven heads. They too were making for the imperial city. Orpheus looked at Babilas. What should they do? Join the other group, or let them go first? He finally decided to join them, quickened the pace of their party, and caught up with the first group just as it reached the monumental gateway.

"*Ga Tai Ma Tai!*" called the guards.

"*Sumor Tet Ga Tai!*" replied the Cispazian leading the first group.

The guards opened the heavy gates and let them through. But when Orpheus, heart beating fast, tried to pass, they stopped him by raising their sword-blades.

"*Ma Tai Ga Tai?*" one of the guards asked.

Orpheus's forehead was bathed in sweat. He gulped, and in what he hoped was a firm voice repeated what he had just heard. "*Sumor Tet Ga Tai!*"

The guards immediately lowered their swords and stood aside to let the little party in. As he passed them Orpheus was trembling all over, but when the gates closed behind his back he heaved a great sigh. The first stage of his plan had gone successfully. Now came the difficult part: finding the Princetta. Always supposing, of course, that she was still in this harem. Orpheus hoped so.

All was quiet on the other side of the wall. In the moonless night, the lanterns and torches along the avenues and over the doors of buildings shone like hundreds of fireflies, and other lights fell from the tops of the towers, casting pools of yellow light over the gardens. A chorus of frogs could be heard croaking, and further away a kind of lament that sounded like singing.

"We mustn't be separated," Orpheus whispered. "Follow me."

They went along the avenues in silence, until they reached a strange kind of hall open to the sky and lined with pillars. They followed the pillars and came to a long, sandy path. Here Orpheus stopped. Nothing was stirring anywhere, not even the leaves on the trees. The eerie calm made him nervous.

"This way," he decided.

The sand underfoot muted their footsteps, and they could see where they were going.

Further on, they found a gate with two white lanterns hanging over it. To one side there was a window with ornamental shutters. Orpheus went up to the window and cast a quick look inside. He saw a dimly lit room where dozens of girls were sleeping on bamboo mats on the floor. Orpheus felt his heart leap. If the Princetta really is in this harem, he thought, she must be here.

To his surprise, the door of the dormitory was not locked. Orpheus pushed it gently open, and signalled to his companions to follow him in.

Once inside, they dispersed and separately went in search of the Princetta. Like all Galnicians, they would have known her among a thousand other girls. Her magnificent flowing black hair made her unmistakable.

They passed between the rows of sleeping girls, leaning cautiously down to look at them, noting every face. At the end of one row Orpheus saw an empty mat. A girl lay face down on the mat next to it, sobbing quietly. Intrigued, he went closer. She was not the Princetta; this girl's hair was as fair as wheat in August. He was about to move on, but as he retreated he stepped on a comb lying on the ground and broke it with a sharp crack.

The girl sat up. "Amun Lin?" she whispered, looking at Orpheus in terror.

He put a finger to his lips, to show that he didn't want her to cry out. "It's nothing," he murmured. "We mean you no harm."

The blonde girl looked at him intently. "You Galnician speak?" she said in amazement.

Orpheus knelt down beside her. "I'm looking for someone. A girl with hair like ink. Her name is Malva."

At these words the little blonde girl leaped to her feet and grasped Orpheus's tunic. "You come rescue Malva? You not preunuch?" she asked, pointing to Orpheus's yellow headband.

"It's a disguise," he said. "Do you know Malva? Where is she?"

"You friends of her?"

"Yes, yes," said Orpheus in urgent tones. "Where is she?"

"In Cage of Torments!" breathed the girl. "You come with me, quick!"

She hastily flung a garment of some kind round her and made for the doorway on tiptoe. Orpheus followed, alerting his companions with a snap of his fingers.

When they were all out in the cloisters, Lei examined the odd group before her with great surprise. Babilas and the two sailors looked strong, but the young man didn't look much like a warrior. As for the two boys, they were as thin as incense sticks.

"You have weapons?" she asked.

"No," said Orpheus. "Only knives."

"Too dangerous!" groaned Lei, aghast. "Many difficulties leaving harem!"

"Take us to Malva," Orpheus told her, "and then we'll see."

Resigned, Lei led them through the gardens. As they walked on, that strange, song-like moaning seemed to rise into the dark night more and more clearly.

When she saw the platform of the "slaughterhouse," Lei stopped and hid behind a hedge.

"Malva there," she whispered. "Locked in Cage of Torments. And guarded by Galnician man, guest of Temir-Gai."

"A Galnician man?" repeated Orpheus, frowning.

Dismayed, he carefully parted the branches of the hedge and looked at the scene. A torche was burning at each corner of the platform. He had a clear view of the row of cages. They were all empty . . . except one. And it was from this cage and the form crouching inside it that the moaning came. Just behind it, the tall silhouette of a man was pacing to and fro to a strange rhythm. In the torchlight, Orpheus recognised the Archont's smooth, domed head.

"By Holy Tranquillity!" he murmured. "The twins were right!"

Peppe and Hob stood on tiptoe, trying to see what Orpheus was talking about. When they caught sight of the Archont they nudged each other. The fortune-teller who read the cards for them had not been wrong!

"What's he doing?" asked Hob uneasily, pointing to the Archont.

"He turn handle of Cage of Torments," Lei told him with suppressed fury. "Malva soon crushed and die."

All their faces paled.

"We must act at once," said Orpheus, with a lump in his throat. "But how are we going to get the Archont out of the way?"

A heavy silence fell on the little group. The two sailors, clenching their fists, were already preparing to fight, but Babilas calmed them with a gesture. The moment the Archont uttered a sound the guards would intervene, and all would be lost. After a moment, Lei went up to the twins. Her pearl-like eyes examined them closely, and they blushed.

"In my land, in kingdom of Balmun, we think twins lucky," she murmured. She put her hands on their shaven skulls, and they jumped.

"Hey, paws off!" said Hob indignantly. "We're not *cornalinos!*"

Lei laughed, and took her hands away, saying, "Shaven heads work well. Everyone here think you two apprentice pre-unuchs!" She turned to Orpheus. "Twins go see foreign man, they take him away. Foreign man think they messengers from Temir-Gai."

Peppe and Hob were breathing fast. "But . . . but we don't speak Cispazian! What do we say to him? And then *where* do we take him?"

"No need speak," Lei reassured them. "Preunuchs always silent, except for singing before Bath of Purity. You lead man away from Malva, that all."

The moaning in the cage suddenly stopped. Orpheus froze. Suppose Malva had fainted? Or worse? He took the twins by the shoulders and pushed them towards the end of the hedge.

"You must hurry! If something goes wrong we'll come and help you!"

Walking unsteadily, Peppe and Hob went up to the platform. They climbed the steps and went round the cage to present themselves to the Archont. When they reached him, he was leaning all his weight on the handle with elation in his eyes.

"Who's there?" he asked.

The boys went closer, heads lowered, and the Archont stopped working the handle.

"Oh, two apprentice preunuchs!" he said.

Going up to them, he abruptly raised their chins. Hob and Peppe met the Archont's eyes. In the dim light, the man's eyes seemed to shine like two pieces of white-hot metal.

"What are you doing here?" he growled. "Can't you see I'm hard at work?"

Hob opened his mouth, but it was Peppe who murmured, "Temir-Gai."

177

"What do you mean, 'Temir-Gai'?" asked the Archont impatiently. "The emperor wants to see me—is that it?"

Peppe simply repeated, "Temir-Gai."

The Archont heaved a sigh of exasperation. "Very well, I'll go with you. I will tell the Emperor how honoured I feel to be allowed to turn this handle myself. I owe him that!"

The Archont pushed the handle down again, bringing the walls crushing Malva a notch closer together. A cry came from inside the cage, chilling Peppe and Hob to the bone.

"Come on, then!" said the Archont, laughing. "Take me to the emperor!"

The twins climbed down from the platform, set off in the opposite direction to where Orpheus and the others were concealed, and disappeared into the night, followed by the Archont.

Lei immediately ran out of hiding. "Malva! You hear me?" she whispered. "Lei is here. We set you free!"

A faint groan came from the cage. Meanwhile, Orpheus and the two sailors had grasped the handle and were trying to reverse the mechanism.

"It's stuck," said the first sailor nervously.

Babilas pushed them aside. Bracing himself, he tried to unjam the interlocking wheels. At that moment a dull and distant rumble like a roll of thunder came through the air. Orpheus looked up in surprise. There was not a cloud over the stars.

Suddenly, as Babilas stood with legs apart, exerting all his strength, the handle broke off in his hands.

"Oh no!" cried Orpheus, appalled.

"Malva!" groaned Lei, kneeling down. "She fainting!"

Babilas angrily flung down the handle and went up to the cage. Clenching his jaws, he took hold of two of the bars and tried to pull them apart. The mesua wood resisted, and Babilas's muscles quivered with the effort.

Another rumble, closer than the first, made the leaves of the trees around them shake. Orpheus turned his head. Over in the west he thought he saw flashes of light. Yet the sky was still clear. There was something disturbing about these strange phenomena.

Meanwhile Babilas was exhausting himself, tugging fruitlessly at the cage. The bars would not move. Orpheus took out his knife and tried to force the lock. He worked on it for some time, but jumped when he heard more thunder. There was a clamour in the west, beyond the city wall.

"Cage too strong!" said Lei. "Impossible get Malva out now! You leave—too dangerous here."

At that very moment the twins came running back to the platform, looking scared.

"We shut the Archont in a room in the palace, but now he's raising the alarm!"

As if confirming their words, shouts rang out, disturbing the serenity of the gardens. Red lights were rising to the sky over them.

Orpheus looked desperately at Babilas. What could they do? They must escape, but they couldn't possibly abandon the Princetta!

Suddenly the giant pulled the yellow headband from around his forehead. Taking a deep breath, he crouched down, put his mighty arms round the bars and lifted the cage from the platform. Orpheus, Lei and the twins watched him in astonishment. The giant's legs were shaking, thick veins stood out all along his arms, but he succeeded in hoisting the cage up on his shoulders. When he had recovered his balance, he signalled to Orpheus.

"Right," Orpheus whispered. "Let's get out of the city, fast!"

"I come too! I escape with you!" announced Lei.

All seven of them made for the gateway. Babilas led the way with Malva's cage on his back. It was an amazing sight. Oh, Holy Harmony and Holy Tranquillity, Orpheus prayed in silence, let him be able to carry the weight as far as the ship!

As they approached the gateway, the confused rumbling noise they had been hearing for some time grew louder. Preunuchs and guards had gathered in a great mass in front of the huge wall. Outside, flames were licking at the wood, and shouts and the sound of horses' hooves filled the air.

"A fight!" exclaimed Hob.

"A war!" said Peppe. "It's the captain and the men of the *Mary-Belle*!"

"But . . . but why have they launched their attack?" stammered Orpheus. "It's too soon! Much too soon!"

Suddenly the gates swung violently open, and tongues of flame shot inside the city walls. The preunuchs and imperial guards fell back, panic-stricken, shouting up at the buildings and towers.

"We must get out!" yelled Orpheus.

At that moment a horde of mounted men appeared. There were dozens of them, riding caparisoned horses, dozens of black shapes opening up a passage through the glowing conflagration. They galloped through the flames towards the harem.

"That's not . . ." Peppe murmured.

". . . the captain!" Hob finished for him, his jaw dropping.

The horsemen raced in close formation through the city gardens, trampling everything in their path. Sheltering behind a row of columns, Orpheus and his companions watched the mounted men pass. They were brandishing spears and whips.

And alone at their head, leading the attack, a young and vigorous man stood erect on his horse's back.

"Hunters from Great Azizian Steppes!" Lei shouted into Orpheus's ear.

The noise of the fire, the galloping horses and clashing weapons was deafening. Why were the hunters attacking Temir-Gai's city? Who were they? What did they want? Fascinated by their proud bearing, Orpheus stood transfixed for a moment. But once the horde had gone by, he collected his wits.

"Our way's clear ahead—quick!"

He raced for the gateway. The flames were now racing up to the top of the wall, consuming the statue of Temir-Gai and his mythical mount. Shielding his face with his arm, Orpheus held his breath and ran through the fire, gasping with terror.

The others followed him, and soon they were all outside the city, standing dazed in the grassy place beyond the wall. Babilas was still carrying the cage on his back. His face was blackened by the smoke and he was breathing hard, but his powerful muscles did not give way.

Behind them, in the streets of Cispazan, the alarm had been raised. Amidst general turmoil, human chains were forming to carry water to the burning city.

"The Princetta is safe!" sighed Orpheus. "Let's not hang around here."

As they moved away from the burning city, they failed to notice the figure of a man emerging from the fire. A man with a smoothly shaved head and eyelashes singed by the flames, holding the broken handle of the Cage of Torments in his hands . . .

Back on the ship, the captain was in a towering rage. The surprise attack mounted by the horsemen from the steppes had upset his plans, particularly the work of the divers whom he had sent into the harbour to sabotage the emperor's fleet. Seeing a crowd of Cispazians armed with buckets flock down to the quaysides, the divers, had abandoned their mission and returned to the *Errabunda*. Most of the Cispazian ships were in no state to put to sea, though some of them were.

"Who are those barbarians who attacked Temir-Gai without warning?" the captain barked at Orpheus when he was up on deck. "They've wrecked my plans, the fools! Did you see them?"

Still out of breath, Orpheus simply nodded. Then he turned and threw a rope down to Babilas, who was waiting in the dinghy with the others. Orpheus leaned over the rail. He saw the twins hurrying to fasten it to the cage, and Babilas signed to him to haul it up.

"Look here, quartermaster, are you going to tell me what's going on?" the captain continued. "Where's the Princetta?"

"Coming up, Captain," replied Orpheus, passing the other end of the rope through the mortise of a large pulley. "Help me to heave her aboard!"

The captain raised an eyebrow, but he lent Orpheus a hand to such good effect that the cage soon appeared above the rail of the poop deck.

"What the . . . ?" exclaimed the astonished captain. "But . . . but . . ."

Babilas climbed the rope ladder, jumped aboard and lent a hand hauling up the cage, and finally got it on deck. Behind him the sailors, the twins and Lei scrambled over the rail. The captain's eyes narrowed.

"Who's that fair girl?" he asked.

"I'll explain later," Orpheus apologised. "The Princetta is dying in there."

He told the twins to find buckets and draw as much water as possible, and then went down through the central hatch to his cabin, where he collected his entire stock of candles and ran back up again.

"Quartermaster!" the captain said again. He pointed to the heights of the city. Even from this distance, it was easy to see that the flames had engulfed the harem and the entire imperial city. "I doubt if Temir-Gai will be after us just yet. Since the Princetta is on board, we will set sail at once!"

Orpheus absently agreed, before making for the cage, where he handed candles to Lei and Babilas.

"Set fire to the bars," he said. "If this cage is made of the same wood as the city it will burn. Only when the flames get too close to the Princetta do I want the twins to pour buckets of water on them, understand?"

Orpheus lit the candles, and Lei and Babilas each held a flame to one of the bars. The wood began to smoke, suddenly, several of the bars caught fire.

"Do we pour water now?" asked Hob, sounding worried.

"Wait!" Orpheus told him. "Only if it gets dangerous."

Lei was anxiously watching the cage burn. Malva could hardly be seen in the middle of it, jammed between the walls and the movable ceiling. Only one hand and a few locks of her hair showed.

"Water!" Orpheus suddenly cried.

The twins feverishly emptied two buckets at once. The flames went out, the wood hissed and a small cry was heard.

"Malva!" said Lei. "You can hear me?"

A faint reply came from the Princetta.

"The cold water has brought her round," rejoiced Orpheus.

He turned to Babilas and showed him the half-charred bars.

The giant signed to the others to stand well away. He grasped one of the bars with both hands and finally cracked it with a powerful heave. He repeated this operation several times, and as each bar broke their hopes grew. Finally Babilas was able to get at one of the wooden panels compressing Malva's body and pulled it out.

"Done it!" cried Orpheus in triumph.

He helped Babilas to lift the Princetta out of her prison, and they laid her gently on the deck. Lei and the twins gathered around her. Orpheus looked at the girl's anguished face. Seeing the Princetta here, alive and safe, he realised that he had just done the first notable deed of his life.

"She's so beautiful," whispered Hob.

"Is she dead?" asked Peppe.

"Don't talk nonsense," Orpheus told him. "But she's not in good shape. We'll have to send for the surgeon on board the *Mary-Belle*."

"The *Mary-Belle*?" said Hob, taken aback. "But we're much too far from her. Look!"

Orpheus raised his head. In all the excitement he had completely forgotten to watch the ship's manoeuvres. The sailors had raised the anchor, hoisted the fore and topsail, and the *Errabunda* had left the creek, all while his mind had been somewhere else entirely.

The ship was now beating westward, followed distantly by the *Mary-Belle*. Further away, it seemed to Orpheus that there was another small white dot. Was it the sail of a third ship? And if it was, ought he to worry about it? He shook his head and looked again, more intently, but he saw nothing. Exhaustion was probably playing tricks on him.

"I know medicine," Lei said softly. "Medicine from

184

kingdom of Balmun. Very magic, very good. Already healed Malva's leg."

Orpheus looked back at the Princetta. Her lips were moving, but she was barely conscious. Her wet hair, spread out on the deck, crowned her head more beautifully than any diadem.

"She's thirsty, isn't she?" said Hob, anxiously.

Orpheus straightened up. He felt worn out. "Give her something to drink and take her to my cabin," he said. "She needs to rest, but keep watch on her all the time." He turned to Lei. "Yes, please use your medicine. I have to go and see the captain."

As Orpheus rose to his feet, he saw mist on the horizon. Bad weather was coming, and that mist boded no good.

21

Surprises and Secrets

When Malva came round she saw two young preunuchs bending over her. They were looking at her with mingled alarm and devotion.

"You've broken three ribs," the first told her. Oddly, he spoke to her in Galnician.

"And your left wrist is sprained," added the second. "Does it hurt?"

Malva tried to raise her head, but this simple movement made her cry out. Pain suddenly shot through her body, and she almost fainted.

"Take it easy," murmured one of the preunuchs. "Lei said you weren't to move."

"Lei," repeated Malva weakly. "Where is she?"

"She'll be back," the second preunuch reassured her. "She's gone to the galley to find ingredients for her medicine."

"We're to keep watch over you," the other boy said. "If you feel thirsty we're to give you a little myrtle brandy." He waved a flask full of transparent liquid in front of Malva's nose. "Want some?"

She nodded. Her throat was so dry, her mind so empty, her body so battered!

The preunuch helped her to swallow a mouthful of brandy. Malva coughed, choked, felt first dizzy and then a burning sensation in her stomach. But in the end she felt rather better.

"I didn't know that preunuchs spoke Galnician," she said. "In fact I didn't think they spoke at all."

The two boys smiled at her. She was suddenly struck by their likeness to each other.

"You're twins?"

"Yes," said the first. "And we're not . . . not prunks or whatever it is. I'm Hob. This is my brother Peppe. We rescued you."

Malva frowned. Memories were slowly surfacing again. She recalled the harem, the Baths of Purity, and then . . .

"The Archont!" she cried, sitting up on the bunk.

"Don't move!" exclaimed the twins.

Malva fell heavily back, racked by pain. Her eyes filled with tears, and it took her some time to get her breathing back to normal.

"The Archont can't hurt you now," Hob soothed her. "Peppe and I shut him up in the imperial city, and then the whole place burned down! He must have been roasted like a pig!"

"You missed a terrific sight!" Peppe confirmed. "There were barbarian horsemen, and flames going up to the stars, and people running all over the place. But Babilas is the strongest giant in the Known World, and he picked up your cage and carried you."

All these explanations seemed extremely confused to Malva. But when she heard the word "cage" she remembered the celestial-charioteer and how Temir-Gai had condemned her to be tortured. More tears ran down her cheeks, and she asked for another mouthful of brandy.

"I want to see Lei," she moaned. "Where is she?"

"She can't be far away," smiled Hob. "She's here, on board the *Errabunda*."

Malva started with surprise. "Are we on a ship?"

The twins spluttered with laughter. There were so many things to tell her, so many nice surprises to come.

"Wait till you see her—she's a big three-master frigate," Hob explained knowledgeably. "She's fast. It took us only seventy days to get here from Galnicia! The voyage home should be about the same."

Malva dared not move a muscle, but her eyes were wide in terror.

"Voyage home?" she said in alarm. "Are you telling me that I'm being taken back . . . back to Galnicia?"

"Of course!" said the twins enthusiastically. "That's our mission!"

Malva closed her eyes. Her dismay was boundless. Now that she had collected her wits, her thoughts were racing like wild horses. She saw moments from her journey again: the shipwreck on the reefs off Sperta, her wound, her long trek to Gurkistan with Philomena, their meeting with Uzmir, the Amoyed attack . . . so much suffering, so much fear, so much hope and so many dreams still to be realised! And all that, just to be taken back to Galnicia by force?

"No! No!" she shouted.

The twins flinched in surprise.

"I won't go back!" Malva shouted. "Leave me alone! Go away! Get out!"

"But—" Peppe protested.

"We're supposed to . . ." Hob stammered.

"I said get out!" Malva interrupted furiously.

The two boys hurried to the cabin door. They could make nothing at all of this sudden violence. Wasn't the Princetta supposed to embody the precepts of Tranquillity and Harmony? They remembered the portrait that had gone all round Galnicia: the Princetta calm and smiling, her hands in her lap, sitting in one of the sumptuous gardens of the Citadel. Just now the likeness wasn't very striking. Malva was pale, her features ravaged by anger, her legendary hair all greasy and tangled.

"If you ask me . . ." murmured Peppe.

". . . she's going too far," Hob finished his sentence.

Offended and disappointed, they left the cabin.

Once on her own, Malva heaved a huge sigh. Not only was she crippled by pain, she was a prisoner once more! She closed her eyes and began to sob.

Suddenly she felt something warm and moist touch her hand. She yanked her hand back. What now? Leaning a little way out of the bunk, she saw a large dog lying on the floor. He looked placidly up at her, tail hanging down. Malva smiled.

"Hello, what are you doing here?" she asked. "Did I wake you up yelling like that? Poor big dog . . . it was all the fault of those two boys. They made me cry, you see."

Putting out her hand, she patted the dog's head.

"At least you don't talk. You don't have any bad news to tell me, do you? And I'm sure you understand me. You can't be happy on this ship either . . . I'm sure you'd rather be running about in the open air, wouldn't you?"

She went on patting the dog. Ears pricked, he seemed to be listening to her attentively.

"I know a wonderful country," she told him. "Its name is Elgolia. You'd be happy there, old boy. You could run around the meadows and chase the red birds. You could swim in Lake Barath-Thor and come to the Bay of Dao-Boa with me . . ."

Malva felt a lump in her throat. Why did everything conspire against her? Why was the Known World full of greedy, cruel people? She didn't ask much: just to be allowed to go away to the east. She was about to collapse in tears again when Lei entered the cabin with her arms full of jars and bags.

"Malva! You wake up! How you feel?"

"Oh, Lei!" Malva groaned. "I'm so glad to see you!"

They began laughing and weeping together, hugging each other before the eyes of the startled Zeph.

"I thought you die in Cage of Torments. But now I make new medicine," said Lei, once she had calmed down. "Cook not happy give me different foods, but too bad!" She glanced at Zeph. "Dog very useful too," she added, patting his head. "In medicine of Balmun, we use hairs and saliva of animals."

Malva made a face, but she didn't protest. Lei's talents had already healed the wound in her leg; she trusted her to do anything now. And once she was well she was sure she'd find some way to leave the ship before it reached Galnicia.

While Lei began mixing the ingredients of her recipe, Malva asked her what had happened in the harem. "And who were those horsemen who started the fire?"

"Riders from Great Azizian Steppes," replied Lei.

"From the steppes? Are you sure?"

"I know customs and habits of all peoples," said Lei. "They wearing fur caps and oryak-skin coats."

Malva felt her pulse beat faster. "Baighurs!" she exclaimed.

190

"The Baighurs came to attack Temir-Gai! Did you see . . . did you see their leader?"

"Yes," replied Lei. "Man strong, very agile. He stand on his horse."

"Uzmir!"

"You know him?"

"It was Uzmir!" hiccupped Malva. "He came looking for me, and perhaps Philomena . . ."

So strong were her emotions that she lost consciousness again.

Meanwhile, on the fo'c'sle, Orpheus was standing beside the captain and scanning the horizon.

"Those mists will lift," the captain repeated. "Believe me, I'm experienced and I know."

Orpheus reddened on hearing the word "experienced." Was the Captain telling him that he'd seen through him, and his inexperience was as plain as the nose on his face? Orpheus dared say no more. However, the mists still troubled him. They seemed to be rising higher and growing denser the more the sun rose in the sky.

"Good!" said the captain, folding up his telescope. "It looks like a fine day, and we can boast of bringing our mission to a satisfactory conclusion. How's the Princetta? I didn't want to bother her, but I hope she wasn't too badly treated by that barbarian Temir-Gai."

"Well . . ." Orpheus began. "I hope she'll recover quickly too."

He was gazing at the horizon with growing concern, but the captain seemed to take no interest in it. He appeared to be in a chatty mood.

"In any case, quartermaster, let me congratulate you on the courage and skill you've shown. I'll admit it now: I wanted to give you a challenge to face when I entrusted this mission to you. The lads didn't seem to appreciate your merits, but I think you've scored points. Even Babilas seems to think highly of you now!"

Orpheus took his eyes off the horizon. These words were very encouraging, and he managed to smile.

"Do you think they'll go on calling me 'greenhorn'?"

The captain laughed uproariously and placed a hand on Orpheus's shoulder.

"Seamen are often suspicious, you mustn't bear them a grudge. Be that as it may, your father would be proud of you! I heard that he's dead, but if he could see you now . . .'"

Orpheus turned pale. "You knew my father?"

"Who didn't know Hannibal McBott? You're not very like him physically, but I can tell that you have the same determination, the same desire to succeed! Am I wrong?"

"Well, I . . . I have to say that . . .'"

"Come, come," murmured the captain into Orpheus's ear. "Don't act the innoc—"

He was interrupted by an irate voice calling to him. "Captain! Do something or I'm handing in my notice! This is organised looting! A raid!"

Orpheus turned and saw the cook Finopico. He was stamping his feet, while his nervous hands twisted his apron.

"First that dog and the herring-thieves, then you take aboard a . . . a foreign girl who looks like a witch! It's just too much!"

"Lei is not a witch," said Orpheus. "She's nursing the Princetta. I authorised her to take everything she needed."

"My pork lard! My preserved lemons! My date cream! My brimble jam and my myrtle brandy!" said Finopico, enumerating these items in pitiful tones. "And to top it all, she's just gone off with my chicken's-tail soup with beans! What's she going to do with all those things? It's against all the rules of Culinary Harmony!"

In his fury he tore off his apron, trampled it underfoot, and when the captain said nothing to calm him turned on his heel and marched away, shouting back, "And don't blame me if it's dry ship's biscuit to eat all the way back to Galnicia!"

The captain sighed in resignation before resuming the conversation where he had left off. "Listen to me, McBott," he said. "If you're as ingenious and intelligent as your father, we can do business, you and I."

Orpheus had a sinking feeling. All these references to Hannibal were making him deeply uneasy. He had left Galnicia to forget his father, and now the memory was coming back to haunt him.

"Just think," continued the captain in confidential tones, "just think how much the Coronador would be prepared to pay to get his daughter back . . ."

Orpheus opened his mouth to speak, but thought better of it. The captain's crafty smile was sending a cold sweat down his back.

"You'll keep your mouth shut, won't you? I understand you! What a fine chance! The Princetta is at our mercy . . . if you ask me, we ought to put the ransom at millions of galniks!"

"The ransom . . ." repeated Orpheus, utterly stupefied.

"Of course!" said the captain, laughing. "That's what your father would have done, I feel sure! When I knew that you were coming aboard, I saw you as my future partner at once. Like father, like son, I always say. The apple doesn't fall far from the tree!"

Fortunately another interruption meant that Orpheus didn't

have to reply. This time it was the lookout man, scrambling down from the crow's nest as fast as he could.

"Captain, see that! Right ahead! There's a terrible squall coming!"

Orpheus turned at the same time as the captain. The entire horizon was covered by an enormous mass of dark clouds, stretching over an impressive distance. It was like a gigantic octopus hanging in the air above the water. The captain's face hardened.

"Take in the mainsail!" he shouted. "Every man to his post!"

22

The Master of the Errabunda

All at once the wind rose. The ocean, which had been rocking gently, began to pitch and toss. The sky grew darker still, and larger and larger waves rolled in. Lightning tore through the darkness, thunder made the sky tremble and a pitiless rain began to hammer the deck.

Orpheus hurried to his cabin. When he got there, dripping and breathless, he found Malva and Lei huddling together on the bunk. There was a strange aroma of mingled lemon, alcohol, pork lard and wet dog in the air. He sneezed several times before asking Lei if her medicine was ready.

"Malva already drink brew," replied Lei in a whisper. "She get better now. But I afraid ship sinking . . ."

"It's only a storm," smiled Orpheus, picking up his water-proof cape. "Where are the twins? And Zeph?"

"Dog go away. He not like it when I pull out hairs. And twins gone too."

Orpheus felt Malva's anxious gaze resting on him. She was

very pale, but even when marked by exhaustion, her legendary beauty illuminated her features.

"Are you the captain?" she asked.

"Oh no!" said Orpheus, blushing. "Only the quartermaster. Welcome on board, Princetta. I am deeply honoured to—"

The ship lurched violently, throwing him suddenly off balance. He caught hold of the table.

"The storm's getting worse," he said. "I must get to my post, but I'll be back to see you. Keep calm and don't worry. The *Errabunda* can stand up to this."

He left the cabin, taking care to close the door after him, and went up on deck again, shrugging his shoulders to shake off the embarrassment that the Princetta's glance had caused him. It wasn't every day that a Galnician spoke to the Crown Princetta, but this was not the time for bowing and scraping and pretty words.

Back on deck in the pouring rain, the crew were running about in all directions. The men raced along the foremast, took the main topsail by force and strapped down everything they could. The captain went from one part of the deck to another, shouting orders. His voice could hardly be heard above the howling wind and the creaking of the ship.

Orpheus made his way to the wheelhouse. The storm was raging all around him, but he was not afraid. And he wasn't seasick either! On the contrary, he felt a kind of intoxication at finding himself here, under this angry sky, with the enormous arms of the sea rocking the ship like some demonic nurse. He had dreamed of experiencing such moments all his life!

The ropes slapped on the deck, the masts groaned. The sea was breaking against the ship's sides with fearsome regularity.

Orpheus made for the poop with determination, like a matador entering the arena to pit himself against the bull.

Despite their number and agility, the men had no time to take in all the sails. The wind grew stronger yet, and the sky seemed to merge with the furious mass of the water so that soon it was hard to say whether the ship was floating or flying. It rose and fell, it rocked from port to starboard.

When Orpheus finally reached the poop the sails had torn like pieces of paper. He climbed the steps, slipped, and crawled over to the helm . . . the pilot was no longer at his post! The *Errabunda* had no helmsman!

"Get under cover! Go down to the hold!" shouted the Captain, making for the central hatch.

Orpheus seized hold of the tiller and, bracing his legs, tried to right it. The rain lashed his face, sticking his hair to his forehead and blinding him. Hands welded to the helm, he stared at the waves as if hypnotised. All the sea stories he had read as a child flashed through his mind. He saw the heroes of the past who had discovered the distant Lands of Aremica and the Orniant, he saw their hard faces, their fevered eyes, and at last he felt close to them.

"You won't sink us!" he shouted to the storm, feeling an extraordinary sense of exhilaration. "I am Orpheus, of the proud line of the McBotts of Galnicia!"

The waves soon rose so high that when he looked down into their troughs it was as if the sea were opening up to its very foundations. With horror, Orpheus saw several sailors swept away by huge waves. Others, clinging to the ship's rail, were crawling over the deck as they tried to get to the hatches.

Flashes of lightning shot across the black sky one after the other in an astonishing rhythm. The captain had disappeared, too, and only Orpheus seemed to be in any state to keep the *Errabunda* under control. There was water everywhere; he couldn't even see the prow of the ship any more. His cape flapped like a sail in the gusts of wind. Whatever happened he must hold on course westward—towards Galnicia!

Suddenly, with a crash like the end of the world, a bolt of lightning struck the ship. The mainmast snapped in two under the impact, and fell forward, dragging with it rigging that struck the deck like a whip. Three men were crushed under the mast, others were swept overboard by the rigging. The howling of the wind drowned out all cries of pain and distress.

"Holy Tranquillity!" gasped Orpheus.

Soon the waves were engulfing everything. In Orpheus's hands, the tiller offered no more resistance; its axis had just broken. The ocean, he realised, was laying down the law now. He got rid of his cape and, leaving his post, flung himself forward. His feet slipped on the steps, and he just managed to catch the handrail, but the waves were sweeping the deck with such force that he was carried along with them. His nails scrabbled at the planks of the deck. Then his back struck an obstacle. It was the entrance to a hatch. Half drowned by the sea water flooding into his nose and mouth, he managed to raise the trapdoor and let himself fall into the interior of the ship, hardly knowing by what miracle he was still alive.

Water was flooding between decks everywhere. Barrels were rolling about in the midst of broken beams. Provisions were swinging from their hooks in the ceilings: hams and blackened quarters of meat that looked like hanged men. Panic-stricken rats were swimming around in this mini-sea that had invaded the hold. A deathly silence reigned inside the frigate. Was Orpheus the last survivor?

Up to his armpits in water, he started moving forward as the ship rocked from port to starboard without a moment's respite. Exhausted, Orpheus finally reached his cabin door, but the pressure of the water was so strong that he couldn't open it. Through the door, however, he heard cries.

· "Princetta!" he called.

He looked around him. Among the floating objects he saw part of a beam and a strong rope. Tying one end of the rope round his waist, he fixed the other end to a hook in the ceiling. Then, bracing his feet against the door, he rammed it with the beam as hard as he could. Ten, twenty times. The wood of the door began to give way. The cries of distress were louder than ever.

Soaked and breathless, but full of hope, Orpheus continued like this for several minutes. His hands were bleeding all over the beam, and the seawater stung them horribly. But at last the door gave way, water pouring through the opening like an animal ready to devour everything in its path. Orpheus cut the rope holding him to the ceiling and went through the doorway.

When he came down on the other side of it, the water was up to the table-top and washing around the bunk. He saw Lei, pale with terror, standing on a chair. Her forehead was bleeding. Orpheus went over to her and gently took her hand.

"Where's the Princetta?" he asked in a stifled voice.

Lei shook her head.

"She left the bunk? What happened?"

Lei put a trembling hand to her forehead. "Man come. He hit me with telescope. Afterwards I know nothing. Malva disappeared."

Shattered, Orpheus closed his eyes. His conversation with the captain just before the storm came back to him, and he realised that the man had tricked him. How could he ever have trusted him? His anger was mingled with weariness. Whatever the captain had intended to do, he wouldn't risk taking the Princetta very far away. At worst, they would both be drowned . . .

Orpheus went over to sit beside Lei. The water went on rising around them, and the *Errabunda* groaned like a beast in its death throes. They did not exchange a single word, but just stayed there side by side, resigned to death.

Soon afterwards, however, the sea stopped beating so savagely against the ship. The rolls of thunder came less frequently. The clouds parted, letting pale rays of sunlight fall through. The storm was dying down as suddenly as it had broken.

In the cabin, Lei started crying. Orpheus felt his own eyes prickle, but he refused to break down. He simply made for the broken door, saying, "Let's go and help the others, if there's anyone still alive."

In spite of her exhaustion and her dazed state, Lei followed him, struggling against the water.

When they came up the steps to the central hatch and out on deck, they felt the gentle warmth of the sun on their faces. The sky seemed to have been washed clean. The whitecaps broke so lazily on the vast seas that it was as though there had never been a storm at all. There were no corpses in sight. They had all gone to the bottom. As for the *Mary-Belle*, she had simply disappeared.

Orpheus stood in the middle of the devastated deck. The green and yellow flag of Galnicia lay at his feet in tatters.

23

The Fabula

The first thing Malva felt when she recovered consciousness was a shooting pain at the back of her skull. Her temples were throbbing, and it felt as though her head had doubled in size. Then she remembered that a man in uniform had come into the cabin and hit her with his telescope. Who was he? Why had he taken her away with him?

Finally, Malva opened her eyes. In spite of the dim light around her, she guessed that she was lying on a pile of ropes. Beneath her, moist planks gave off a strong salty, vinegar smell, nearly suffocating her. Something was weighing down on her legs, but she could move her arms. Raising herself on her hands, she managed to turn slightly so that she could breathe more easily. Once lying on her side, she realised that the weight over her legs prevented her from moving any further.

She raised her eyes, and saw that she was lying under a tarpaulin stretched over the high sides of a dinghy. A little daylight filtered through gaps in it, and a slight rolling movement rocked the boat. Malva breathed deeply, remembering the terrible storm that had struck the *Errabunda*. At least the sea seems calm now, and I'm alive, she thought.

However, the weight on her legs still troubled her. Twisting her neck and raising her head as far as she could, she saw out of the corner of her eye the face of the man who had knocked her out. She uttered a stifled cry and fell back on her side.

"Who are you?"

The man did not reply. He was lying almost on top of her, with his chest apparently resting on the oarsman's seat, but the rest of his body was pinning her legs.

Heart thudding, she made the effort to turn her head again to get a better view of her attacker. He was smiling with satisfaction, eyes fixed on his captive. Malva recognised the Galnician insignia of the Maritime Institute on the collar of his uniform, but she didn't feel strong enough to pursue that train of thought. She fell back on her side.

"Are you . . . are you the captain of the *Errabunda*?" she asked in a faltering voice.

The man still didn't deign to reply. As far as she could make out, however, he was nodding.

"I don't know why you hit me," Malva went on, trying to calm the racket her heart was making in her breast, "but I suppose you wanted to . . . to rescue me, didn't you? Is that why we're here in this boat?"

The man's persistent silence was disturbing. Malva saw a certain malice in it. She twisted her neck again, and saw that he was still smiling imperturbably, no doubt enjoying the sight of her impatient wriggling.

"Well, if it amuses you," she said tartly, "have fun! But let me tell you, whatever happens, I'm never setting foot in Galnicia again."

The man was still nodding, and didn't bother to reply.

"I shall jump into the water rather than go with you, do you hear me?" said Malva, losing her temper. "My life doesn't belong to anyone. Certainly not to the Prince of Andemark, or the Coronador, or even the people of Galnicia. If you're a man of honour, go back to my father and mother and tell them this: Malva is not interested in the throne, or power, or balls in the Citadel, or the plots and conspiracies that so many people of their rank indulge in, like the Archont, for instance. Malva was made to live in freedom. And whatever the Coronador may think of it, to read and write and study! She was made to live in the Bay of Dao-Boa. I hope you'll remember that name!"

Running out of breath, she stopped for a moment to see the captain's reaction. Then, suddenly, she felt something warm dripping on the nape of her neck. Passing her hand through her hair, she brought it back and looked at the palm . . .

"Blood!" she screamed.

Panic-stricken, she contorted herself so hard that she managed to turn on her back. Suddenly she was face to face with the captain's flabby face. A trickle of blood was running from his twisted mouth, and his glazed eyes no longer seemed to see anything.

"He . . . he's dead!" said Malva in a strangled tone, her stomach heaving with disgust.

Struggling awkwardly, she managed to pull her legs up. Bracing her forehead against the oarsman's seat, she succeeded in working herself free, while the captain's blood ran over her clothes, her arms, her hands. At last she was huddled at the front of the dinghy. The dead man's presence terrified her.

Shaking with sobs, she pushed against the tarpaulin with all her might.

When she finally emerged into the open air and stood up she had an attack of vertigo. She almost fell into the water, but caught herself just in time and collapsed against the side of the dinghy, giving way to uncontrollable nausea. She stayed there for a moment without moving, leaning over the water, her mind blank, until shrill cries made her look up.

The sun was high in the sky. Dazzled by the light, at first Malva could make out nothing in front of her but a dark shape a little way off. Then, narrowing her eyes, she saw Lei standing on the *Errabunda* and waving to her.

"Malva!" cried the daughter of Balmun. "We come fetch you!"

Still mute from the shock, Malva could only raise her hand in reply. She saw Lei disappear, no doubt to go and get help. That suggested that she wasn't the only survivor of the storm.

Without realising it, Malva had started to cry. Tears ran down her cheeks as she gradually took stock of the situation. The dinghy was still attached to the ship by a rope; the captain had not had time to cast it off. The unfortunate man was lying under the tarpaulin, his back pierced by the hook of an enormous pulley which, carried away by the furious wind, had been driven between his shoulder blades. Malva began trembling like a leaf at the thought that, if the captain hadn't been in the way, that deadly projectile might have gone straight into her own breast.

Other figures appeared at the stern of the *Errabunda*. When Lei pointed to the dinghy, two men began hauling in the rope holding it. Malva looked around her in amazement. The sea was almost dead calm now, deep blue and strangely still. There was no land on the horizon, not a bird in the sky, not a breath of wind to ripple the surface of the water. She began to wonder if there had really been a storm at all, but when she looked back at the *Errabunda* she saw all the damage that had been done: the broken mainmast lay on deck, there was splintered wood everywhere, frayed rigging, tattered sails . . . and as the dinghy came closer Malva saw that even the golden lettering painted on the stern had been partly scoured away by the waves: the bottom stroke of the E had gone, turning it into an F, the two Rs were entirely wiped out, and so was the letter N and the curve of the D. Her heart suddenly leaped. The lettering on the ship's battered hull no longer read *ERRABUNDA* but *FABULA*!

"Good gracious," murmured Malva, dumbfounded. The ship now bore the same name as the vessel of the old sailor Bulo's story!—the same name as the ship that had been wrecked on the shores of Elgolia!

"It's a sign!" she told herself out loud. "By all the Divinities of the Known World! It's the sign that this ship will take me where I want to go!"

In spite of her weariness and all that she had been through, Malva suddenly felt happy and confident. A wide smile lit up her face, spattered as it was with the captain's blood, and she started dancing about in the dinghy.

"Lei! Lei! This is amazing! We've had incredible luck!"

Leaning over the stern rail, the fair-haired girl returned her smile without really understanding. "Faster! Faster!" she told Orpheus and Babilas, who were hauling in the dinghy.

A moment earlier the giant had emerged from the hold, where he had been buried under a pile of fallen barrels. His left hand was broken, but the strength of his other hand was enough for him. Orpheus hoped they would find other survivors, but the presence of Babilas was a great relief in itself. As for the Princetta, it was a miracle to see her on her feet.

"Are you all right?" he called to her when the bows of the dinghy came up against the *Errabunda*'s hull.

When Orpheus saw the motionless body of the captain lying over the tarpaulin, he only hoped that at the moment of death the swindler had tasted the bitterness of treachery on his tongue.

"I'm fine!" replied Malva. "Send down a ladder!"

Orpheus did so, and admired the girl's agility as she climbed the ropes. But when she set foot on deck in front of him he looked anxiously at the bloodstains on her clothes.

"Don't worry," said Malva, smiling at him. "I'm not injured. It's the captain's blood . . . and he's stone dead."

She began laughing, rather nervously, and then went over to Lei and hugged her.

"Where are the others?" she asked.

An awkward silence met her query. Malva frowned.

"You mean we're . . . we're the only . . ."

"For the time being, yes," Orpheus admitted. "The four of us are the only survivors."

Appalled, the Princetta looked Orpheus up and down. Then she raised her eyes to Babilas. "Well, at least you look very strong," she murmured. "But you won't be able to repair the *Fabula* and sail her single-handedly."

"The *Fabula*?" asked Orpheus in surprise.

"Our ship!" said Malva. "I know it may sound odd, but her name changed during the storm. Look for yourselves!"

The other three leaned over the rail, and managed to read, upside down what remained of the golden letters on the hull.

"The *Fabula*," sighed Orpheus. "I don't know if the name suits a wreck like this. We have no mainmast, no sails, the tiller's broken and I don't suppose the instruments are working either.

The *Fabula* will have her work cut out to take us back to Galnicia."

At these words Malva looked hard at Orpheus with her amber eyes.

"I'm not going back to Galnicia," she said firmly. "I know the Coronador sent you on this mission, but . . . but I have other plans. First I have to find my chambermaid Philomena, who was left behind on the Azizian Steppes. Then we're going on to Elgolia, east of the Known World. And my friend Lei has to get back to the kingdom of Balmun."

Orpheus took a step back. The Princetta's words astonished him.

"All you have to do is put us ashore on the first land we come to," suggested Malva, "and tell my father that I died in the storm. After all, I very nearly did. It won't be such a big lie."

"I . . . I don't understand, Your Alteza," stammered Orpheus. "The people of Galnicia are awaiting your return . . . the country has no future without you. We lived in mourning and a state of terror for months, until the day we heard that you were alive, and—"

Malva shook her head. Orpheus, distraught, glanced at Babilas and then at Lei.

"You can't ask me to lie to the Coronador," he said. "I took an oath before the Altar of the Divinities, I—"

When Malva still shook her head, he gestured despairingly at the ship.

"Men have died for you, Princetta! They believed in their mission! How dare you—"

"You don't understand," Malva interrupted him rather sharply. "If I go back to Galnicia now my life will be a failure. I will go to Elgolia or I will die!"

Orpheus passed his hands over his face. It was beginning to get hot. Very hot. And this ridiculous argument was giving him a headache.

"I don't know this place Elgolia," he said. "I've never heard of it. And anyway, I'm not going to abandon you on unknown land."

Malva heaved a sigh of exasperation. "Someone else who wants to make up my mind for me," she muttered.

Suddenly she fell into a temper. She remembered the day when her father had publicly humiliated her in the Council Chamber, the day when her mother had confirmed that she was to marry the Prince of Andemark, the day when the Amoyeds had sold her to Temir-Gai. Was she going to have to fight all her life to be left in peace? In a fury, she turned to Babilas.

"And how about you?" she asked him. "Why don't you say anything? I'm sure you have plenty of plans for me too! Come on, make your offer! The Princetta is up for sale!"

The giant lowered his eyes.

"Babilas is mute," Orpheus said roughly. "He carried you on his shoulders to free you from Temir-Gai's harem! He walked through the flames consuming the imperial city, and he broke the bars of the cage where you were imprisoned. That's no way to speak to him, Princetta."

Disconcerted, Malva bit her lip. Her anger died down.

"And that will do!" said Orpheus shortly. "There's no point in this argument. We're lost in the middle of the sea. Let's have no more talk of Galnicia, or this Elgolia. We have to stay alive, that's what matters."

He looked at the horizon. The air shimmered in the heat. The temperature was rising by the minute, and the flat calm of the ocean worried him. He went to the rail to look at the dinghy where the captain was lying. Taking out his knife, he cut the rope that still moored the little boat to the ship, and without so much as a word of farewell watched the body float away. Then he turned back to Babilas and Lei.

"Search the hold again," he told them. "We'll need food and fresh water."

Malva was looking sullen. She suddenly felt weak, and very tired. The bump on the back of her head was hurting, and the sight of this pitiful crew lowered her morale. Who did this quartermaster think he was, speaking to her like that? She went and sat on the capstan, crossed her arms and did not move.

As Babilas and Orpheus made their way to the central hatch, a strange sound broke the silence. It was like a foghorn, a long note sinking deeper and deeper. The passengers listened, transfixed, expecting to hear the sound again, but it was not repeated.

"It must have been thunder," said Orpheus at last.

"Or perhaps other ship?" suggested Lei.

"I don't think so," Orpheus replied. "The *Mary-Belle*'s foghorn has a higher note."

He didn't try to make sense of it, but shrugged and led Babilas down into the hold. When they reached the foot of the second stairway, they saw that the water level had gone down a good deal. Whereas not long before they had almost had to swim to get around the ship, now they could wade, paddling through shallow water full of drifting seaweed.

They went through several of the holds in succession, without finding anything but gutted barrels, broken beams, canvas bags soaked with water and rats that fled at their approach. At last they opened the door of the galley, hoping to find a few dry provisions, but they saw that the water had spared nothing in there either. Finopico's cookbooks had fallen off their shelf and lay all jumbled up, mingling with broken spice jars and spoilt herrings.

They were about to leave the galley when Orpheus saw a mop of red hair showing from behind the enormous cast-iron stove, which had toppled over at the back of the cabin.

"Finopico?" he called, heart thudding.

There was no reply. Orpheus walked towards the stove. The cook was huddled behind it, crouching in the water, his face buried in Zeph's sodden coat and holding the dog in his arms. The St. Bernard gave a low growl on seeing his master. Finopico immediately raised his head. His eyes met Orpheus's.

"It's the greenhorn!" he breathed, amazed. "By all the Divinities of the Known World . . . he survived!"

Orpheus smiled. He didn't mind being nicknamed the greenhorn any more—he was so glad to see Zeph still alive! He was even glad that the irascible cook had escaped the devastation.

"I see you've been getting to know my dog better," he said. "He seems to like you."

Finopico shrugged, but he did not refuse the hand that Orpheus held out to help him to his feet. He had a bleeding gash on one cheek, and he was limping slightly.

"I thought it best to wait here," he muttered. "To be sure the storm was really over . . . by Holy Harmony, my books!"

The cook picked one of them up, and uttered a groan of dismay when he found that it was soaking wet.

"Well, that makes six of us," sighed Orpheus, patting his dog's head. "And perhaps that's not all."

He left the galley to go down into the belly of the ship. He was thinking of Peppe and Hob. Resourceful as they were, perhaps those two lads had found shelter. But where?

"Never mind your books! Try to find something edible, and take it all up to the deck to dry out," he told Finopico before leaving him.

Down below he was met with a terrible sight. Up to his thighs in water, Orpheus made his way past the bodies of drowned sailors. There were eight or nine of them, floating face downwards in dark and stinking corners. Orpheus put a hand over his mouth, nauseated and sick with grief. A few hours earlier these men had been running around on deck, hauling in the sails. They had been alive, strong and confident. They had followed the captain's orders, and this was what had become of them . . .

"Hob!" called Orpheus in a voice strangled with emotion. "Peppe!"

Holding his breath, he wandered around in the dark, losing hope as he discovered more dead bodies. When he reached the tiny doorway of the sail locker, he called again.

"Hob!"

At last there was a muffled reply. "We're here! Inside the locker."

Orpheus leaped forward and put his mouth to the door. "Hold on! I'm coming!"

He lifted the latch, expecting to feel resistance, but the door opened easily.

"You weren't stuck in here!" he said in surprise, seeing the twins sitting on the spare sails.

"We never said we were," replied Hob.

"Then why didn't you come out?"

Peppe leaned over his brother's shoulder, and cast a glance at the hold. "It's all dark out there," he whispered.

211

"And full of dead men," added Hob, making a face.

Orpheus smiled. He was delighted to have found the two lively rascals.

"Afraid of dead men, are you?" he mocked them.

Hob and Peppe raised eyes full of alarm to him. "It's unlucky to touch a corpse!" they cried in unison.

Orpheus managed to convince them that it was all superstition, and the two boys, trembling, followed him through the hold and up the steps. When they came out into the sunlight they collapsed on deck, pale and nearly fainting.

"That makes eight of us!" said Orpheus proudly.

Malva and Lei, who were busy spreading some provisions on a scrap of sailcloth to dry it out, cast a sardonic glance at the twins.

"Hm," sighed Malva, "with a crew like this we won't be reaching Elgolia in a hu—"

No one heard the end of her comment. It was drowned out by another note on the horn, echoing through the air, long-drawn-out and, this time, rising to a higher register. The survivors were rooted to the spot. When the sound died away they looked at each other, puzzled. The horn sounded closer than before.

"That wasn't thunder," murmured Malva.

Hob and Peppe started trembling again. "The dead men!" they whispered. "It's . . . it's their souls weeping! We told you not to touch the corpses! They've come for us!"

At that moment Zeph raised his head to the sky and began howling, while the twins put their hands over their ears and huddled close together. They looked terrified.

"Make that dog shut up!" yelled Finopico, brandishing one of his books above his head. "And tell those two idiots to keep their stupid prophecies to themselves! They'll bring bad luck down on us!"

But Orpheus wasn't listening. He was gazing at the horizon, his eyes wide and baffled.

"Too late," was all he said, pointing to the thing that had just appeared.

24

The Patrols of Catabea

A dark shape had just emerged from the water, some twenty kilometres away from the *Fabula*. At this distance there was no way of saying what it was, but *whatever* it was, it was gigantic. And even stranger, *whatever* it was seemed to be multiplying. A second, identical shape appeared with the faint sound of cascading water, and then a third and a fourth. Before the eyes of the survivors, these colossal things emerged from the water, and then were immobilised.

Zeph had stopped howling. Exhausted, he was lying full length on the deck with his tongue hanging out. Total silence reigned on board now. Malva and Lei dropped their sacks of flour and went over to the bulwarks. They could feel the fragile hulk of the ship quivering beneath their feet. Orpheus joined them, and looked at the waterline. Something was making the sea foam just below the ship's hull.

When he raised his head again, Orpheus saw with amazement that the black forms were still rising out of the sea at the same pace.

"They . . . they look like statues," murmured Malva.

"They have human shape," added Lei. "I see heads, necks, arms . . ."

Fascinated, Orpheus watched the birth of these immense stone men. The statues were visible from their waists up in the sea. They faced each other in pairs, gradually forming an alarming kind of line that seemed to be coming closer to the ship.

"It's all because of that witch!" cried Finopico in sudden panic, pointing at Lei. "It's her! It's because of her magic!"

"Be quiet!" Orpheus told him firmly.

He leaned over the rail again, and saw that the *Fabula* was indeed being drawn towards the line of statues by a current that had come up out of nowhere. He cast a brief glance at Babilas, but the giant made a sign to show that he was powerless. The *Fabula* had no anchor and no sails now; even he couldn't do anything. The members of the crew gathered silently around Orpheus, apprehension written plain on their faces.

The ship gained speed. The stone men stood erect in the water like sentries on guard, and when the *Fabula* began to make her way through the narrow corridor they had formed, Orpheus could better estimate their size. Their faces, which seemed to be carved from copper-covered stone, rose at least twenty metres above the deck of the ship.

"No human peoples able to make such things," murmured Lei, marvelling rather than frightened. "This work of heavenly powers!"

Beside her, Malva was feeling a vague terror. Not one of the hundreds of travellers' tales she had read mentioned anything like this. Had the storm driven the ship beyond the borders of the Known World?

215

The current carried the *Fabula* on for what seemed to all on board like eternity. The twins were beginning to moan and make gloomy predictions again, while Finopico cast a dark gaze at Lei.

Then, suddenly, the line of statues came to an end. The prow of the ship entered waters of an astonishing turquoise blue. Far away, Orpheus could see the outlines of land, but he had no time to say anything, for a flock of birds was making for the *Fabula*, skimming the waves. The beating of their wings made a harsh whistling sound.

Zeph immediately got to his feet and trotted to the prow of the ship, growling. When the birds were close enough he barked at them, but they were not in the least alarmed, and settled on the deck of the *Fabula*.

And now the survivors of the storm realised that they had indeed entered an unknown world. For these creatures, perching on the gnarled claws of wading birds, had metal wings, and their graceful necks ended in tiny human heads.

"By all the Divinities of the Known World!" choked Finopico.

He was the only one of them able to say anything at all. The others were as mute as Babilas.

"Well, well," remarked one of the birds. "They speak Galnician too."

"Catabea will be amused," said another bird.

And all the human-headed wading birds opened their mouths to burst into laughter as lugubrious as the croaking of frogs.

Malva felt cold sweat trickling down between her shoulder blades. Since her flight from Galnicia she had seen many strange creatures, but the shrunken heads nodding at the ends of those birds' necks were the scariest of all. When one of the birds approached, spreading its metal wings, she stifled a cry of alarm.

"Don't be afraid," cooed the bird. "We are the Patrols of Catabea. You have just entered the Archipelago, and the Procedure must be followed. What is the name of this ship?"

The travellers exchanged glances of panic. Archipelago? Catabea? Procedure? They didn't understand a word of it.

"The name of this ship!" repeated the bird in a menacing tone.

"The *Errabunda*," replied Orpheus in a strangled voice.

"The *Fabula*," replied Malva at the same moment.

The human-headed birds craned their necks.

"Does this ship by any chance have two names?" asked one of them. "Beware if you are trying to deceive us!"

The others creaked their wings.

"Its name is . . . the *Fabula*," Orpheus quickly corrected himself.

The Patrols relaxed. "Who is in command?" one of them asked.

There was silence. Peppe and Hob, leaning against the foot of the broken mainmast, seemed dead on their feet, while Finopico's teeth were chattering. He didn't seem to realise it. Babilas had narrowed his dark eyes, and Malva shook her head. Facing these alarming birds, none of them was keen to take on the job of captain.

"Our captain is dead," Orpheus explained.

The Patrols waddled from one large foot to the other, and a disapproving murmur rose among them.

"The Procedure insists on our knowing the captain's name!" said one of the birds. "If we don't get it we have to send you to the Immuration."

"The Immuration!"

"To the Immuration!" repeated the other birds.

"What *is* the Immuration?" Orpheus ventured to ask.

A Patrol came out of the ranks and shook its dreadful little head back and forth in front the young man's face.

"The Immuration is the centre of our Archipelago. It's a prison into which we throw all who fail to respect the Procedure."

At these words Hob and Peppe were panic-stricken. "Not prison! Not prison!" they begged, falling to their knees on the deck.

"We've been in too many cells already!" said Hob tearfully. "It's cold and damp and all dark there! We'd rather die than go to prison!"

Malva tugged at Orpheus's sleeve, and looked imploringly at him. "You saved Lei and me from Temir-Gai's harem. I couldn't bear to be shut up again."

The Patrols obviously expected a swift answer. Menacing sounds emerged from their mouths. Orpheus turned to Babilas and then Finopico. Both men lowered their gaze.

"Oh, all right," Orpheus said, resigned. "I'm the captain of the *Fabula*. My name is Orpheus McBott, and we were on our way to Galnicia when an infernal tempest broke over us and—"

"Enough!" announced another bird, narrowing its eyes, which were no bigger than pinheads. "What you call an infernal tempest was the wrath of Catabea!"

"All the same," Orpheus continued, "this tempest—"

"Silence!" cried a third bird. "Listen to what you're told, and don't speak of that tempest as if it were an ordinary natural event. Catabea is sensitive, you know. You've already felt the force of her anger when you passed the Great Barrier.

I wouldn't give her further reason for annoyance if I were you."

Finopico had come over. His skin had taken on a greenish hue beneath his mop of red hair.

"What are you talking about, you ill-omened birds!" he exploded. "Go back to wherever you came from and leave us to follow our own route in peace. We're going home!"

The Patrols instantly turned their tiny heads towards the cook, narrowing their little eyes at him.

"He wants to go home!" exclaimed one of the birds.

"Wants to go home!"

"Wants to go home!"

And all the others fell about laughing, scraping their metallic wings together. It made Malva's hair stand on end.

"When a vessel wanders off course into the Archipelago," said one of the wading birds, suddenly serious again, "no one ever knows what becomes of its occupants. What was once known is known no longer. Your home doesn't exist any more."

"And now," said the bird who had spoken first, "we will take you to Catabea. She will tell you all you need to know about your future."

It unfolded one of its wings and pointed to the bows of the *Fabula*.

"Tow this vessel!"

At this signal, the flock took off from the deck, with a great mechanical din, flew around the broken mainmast, and came down again, but this time at the stern of the ship. Then, moving perfectly in unison, the Patrols unfurled their wings.

As they beat their wings, the *Fabula* was propelled forward. She gained speed, cutting through the turquoise water surprisingly fast, and finally came ashore on the beach of the island that Orpheus had seen.

One of the Patrols cried, "Welcome to the realm of Catabea, strangers!"

With that, the flock of birds suddenly flew up, and hovered over the tops of the skeletal trees that covered the island. Then they disappeared, leaving the passengers of the *Fabula* behind them, stunned.

The prow of the ship had run into greyish sand that contrasted with the intense blue of the water. The island was small, dry and rocky. There were no leaves on the trees, the bushes looked like the rocks, and total silence reigned. The place had obviously been deserted by all animals and insects. There was dismay on board the *Fabula*.

"This is some kind of joke," Finopico said at last. "A hallucination. A hoax . . ."

Before he could finish speaking, a sudden gust of wind made the branches of the trees closest to the shore rustle. Then it died down again.

"No one's ever heard of the Great Barrier, or this stupid Archipelago," added the cook, in a voice that was not as firm as before.

Something cracked in the thickets of the dead forest higher up on the hills: a sound like dry wood snapping, a sonorous and melancholy noise.

"No one has ever—"

"Oh, do stop talking!" Malva suddenly interrupted.

"Yes, be quiet, by Holy Tranquillity!" begged the twins. "You'll arouse the wrath of Ca—"

"Oh, for goodness' sake!" snapped Finopico. "This is ridiculous! Those birds were obviously making fun of us!"

The others didn't think so. The strange sounds of the horn, the gigantic statues with their stony eyes, the human-headed birds all suggested that they were in a world where they had entirely lost their bearings. Even Zeph was pointing a suspicious muzzle at the island.

"Come on!" said Finopico, losing his temper. "Be sensible! This is just a hallucination brought on by hunger and thirst!"

"But suppose we have indeed crossed some kind of frontier?" murmured Malva. "Suppose this Great Barrier really does exist?"

She sought an answer in Orpheus's eyes, but he shook his head, undecided and uneasy.

"I don't know, your Alteza."

"Well, since no one knows anything," Finopico went on, "I suggest we go ashore. This may look like a desert island, but perhaps we can find fresh water and fill some barrels? And there may be berries or roots that we could eat."

The survivors of the storm looked hard at the grey, dismal shores. Finopico shook Babilas. "We'll have to repair the *Errabunda* . . . or the *Fabula*, never mind which. Don't you think so?"

The giant nodded in agreement.

"Right," said the cook. "Let's get going. And then we'll leave this spot! If Galnician blood still flows in our veins, let's prove ourselves worthy of it!"

Orpheus sighed. No doubt Finopico was right. And now that he had appointed himself captain, he had to make a decision.

"We'll need a gangplank," he began. "Firewood, tools, and—"

"As you know, I'm an excellent fisherman," Finopico interrupted, rolling up his sleeves. "I just need to make a harpoon, and then I'll dive in and bring back the ingredients for a good soup. By Holy Harmony, these clear waters must be teeming with fish! And at the moment I don't see any Catabea who—"

But at these words a low sound shook the trees and rocks. The whole island seemed to snarled like an animal, and a hoarse voice could be heard.

"You have spoken my name."

Malva jumped, and without thinking clung to Orpheus's jacket. Before their eyes, an enormous woman emerged from the forest of dead trees. She moved slowly over the sand, with a voluminous black tunic covering her body. Her limbs were so heavy that they seemed to be a burden to her: her legs and arms were like tree trunks, thick, gnarled and wrinkled like bark. Only her face, which was smooth and luminous, retained a human look.

"I am Catabea," she announced. "Catabea, Guardian of the Archipelago."

And as she spoke, grey vapours swirled out of her mouth.

25

The Law of the Archipelago

Catabea's face was almost entirely hidden behind a curtain of mist. Even standing on the deck of their ship, the survivors had to narrow their eyes so as not to lose sight of her.

"You have accepted the Procedure," said Catabea, "and you have spoken my name. In passing the Great Barrier you crossed the frontiers of our world. You have sailed into the Archipelago, and now you must submit to our Law. Listen well, strangers. Your survival depends on what I am about to tell you."

Hob and Peppe went pale at these words. They closed their eyes and began moaning again. But Catabea went on, and her cavernous voice drowned out their lamentations.

"The rules I am about to tell you are inflexible, and I must warn you: to this day, no traveller has ever succeeded in what he set out to do. Not one! Knowing that, you still have a choice: you can give up your freedom and remain prisoners of the Archipelago forever. If that is your decision, you can take advantage of the great riches of our sea and our islands. We will ask nothing of you. On the other hand, if you wish to cross the Archipelago and come out again, you must submit to our Law."

A silence followed this announcement, and the survivors on the *Fabula* silently consulted each other. Bafflement was written on all their faces.

"Well?" said Catabea impatiently. "What is your decision? Do you wish to stay here for ever? Or would you rather make the impossible attempt to return to your homes?"

Orpheus he timidly cleared his throat, before venturing to ask, "What happens to us if we don't succeed in what we set out to do?"

"You will be thrown into the Immuration," Catabea calmly replied. "That is the most common fate, and a terrible one too. But you can still decide to become ordinary inhabitants of the Archipelago. There are many islands here. You are sure to find one that suits you, and you can live a long and easy life there."

"But we can never go home again?" persisted Orpheus.

"That is so. I must point out that the choice you are about to make holds good only if all the passengers on your ship agree."

In a panic, Malva tugged at Orpheus's arm again. "I won't stay a prisoner here!" she murmured. "Let's accept their Law if that's the only way of escape!"

Hob and Peppe had risen to their feet. Tottering, they went over to Orpheus. A little further off, Babilas still leaned over the rail.

"I in agreement with Malva," said Lei in a firm voice. "Impossible for me stay here, so far from kingdom of Balmun."

"Your reply!" Catabea commanded them.

Babilas straightened up, and signed to Orpheus that he would go along with his decision. But it was Finopico who spoke first.

"We want to go home, you madwoman!" he snapped at the

Guardian of the island. "We came to the outskirts of your Archipelago only by bad luck, and I've already seen too much of it! If we're to come across human-headed birds every other day, I'd prefer your Immuration!"

The twins cried out in terror. Catabea's mouth opened, and mist poured out once again, leaving the passengers on the *Fabula* pale with amazement.

"So that is your decision!" cried the creature. "Then here is our Law!"

The mists surrounding her began to disperse and then, with a slow movement, she brought something out from the folds of her tunic and showed it to them.

"This is a Nokros, a Killer of Time. Look at it carefully, for it will accompany you as you cross the Archipelago."

The Nokros looked like a very large hourglass, except that one end had a clear chamber filled with red liquid.

"This chamber contains morbic acid. It will flow through, drop by drop, until . . ."

Here Catabea interrupted herself, and withdrew a brown stone from the folds of her tunic. She showed it to the passengers on board the *Fabula*.

"Is obsilix!" said Lei in amazement. "Very rare stone. I think it found only in core of volcanoes."

"It is indeed an obsilix," Catabea replied. "More often called the Stone of Life! This mineral is so hard that it can resist molten lava."

She opened the top of the chamber, put the Stone of Life down in front of her, and let a little of the red acid trickle on it. At once the stone split in two. It smoked, became covered with blisters, and then, before the astonished eyes of the survivors, began to dissolve. Her demonstration over, Catabea closed the chamber and said, "There are eight of you. I will place eight Stones of Life in the upper part of the Nokros. Each one symbolises one member of your crew."

In spite of the mist that swirled around Catabea, Malva could see her manipulating the fragile Nokros. The woman's tree-like hands worked slowly, but with surprising precision as she unscrewed the Nokros, picked up the Stones of Life and put them in the glass compartment at one end.

"There," she said at last, raising the large hourglass. "The eight Stones are in place. Soon a drop of morbic acid will fall on the first. Once the destruction begins, no one will be able to stop it until all the stones are reduced to powder. When nothing is left of the eight Stones, the powder will then fall into the lower part of the Nokros and your time has run out."

The passengers on the *Fabula* exchanged glances. Orpheus bit his lip before asking, "And what happens when that moment comes?"

"There are two possibilities," replied Catabea. "Either you have failed, in which case you will be thrown into the Immuration. Or you have succeeded, and then you can leave the Archipelago. But as I told you, no one, no ship's crew, has ever succeeded."

"Succeeded in what?" cried Finopico. "I don't understand a word of all this!"

Catabea approached the ship. She looked hard at the cook with her misty eyes, and when she opened her mouth Finopico was immersed in a fog, and began coughing.

"Be wise, hot-tempered Galnician!" she told him. "I know your temperament. I know what obsesses you, for I know everything about you."

"This makes no sense!" gasped Finopico, brushing the fog

away with the back of one hand. "What must we succeed in doing?"

The Guardian of the Archipelago smiled. "You must succeed in satisfying your wildest and most secret desires."

Turning her head slowly, she looked hard into the eyes of Orpheus, Malva, Lei and all the others in turn.

"I know your histories! I know your vulnerabilities! You all have profound dreams, terrible flaws, devouring ambitions! You are never satisfied with what you have."

Malva shivered. Every word Catabea spoke seemed as barbed as an arrow, and each arrow found its target. The prophetess stopped in front of Zeph, who was still lying flat on deck with his nose between his paws.

"Even dogs have their desires!" she said. "Here in the Archipelago you will find the vast mirror which reflects your desires and fears, your dreams and nightmares. That mirror grows larger or smaller by virtue of those passing over it. It is always changing shape. Every day new islands appear or are submerged. I myself don't know their exact number. They are welcoming or dangerous, light or dark, humid or arid, deserted or over-populated, but there is a treasure hidden on each one."

As she spoke, mist poured from her mouth, and Catabea swayed her enormous arms as if in time to some inaudible music. Her hair, thick, bushy and ashen, shook whenever she moved her head, and the trees on the hills bowed or raised their tops to the same rhythm. Catabea *was* the island.

"This is what our Law demands," she continued. "In crossing the Archipelago you must succeed in fulfilling yourselves. As you sail our sea, you will be confronted with yourselves, and you must fight your own worst terrors. If you refuse to face the ordeals waiting for you, you are lost. There will be nothing left for you but the Immuration."

Catabea went towards Orpheus, raised one enormous arm and handed him the Nokros over the ship's rail.

"Captain, I entrust the Killer of Time to you. It takes two days for the morbic acid to dissolve a Stone of Life. You will be responsible for the Nokros throughout the sixteen days allotted to you. If you or one of your companions should try to interrupt the process, your sentence will be carried out at once. Take good care of this instrument."

Orpheus felt cold sweat break out on his forehead. He took the Nokros in his hands and then, without taking his eyes off the acid in the chamber, put it down on deck and wedged it against the mast. Meanwhile Catabea had turned to the Princetta and was inspecting her closely. Vapour steamed from her mouth.

"I should warn you, young Princetta, of the danger that threatens you in particular. Another ship has come ashore here. No doubt you heard the two horns: each signalled that a visitor had just crossed the Great Barrier. This solitary visitor was on board a Cispazian ship, but he spoke Galnician, your language. He has made the same choice as you, preferring to risk the Immuration rather than remain a prisoner of the Archipelago. I have probed his soul. I found nothing there but hatred, and that hatred is for you."

"The Archont . . . the Archont is here?" Malva asked, her face turning pale.

Catabea's tree-trunk body swayed back and forth in assent.

"But that's impossible!" cried Hob. "We shut him up in Temir-Gai's harem!"

"Locked in a small room," Peppe agreed. "And the fire spread so fast! How could he possibly have—"

"I know everything that happens in my Archipelago," Catabea interrupted him, "but nothing of what goes on outside it."

She stepped slowly back.

"Now I must go, and you must leave this shore. The morbic acid is already beginning to work . . . look!"

Inside the Nokros, the first stone was smoking faintly and tiny blisters appeared on its surface.

"Do not lose a moment!" Catabea advised. "Sixteen days, don't forget. That is our Law."

And with these words she turned and made slowly for the forest.

"Oh, please don't leave us!" cried Malva, flinging herself at the rail with all her might. "We have more questions to ask you!"

But Catabea was not to be stopped. Her echoing voice was already fainter.

"There are treasures to be unearthed on as many islands as you like, strangers. Above all, be true to yourselves! Then perhaps you will find the gateway of the Archipelago." She made a final gesture with her enormous arms. "And now, leave."

At that, total silence descended upon the island.

Then everything seemed to happen at once: small waves made the *Fabula* pitch, waves going the wrong way, starting from the shore and rolling out to sea. To the utter amazement of the crew, foaming breakers swept the ship away from Catabea's island. In moments, its outline became blurred, and then completely invisible. The trees, the rocks, everything had disappeared.

Stunned, the survivors gathered around the Nokros. A second drop of red acid was forming at the opening of the chamber.

"What does all this mean?" Finopico suddenly exploded. "I

didn't understand a word of it! A mirror, islands appearing and disappearing! Hidden treasures! Personally I don't mind digging, but where? I see no land in sight anywhere on the horizon!"

"Catabea speak in riddle," Lei said. "Treasures perhaps not really exist. She mean treasures hidden inside us."

The twins knelt in front of the Nokros.

"Captain," murmured Hob, "tell us what to do."

"We don't want to die," said Peppe. "We're too young."

They turned distressed faces towards Orpheus. "We don't want to be thrown into the Immuration!" they groaned in chorus.

Orpheus sighed, at a loss. Catabea was going to put them to the test, but he had no idea in what way. All he could see was that the *Fabula* needed repairs, and its crew was in danger of dying from hunger and thirst.

At that moment, inside the Nokros, the next drop of morbic acid fell on the Stone of Life and dug a small, smoking crater in it. Everyone jumped.

"We must find an island where we can take on provisions," said Orpheus in a sombre voice. "That's all that matters for the moment."

26

Torments and Delights

The sun had reached its height, and didn't seem to want to move on. For a very long time, no one knew what to say, what to do, even what to think. Each felt the crushing weight of fate on their shoulders, while the Nokros mercilessly marked the passing of seconds, minutes, hours . . .

The *Fabula* went with the current, obeying its whims. No one tried to steer it any particular way, and anyway, what way would they go? Without a map, without a compass, in an Archipelago of changing dimensions, no sailor, not even the most experienced old salt, could get his bearings.

So the ship drifted aimlessly, delivered up to the currents of this strange sea, which was soon covered with a thick layer of slimy seaweed. It sucked at the hull like leeches, clinging so tenaciously to the stern and the fallen rigging that the ship slowed, then came to a halt, mired in a green mush that stretched as far as the eye could see.

What's more, it was getting hotter and hotter. A fetid smell rose to the nostrils of the crew.

"What's going on?" asked Finopico, leaning over the side. "It's as if the sea were rotting."

A shiver passed through Orpheus, and he recognized the bitter taste of fear and thirst in his mouth. It wasn't a sea that he saw around him any more; it was a dense puddle of algae, vast and hopeless.

"Captain!" groaned Hob. "I'm hungry! I'm thirsty!"

"Do something!" begged Peppe.

Orpheus turned round slowly, as if his mind and body were caught in the seaweed too. The twins were lying on deck beside the old St. Bernard, who was panting heavily. Malva and Lei, seated on a sea chest, were staring into space, their arms dangling listlessly. Only Finopico and Babilas were still on their feet. They stood side by side, eyes downcast, hands clutching the rail. Orpheus ran his tongue over his lips, which were dry with sun and salt. He saw the day of his departure again, the day when he saw the coasts of his own country recede, and felt proud and impatient. Hadn't he sworn then to win back the lost honour of the McBotts? Hadn't he made a thousand promises of glory and adventure to himself?

"And look at me now!" he murmured.

A sudden pain shot right through his head. He raised a trembling hand to his brow. The memory of his father's face on his deathbed came to him, and he thought of the injury which he had been led to believe he'd suffered from since childhood. Was it coming back?

"No!" he cried out loud.

His companions jumped. Slowly they turned dull, hollow eyes towards him. Orpheus sensed that they were abandoning themselves to the decay all around them, were simply letting themselves die. Panic suddenly took hold of him.

"Babilas!" he shouted, making for the giant who leaned listlessly against the rail. "Stand up straight! Come on! We have to get out of here. I need your strength, Babilas!"

When the giant still did not react, Orpheus shook Finopico. The cook swayed in place and fell to the deck like a broken puppet, his eyes reflecting nothing but the dismal sky.

"Hey!" Orpheus tried provoking him, putting his face close to the cook's. "You promised to catch us fish, Finopico! Go on, dive in! Dive in and bring us back something to eat!"

Still, Finopico did not reply. His chest was rising and falling with his breathing, but his strength had gone.

"Princetta!" called Orpheus.

Turning away from Finopico, he went towards Malva. She was still sitting on the sea-chest, one shoulder leaning against Lei, but her eyes were lifeless. Orpheus knelt down in front of her and took her hands. They were cold as death.

"Princetta, speak to me! Say something! Just a word, by Holy Tranquillity!"

To his dismay, not a sound passed her lips. As for Lei, she had slipped into a profound slumber. It was no good pleading with her, shaking her—nothing worked. Orpheus tried the twins, drew them towards him, shouted their names, threatened and cajoled them, with no result. They too had been overcome with a morbid languor, their eyes drained of any desire to live.

"We're not going to die here," muttered Orpheus, casting the Nokros a panic-stricken glance.

He was horrified by the situation. He turned to Zeph and ran one hand through the thick fur on the dog's head. Beneath it he saw the St. Bernard's eyes light up.

"Zeph—can you hear me?"

The dog looked straight at him.

"You *can* hear me!" cried Orpheus, greatly relieved. "You're alive at least! Silly old mutt!"

He put his arms lovingly around the dog as tears sprang to his eyes.

"Can you feel Death on the prowl, Zeph?" he asked. "We must chase it away, do you hear? I refuse to abandon my post. I won't let my life end in a place like this . . ."

Orpheus leaped to his feet and ran to the fo'c'sle. His fear had suddenly turned to revolt. He hung from the rigging, shouting furiously at the sky.

"By all the Divinities of the Known World—and the Unknown Worlds too!" he cried. "I'm alive and I'll fight to stay alive! This ship is afloat! I'm its captain! And I swear that it will take me where I want to go. I refuse to break my word."

He was getting his breath back. Nothing in the sky had changed, but Orpheus felt the blood racing through his veins. Picking up a piece of timber torn loose in the storm, he flung it into the seaweed with all his might.

"Be gone, spirits of Death!" he cried. "Let us go on our way!"

And he threw more and more debris into the murky waters, cursing the whole time. Sweat ran down his temples. He was gasping for breath, and his throat was sore with shouting, but his anger would not die down.

"I want water! Clear water!" he shouted, as if it were a feverish incantation. "Something to drink for our dry throats! Something to eat for our empty bellies! Wind for our ragged sails! Hope for our broken hearts!"

He suddenly stopped, opened his mouth and sneezed violently. He had just felt a breath of fresh air on his face.

Muzzle raised, Zeph barked two or three times. Now the wind was rippling the spongy surface of the water, creating movement that broke up the thick layer of seaweed here and there. Patches of turquoise water appeared, and the *Fabula* moved gently.

"Look!" shouted Orpheus. "Look at this!"

The other passengers didn't move. But suddenly the seaweed parted, drifted away on the sea, and a pathway appeared in front of the ship's bows.

"We're moving!" marvelled Orpheus.

A mysterious force was pushing the *Fabula* forward. Clinging to the rigging, Orpheus looked along the line of blue water that cut through the layer of seaweed. Soon he saw the blurred shape of another island in the distance.

"Land! Land ahoy!" he rejoiced. "We're saved!"

As the ship drew closer, Orpheus could make out trees, flowers, rocks and a waterfall cascading down a mossy hillside. Zeph started barking, but the other passengers still didn't react.

A moment later the *Fabula* entered the calm waters of a large bay. Intoxicated with hope, Orpheus seized one of the mooring ropes.

"Wait here!" he told his companions. "I'll be back!"

Diving off the fo'c'sle, he swam as strongly as he could to the beach. An enormous trek grew a little way from the water, and Orpheus wrapped his mooring rope firmly round its trunk.

Unlike the island where Catabea lived, this one was teeming with life. There were insects, birds (not with human heads this time), fruits and berries—something to satisfy all their appetites.

Orpheus went on up the beach towards some undergrowth. But as he skirted a large rock he suddenly stopped, stifling a cry of surprise. A man was sitting on a tree stump looking at him.

"I'm so sorry," Orpheus apologised. "I . . ."

The man was much older than him. His face was covered with brown age spots, and white hair flowed over his shoulders. He was holding a small knife in his left hand and a reed between his knees.

"I'm so sorry," Orpheus repeated. "I . . . we need food and water. My companions . . ."

He pointed to the ship, unable to finish his sentence.

"Take anything you like," the man calmly replied in perfect Galnician. "This island belongs to no one and everyone. It's full of riches, and I don't know what to do with them. Do you have a knife?"

Orpheus pointed to the knife at his belt.

"Then you can cut fruits and roots," the old man smiled. "Help yourself."

Then he bent his head, and went on with his work, whittling. Disconcerted, Orpheus hesitated for a moment, wondering which way to go.

"Oh, and as for water," the man went on, "I have a little keg over there in the shade of the araucaria. You can borrow it."

Orpheus nodded his thanks, and then, holding his questions for later, went up to the tree. Its branches bristled with thorns. The keg contained clear, cool water, and there was a wooden ladle beside it. He picked up the ladle, had a long drink, and suddenly felt his weariness vanish. Waiting no longer, he picked up the keg, made his way back to the *Fabula*, and hauled himself up the rope ladder with one hand. Once on deck, he hurried to Malva first.

"Drink this, Princetta," he murmured, pouring water into her mouth from the ladle.

Malva drank, clumsily at first, then greedily. She reopened her amber eyes at last and looked gratefully at Orpheus. He smiled.

"I'll bring you something to eat soon."

Then he went to Lei, the twins, Babilas and Finopico, and finally poured a little water into a bowl for Zeph. Each time the same miracle happened: the water seemed to bring those who drank it back to life.

Reassured, Orpheus returned to the island to thank the old man.

"It's the clouds you should thank," replied the man, never stopping his work. "It rains every night here." He cleared his throat. "You'll find a big basket for collecting fruits under the latania tree. You can borrow it."

Orpheus thanked him again, replaced the water keg under the araucaria, found the basket and went into the outskirts of the jungle. Trees of all shapes and sizes were bowed under the weight of their fruit. Orpheus bit into a kind of tender-fleshed apple which tasted delicious. He picked so much that his basket was very soon full, then hurried back to the *Fabula* with his harvest. The colour came back into his companions cheeks.

"That's good!" sighed Hob.

"Thank you, Captain, said Peppe.

Malva just smiled.

"When you feel strong enough," Orpheus told her cheerfully, "come and join me ashore. There are hundreds of fruits waiting to be picked!"

Then he clambered down the side of the *Fabula* again. He wanted to talk to the old man and find out his name and what he was doing on the island.

"My name is Jahalod-Rin," the man replied when Orpheus

asked him. "I've lived on this island for more years than I can count. I make flutes."

"Are you a musician?" Orpheus asked.

"No, I make flutes, that's all."

"Do you never play them?"

"Never."

Orpheus frowned. "Then who are the flutes for if you don't play them yourself?"

Jahalod-Rin narrowed his eyes. "Making flutes is no sillier than wanting to leave the Archipelago."

"How do you know that's what we want to do?"

"You're just like all the others," said the old man, laughing. "You arrive here with a great deal of noise, you set off the warning sirens, you bring the Patrols flying along, and then all you want to do is go away again! Personally I preferred to use my time in other ways. This island is full of pools and rivers; reeds grow freely everywhere, so I make flutes."

Orpheus looked at Jahalod-Rin in surprise. "You didn't want . . . ?" he began.

"No, no," smiled Jahalod, anticipating his question. "Why go round and round among all these islands and risk ending up in the Immuration? I'm better off here. I don't expect anything more of life, but at least I'm not disappointed."

Orpheus sat down on the sand in front of the old man. He took off his quartermaster's jacket and mopped his brow. He said nothing for a moment, lost in contemplation of the island. The distant sound of the waterfall was enough to soothe and refresh him. Jahalod-Rin had gone back to his work, giving it all his attention.

"But Catabea did tell us there was a way out of here," sighed Orpheus.

"I haven't believed in that for a long time," replied the old man. "Those who tried to get out are all dead now."

"Have you seen them?" Orpheus asked timidly. "I mean . . . have you seen the Immuration?"

Jahalod shrugged. "Of course not! Only those thrown into the Immuration know what it's like. There, look! This one's finished."

He proudly showed the new flute. When Orpheus nodded admiringly, he handed it to him.

"Here you are, a present," he said. "When you leave you'll remember me."

Orpheus, who was not used to getting presents, readily accepted it. Everything seemed so easy in this wise old man's company.

"Having said that," added Jahalod, "I'm not chasing you away. You're very welcome. Stay as long as you like. You'll be company, and that will be a nice change for me. I haven't had any visitors for so long!"

Orpheus thought about the Archont. "Have you seen a man alone aboard a Cispazian ship? A man with a smooth, shaven skull, wearing richly embroidered robes?"

When Jahalod-Rin shook his long white hair, Orpheus felt better. If the Archont had really followed them to this strange place, as Catabea had said, at least he wasn't prowling around these parts. He put the flute to his lips and blew. A pure note came out, making Jahalod smile.

"You know how to play it!" he exclaimed.

"Not really," Orpheus confessed, "but it can't be too difficult to learn."

"Play it again! Please do!"

Orpheus obliged. Stopping the holes with his fingers,

he produced a series of notes that seems to delight the old man.

"Music . . . ah, that comforts me. I feel sad already to know that you will leave again."

Orpheus immediately felt his heart contract. This old man seemed so lonely, so kind. He wanted to help and please him. "We won't be leaving at once," he hastened to assure him. "We need to rest, and we need time to repair our boat. If you will allow it, we'd like to sleep on land tonight."

The old man's face lit up. With a wave of his hand, he pointed out a roof made of planks that he had built close to the araucaria. "It rains hard at night here, so by all means take shelter there."

Orpheus, who didn't like the damp or draughts, appreciated the old man's hospitality. He ran back to the *Fabula*, told his companions about Jahalod and showed them the plank shelter.

"We won't stay long," he told them, casting a quick glance at the Nokros, "but I'm sure there are things on this island that will do us good."

27

The Flutes of Discord

And so the crew of the *Fabula* recovered their health. Lei found the plants and insects she needed for her medicine in the undergrowth. She made potions and ointments to treat Babilas's injured hand, and once again the giant was able to lift and carry, cut wood and dig. He worked so well that the leaks in the hull of the ship were soon plugged, the deck was cleaned, the masts replaced.

Meanwhile, Orpheus asked Jahalod-Rin's permission to bury the bodies of the sailors who had died in the storm. With help from the twins and Finopico, he dug graves not far from the source of the waterfall.

"May Holy Tranquillity and Holy Harmony protect them forever," he said, once the dead were buried. Then he mopped his brow, and looked at the sky above the trees.

"This is a wonderful place," he said. "And Jahalod-Rin is a remarkable man, don't you think?"

"He's strange," said Hob. "Kind, though."

"More than that!" said Orpheus. "He's . . . delightful."

He had seen so many men reveal their base, deceitful natures: his own father, of course, and then the Archont and the Captain of the *Errabunda*. Jahalod-Rin, on the other hand, seemed kind and simple. In his company, Orpheus felt confidence in his fellow humans. He sensed that this time he had found a really good example.

"Jahalod is so wise," he said as they followed the path leading back to the beach. "He's not strange just because he spends all day making flutes. He's a craftsman. And his fingers are remarkably nimble for a man of his age."

With that Orpheus picked up the flute the old man had given him and played a few notes. When they reached the spot where the *Fabula* was moored he sat down on the sand and continued to play. Babilas and Malva, who were busy sewing the sails together again, looked up from their work.

"Don't you think you ought to be repairing the navigational instruments, Captain?" Malva suggested.

Orpheus stopped playing for a moment. "Later!" he said. "There's no hurry."

Malva turned to the Nokros. The first Stone of Life was half dissolved. How could Orpheus be so carefree? She looked down the beach, to where old Jahalod sat on his rock, cutting his reeds. He looked serene, but there was something about him that made Malva uneasy. She couldn't help looking at the old man with a touch of suspicion. She couldn't understand how anyone could choose to stay in the Archipelago, as he had done.

"Spending his days cutting flutes!" muttered Malva. "It's absurd. What's the point of sitting on the ground doing the same thing day after day?"

Two days passed very quickly. Hob and Peppe, who had chased rats and stray cats on the streets of Galnicia, caught game. Small rodents, birds, long-tailed marsupials. Finopico restocked the galley of the *Fabula*, made fishing rods from bamboo in the forest, and invented all kinds of delicious dishes, which the crew shared with old Jahalod.

On the second evening, Orpheus lit a big bonfire on the beach. When they were all sitting around it on the sand, he raised a goblet of mangava juice to Jahalod-Rin.

"To our host's good health!" he said, his eyes shining. "To his great wisdom and his hospitality! If not for him we'd all be dead of hunger and thirst by now!

The others gravely nodded, remembering the poor state in which they had come ashore. Only Malva was unwilling to drink to Jahalod's health. She drew her knees up to her chin and looked sulky. While his companions ate heartily, Orpheus took out his flute. He played for a long time, and the old man listened with delight.

"You are wonderfully gifted!" he exclaimed, between mouthfuls. "I never heard such sweet melodies in my life!"

The others exchanged doubtful glances. Orpheus wasn't doing badly for a beginner, but they thought Jahalod's compliments were rather over the top.

"We're gifted too!" announced the twins.

They got up and were about to sing some Galnician songs, but they had hardly begun on the first when Jahalod began coughing.

"Excuse me!" he said as he got his breath back. "But I think I like the sound of the flute better."

"Maybe you do, but Orpheus hasn't had a chance to eat," objected Hob, slightly annoyed. "We just wanted to let him—"

"Oh, I'm not hungry," Orpheus assured them. "Do go on eating, all of you. I'll just play for a little longer."

Hob and Peppe stopped singing, disappointed, and glanced at Malva. She was boiling with fury inside. The sound of the flute got on her nerves, but she didn't like to say anything. Jahalod-Rin, eating his fill of grilled game, fruit and the fish caught by Finopico, was nodding his white head in time to the music and beaming happily.

"If I had ever had a son," he suddenly said, "I'd have liked him to be like you."

At these words Orpheus stopped playing. There was a sudden lump in his throat.

"I had a father," Orpheus murmured, putting the instrument down on his knees. "He's dead now. I buried him a few months ago in Galnicia. I wish so much . . ."

He hesitated, suddenly looking into space. Zeph gave a little yap as he burned his nose on a live ember. Orpheus jumped.

"You were talking about your father," Jahalod gently reminded him.

"Yes, my father," murmured Orpheus. "He was a man who . . . who sad to say was not as wise and honest as you."

He looked at the flute, shook his head as if to shake off his melancholy, and began playing again. Malva shuddered.

"I've had enough of this music!" she said. "I'd like to eat in silence."

Jahalod and Orpheus turned to her at the same moment, looking vexed.

"There's no reason why you have to stay here," the old man told her sharply. "If you can't appreciate beauty—"

"That flute is dreadful!" complained Malva. "I've heard much better tunes in my time, if you really want to know." She threw a handful of sand on the fire. Her hands were trembling. "I've heard the *lamento* of a sailor from Lombardaine. I've heard the voices of Baighur women in the evening on the Great Azizian Steppes. I've heard the sweet singing of Temir-Gaï's preunuchs! Even the serenades my father's musicians played were easier on the ear than this shrill flute!"

"All the better for you, young woman!" retorted Jahalod-Rin. "You're lucky, you can go all over the world! But here all alone . . . well, I have nothing but my flutes!"

Irritated, Orpheus leaped to his feet and planted himself in front of Malva.

"You have a very hard heart, Princetta!" he said angrily, towering above her. "Jahalod welcomes us to his island, gives us his fruit and his water—you might make an effort to thank him. I've been watching you since we came here. You sit about as if you were the unhappiest girl in the world, but just look around you! This is a wonderful island. We can eat and drink. Jahalod has lived here all alone for years, without any entertainment, with no one to talk to. So if a few tunes on the flute can be a little comfort to him in his loneliness, I—"

Malva threw the piece of meat she was eating into the fire and rose to her own feet, fixing her amber eyes on Orpheus. "Jahalod chose to live alone on this island!" she replied. "It's not up to us to console him for being a coward!"

"A coward?" gasped Orpheus. "How dare you insult our host?"

His breath was coming fast, his neck was stiff with anger and blue veins stood out on his forehead. He seemed about to fling himself on Malva. The others watched the scene at a loss, not knowing what to do. The game was still roasting over the fire, sending showers of sparks up to the dark sky now and then. Jahalod coughed again, and then said, in a quavering voice,

"Never mind. I am sure the young lady is right. I was a coward in the past, when Catabea received me into the Archipelago. I wasn't brave enough to accept her challenge, and that's the truth."

Disconcerted, Orpheus turned to the old man. "Don't say such things!" he begged him. "You are so good, so generous! The Princetta doesn't know what she's saying. She's . . . she's just a spoilt child."

Malva opened her mouth, but she was too stunned to say anything. Jahalod-Rin gave her a sideways glance and nodded. A sly smile touched his lips.

"Perhaps the young lady is jealous," he suggested. "If I understood you correctly, she is of high lineage. She is used to being pampered, surrounded by solicitude, and she likes giving orders. Now she sees you paying attention to me, she feels she isn't as powerful as she once was . . . and she feels slighted."

Malva went scarlet in the face. "You think I'm jealous?" she shouted. "How could I be jealous of a poor old lunatic?"

Orpheus seized her by the shoulders and shook her roughly. "Shut up!" he spat. "If you call my father a lunatic again, I'll—"

Orpheus sounded so angry that Babilas and the twins got between him and Malva.

"Your *father?*" she cried, laughing. "What are you talking about, Captain? Your father's dead! You said so just now."

Orpheus took a step forward, his mouth twisted with rage, but Babilas stopped him with one hand. The twins were on each side of Malva, tugging her back.

"Make her shut up!" said Orpheus, foaming with fury. "Get her out of here, or I'll murder her!"

Lei and Finopico rose to their feet too, stunned. Such sudden violence left them speechless. Only Jahalod-Rin stayed peaceably sitting by the fire, licking his fingers and nibbling fruit as if nothing had happened.

"Come over here, my son," he murmured to Orpheus. "Sit down by the fire and let the anger in your heart die down."

Held back by Babilas's powerful arms, Orpheus watched Malva and the twins move away. When he heard Jahalod's voice he suddenly relaxed.

"Come here, come here," the old man insisted. "If those people are still your friends, they will understand. Give them time. Sit down and play me a little tune . . ."

Babilas frowned when Orpheus shook free of his grasp and went back to Jahalod. The giant stood there motionless, looking anxious, his impressive shoulders casting a shadow on the flames, while Orpheus went back to sit beside old Jahalod and prepared to play.

Lei and Finopico took Zeph by the back of the neck and led him away from the fire. "Looks like we're not welcome any more," said Finopico. "And it hurts our ears too!"

Orpheus played the flute as loud as he could, making such a harsh sound that Lei cried out. Jahalod-Rin burst into laughter.

"Excellent, my son!" he said, smiling, as the others moved away. "Now we can be at our ease, you and I!" He put his freckled hand on Orpheus's shoulder. "I have eaten well. I feel sleepy, I will lie down. But go on playing to me, please. The music will lull me."

The old man lay down at the threshold of his hut and closed his eyes. Sitting by the fire, Orpheus played, and played, and played. Night enveloped the island, black and heavy as a velvet cape. It had begun to rain. Malva, Lei, Finopico, Babilas and the twins had taken shelter beneath the plank roof a little way off.

They were talking in low voices, glancing anxiously at Orpheus from time to time. He ignored the rain and played on, his hair dripping wet, sitting beside the fire as it went out. Now and then he sneezed. Whenever he stopped, Jahalod sat up with a start.

"Go on, please go on!" he begged plaintively. "The flute does me so much good!"

Orpheus obeyed, struggling against exhaustion to please his host. Hour followed hour, tune followed tune, sneeze followed sneeze.

At dawn, red-eyed and with stiff fingers, Orpheus was still playing.

"Thank you, my son!" said Jahalod, stretching. "I have slept well, thanks to you. Now I feel hungry."

Orpheus slowly put down his flute. His teeth were chattering. The sky was pale, and a cool breeze stirred the leaves of the tall trees. Dazed, Orpheus went off to the forest to pick fruit. He could hardly stay on his feet, but he took no notice of his aching muscles, which were telling him to rest. He had to find food for Jahalod, at any cost.

Further away, under the plank roof, his companions were watching. The sound of the flute had kept them from getting a wink of sleep all night.

"Holy Tranquillity, our Greenhorn would bring down the moon to please that cutter of reeds," grumbled Finopico. "If I hear any more of his ghastly music I'll make him eat sand!"

Babilas, clenching his fists in rage and impatience, evidently agreed.

The sun had risen. It was now three days since Catabea had placed the Stones of Life in the Nokros, and the passengers of the *Fabula* were downcast.

"We must leave," said Malva. "The *Fabula* is ready to sail. We've waited too long already."

"I think same," agreed Lei. "We leave! But Orpheus?"

"Let's leave him here!" said Finopico aggressively. "If he *wants* to die of exhaustion to please that old tyrant, that's his choice!"

But Babilas shook his head, and the twins protested too.

"Catabea told us we must stay together," Peppe reminded the others. "If we don't, we get thrown into the Immuration anyway!"

"He's right," Malva agreed. "We must all go on with our voyage together."

Jahalod-Rin had gone back to sit on his rock. Knife in hand, he was beginning his pointless work, examining the pile of reeds that Orpheus had just brought him.

"This reed is broken," he complained, holding up one of them. "And this one is too green! These are too dry. Listen, my son, how do you expect me to make good flutes with reeds like this?"

"I'm sorry, Father," Orpheus replied. "I'll get some more."

Obviously on the point of collapse, he made for the trees all the same.

"This island is our first test," said Malva, watching him go. "And Orpheus is failing it."

At that moment Orpheus emerged from the forest with another armful of reeds. Staggering, he went back to Jahalod and put the reeds down at his feet like a pilgrim making an offering before the statue of a deity.

"Good, my son," Jahalod told him. "Now play me something on the flute. I have stomach pains. Perhaps the music will soothe them. I wonder if it was the game your cook served us? It had a strange flavour."

The old man had said this in a voice deliberately loud enough for everyone to hear. Finopico shook with anger.

"My game? It was perfect!" he muttered. "This old man is getting on my nerves!"

Lei took a step forward and emerged from the shelter of the roof above them. "Jahalod want separate us," she said. "He sow discord."

Malva joined her. "That's quite enough! Come on!" she said.

She walked towards Orpheus, who was crouching in front of the rock with the flute to his lips. She looked at the young man's face: his pallor, his features drawn by weariness, his chapped lips, his fevered eyes.

"Go away!" he snapped. "Jahalod-Rin doesn't want anyone but me!"

Malva assumed a severe expression. "Since when do you speak to your Princetta in that tone?"

"He told you to go away," the old man interrupted, without even looking at Malva. "Leave us in peace."

Malva didn't favour Jahalod with a glance either. She took a deep breath and knelt on the sand. "We're leaving," she murmured in Orpheus's ear. "We're only waiting for you."

"I'm not going anywhere," the young man replied. "Jahalod needs me here. He's frail, and I must look after him. I am a good son to him, and a good son doesn't abandon his father."

Behind Malva, the rest of the crew of the *Fabula* had gathered. They were all looking at Orpheus.

"Leave us!" repeated Jahalod, raising his knife blade.

"You'll make him angry!" Orpheus told Malva. "Go away!"

"I don't fear Jahalod's anger," Malva replied. "We're the ones who need your help, Orpheus. We can't sail the *Fabula* without you. Remember what Catabea said: if we are to find the gates of the Archipelago—"

"I don't want to leave the Archipelago now!" shouted Orpheus, his face flushed. "I've changed my mind! I want to stay here with my master, Jahalod!"

Jahalod-Rin suddenly rose from his rock. Babilas made a movement, but the old man pointed his knife at him. The giant remained at a prudent distance.

"Play me a tune, my son!" demanded Jahalod. "There's a ringing in my ears. I need music!"

Orpheus was about to start playing the flute when Malva leapt at him. She snatched the instrument from his hands and held it above her head.

"No more flute music!" she cried. "Here's an end to it!"

And with a little crack, she broke the reed in two. Orpheus uttered a cry, but stayed crouching by the rock as if paralysed.

Jahalod-Rin immediately fell into a terrible rage. He rushed at Malva, shouting and holding out his knife. Babilas launched himself forward and disarmed the old man. Malva took the knife.

"Curses on you!" cried Jahalod, on his knees. "How dare you break my son's flute? You deserve to die!"

Staggered, Orpheus looked in turn from the old man to his companions and then the two halves of the reed. When the flute broke, something inside him had broken too.

"Other reeds!" cried Lei suddenly. "On the fire, quick!"

While Babilas firmly held Jahalod by the shoulders, Malva, Lei and the twins hurried over to the pile of reeds, ran to the dying fire and threw the flutes on the embers.

"No, not my flutes!" begged the old man. "My music! My son! Curses on you all!"

The reeds immediately fed the embers again. Sparks rose to

the sky in clouds. At last Orpheus rose to his feet, dazed, and put a trembling hand to his brow.

"Avenge me!" Jahalod ordered him, still struggling in the arms of Babilas. "You can see they're trying to separate us! Avenge your father!"

Zeph, who had been hauling his old hindquarters over the sand, went up to Orpheus, grunted and licked his hand.

"I'm thirsty," murmured Orpheus. "I'm so thirsty!"

Hob made haste to bring him water. He gave him a drink and then held out a friendly hand. "Come on, Captain. Please . . . it's time to leave."

Orpheus took Hob's hand and let the boy lead him to the *Fabula*.

"You can't abandon me!" the old man shouted after him. "You have to look after me! I gave you water and fruit!"

Orpheus was in a state of shock, but Jahalod-Rin's hysterical cries no longer had any effect on him. As he took hold of the rope ladder, Jahalod called to him, "Why did you summon me if it was only to betray me?"

Orpheus stopped in mid-movement. He turned to Hob, who was waiting anxiously down on the beach. "Did I really summon that man?" he asked. "Did I betray him?"

"Don't listen to him, Captain," the boy gently advised. "It was he who betrayed you! He'll say anything to keep you here. Climb up now. We must put out to sea!"

Orpheus nodded gravely and went on climbing. Finopico, Lei and Malva came up behind them, while Peppe dragged Zeph along by his neck. The old St. Bernard, who had unearthed a remnant of meat among the ashes, was refusing to let go of his find. He growled and yapped.

At last, when everyone was on board, Babilas let go of

Jahalod. He made haste to cast off the moorings before bracing himself against the hull of the *Fabula*. With a great shove, he pushed the ship well out from the beach, and then caught hold of the rope ladder and clambered aboard.

On his knees by the embers of the fire, Jahalod-Rin was trying to save some of the half-charred flutes. He was burning his fingers, and moaned like a wounded animal. As for Orpheus, he had collapsed on deck, and was covering his ears to shut out the old man's lamentations.

"I wish he'd be quiet! I wish he'd be quiet!" he groaned, writhing in pain.

Lei had knelt down beside Orpheus. She passed her hands over his burning forehead, uttering strange, soothing words.

The twins and Finopico hoisted the mended sails. They flapped as they unfolded in the clear air.

"Here's to a favouring wind!" cried Hob.

Standing at the stern of the ship, Malva watched the figure of Jahalod-Rin grow smaller as the island receded. What had happened to them? How had that inoffensive-looking old man been able to exert such power over Orpheus? How had a few notes of music managed to sow such discord among them all? Malva couldn't explain it, but she sensed that she and her companions had just had a close brush with disaster.

Red acid continued to drip on the Stones of Life in the Nokros. There were only seven left now.

28

Orpheus's Logbook

I found my logbook under a pile of damaged maps and pieces of paper all crinkled up by seawater. I gave the spare sheets of paper to the Princetta, who has told me she needs them to write a record of her travels.

My logbook has suffered, and the notes I made in it before the storm are illegible, but it's time for me to take command as Captain again. My high temperature has miraculously gone down; I feel myself again.

My experience on Jahalod-Rin's island obsesses me. I keep wondering about it. Lei, who knows a great deal about strange phenomena, thinks I was bewitched by the sound of the flute. So does Malva. It's true that when she broke the flute the spell was broken too. They are probably right, but I think most of all it was that Jahalod-Rin guessed my weakness. With him, I was as submissive and obedient as I was with my real father. When will I manage to shake off my childish fears?

Just now I assembled the crew on the fo'c'sle of the ship. I thanked everyone for rescuing me from Jahalod's clutches, and I apologised for the stupid things I said on the island, particularly to Malva.

The Princetta accepted my apologies, and I'm grateful to her. As far as I

*can remember, I called her a spoilt child. Holy Harmony, I'm really cross
with myself! She, who has survived so many insults and deadly dangers
recently—how did I dare? Malva is not a spoilt child, far from it. She is
proud and brave, determined, upright and . . .*

Orpheus let his pen hover in the air above the crinkled pages.
Malva's luminous face danced before his tired eyes. Her delicate
features, her heavy black hair, her amber eyes. He had to admit
that her reputation for beauty was well-earned. He shook his
head, and went on writing.

*Time is passing. The second Stone of Life has just split in two.
Tomorrow night it will have dissolved.*

*A moment ago Hob asked me what hidden treasure I found on Jahalod's
island. "Catabea said there'd be one on every island, didn't she?" he added.*

*I hesitated, and then I remembered that Catabea had advised us to be
honest, so I made up my mind. I said, "I found two things on that island.
First, I understood that I really had lost my father, and no one could replace
him. Not Jahalod or anyone else. Hannibal McBott was not a good father to
me. He was my father, that's all. Now I have to lead my life without him,
just as I've lived without a mother since my birth." Then I paused. Hob and
Peppe were whispering to each other, and then Peppe said that meant I was
an orphan, like them. The brothers seemed very pleased to think of me being
the same as themselves.*

*"And the second treasure I found on the island," I went on, "was you.
All of you. Without your help, I'd still be there playing that flute."*

*Finopico has told me that he felt like leaving and abandoning me to my
fate. I'm not surprised! That oddball has never much liked me, but I don't
bear him any grudge. He calls me Captain, like the others, and I know that
at heart he wouldn't hurt a fly.*

*Now we have to go on wandering through this eerie Archipelago. We
know that the dangers lying in wait for us may take unexpected forms, and I
feel great tension among the members of the crew. At the moment it's night,*

and I suspect that no one's sleeping, except for Zeph, who has always fallen asleep easily. Babilas and Lei are keeping watch on deck. I think I'll go and relie—.

29

Six Toothless Men

Cries of distress came through the darkness. Terrible, raucous, deep and terrifying cries that shook Orpheus to his bones. He raced headlong out of his cabin, met Hob, Peppe and Malva on their way up to the deck with storm lanterns, and when they all came up through the hatch together in panic they found Babilas and Lei crouching by the poop rail, hands over their ears. The howls were so loud that they were almost unbearable.

"What is it?" asked Peppe and Hob in terror.

Babilas shook his head. He had no idea. His face set with pain, Orpheus took a lantern from Peppe and went over to the rail. The cries seemed to come from somewhere off starboard. He raised the lantern and leaned over the rail. Down below, phosphorescent foam was washing against the hull of the *Fabula*—and further off, in a beam of lantern light, Orpheus thought he saw a human form. It was waving its arms and shouting.

"Quick!" shouted Orpheus. "More lanterns!"

Malva and the twins joined him.

"Over there!" said Orpheus, pointing to the shape he had seen.

The others narrowed their eyes. "Shipwrecked sailors!" exclaimed Malva. "They're calling us to help them!"

In spite of the darkness, Orpheus could almost count the unfortunate men drifting a short way from the ship. But there was little that sounded human about their cries.

"Five or six of them," he said. "Take in the sails! We must help them!"

In spite of their fear, the crew of the *Fabula* obeyed his orders. Babilas took his hands away from his ears and climbed to the shrouds. The sails slackened and the ship slowed down. Meanwhile Orpheus had taken the tiller. It was still fragile even though Babilas had repaired it. He handled it gently, setting a course for the shipwrecked sailors before turning to the bows of the ship.

Finopico had just arrived, eyes puffy with sleep, hair tousled. "What's going on?" he grunted.

Malva pointed to the men swimming in their wake. Their cries were becoming fainter, but there were indeed six of them.

"Throw them ropes!" Orpheus ordered.

Babilas was first to react. In a moment he fastened all the hawsers and sheets he could lay hands on, and with his powerful arms threw them overboard one by one in the direction of the shipwrecked sailors. The twins, Malva and Lei held up lanterns to give as much light as possible, their eyes wide and hearts beating fast.

Babilas hauled in two men who had caught the same hawser at once. He pulled, breathing hard, pulled again, and when the two unfortunate men collapsed on deck he hurried to help the next of their companions.

Orpheus and Finopico took charge of the shipwrecked sailors, wrapping them as well as they could in old sails and offering water and words of reassurance. When the last man collapsed on deck, exhausted, Babilas coiled up the ropes and then disappeared down the steps of the central hatch.

The twins, Lei and Malva formed a circle around the men they had rescued, casting light on their soaking faces at last. They were startled to see the six dazed men open their mouths to reveal bleeding gums. They had no teeth left!

"By Holy Harmony!" murmured Malva, turning pale.

Not only had they no teeth, some had no hair either, while others, whose eyelids were closed, seemed to be blind.

"Their hands!" said Hob in a strangled voice, repressing nausea. "Look at their hands!"

The six men's fingers were curved like the claws of birds of prey, but all the same, the crew of the *Fabula* could see that they had no nails left.

"How horrible!" gasped Finopico, turning away.

"They must have been in the water a very long time," Orpheus suggested, trying to explain their present state. "How sad . . ."

Bravely, Lei crouched down beside the man who seemed the least exhausted. He was leaning against the rail, and although he had no teeth or nails, he still had his eyes.

"*Ydroim fwr graich?*" asked Lei.

The man looked at her with a certain astonishment. A gurgling sound came from his throat, and a bubble of blood formed between his bruised lips.

"*Ysgybolg fwr graich?*" Lei persisted.

This time the man just nodded. Then, making a great effort to speak, he added, "*Dillwisg . . . nozg . . . nozgeidim.*" And he pointed to the darkness with a weary gesture.

"What's he saying?" asked Orpheus anxiously.

"They sailors from Dunbraven," said Lei, putting a hand to her troubled breast. "Lost in Archipelago like us. Ship wrecked on reefs, over there."

Lei pointed in the direction the *Fabula* was sailing. Orpheus made for the tiller, calling, "Babilas, the sails! Quick! We must change course!"

But the giant had disappeared, and did not respond to Orpheus's order.

"We'll do it, Captain!" offered the twins, glad of a chance to take their eyes off the mutilated men.

Meanwhile, Lei went on questioning the sailor in his own guttural language. Malva, kneeling beside the daughter of Balmun, tried to understand the situation.

"Ask him what happened to their teeth—and their nails," she whispered in her friend's ear.

Carefully, Lei managed to get a few scraps of information out of the man, but he was so exhausted that he often lost his train of thought. However, Malva caught a few words that she knew only too well: Catabea, Nokros . . . Finally Lei translated what she had learnt for Malva's benefit.

"They more than twenty men when they enter Archipelago. Catabea gave them Nokros with Stones of Life, like us. If I understood, they go through many terrible ordeals. Some sailors fight. Yesterday only one Stone of Life left, and then they driven on reefs. Nokros sink with ship. Most of the men dead."

Having changed course, Orpheus had come back, and so had the twins. They listened to Lei's account frowning, their lips pressed tight.

"Man say Patrols of Catabea arrive a little before night. Come down on survivors of shipwreck. Two sailors carried up in the air to Immuration. But these others resist. Then Patrols blind eyes, pull out teeth, pull out nails . . ."

Lei was choking as she spoke, and trembling like a leaf. The horrified twins were leaning against each other, feeling sick.

"When night fall," Lei finished in a whisper, "patrols fly away and disappear."

Orpheus shuddered. Looking at the poor men lying on deck, he felt he was seeing the future: this was the fate in store for those who failed Catabea's tests! First mutilated, then thrown into the Immuration!

"What we do?" groaned Lei, turning her pearl-like eyes to him. "They doomed! No Nokros left, no Stone of Life!"

"If I understand this correctly," murmured Malva, "the Patrols don't fly by night. Perhaps they're afraid of darkness. So we have until dawn to come to a decision."

Hob uttered a little wail. "You think the Patrols will come back, Princetta?"

No one replied, yet it seemed inevitable that those ill-omened birds would reappear at dawn to finish their work. For a moment silence reigned. The shipwrecked sailors were shivering and bleeding under their sailcloth wrappings, but they did not cry out any more.

"We'll hide them," Orpheus suddenly decided. "We've saved these poor men from drowning, we're not going to abandon them to the mercy of the Patrols! If we hide them in the hold of the *Fabula* no one will know. The Patrols will think they've drowned."

Malva, Lei and the twins exchanged worried looks. Finopico shook his head vigorously. "In the hold?" he protested. "But . . . but these men are sure to have sicknesses! They'll bring vermin down on us! I don't want to be infected!"

Orpheus consulted the others.

"I don't know, Captain," said Peppe hesitantly.

"I don't either," Hob admitted. "Perhaps if we scrubbed the hold out with vinegar . . ."

"That's it!" exclaimed Orpheus. "We'll disinfect the hold to kill any vermin. Do you agree to that, cook?"

"I do," Malva put in. "We have no choice but to save them! The Patrols are our enemies as much as theirs, after all!"

Finopico, running out of arguments, bowed his head. Lei leaned over the man and translated their plan. Something like a smile crossed the sailor's face.

"Babilas!" Orpheus called again. "We need you! We have to get these men below decks!"

But the giant did not appear.

"By Holy Tranquillity!" grumbled Orpheus. "He works like a madman to save these poor fellows, he coils up the ropes . . . and then he walks out on us! Funny . . ."

"We'll go and find him!" said the twins, running to the top of the hatch. But when they came back a moment later they looked crestfallen.

"Babilas is in his bunk. He won't come," said Peppe.

"And . . . and he's in tears," added Hob in astonishment.

"Tears?" repeated the others, baffled.

The twins nodded. "Floods of tears."

30

Why Babilas Wept

Malva offered to go and talk to Babilas. The giant might have refused to let the twins into his cabin, but he wouldn't dare to send his Princetta away.

She spent part of the night beside him, trying to comfort him and find out the reason for his sudden flood of tears. When she returned to her bunk it was nearly dawn. Although there were dark circles under her eyes, she didn't lie down. What she had learnt from Babilas deprived her of any wish to sleep.

A few days earlier she had asked Orpheus for paper and ink. He had given her some sheets of paper torn out of his captain's logbook, a little the worse for the sea air, but Malva had not written anything on them yet. Writing, telling stories . . . what was the use of it, if all her words were bound to be lost in the end? The Coronador had made her burn her first notebooks, the *Estafador* had carried the others down with it when it sank. What would happen to what she wrote next?

That night, however, she picked up her pen again, hoping to free herself of the burden weighing on her heart by writing.

When I entered Babilas's berth, she wrote, *he was lying face downwards. His legs hung a long way out over the end of the bunk. He's so tall! But what struck me was that he still looked small, lying there sobbing. You'd have thought he was a child. I went over and touched his shoulder.*

In the old days when I lived in the Citadel, protocol meant I couldn't touch anyone of lower rank than myself, except Philomena, of course. That was a strict order, but I didn't always obey. When I hid in the kitchens with the maidservants, for instance, I sometimes sat on their laps to help them shell peas.

Babilas was surprised to find me there too. He opened his sad eyes wide, and I saw that he was ashamed of himself. I asked if he was afraid of the Dunbraven men. He shook his head. Then he made a face and pointed to his heart. "Those men have hurt your heart?" I asked. Babilas sat up in the bunk and sighed wearily.

Then he tried to explain to me, in gestures, what had upset him so much. I think I guessed most of it, and that is what I must describe here.

Malva stopped writing for a moment. Her hands were damp, and there was a lump in her throat. The paper was covered with her still childish handwriting, and the lines blurred before her eyes, but she had to go on.

Babilas wasn't always mute. He had a fiancée, whom he'd met in a sea port in the country of Dunbraven. It was love at first sight, I think he told me. They both loved the sea. They often spent days fishing and boating together. One summer day it was so hot that Babilas's fiancée wanted to swim in the sea.

Babilas began weeping again when he remembered all this, but he showed me that he wanted to get to the end of the story, to tell me everything as best he could. His grief went to my heart.

That summer day, his fiancée dived off the boat. He called to her to be careful, not to go far away. She was a good swimmer and wasn't afraid. She amused herself by diving under the boat and coming up on the other side, staying under water longer and longer each time.

A moment came when Babilas couldn't see his fiancée any more. She didn't come up again. He fastened himself to the boat with a rope and jumped into the water. He swam, dived, searched, called her for hours. But she never came up to the surface.

Malva wiped away a tear caught on her lashes, and turned the page over to write on the other side.

Somehow Babilas found the strength to get back to land, alone in that boat. When he set foot on the shore he felt as if he were dead.

He went to the house where his fiancée's parents lived. The last words he ever spoke were to tell them that their daughter had drowned.

After that, Babilas became mute.

The candle lighting Malva's cabin was almost burnt out, but some light came in through the porthole. Day was about to dawn. She dipped her pen in the inkwell again.

When Babilas saw the sailors calling for help as they drowned, it must have been like living through that dreadful scene again. Except that this time he managed to save six men! Six men of Dunbraven whom he didn't even know . . . while he hadn't been able to save one woman whom he loved. That's why he was crying . . .

After confiding all this to me, he collapsed on his bunk, exhausted. I stayed beside him for awhile, my head full of terrible images. I thought of Philomena and Uzmir. I wondered where they were, if they were still looking for me, and if they had been injured after the attack in Cispazan. I miss them so much! How can you survive without the people you love around you?

Babilas fell asleep at last, and I went back up to the deck, where I found Orpheus. He had finally managed to get the sailors down into the hold with the help of Finopico and Lei. I gave him a little of this information about Babilas, and he understood. I know he won't hold it against him for giving way to grief. Orpheus is a decent, sensitive man. Since he shook free of Jahalod-Rin's influence, I've found him really . . .

But she suddenly couldn't think of the words to describe Orpheus. Malva crossed out the last line, put down her pen, folded the sheets she had written and put them in a drawer under her bunk. Her eyes were red. The sun would soon rise now. She felt as sad and empty as a deserted house.

At that moment someone knocked at the cabin door. It was Orpheus. When his face appeared in the doorway Malva's heart leaped.

"I was just thinking," she said, to explain her surprise.

"You could get a little sleep," suggested Orpheus, smiling. "The twins are on watch, so I came to see how you're feeling, Princetta."

"I'm quite well, thank you. But please stop calling me Princetta. I'm Malva. Just Malva."

She nearly added *a girl of no importance*, as Philomena had done on the evening of their escape from the Citadel, but the words did not pass her lips. A strange, vague emotion was stirring in her heart.

"All right," said Orpheus. "I'll watch my tongue! We've hidden the sailors in the hold. I'm sure that some of them are ill; I wanted to ask you not to go down there. I don't want you to catch any deadly disease."

Orpheus spoke quietly, but with touching kindness. Just as he was about to close the door again the first ray of the sun shone

266

into the cabin through the porthole, and rested on his face. He smiled.

"It's morning," he said. "Be careful."

Then he left, leaving Malva dazzled and exhausted.

31

Danger on the Horizon

Back on deck, Orpheus found Peppe and Hob leaning against the mainmast, asleep.

"Well, this is a nice way of keeping watch!" he told them, shaking them awake.

The twins leaped to their feet, rubbing their eyes. They stammered some confused apologies, but Orpheus didn't reprimand them. Luckily the *Fabula* had not been driven on any reefs or sandbanks, so their moment of weariness could be forgiven. Orpheus looked at the Nokros, still in place close to the mast. It was slowly sifting time: another Stone of Life had been reduced to powder, so that now there were only six. A fine layer of brown sand had dropped to the bottom of the hourglass. Orpheus thought of the sailors from Dunbraven, their toothless mouths and bleeding fingers . . . and when his eyes met those of Hob and Peppe he knew that the twins were thinking just the same.

"Come on!" he told them. "Let's not be discouraged. Day has

dawned, the weather is fine and . . ." He looked at the sky. "And there are no Patrols in sight!"

But as he went to the port rail and looked out to sea, he trembled. A triangular sail had appeared some ten kilometres away from the *Fabula*. The look of the sail and the ship's flat-bottomed hull left him in no doubt: this was a Cispazian junk. One of the vessels that the divers hadn't had time to scuttle before the battle against Temir-Gaï. And without doubt, it was carrying . . .

"The Archont!" murmured Orpheus.

A shadow fell on his face. The junk, lighter than the *Fabula*, was sailing before the wind, and its large sail seemed to be in perfect condition. It would catch up with them quite soon. Remembering Catabea's warnings, Orpheus turned to the twins.

"I want everyone on deck in two minutes' time!"

Hob and Peppe raced to the hatch without asking for explanations. While they raised the alarm, Orpheus took stock of the situation; they had no carabins or musketoons on board the *Fabula*, no arbapults or cannon. They had all been lost in the storm. The only weapons they had to fight with were their fists and the kitchen utensils! If the Archont still had Cispazian weapons on board, things were going to be difficult.

One by one the members of the crew appeared on deck. Even Babilas had responded to the call. He looked pale as death, but Orpheus was grateful to see him.

"I have bad news," he announced. "The Archont is close on our heels."

As he spoke, his eyes lingered on Malva. She stiffened, while the others exclaimed in despair.

"I'm sorry, Princett—" he began, then remembered the promise he had made and corrected himself. "I'm sorry, Malva."

He pointed to the triangular sail, which already seemed to have gained on them.

"Let's get moving, Captain!" suggested Peppe.

"Yes," Hob enthusiastically agreed. "Let's hoist the foresail and the fore topsail! We'll show him what speed the *Fabula* can make!"

Malva, shattered, closed her eyes. "I used the foresail to repair the mainsail," she said gloomily. "We only have the fore topsail left."

"Hoist it," Orpheus told the twins. "I doubt if it will be enough, but we must try to keep a fair distance away." He turned to Babilas. "Can we count on you?" he asked, a little uneasily. "If the Archont does catch up with us, will you be able to protect the Pri—to protect Malva?"

The giant nodded. He straightened his back, placed himself behind Malva, and struck his chest with a fist to show that he would keep her safe.

"Good," smiled Orpheus, turning to Finopico this time. "I think it might be a good idea to collect anything that could serve as a weapon. What have you got in the galley?"

The cook made a face, but thought about it. "Two iron casseroles, a pan, a large cauldron. And I think I still have two large ladles, some blunt knives and some forks."

"Find me anything you can," Orpheus told him.

"Excuse me, Captain, but is there any point in this?" Finopico protested. "What do we have to fear? Catabea told us that the Archont was alone on board!"

"You don't know him!" Malva put in. "He's wilier than an old monkey and more dangerous than a snake! He's tried to kill me three times. He almost drowned me in the Sea of Ypree, he nearly strangled me in Temir-Gai's harem before crushing my bones in the cage where you found me! His hatred is so powerful that—"

"But you're still alive!" Finopico interrupted her. "You were alone those other times, but today there are seven of us to defend you."

"Yes, indeed," Malva admitted. "But the Archont has sworn to kill me, and he's been nurturing his obsession for so many years he's capable of anything now."

Babilas suddenly laid his large hands on the Princetta's shoulders.

"I know, Babilas," she murmured with a sad smile. "I know you aren't afraid to pit yourself against him. But if only you knew how frightened I am!"

She slowly went over to the rail and looked to the Cispazian ship in the distance.

"The Archont set his trap with such care," she went on. "First he won my father's confidence by pretending to be a faithful servant of the Galnician crown. Then, when he was put in charge of my education, he began weaving his web like some evil spider. He knew that my parents planned to marry me to the Prince of Andamark, but he said nothing at all about it to me. On the contrary! He did all he could to give me a taste for freedom and independence. He knew that when the day came, I'd rebel against the idea of my marriage, he opened the gates of the Citadel wide for me." She sighed. "The worse of it all is that I almost have to thank him! If not for him I'd never have set out on my journey. I'd just have let my parents shut me up, like a good girl . . ."

She leaned a little further forward, hands clamped on the wooden rail, and her voice shook with anger.

"Thank you! Thank you, Archont!" she cried in sudden fury. "I owe it all to you that I've come to see the world as it is: vast, magnificent, surprising, dangerous and cruel! I owe it to you that I know of the existence of Elgolia, and I owe my good fortune to you too!"

Spinning abruptly round, she turned her amber eyes on Orpheus, and made a sweeping gesture with her arm.

"If not for you, Archont," she went on, "I'd never have met Uzmir and the Baighur people, or Lei, or Babilas, or those two rascals the twins, or Finopico, or Captain Orpheus . . . or even that half-paralysed old dog! Yet all the same I hate and detest you, Archont!"

At that, Malva staggered and sat down on deck.

"He'll never forgive me for still being alive," she finished in a low voice. "I've become an obsession with him. As long as I'm alive he'll resent me. Even if it's impossible for him to seize power in Galnicia now. He's after me because I represent his failure. Believe me, there's no stopping a man like that."

She raised her eyes. Up in the rigging, Hob and Peppe were gazing down at her. Around them, the mainsail and the fore topsail were billowing in the wind.

"You can't give up!" Peppe shouted down to Malva. "That's impossible!"

"He's right!" Hob shouted in his own turn. "And do you want to know why?"

Malva sighed.

"Do you want to know why, Princetta?" Hob repeated, scrambling down from the rigging. He went up to her. "You can't die here because it's not your fate! We know your future, Peppe and I do!"

"Oh, come on!" laughed Finopico. "Who can know the future? No one!"

"Oh yes, they can," said Peppe indignantly, joining his

brother. "In the city below the Citadel there's a fortune-teller who—"

"Oh, a clairvoyant!" mocked Finopico. "I've heard you lads say some silly things, but this one is ridiculous!"

"She warned us that the Archont had set off to look for the Princetta. We told you so, didn't we, Captain?" Hob said, defended himself.

Orpheus had to agree.

"Certain people have strange powers, but real!" Lei added. "In kingdom of Balmun, we think visions can tell truth."

The twins nodded, delighted to find an ally in their argument with Finopico.

"Well?" said the cook, sneering. "So what did this fortune-teller predict about our Princetta?"

Peppe and Hob exchanged glances. "We swore not to say," they said apologetically. "If we give the secret away it will all change, and some important things won't happen!"

"How very practical!" laughed the cook. "The clairvoyant pockets your galniks and swears you to silence! A neat little swindle!"

"Not at all!" said the brothers indignantly. "The only thing we *can* tell the Princetta is that she won't die here. Her fate lies elsewhere."

"I believe you," said Orpheus, thinking it was time to put an end to this argument. "I feel sure that Malva has nothing to fear." He went over to her, holding out a hand to help her to stand up. When she was on her feet in front of him he said quietly, "Do the twins a favour, Malva. Don't die!"

She smiled. "I'll try not to, Captain."

"And please don't call me Captain any more. I'm Orpheus. Just Orpheus."

At that moment Zeph started barking. He had padded over to the fo'c'sle, and now had his front paws on the steps, nose in the air, growling and barking vehemently. The crew of the *Fabula* looked up.

"There!" cried Lei, pointing to the east.

A cloud had appeared on the horizon—a black cloud made up of small moving dots.

"The Patrols!" cried the twins. "They're after us again!"

"Not yet!" replied Orpheus. "They're looking for the sailors near the reefs where their ship sank." He made for the tiller, took hold of it, and ordered, "All of you to your posts! Babilas and Malva to my cabin! The twins up to the crow's nest! Finopico, collect anything we can fight with! And Lei, you go down to the sailors from Dunbraven. They mustn't move, mustn't say a word, mustn't do anything!"

He swung the tiller vigorously over to starboard, and the *Fabula* changed course. At the same moment an explosion was heard. A cannonball whistled as it flew through the air—and hit the water just off the ship's prow. There was no doubt, the Archont had weapons.

32

Battles

Shut up in the cabin, Malva and Babilas could hear sounds of cannon fire. A whistle preceded the impact of the ball in the water. Each time Malva hunched down and held Babilas's hand tightly. She didn't take another breath until the cannonball had struck the water. The giant, feeling tense and nervous himself, was craning his neck and trying to see out of the porthole, but he couldn't leave Malva. All he saw were foaming waves and scraps of blue sky turning above them.

"What's going on?"

As if in reply, there was a sudden sharp sound followed by a jolt. Then came cries. More small shocks, long-drawn-out or sharp like the first one. Malva, still clutching Babilas's hand, strained to hear.

"Captain!" she heard someone shouting. It was the twins' shrill voices. "Grappling irons!" they called.

"Grappling irons!" Malva repeated as she began to comprehend. "The Archont! He's going to board us!"

On deck, Orpheus swung the tiller violently to port, but the grappling irons had dug themselves firmly into the deck wood, catching the handrail and pilasters at the stern. The *Fabula* was tethered like a dog on a leash.

"Come down!" Orpheus shouted up at the twins. He was afraid they might fall from their perch if there were more jolts. "Come on down and lend Finopico a hand!"

The boys dropped to the deck and hurried to the catwalk where Finopico was standing ready to do battle, although the artillery at his feet suggested that he was preparing for a cooking competition. Chin jutting out, he was staring at the enemy ship as he brandished a casserole.

"Come on, then!" he shouted to the Archont. "I'm ready for you, you wicked pirate! I'm not afraid of you!"

The twins picked up skewers, tin bowls and tongs. Thus armed, they marched forward, bravely hurling insults at the Archont.

The Archont himself, standing in the prow of the Cispazian vessel, was clinging to the rope of one of the grappling irons. He still wore his richly embroidered robes, but his tunic was torn, and showed the muscles of his arms straining with effort. He was grimacing as he hauled on the rope. His smooth skull glistened with sweat.

"Just let him get a bit closer!" growled Finopico. "Then I'll stun him!"

"And we'll skewer him!" Hob assured the cook.

"And tear his nose off!" added Peppe, snapping the tongs.

Meanwhile Orpheus had drawn his knife and was trying to cut the ropes as the Cispazian junk drew closer.

"Here goes!" shouted Hob suddenly, and with all his strength he threw a fork, which brushed past the Archont's face. The

Archont did not flinch, but imperturbably went on pulling the rope, which Orpheus's blunt knife had not managed to sever.

"Again!" ordered Finopico.

He flung his casserole at the Archont. It fell at his feet with a clatter. The twins began bombarding him with anything they could lay hands on: fish knives, nutcrackers, pie dishes and spatulas flew through the air. A pewter tankard struck the Archont full in the chest. This time he grunted. Still holding the rope in one hand, he unsheathed the sword at his belt with the other.

"And again!" cried Finopico.

Down in the cabin, Malva was huddling close to Babilas. The clinking noises she heard made her tremble. At one point she even thought there was a stampede in progress on the steps down from the hatch.

"He's coming!" she cried, clinging to Babilas.

But the footsteps stopped, and Babilas smiled reassuringly. It had probably just been Finopico and one of the twins coming down to look for more ammunition.

A few moments later, however, Malva and Babilas heard more noise on the steps, accompanied by groans, and suddenly the cabin door shook.

"No!" cried Malva. "Go away!"

"Malva!" called a voice on the other side of the door. It was not the Archont.

"Lei?" asked Malva in alarm. She ran to open the door. The daughter of Balmun was lying on the floor, close to fainting. Malva took her under the arms and tried to raise her.

"Dunbraven sailors," Lei breathed. "They . . . they hit me. They . . . escape!"

Babilas straightened up, his face suddenly hardened. When Lei pointed to the steps, he ran from the cabin, leaving the two girls alone and stunned.

Up on deck the situation had deteriorated. The Archont had succeeded in jumping aboard the *Fabula*. He was standing on the rail, clinging to the rigging with one hand, while in the other he brandished his sword, keeping Orpheus, Finopico and the twins at bay. The twins were still hurling various kitchen utensils, which the Archont did not always manage to duck. His forehead was bleeding, but not a word or cry emerged from his mouth. He was all hatred, a fighting machine. Orpheus, his knife extended ahead of him, regarded him with awe. At close quarters, the Archont impressed him to the point of paralysing him.

As Babilas emerged through the central hatch, he immediately saw the Archont. But his focus was on the six Dunbraven sailors who had escaped from the hold.

One of them had seized the Nokros.

The others were forming a ring around him, and in spite of their pitiful condition they seemed ready to do anything to defend the treasure they had stolen. The Nokros contained exactly six Stones of Life: it was their safety raft!

Babilas did not hesitate. Without the Nokros, he knew that there was no chance of their own party's survival. He made for the toothless man clutching the precious hourglass to his chest.

"*Balbh tafaod*" snarled the man.

The others turned their bleeding faces on Babilas. The blind ones took their bearings by sound alone. Those without finger-nails raised their red hands, curving their fingers like claws.

"*Gwewyn pluchtar ahim!*" spat one of them, flinging himself at Babilas.

The giant caught him in mid-leap. He raised the man above his head like a piece of wood and flung him to the deck. Two more sailors made for him at once. Babilas punched, struck and repelled them. He felt such rage that his strength was redoubled. He didn't even hear the cries of his companions as they fought the Archont. Using his fists, he made for the man holding the Nokros, who had retreated to the mainmast in alarm. But just as Babilas reached for the Nokros, the man took another step back, stumbled and rolled to the deck. As he fell, the Nokros made an odd tinkling noise. Babilas went pale. If it broke, they were doomed!

He fell on the sailor, pinned him to the deck and struck him again and again. Finally he got hold of the Nokros and rose up. A Dunbraven sailor now clung to his shoulders, trying to strangle him with one arm, but Babilas managed to shake him off, holding the Nokros above his head with his other hand.

When he turned, he saw Malva and Lei at the opening of the hatch. He ran to them and thrust the hourglass into their hands.

Near the stern, the Archont was making progress, and Malva cried out when she saw him. At the sound of her voice, the Archont raised his grey eyes to her, and the light of madness flared in his face. He waved his sword in the air and leaped forward.

"Watch out!" Orpheus shouted.

Then everything happened very quickly. Orpheus blocked the Archont's way, plunging his knife deep into the man's arm. The shock made the Archont stop. At the same moment Orpheus felt a dreadful pain shoot through him.

The sword . . . the Archont's sword! As he leaped between the Archont and Malva to protect her, he had impaled himself on it.

In the general panic no one noticed Orpheus' distress. Malva and Lei had fled back into the ship with the Nokros, and while the twins and Finopico were gathering their weapons, Babilas fought the Dunbraven sailors. Driven to despair, they were becoming more and more aggressive.

Suddenly Babilas realised that he had no choice: the men no longer deserved his pity. They were endangering the *Fabula*. At that he seized one of the sailors and with a mighty movement threw him overboard.

"*Lambrog! Eidath!*" the others howled. Terrified, they were crawling around everywhere and groaning, leaving bloody trails on the deck.

Babilas caught them one by one.

One by one, he threw them into the sea.

As Babilas went in search of the last sailor, the twins suddenly called to him in terror. They were clinging to the Archont's legs, while Finopico barred the opening of the hatch as best he could.

Babilas struck the Archont like a cannonball. The twins let go, only just getting out of the way in time. Destabilised by the giant's attack, the Archont fell on the deck with a yell.

Somewhere Zeph had begun to bark.

Babilas seized the Archont, who struggled and howled with rage. He made his way to the railing, intending to throw his adversary overboard, but the Archont managed to cling to the rail, his eyes shining with hatred. With a mighty blow, Babilas struck him full in the face, and at last the Archont tumbled over the side of the hull. As he fell into the water, Babilas opened his mouth and a strange, deep cry emerged from his throat.

The giant turned, breathless and dripping with sweat. He had to find the last sailor, the sixth, the man who had succeeded in escaping him. He listened. Zeph's barking had turned to growls. Babilas made his way over the deck, fists clenched. The growls came from the fo'c'sle. He ran that way and found what he was looking for behind a pile of barrels: the blind sailor on his knees on the planks of the deck, struggling in Zeph's jaws. The St. Bernard had closed his teeth on the man's arm, preventing him from going any further.

Babilas seized the blind man by the throat and flung him into the air. As the man plunged into the waves, a second heart-rending cry escaped Babilas's throat. A rasping, hoarse, painful cry that seemed to come from the unfathomable depths of time. Finopico and the twins were transfixed.

The sailors and the Archont were trying to keep afloat in the tumultuous seas. Spitting water, coughing, shouting, they scrabbled at the *Fabula*'s hull, calling for help, and their eyes searched the sky as if pleading with the divinities to aid them. But it was not the divinities who answered them . . .

"Look!" Peppe suddenly cried, pointing to the west.

The Patrols were arriving in close formation. Babilas joined the others, ready to go on fighting, while Zeph limped to the back of the ship. Malva and Lei, having put the Nokros in safety, emerged from the hatch again.

As they watched, the Patrols swooped down between the two ships. Lively and agile despite of the imposing span of their mechanical wings, they seized their prey in their claws. Letting out dreadful screams, the sailors were plucked from the waves and carried up into the air.

"Not me! Not me!" begged the Archont, as he swam for the rope ladder on the side of his ship.

The Patrols, who presumably had no reason to bear him a grudge, spared him. Once they had fished the six sailors out of

281

the sea they rose above the *Fabula*, circled for a moment in the azure sky, and then flew away at great speed.

"They . . . they're going to the Immuration," said Hob, shivering.

A horrified silence fell over the ship again. Babilas slowly came forward, and once more gave evidence of his amazing strength by pulling the hooks of the grappling irons thrown by the Archont out of the deck, one by one. The *Fabula* was free of the Cispazian junk now, and immediately the space between them widened.

The Archont, dripping and half dead, struggled to climb aboard his vessel. Malva watched him for a moment, torn between a wish to laugh and a wish to cry. She looked down.

And only then did she see Orpheus. He was lying on the deck, his breath whistling as it left his lungs, his face pale. A pool of blood was spreading beneath him. Before she could even cry out, Babilas did so first.

"Orpheus!" said the giant in a grating voice. "Orpheus *gwisdall esdog!*"

Everyone jumped. By what miracle had Babilas recovered the power of language? Eyes wide with surprise, Lei replied to him in the strange language of Dunbraven.

"*Nhot gwisdall esdog! Orpheus crogoil!*" She cast a desperate glance at the others. "Orpheus not die! I make medicine!"

She knelt down beside the Captain's body and carefully turned him over. The Archont's sword had left a gaping wound in the middle of his stomach.

33

Malva's Journal

As I write these lines, Orpheus is struggling with Death. We have put him in Lei's berth. With Finopico's assistance she has made one of those potions which has already cured me. I had sheets boiled in seawater, and Lei soaked the fabric in a sticky ointment with an unpleasant smell. She used it to put a dressing on his wound. He lost consciousness. Oh, Holy Harmony, Holy Tranquillity . . ..

Malva wiped her tears away, and went on:

. . . let him survive his injuries! If I had known the sufferings ahead when Catabea offered us her dreadful bargain I'd never have accepted her conditions.

We're all worn out. I am worried about Lei. The sailors from Dunbraven knocked her about so badly that she has bruises on her arms and forehead. She's so busy looking after others that she forgets to care for herself. The twins are badly shaken by their confrontation with the Archont. Just now they were showing off a little as they told the tale of how they bombarded him, but I could see that they were still trembling. Finopico, usually so talkative, isn't saying anything. He's shut himself in his galley

283

*where he's reading his books about fish! I suppose it's his way of dealing with
the shock. As for Babilas, it's a mystery . . . what with all that's happened,
we've hardly had time to think about him, but one thing's certain; he's
talking. The trouble is that he only speaks the language of Dunbraven now.
He's forgotten Galnician, though it was his mother tongue, and has adopted
the language of the sailors whom he threw into the sea. It was his fiancée's
language as well . . . should we see this as a kind of cure?*

Malva stopped writing and leaned over Zeph, who was
stretched at her feet. She patted the St. Bernard's warm flanks.
The animal's company did her good.

"You're a hero too," she whispered to him. "I hear you bit
one of those men stealing the Nokros."

She sighed, and looked at the Killer of Time, which was now
standing on the shelf in her cabin. When it fell, the hourglass had
cracked. A little more and it would have broken . . . Malva
shuddered to think that then their fate would have been
irreversibly sealed.

The amount of morbic acid had already decreased a good
deal. By the following evening there would be only five Stones
of Life left, and just ten days to find the gates through which
they could leave the Archipelago. She put her pen to the paper
again.

*Our trials aren't over, far from it. If Orpheus lives I think we shall hold
out. But if he dies? I can't imagine the rest of the voyage without him,
without his strength, his courage, his kindness and intelligence. I can't bear
to lose any more of those I love. In the face of these torments, even my dream
of Elgolia gives me no strength. It's all very well for me to shut my eyes when
I lie on my bunk and conjure up the images of Mount Ur-Tha, the Bay of
Dao-Boa and Lake Barath-Thor. But I can hardly manage to picture them
now. It's as if I have lost the power to dream.*

When I saw the Archont so close to me, such terror came over me that

Lei had to drag me away to shelter. Later, I was alone on deck watching the sail of his ship drifting away. Babilas had lashed the tiller of the Fabula *on course, and we were sailing west. I felt calmer. Before I came down here again, I went to look once more, but night had fallen and I saw nothing. All I want is for the Archont to be thrown into the Immuration.*

Malva felt a cramp in her hand, and had to stop writing. She was nearly dead with fatigue anyway. Without even taking the trouble to fold the paper, she staggered to her bunk and let sleep overcome her.

34

The Island Beyond the Mists

Only Lei did not sleep that night. She sat up beside Orpheus, silent and attentive, changing his dressings every hour, making him drink a concoction of boiled plants and roots that she had collected on Jahalod's island.

At dawn she saw that he seemed more peaceful, and deduced that he was no longer suffering pain. The bleeding had stopped, the wound was clean, so Lei rubbed his face with marguerilla stalks, left the cabin and went on deck to greet the sunrise. The healers in her distant country thought that when a wounded or sick patient survived the first night it was a good sign, and you must pay your devotions to the natural world by giving thanks.

But when she emerged from the hatch, the deck was enveloped in an extraordinarily thick mist. She could hardly see her hand in front of her face! Lei took a few cautious steps, trying to reach the rail. It was cold. Moisture was already soaking into her clothes and making her teeth chatter.

It was useless leaning over the side of the ship; she couldn't make anything out. The *Fabula* seemed to be wrapped in cotton wool. She would have to wait to pay her devotions to the sun.

Annoyed, Lei went back down to her cabin. Still shivering, she searched everywhere and finally found a dry blanket in a corner of her berth. She wrapped it around Orpheus. In his present state any chill could be fatal to him. Particularly since, as Lei had already noticed, the slightest draft seemed to give Orpheus a cold. Once she was reassured of her patient's condition, she wondered how to cover herself. Most of their clothes had been ruined in the baggage at the bottom of the ship's hold. Then she saw the quartermaster's jacket that she had taken off Orpheus the night before so that she could tend to his wound. The thick canvas had a slit a dozen centimetres long where the sword had slashed it, and worst of all it was still badly bloodstained. But the air was suddenly so cold! Lei no longer hesitated; she put on the jacket, which was much too big for her, turned up the sleeves, and left the cabin again. Between decks, she saw Finopico searching all the chests and crates.

"It's so cold!" he was complaining. "Let's get out of this cursed Archipelago as quickly as we can!"

When he saw Lei he calmed down. "How is Orpheus?" he asked, still searching the chests.

"He not so ill," said Lei. "Blood stop flowing. I think he live."

"For a Greenhorn, I must say he has guts," Finopico remarked. "And for a foreigner," he added, raising his head and smiling at Lei, "I must say you have guts too!"

"Thank you!" she murmured.

"Ah, here we are!" exclaimed Finopico, laying hands on a worsted jersey. He buried his nose in it, made a face, and then, shrugging his shoulders, put it on. Then he rubbed his arms vigorously before saying he would make some good hot soup for everyone.

"I don't know what in, seeing that all my pans went flying at the Archont or dropped into the sea, but I'll find something. What filthy weather!"

As Lei was about to go up on deck again, Malva opened her cabin door and called to her. "What's going on? I'm frozen!"

"Mist," replied Lei, indicating the deck outside with her chin. Malva joined her on the steps. Her lips were blue with cold. She asked how Orpheus was, and when Lei had reassured her, Malva smiled. But suddenly she looked annoyed.

"Is that his jacket you're wearing? Orpheus's jacket?"

"Oh . . . yes," said Lei. "I no find any warm thing to wear." Malva looked disapprovingly at her.

"If you like, you take jacket," added Lei. "I find something else."

"No," snapped Malva. "Keep it. I don't want that jacket. Philomena always told me it's unlucky to wear anything blood-stained!"

She turned on her heel and closed her cabin door crossly. Lei sighed, vaguely understanding why Malva was in a temper, but decided not to bother about it. Her main aim was to reassure herself that Babilas had taken the helm of the *Fabula* again. It was essential to be on their guard in this mist.

Up on deck the mist hovered heavy and silent. When she breathed in, air tasting and smelling of dead leaves seemed to trickle into her mouth and nostrils. Lei drew the jacket together over her breasts and took a few steps towards the stern of the ship. She thought the deck was sloping slightly, and it struck her as odd. There was no wind, and so no reason for the ship to tilt.

Babilas wasn't there. The tiller, still lashed into place, was taking them on course . . . all the same, Lei was wary. She glanced first to port and then to starboard. At that moment she saw shadows through the curtain of mist.

Her heart sank as she went closer, squinting to see. No, it was not an illusion! There really was something there, very close to the ship! Had the Archont managed to follow them? She stood motionless, on guard. And suddenly the gap in the mist widened . . . to reveal an enormous rock. Lei went pale.

"Reefs!" she shouted.

She raced towards the hatch, catching her feet in the coiled ropes on deck as she ran.

"Reefs! Reefs!"

All the other members of the crew except, of course, for Orpheus, heard her cries. Finopico and Babilas were the quickest to react. They came up through the hatch and found themselves face to face with Lei, who was still shouting at the top of her voice.

"*Brogsgin!*" she told Babilas in the language of Dunbraven.

The giant made straight for the tiller and freed it from its lashings, but when he tried to manoeuvre it he couldn't.

"*Hufeneth gwar!*" he gasped.

"What's he saying?" asked Finopico anxiously.

The twins, wrapped in blankets, had just emerged on deck with Malva. She had found an old knitted wrap with holes here and there, and put it on, but she was still shivering. She wished she had the oryak-skin coat that Uzmir had given her, but Temir-Gai's preunuchs had taken it.

"Tiller no respond!" Lei translated, desperate.

They all ran to the ship's rail, expecting to hear a crash and feel a violent shock as the boat struck the reef.

It never came. The silence seemed to last forever. They

couldn't even hear the familiar sound of the waves retreating from the reefs. Not a murmur, no sound of lapping water, nothing.

After a moment the seafarers relaxed. They exchanged baffled glances and then began searching the fog, which was thinning here and there.

"There!" cried Malva suddenly, leaning overboard. "Sand! There's sand under the ship!"

The others looked too, and saw with amazement that she was right.

"We ran ashore during the night!" said Finopico. "The *Fabula* is stuck in the sand."

At that moment a great patch of mist drifted away to reveal the rocks, tall and dark, trickling with moisture. They were so close to the hull that it was a miracle the ship had avoided them.

"Rocky cliffs, sand," murmured Malva. "This is another island in the Archipelago."

The mist was parting into long wisps now, striping the scene with white. Trees appeared, then rows of neatly trimmed bushes and paved roads winding up the cliffside. This was not the work of nature; they had obviously come to an inhabited island.

"Let's go ashore," suggested Hob.

"We ought to cut wood and make a fire," added Peppe. "If this goes on I shall die of cold."

As he spoke, a ray of sunlight pierced the thick clouds. The passengers on the *Fabula* looked up at the sky. And suddenly the mists rose entirely, revealing an amazing sight!

The whole island was conical in shape, with the cone eroded at sea level and almost pointed at the top. It rose so high that the travellers had to crane their necks to see the summit. The rocky cliffs led to meadows full of flowers, then the meadows gave way to a ring of trees, and finally a town of red-brick houses rose in terraces to the peak of the island. Roads with low walls beside them criss-crossed each other, dividing up the landscape and making it look neat and well-ordered. At the top of the island, high above the town and the sea, rose a lighthouse.

"*Kigchupen*," said Babilas.

"My word!" exclaimed the twins in unison.

The beauty of the island took their breath away. In the sunlight the tiniest details stood out as if outlined by a fine brush: here a bed of mauve flowers, there a washhouse under a thatched roof, a freshly ploughed field, an ox-cart, animals in an enclosure, and higher up streets and squares with fountains in them.

"The people of this island seem to be perfectly civilised," said Finopico happily. "They make use of every corner of their land!"

"No doubt," said Malva, "but . . . where are they?"

"They perhaps not like mist?" suggested Lei.

"It's all gone now," Hob pointed out, letting his blanket drop at his feet.

Sure enough, the sun was gradually warming their bodies and cheering their minds.

"It's even getting hot," added Malva, with a pointed look at Lei, who had not taken off Orpheus's jacket. Setting an example, she took off the moth-eaten shawl she had found, but the daughter of Balmun paid her no attention. She stood there looking at the island.

"I want explore," she said. "I certainly find more herbs here to treat Orpheus."

"You told me he was better," objected Malva.

"Better, yes. But he not well yet. Good medicine need bromella leaves, buflon milk and scorpiphore shells. Maybe here . . ."

"Let's all go!" suggested the twins. "Zeph can stay with the Captain."

Malva, Babilas and Finopico still hesitated. The shores certainly seemed welcoming. Looking at the landscape, they felt an irresistible urge to walk beside the streams and wander through the meadows, to refresh themselves at the fountains, sit in front of the houses, lean against the low stone walls and warm themselves in the sun.

"Come on!" cried the twins impatiently. "What's the risk? The inhabitants of this island must be nice people!"

"Jahalod-Rin was a nice man too," Malva intervened. "Are you so naive that you didn't learn your lesson from the last place we visited?"

The twins sighed.

"We're not naive," they pleaded, "but we're tired of being suspicious all the time!"

"We don't necessarily have to have enemies everywhere in this Archipelago!" said Peppe.

"Catabea mentioned treasures," argued Hob. "If you ask me, this island is one of them. It reminds me a little of Galnicia."

Suddenly Babilas pointed to the houses with their red-brick facades, and said something which Lei translated as, "See shutters! They opening!"

One by one, the houses were coming to life to greet the new day. It was impossible to see the faces of the inhabitants from the deck of the *Fabula*, but life was indeed beginning to stir in the town. Somewhere, a bell rang. The sound of wheels jolting over the paved roads could be heard.

"I agree, there's nothing wrong with this island," Finopico decided at last. "Let's take advantage of this sunny spell and go ashore."

They all decided to go, except Malva, who said she would rather stay on board.

"I'll keep an eye on the soup," she said, "and then if Orpheus wakes up he won't be alone."

She watched her companions climb down the rope ladder.

"Don't hang about!" she advised them. "There are only five Stones left in the Nokros!"

Seabirds were soaring above the cliffs, now and then diving down to the crevices in the rocks where their chicks were nesting. A breeze had risen, and the temperature seemed all the more pleasant because a moment earlier they had all thought they were going to freeze where they stood.

Light at heart, Lei led her troop of explorers up a steep path and then along a road rising to the meadows. As she walked she looked at the green banks along the road. Her expert eye found herbs, plants, roots and useful berries. The pockets of her tunic were soon bulging.

"Kinds I not know," she said out loud, "but I find out how mix them all. Knowledge of Balmun very great!"

They soon arrived near a paddock where animals were grazing. They were not goats, or sheep, or cows. Finopico stood by the fence, resting his elbows on it and searching his memory to decide whether he had ever seen such beasts before. They had short legs, and were stocky and muscular like little bulls, but without any horns. Long, hairy ears hung beside their wide, flat muzzles.

"Never seen anything like them," the cook admitted at last, "but I wouldn't mind trying a steak from one!"

They left the paddock and meadows behind and climbed on towards the town. As they passed through the forest, Lei picked a great many more mushrooms and fruits. The closer they came to the houses, the more noises they heard: little bells, shutters banging in the wind, voices answering each other. They stopped on the outskirts of the forest and waited.

There wasn't a single inhabitant to be seen. The streets echoed with happy cries, the hammering of tools and merry laughter, but no old gossip, no craftsman, no child came to meet the new arrivals.

"Perhaps they're . . . well, very small?" suggested Hob. "So small that we can't see them?"

"Don't talk such nonsense," replied Finopico. "Their houses are the same size as ours. We must go closer, that's all."

He started along the first street, with Lei and Babilas. The noises sounded so close . . . all of a sudden a handcart came up in front of them. Lei uttered a cry. The cart stopped. Its two wooden handles remained in the air on their own, as if by magic. The cart was full of neatly tied bundles of firewood, but who or what was pulling it? There was no one in sight!

"Hey!" shouted Finopico. "Where are you?"

The handles of the cart immediately dropped to the paving stones with a clatter. There was a sound of running, and then a voice which came from nowhere, speaking a language that no one could understand . . . no one but Lei.

"He go tell others!" she translated in a voice quivering with emotion. "He say that . . . that saviours have come!"

"Saviours?" repeated Finopico.

"But who was it?" groaned the twins. "Who said that? Who was pulling the cart?"

Lei turned her pearl-like eyes on them and shook her head. "*Lloedzar a smigoim*," said Babilas. "*Cnohmbelb brogez!*"

"And what about him?" cried the twins in panic. "What's *he* saying?"

"Babilas think people here invisible," Lei translated.

She didn't have to offer any more arguments to persuade her companions that Babilas was right. The street was soon full of murmurs. Under the frightened eyes of the five travellers, wicker baskets and wooden tubs floated through the air, while a small toy horse on wheels wheeled itself over the paving stones without anyone to push it. A pitchfork rose over the crowd of invisible people by itself. Peppe tugged Finopico's sleeve.

"Let's get out of here," he begged.

"Wait!" said Lei. "These . . . these people means us no harm. Let me listen!"

The murmuring voices of the unseen men, women and children mingled, making a racket that echoed through the streets. Lei frowned and tried to follow what they were all saying. She translated as she went along.

"They say great epidemic strike their island once. No medicine . . . no one have cure."

Suddenly a fabric ball rolled to the twins' feet. They trembled. A moment later the ball rose from the ground and swayed back and forth under their noses.

"Go away!" moaned Peppe, pushing at the air in front of him. "Shoo! Shoo! I don't want to play!"

A small voice gave some kind of reply.

"Child say he never seen one of Living before," Lei translated.

"One of the Living?" asked Hob. "You mean . . . you mean we're among the dead here?"

Lei nodded.

"They ghosts of dead people. After epidemic, no survivors. They become Unseen. And they wait for saviours every day."

Finopico turned pale. He flinched, protesting that he was no one's saviour, only a cook, and he was going to get out of here straight away.

"No," said Lei. "You wait a while!"

She questioned the empty air at length, receiving answers in the language of the Unseen. Meanwhile Babilas, the twins and Finopico remained in a group behind her, eyes wide with amazement. At last the daughter of Balmun turned round, smiling.

"They want show us something. You come."

"What?" gasped Finopico in strangled tones. "Go with them? Nothing doing!"

"This island is accursed!" added the twins. "Let's get back to the ship!"

"Why do we have to help these Unseen people?" asked the cook, stepping back again. "They're just air!"

Lei went up to him, fixing him with her blue gaze. "Catabea say we face our fears, and if not, we fail. Cannot refuse now. If you cowardly, you go. I help these people!"

"*Horch ghim!*" said Babilas, following Lei.

Finopico bit his lip and bent his head. He remembered the warnings that the Guardian of the Archipelago had given them. He sighed, grumbled a little, but finally agreed to follow the Unseen.

Beside him, Hob and Peppe had fallen silent. They walked on reluctantly, never sparing a glance for the squares, the fountains, the porches. The town which had looked so charming from a distance had really been frozen in death for years. It was a chilling idea.

The pitchfork, the tubs, the baskets, the fabric ball and the toy horse on wheels led the travellers right through the town along steep roads. At last they made their way round the lighthouse.

Now the five companions saw the other side of the island, its hidden face. The landscape here was nothing like what they had seen from the *Fabula*. The place was one vast graveyard, a field of desolation, full of brambles, littered with dry twigs, covered with grey dust. The graves, scattered all down the slope, were black gashes in the middle of the wild grass.

Lei shuddered, thinking how terrible the epidemic must have been. Some of the graves were no larger than cradles. She felt her heart sink, her throat was dry, and she clenched her fists. Her whole being quivered to think of the long-ago grief of the mothers who had to lay their children in the earth, the distress of the men who had to dig their wives' graves, and the indescribable sorrow of the last survivor. Alone on his island, he must have lain down in a hole to die like a dog.

Tears ran down Lei's cheeks as the Unseen told her what they wanted. It was mad, senseless, terrifying, but if anyone could help them she, the daughter of Balmun, was the one to do it. She swore an oath in the language of the Unseen, and then turned to her companions.

"I come back here tonight," she announced. "I repair what was broken. Thanks to knowledge of Balmun, I unite what was separated."

35

The Hour of the Dead

"You don't even know what they died of!" Malva pointed out.

She was sitting on a sea chest in a corner between-decks. Lei was pacing, sorting out plants and roots, blowing on the fire under the last cauldron they had on board. She had rolled up the sleeves of her tunic, and was in such a state of agitation that her brow was covered with sweat.

"How do you think you can work such a miracle?" Malva went on. "Your medicine can cure bites, set broken bones— even heal sword wounds. But what these . . . these Unseen are asking you to do is something else!"

Lei didn't reply. She was concentrating on her work with unprecedented intensity. She chopped leaves, removed the seeds from wild berries, made calculations, measured out ingredients, mixed them—nothing else interested her.

"They're dead!" Malva cried again. "They've been dead and buried for years! You'll never bring them back to life, Lei!"

Who did Lei think she was? wondered Malva. Who, in the

Two Worlds, could boast of being able to restore the dead to life? At heart Malva knew she was jealous of Lei's knowledge. She felt sure that Orpheus would admire Lei enormously when he was better, and . . .

"I not have choice," said Lei quietly. "This is test for me. If I refuse test, Catabea know. Then Catabea send us to Immuration."

Malva clasped her knees in her arms and looked sullen.

The day had tested her nerves severely. She had paced up and down anxiously for hours while Orpheus slept in his berth. She had visited him countless times, hoping he would open his eyes and recognise her. It was a waste of time: Orpheus slept and slept and slept. Finally, Malva had taken Zeph with her and lay close to him on her bunk to feel less lonely. Acid was still dripping onto the five Stones of Life in the Nokros and the gloomiest of thoughts invaded her mind. Later, when she heard her companions coming back, she had heaved a sigh of relief and ran to meet them.

Once on board, they had told her the whole complicated tale of their discoveries. Malva couldn't believe that they had followed invisible beings all over the island, yet they swore it was the truth. Here, as in the rest of the Archipelago, inexplicable things really happened.

Hob said he had counted sixty-eight graves in the graveyard on the other side of the island. How terrible!

Lei had summed up the tale that the Unseen had told her. Every night the island was plunged deep in mist and the Unseen shut themselves up in their houses. This was the Hour of the Dead. Corpses rose from their graves on the other side of the island. They climbed to the lighthouse, they walked in the streets, the meadows, the fields, the woods. As they do so, the temperature fell several degrees. And in spite of the thick mist, these dead worked: it was they who kept the roads in good condition, repaired the low walls, fed the herds of nuba-nubas, those strange beasts whose meat Finopico no longer wanted to taste. It was these dead who rang the bell in the morning when the mists lifted. Then they went back to their graves on the other side of the island and did not move until the following night. It had been like that since the epidemic had come.

Malva's hair stood on end as she listened to the story. But when the daughter of Balmun told her that she had promised the Unseen to find some way of curing their dead she was left speechless. To repair what was broken and unite what was separated . . . that was what they expected. According to a prophecy, a saviour was going to appear and work that miracle: reunite the two sides of the island, repair the bodies wrecked by disease so that their souls could inhabit them again, and life could go on as it did in the old days.

"If I find cure," Lei had finished, spreading her harvest of herbs and fruits out on deck, "curse on island lifted. Then we go."

And now she was here between decks concocting her potions.

Night was already falling outside. Wisps of mist were clinging to the portholes, and the cold made its way into the *Fabula* again. Lei had taken off Orpheus's jacket and put it on the chest. Malva's teeth were chattering.

"Take jacket," Lei suggested. "If you not fear bad luck because of blood . . ."

Malva shrugged her shoulders and picked the jacket up. Its collar smelled of Orpheus. She breathed it in deeply.

"Babilas say he come with me," added Lei, still stirring the potion bubbling in the cauldron. "We have to give cure to sixty-eight dead before sun rises."

"That's a lot," Malva agreed.

"I need help," Lei added. "Twins too frightened . . . Finopico too, but you?"

Malva's fingers tightened on the lapels of the jacket. She didn't know what to say. At that moment Lei tipped a powder made from roots that she had found in the undergrowth into the cauldron. A disgusting odor began to spread between decks. Finopico emerged from his galley, horrified.

"What on earth is that?" he cried. "It smells horrible!"

"To cure deadly disease," said Lei in learned tones, "potion must be horrible."

Nauseated, the cook shook his head. "Holy Harmony protect our taste buds from sorcery!"

Malva looked at Lei, and they burst out laughing, while Finopico angrily slammed the door.

"I'm not afraid," said Malva, when her laughter had died down. "You can count on me to help you on the island."

Babilas, Lei and Malva left the *Fabula* two hours later, laden with phials and small jars containing Lei's potion. Each of them also carried a storm-lantern, which didn't cast much light anyway. The mist turned night white, night turned the mist black; they could hardly see their own feet when they looked down.

It was so cold that no one wanted to go up on deck to see them off. The twins and Finopico had gathered round the stove in the galley, and Zeph was acting as a blanket for Orpheus: Malva's idea to keep the Captain from catching cold. The old St. Bernard had been perfectly willing to lie full length on top of his master. He was drooling liberally over him too, but Orpheus didn't notice.

Babilas jumped down to the beach and helped the two girls. He walked a little unsteadily before them, but this large frame was reassuring. The three of them went in single file along the pathways and roads. Beyond the little roadside walls, fields and meadows were lost in the mist. Suddenly they heard bleating on their right. It was the nuba-nubas, no doubt wanting to be fed. Lei stopped.

She raised her lantern and scrambled over the wall. The other two followed her in silence, and they set off across the meadow. The grass and flowers were covered with dew. Malva had buried her nose in the collar of Orpheus's jacket to give herself courage. Every time she breathed in, his scent warmed her heart a little.

The bleating of the nuba-nubas was closer now. They could also hear dry creaking sounds, rustling straw and gurgling water. Somewhere in the mist, the dead were giving the flock food and water.

Lei took a phial out of the pocket of her tunic. She cautiously went forward, straining her ears to help her get her bearings. Behind her, Malva was clinging to Babilas. She felt fear in the pit of her stomach.

Suddenly shadows appeared in the light of the lanterns. Malva suppressed a scream.

"Is only nuba-nubas," Lei whispered, still going forward.

The long-eared animals were crowding around them, rubbing against their legs. They seemed perfectly harmless. Malva took a deep breath. But at that moment a taller shadow emerged from the darkness, carrying a bale of hay on its back. Lei immediately raised her lantern and said a few words in the language of the

Unseen. The shadow moved. When it was close enough the three terrified companions saw its face: it was a man, and scarcely more than a cadaver. Above the man's fleshless neck was a grey bloated face, mottled with violet stains. His wide, bloodshot eyes rolled in their sockets.

Meeting that sorrowful gaze, Malva felt her legs about to give way beneath her. Babilas held her up with one hand while Lei talked to the apparition. She held her phial up in the air.

The dead man put down his bale of hay. He looked at Lei with a kind of amazement. She spoke to him again and again, until at last he was prepared to take the phial. He turned it this way and that in his skeletal fingers. Malva closed her eyes: the sight of this man, risen from his grave, nauseated her. When she looked again she saw him taking the stopper from the little bottle and carrying it to his mouth. Lei was close enough to touch him. She kept talking gently.

The dead man drank all the potion in the phial and gave it back to Lei. Then, without a word, he lifted his bale of hay again, turned his back on them and vanished into the mist. Lei, Malva and Babilas looked at each other, heaving sighs of relief.

Now they had only sixty-seven more of the dead to find.

It took all night. Groping her way through the fields, the woods and the streets of the town, Lei led Babilas and Malva on in her determined quest. All the dead looked like nightmares when they emerged from the fog. Empty-eyed, mouths contorted by their past sufferings, their faces bloated, their bodies broken, some even had traces of dried blood on their cheeks. Malva couldn't get accustomed to their sickly, putrefied faces, particularly when they were children. Several times she was on the point of running away or fainting. Babilas helped her to

303

overcome her revulsion every time, while Lei went tirelessly up to the dead and spoke to them until they had drunk the potion. The worst of it was that none of them knew exactly what the effects of her brew might be.

In her heart, Malva felt that her friend's efforts would be in vain, but Lei never showed any sign of discouragement. She wanted to save these people and allow the Unseen to return to their bodies. Above all, she wanted to pit her powers of healing against the infinitely greater powers of Death.

Babilas kept count of the phials, the jars and the corpses they met. When the sixty-eighth dead body had drunk her medicine, the daughter of Balmun turned her weary eyes to him. She was swaying where she stood, her lips dry and her voice hoarse. She just looked at the sky. The mist was already dispersing, revealing a few pale stars. Malva, exhausted, sat down on the ground. She buried her face in her hands and began weeping with fatigue.

Suddenly the bell rang very close. Lei jumped. It was the signal that the dead were returning to their graves.

A moment later the mist lifted as suddenly as it had the day before. Sunlight flooded the island, and the three travellers hid their burning eyes in their hands. Without knowing it, they had reached the foot of the lighthouse. Before them lay the town, with its well-maintained roads and its squares and fountains. Below them in the little bay they could see the *Fabula*, with Finopico and the twins on deck trying in vain to catch sight of them.

Babilas and the two girls waited. The sun rose in the azure sky, the seabirds circled above the cliffs. For some time not a word passed their lips. Lei was looking impatiently at the houses. When the shutters opened, and if her potion had worked, it would not be the Unseen who looked out to greet the new day, but flesh-and-blood people.

Long minutes went by. Malva felt her limbs going numb in the warmth of the sun. She must have slept briefly while her two companions, still on the alert for any sign of life, walked round and round the lighthouse.

In the end, when nothing happened, they too sat down, heavy at heart, their expressions gloomy.

This morning the shutters of the red-brick houses remained closed. The streets were still silent. None of the Unseen came out to draw water from the fountains. No pitchfork turned the hay, no laundry basket floated through the air to the wash-house, no little wooden horse was wheeled along the streets . . .

Something had certainly happened during that terrifying night, but it was not at all what Lei had wanted.

"Is no good. I failed," she murmured at last.

With a lump in her throat, Malva turned her amber eyes on her friend. Lei, so graceful in her light tunic, was looking at the graveyard on the other side of the island. The wind played in her fair hair, and she was crying. It was the first time Malva had seen her look so frail. The daughter of Balmun, her arms dangling in the heart-breaking silence of the island, was simply giving up. The effect of her potion had been the opposite of what she intended: the Unseen had indeed been reunited with their injured bodies, and now they were lying in the ground for all eternity.

"*Newynas ghun!*" Babilas suddenly shouted, pointing at the graves.

Malva leaped to her feet and joined him. Open-mouthed, the three companions watched a strange and terrifying phenomenon: the brambles and wild grass were growing at incredible speed, sending thorny tentacles and thickets of green all the way up the slope. Before their eyes, the vegetation was reclaiming its place and soon the graves disappeared under the foliage.

"Watch out!" cried Malva, flinching.

The undergrowth was climbing rapidly towards the light-house, digging its roots into the paving stones of the streets, clambering up houses, trying to throw its thorny arms around the legs of the Living.

"We must get out of here!" cried Malva, untangling a bramble from her ankles.

Babilas took the girls by their arms and ran through the town with them. Trees were already growing in the middle of the streets, lifting paving stones, cracking walls. The fountains were covered with moss, tiles on the rooftops were being loosened by the ivy attacking the houses. Chimneys fell to the ground and broke, shutters came off their hinges.

"The town's collapsing!" shouted Malva.

They ran without turning to look back. The entire island was changing all around them. When they entered the forest gigantic cobwebs stuck to their faces. Babilas took out his knife and slashed a way through the branches for them.

"Medicine bad! I not saved Unseen!" moaned Lei in terror.

The grass had engulfed everything in the fields. The bodies of nuba-nubas lay beside the roads surrounded by fallen walls. There was a smell of rotting in the air. Death embraced the island.

Babilas led Lei and Malva to the beach. The seabirds were screeching threateningly overhead, while up on the deck of the *Fabula* the twins and Finopico were waving frantically.

"I not succeed!" repeated Lei, collapsing on deck. "I un-worthy of my people!"

"Hoist all sail!" Finopico shouted to the twins. He took the tiller himself, while Babilas pushed the ship well away from the beach.

Trembling from head to foot, Malva clung to the rail, her lungs burning. The dreadful images of the night left her mind feverish. She felt consumed by flames, melted, charred. Raising her head to look at the summit of the island, she saw that even the lighthouse had disappeared entirely under the vegetation. Within a few minutes the island had become wild and deserted again.

As the *Fabula* bravely put out to sea, Malva turned, and saw Lei curled up in a ball on deck, sobbing inconsolably. She went over to her, took off Orpheus's jacket and wrapped it around her friend. Then she took her in her arms clumsily, not knowing how to comfort her in such grief. Lei's failure might have grave consequences for all of them, but one thing was certain: neither Malva nor any other member of the crew would hold it against her. The daughter of Balmun had given all she had to save the tormented souls of the Unseen. She had devoted herself to a cause that was lost in advance.

36

Hope

The fifth Stone of Life had just crumbled into powder at the bottom of the Nokros when Orpheus opened his eyes. His face was sticky with dog slobber, Zeph weighed heavily on his chest, and a strange taste clung to his tongue.

As soon as he came round, he remembered everything: the shipwrecked sailors from Dunbraven, the fight with the Archont, the kitchen utensils, the grappling irons, and finally that stroke of the Archont's sword. He raised the blankets and looked for his wound. It had disappeared; Lei had worked another of her miracles! And if she had the time to nurse him, that must mean that the *Fabula* was sailing calmly on its own, far from the Archont and the Patrols. Orpheus turned to the door.

"Hello there!" he called.

Zeph shifted, and raised his big head.

"Thanks for keeping me warm, old fellow," Orpheus said. "You can get off me now."

Zeph put out his tongue and licked his master's nose, but stayed where he was.

"Go on, shoo!" Orpheus repeated. "Go and find the others! Go and tell them I've woken up!"

Zeph didn't budge. As usual, he was refusing to obey. Orpheus tried to push him off, but he had lost a lot of strength.

"Help!" he called. "I'm being smothered! Anyone there?"

A moment went by before the cabin door opened wide. Hob appeared, fists raised, ready for a fight. When he saw that his only opponent would be the big St. Bernard he stopped short.

"Oh," he said. "I thought . . ."

"You were good and quick," said Orpheus, smiling at him. "Congratulations, sailor! If you can dislodge this drooling mutt I'll make you first mate."

Hob whistled. Zeph immediately jumped off the bed without any more fuss and went to sit at the boy's feet. Orpheus shook his head; that dog certainly took pleasure in disobeying him personally.

"So am I really first mate now, Captain?" asked Hob mischievously.

Orpheus patted the edge of his berth to show that he wanted Hob to sit down, and asked him what had been going on while he was getting his strength back. Hob immediately told him how Babilas had recovered his ability to speak, and went on to describe the events on the Island of the Unseen in detail, delighted with this chance to impress the Captain. But then his face grew dark.

"The trouble is that Lei didn't succeed in bringing the dead to life. She wept for a whole hour, saying over and over again that we were all doomed to the Immuration, and it was her fault. Do you think that's true?"

Orpheus scratched his chin. The lower part of his face was covered by a thick growth of beard, and it itched.

"I don't know," he said at last. "It will all depend on Catabea's decision. After all, Lei did reunite the souls and bodies of those Unseen people."

Hob sighed. "I'm afraid of the Immuration, Captain. Peppe's even more scared of it than I am. He's so sensitive . . . after all the prisons we knew in Galnicia, I'm not sure he'll hold out for very long if he's shut up again."

"What about you?" asked Orpheus gently.

"Me? I sometimes feel I'm tougher than my brother. Physically we're identical, yet . . . oh, I don't know. Anyway, I could never live without Peppe. The two of us are together for life or death!"

Orpheus smiled, touched by the boy's devotion, and reassured him as best he could about the Immuration. Then he threw off his blankets and stood up.

"I feel almost better again!" he exclaimed, stretching and flexing his muscles. "Who's on watch up on deck?"

"Finopico," said the boy.

Orpheus said he would go and relieve the cook. But when he looked for his jacket, Hob explained that Lei and Malva had been competing for it.

"In the end they both went to sleep on deck under it, close to each other. I offered the Princetta my jersey, but she didn't want it. I don't know why—my jersey's no dirtier than your jacket!"

He said this with a touch of regret and jealousy that made Orpheus smile.

"Girls are complicated," he said, pulling his boots on. "They have their secrets, but you mustn't despair."

"Oh, I don't!" Hob was quick to say. "Judging by what the fortune te—"

He stopped short and blushed. Orpheus looked hard at him, narrowing his eyes. "What exactly *did* that fortune-teller say? I'd be interested to know."

At that moment the cabin door opened again. Peppe appeared, hair ruffled and looking sleepy. "Oh, there you are!" he said to his brother. "I don't like you leaving me alone at night. It wakes me up."

"Just coming," said Hob, making off with a certain relief.

He followed his brother, and they both disappeared into their cabin. Peppe hadn't given his resuscitated Captain a glance. Only his brother mattered to him. Those two are as inseparable as the two sides of the same coin, thought Orpheus. You could call them Head and Tail!

Then he decided to go up on deck. Zeph followed, dragging his old body up the steps through the hatch.

The sky was clear, and covered with stars. A steady breeze was swelling the sails of the *Fabula*. Before looking for Finopico Orpheus went over to the rail. His face raised to the wind, he breathed in its salty tang with pleasure. By Holy Harmony, how good it was to be at sea! The ship's speed and the night air made his head spin. He almost forgot Catabea, the Patrols, the Archont, the Nokros and the terrible deadline hanging over the crew. Just for a moment, standing there on deck and lost on the nameless sea, he felt happier than ever before. The burden that had been weighing on him for so many years had been lifted. Here and now, he felt that at last he was alive. Perhaps that sensation was due to the danger itself? Or the silent presence of his companions on the voyage? Or more simply to his miraculous recovery from the swordstroke? No doubt it was all of them.

He bent down and patted his dog vigorously. "I never thought you'd stand up to travelling for so long, you old mutt," he said affectionately. "If we get out of this Archipelago, I'll ask Lei to make you something for your paws. Perhaps she can give you back your youth, who knows?"

So saying, he glanced at the middle of the deck, where the two girls were asleep. They were pressed close together, curled up under his quartermaster's jacket. They had both been through so many ordeals . . . he owed his life to one of them, and to the other the chance to do what he had always dreamed of. Orpheus straightened up and took a few steps in their direction.

"I won't make you go back to Galnicia, Princetta," he whispered. "If we're still alive at the end of this voyage I hope you will find the country that haunts your dreams. Elgolia, wasn't it? You deserve it . . ."

He thought he saw Malva move in her sleep. Leaning down to her, he looked at her luminous face for a moment.

"Too bad about me," he added in a low voice. "Too bad about my oath! Too bad about the honour of the McBotts!"

He raised his head to look at the stars, smiled and went off to the stern rail with a determined tread. He had hardly turned his back when Malva opened her eyes. She had heard everything he said.

"If we're still alive at the end of this voyage, Captain, who knows what I'll decide?" she murmured.

And she went to sleep again, a smile on her lips, holding Orpheus's jacket close to her heart.

Finopico was standing at the helm. He had put a stormlantern down on a chest beside him, and an open book lay under it, its pages fluttering in the wind. As he steered the *Fabula* he was reading with great interest, so absorbed in the book that he didn't see Orpheus coming.

"Learning new recipes?" the latter asked.

Finopico jumped. Then his face lit up.

"It's like a miracle to see you up and about, Captain! We thought your last hour had come, but the Archont may come back!"

"I hope not," replied Orpheus cheerfully. "I trust that by now he's drowned and the fish are feeding on him!"

With these words he cast a glance at the book that Finopico had placed on the chest. It was one of the many works about fish that the cook collected.

"But I'm disturbing you in the middle of your reading," Orpheus apologised. "If you like I can . . ."

Finopico shrugged, and closed the book. "I was passing the time, that's all. The sea is so calm tonight."

Orpheus sat down on the chest and said nothing for a moment, enjoying the soft air and the slight pitching of the *Fabula*. Everyone was asleep, and there was no particular danger on the horizon.

"This is exactly how I always imagined a night at sea," he sighed. "I've dreamed of such moments so long."

"But you have the sea in your blood, don't you?" Finopico asked. "Why did you wait so long before going on board a ship?"

Orpheus felt his heart skip a beat, and bit his lip. "It's a long story," he murmured. "I don't think the time has yet come to tell it."

Finopico, both hands on the tiller, nodded gravely before saying, "It doesn't matter now. You've given plenty of proof of your courage, and no one will ever call you Greenhorn again! I'll make sure of that!"

Orpheus looked sideways at him. His mop of red hair, his

angular and nervous face . . . the cook wasn't such a bad sort after all.

"I'm really sorry that Zeph ate your chicken on the day of the audience with the Coronador," he said.

"Oh, forget the chicken!" laughed Finopico. "That's ancient history too! Anyway, I'm more interested in fish than poultry!"

"Can I look?" asked Orpheus, pointing to the book.

The cook allowed him to leaf through it by the light of the lantern. All the pages had engravings of strange-looking marine creatures; these illustrations accompanied texts describing the habits of the fish and giving information about the seas where they could be caught. The stamp of the Maritime Institute of Galnicia was on the first page.

"My word, you stole it!" said Orpheus in surprise.

"I borrowed it," Finopico corrected him. "That's all."

"What about the others? All the books in your galley?"

"I borrowed them too. The few galniks I'm paid as wages don't allow me to buy books like those. I'll return them once we're back."

Orpheus shrugged. "I don't suppose anyone has missed them. Who'd be interested in those monsters?"

"You're wrong there, Captain! Many Galnician scientists are passionately interested in rare fish. There's even a special scientific committee which regularly sends expeditions out to all the seas of the Known World."

"You ought to offer them your services," Orpheus suggested. "It seems to me you know all about the subject."

The cook looked piqued. "I did approach the scientific committee, several times. But the top brass at the Institute didn't take me seriously, though I've gone diving in all sorts of places, and even brought back some interesting specimens.

314

However, I'm only a cook, you see. I don't have any higher education."

That reminded Orpheus of the day when he had first seen Finopico outside the Institute itself. He remembered hearing him complain about scientists with their moustaches; now he knew why he resented them.

"That's not fair," said Orpheus. "Why would you need diplomas and grand-sounding titles?"

"That's what I think too," replied Finopico. "But I still hope to convince those fine gentlemen the scientists. Here, take a look at page 243 . . ."

Orpheus found the page.

"See that engraving at the bottom, on the right?"

"The big fish with its jaws open?"

"According to the author that fish doesn't exist. He says it's just a legend invented by the ancient seamen of Polvakia. A mythical beast."

Orpheus read aloud the brief text printed in a box under the engraving.

" 'GHOOM OF THE DEEPS, *n*. So called by the crew of a Polvakian vessel coming back from an expedition to the Orniant. According to them, the creature measures between five and ten metres and has a double set of pointed teeth. Smooth in appearance, with a translucent skin, the Ghoom is also said to have two separate tails. It is claimed to have been sighted several sea-miles offshore, at a place where the sea is so deep that it has no bed. No other evidence.' "

"There," said Finopico, cheerfully, "what about that, Captain? Don't you think the Ghoom deserves our attention?"

"Yes, of course," said Orpheus rather doubtfully.

Finopico pursued the subject eagerly. "If only I could find the creature! If only I could bring a specimen home to Galnicia! If only I could march into the Institute, head held high, and put what they say is a mythical beast down in front of those pompous men of science! They'd have to take me seriously then!"

Hearing him speak, Orpheus realised that to Finopico the fish was much more than a simple biological curiosity.

"I'd like to see their faces!" exclaimed the cook, with his own turned up to the stars. "Oh—they'd bow to my discovery! They'd envy me! They'd prostrate themselves at my feet! I, the little cook without any money or any diploma, would make all those idiots eat their scornful words!"

He suddenly let go of the tiller and knelt down in front of the chest, next to Orpheus. A spark of madness lit up his eyes like St. Elmo's fire in a storm.

"I hate those scientists, Captain! There they sit comfortably installed in the Institute armchairs down the generations, from father to son! They despise us, they judge us and mock our ambitions, but one of these days I'll have my revenge! Thanks to the Ghoom!"

He abruptly calmed down, and stroked page 243 with a trembling hand.

"Take it easy, my pretty one," he told the engraving. "I know you don't want to end up in a museum, I know you'd rather enjoy swimming in the black waters of the ocean, but have patience. I'm sure the Divinities will hear my voice at long last and you and I will meet. When that moment comes I'll catch you. And you will go into the official reference books under the magnificent name of *Finopicuum de profondis*!"

He took a deep breath, reluctantly closed the book and rose to his feet.

"We all have our secrets," he added in a less elated voice. "One can't always admit to them, but . . . well, it does the heart good to share them now and then, don't you think so, Captain?"

A hint of dawn was showing, a milky line on the horizon.

Finopico suddenly seemed very tired. Orpheus went to take the tiller and dismissed him. His back bent, the redhead left the Captain without another word and disappeared down the hatch. He was carrying his book in his arms as carefully as if it were a small baby.

Perplexed, Orpheus looked into the vastness of the sky as it turned pale. Had Finopico gone mad in his search for his mythical fish?

He shrugged. No—Finopico was no madder than anyone else. He was pursuing a dream, like the rest of them. For Finopico, it was the Ghoom. For Malva it was Elgolia. For the twins, it was a secret that some fortune-teller had read in the cards. And what about me? thought Orpheus. He remembered his father again. When would he stop feeling ashamed of the past? Finopico might have shown that he trusted him, but Orpheus couldn't shake off the disturbing feeling that he was only an impostor, a usurper, and didn't deserve to be Captain of the *Fabula*.

He stayed like that for some time, deep in his own thoughts. But when the sun rose he saw its first rays with a kind of joy. In daytime, it seemed to him that his ideas were less confused, and he could breathe freely. He placed his hands on the tiller and sighed.

Malva and Lei were beginning to stir. When their heads emerged from under his jacket, eyes blinking, Orpheus waved to them. They smiled.

"It's a new day!" he told them cheerfully. "We have a favouring wind, and we're still alive. Well done the *Fabula*!"

317

The two girls got to their feet and joined him.

"Thank you, Lei. My wound is completely healed," Orpheus went on in the same enthusiastic tone. "I've never felt better! Next time I see the Archont I'll be the one to skewer him with a sword, word of a McBott!"

Lei smiled. Everything looked so beautiful in the rising sun.

"Look!" said Orpheus, opening his arms wide. "The sky is clear. We've overcome our fear and pain. Catabea will have to keep her word! There's not a shadow in sight today."

Malva looked at him with a shy smile. His good humour and enthusiasm did her a world of good. There were only four Stones of Life left in the Nokros, nothing was gained yet, but she wanted to believe that Orpheus was right. Perhaps the gates of the Archipelago were just ahead of them? Perhaps they had only to hold their course?

While Orpheus was shouting and hurling defiance at Catabea, Babilas and the twins appeared on deck, still drowsy. The sun welcomed them. For the first time in ages, they had had enough sleep, and their faces seemed relaxed and at rest. Orpheus shouted good morning to them, and they all gathered by the stern rail to look at the horizon.

This morning, for the frailest of reasons, hope revived in the troubled hearts of the travellers.

37

The Wave

Two more days passed, and nothing happened. The *Fabula* did not come upon any other island, or meet with any ship or ambush. In her berth, Malva watched the morbic acid of the Nokros dripping on the Stones, torn between her hope that the Archipelago had really let them go, and her fear that they would be held hostage here forever. Her mood swings surprised everyone.

"Come on, Princetta," Finopico told her, "don't look so dismal. See what I've brought you!"

Taking advantage of the calm weather to go fishing, the cook showed her his catch. He had a strange assortment of fish. Some were tiny, blue and slender as dagger blades, others were huge and globular like balloons. Finopico tirelessly classified his specimens, drew them, described them, and when he had finished his studies he plunged them into boiling water and made fish soup. He was secretly hoping to find the Ghoom of the Deeps in this strange ocean. But to do that he must fish and fish without stopping.

Orpheus kept on course, not quite sure they were going the right way. In this unknown part of the world the stars were different, the sun made a mockery of the points on the compass, and none of them were able to take their bearings. He had to fix on some objective at random and hope for the best.

On the second night, however, when he went to join Hob and take over his watch, Orpheus felt a change in the atmosphere. First it was the wind, which shifted and grew cooler at the same time.

"What's going on, Captain?" asked Hob anxiously, holding the tiller steady.

Orpheus frowned, and told him they must be very watchful. At the same time there was a strange watery noise, followed by a swell that shook the hull.

In her cabin, Malva couldn't sleep. Now that the morbic acid was beginning to attack the last three Stones of Life she couldn't help thinking with terror of what might lie ahead. She thought of Philomena too, of Elgolia, of the Baighurs, and dreadful nostalgia rose within her. When she felt the shaking hull she sat up straight in her berth.

Without stopping to think, she left her cabin and went on deck. Orpheus was leaning over the prow with a lantern in his hand.

"The *Fabula*'s being carried away by a current—it's getting stronger and stronger," he said when he saw Malva. "Look."

She went over. In spite of the darkness she could guess at the heavy swell of the sea below. There was a continuous growling sound under the hull like an animal purring. It was as if the ship were on rails, following an invisible but inescapable track.

"We've veered off course," Orpheus said. "There's not a breath of wind, so we can't counter the currents."

"What's that over there?" asked Malva, who had raised her head. The sky was growing a little lighter, and they could see a dark shape rising vertically above the water. "Another ship?"

"Perhaps," murmured Orpheus. "It's moving, but . . ."

They stayed silent for a moment, concentrating on the approaching shape. Its outline became clearer; no, it was not a ship.

"It looks like . . . like a wave," said Malva.

Orpheus shivered. A wave? A wave as tall as the *Fabula*'s mainmast? Orpheus turned and called to Hob.

"Go and wake the others! Hurry!"

Without asking for any more explanations, Hob let go of the tiller and ran to the hatch, while Orpheus and Malva watched the strange object rising up in their path. Their hearts beat in unison, very fast. For a moment Malva thought of clinging to Orpheus for comfort, but she didn't dare.

"Are you afraid?" he asked her.

"A little."

He moved behind her and took her gently in his arms. A shiver ran down the back of Malva's neck.

"What about now?" asked Orpheus. "Are you still afraid?"

Disconnected thoughts flooded Malva's mind, but only a sigh passed her lips, and at last she abandoned herself to the gentle warmth of Orpheus's embrace. For a few moments she saw nothing: not the sea, or the coming dawn, or the wave which was still growing. The world didn't exist at all. She felt as if she were weightless in a bubble. Strange as it might seem, she had never felt so close to happiness.

But it didn't last.

Babilas, Finopico, Peppe and Lei ran to the stem of the ship, uttering cries. The bubble holding Orpheus and Malva abruptly burst, its sweetness gave way to terror, and reality took them by the throat: the *Fabula* was making straight for the enormous wave.

"*Gorchnaim ei arthan!*" cried Babilas, leaping towards the tiller. "*Cypell olc bhung!*"

"We lost!" Lei translated in a strangled voice.

Orpheus joined Babilas, who was trying desperately to correct the ship's course. With their combined strength, they managed to turn the tiller, but it wasn't enough. The wave was swelling as it advanced, and its crest of foam was rising higher and higher in the pale sky. In a few minutes it would be right on top of them.

"Lash yourselves down!" ordered Orpheus, when he realised there was no hope of avoiding the wave. "It's our only chance!"

He dashed forward, uncoiled the hawsers and the ropes, passed their ends through the mortises of the capstan and the eye of the fairleads, and then threw the ropes to his companions. Suddenly he realised that Zeph wasn't there.

"Zeph? Zeph!" he called. "Where's that wretched dog?"

"Asleep between-decks," said Finopico, tying a rope round his waist.

Orpheus glanced at the wave. If he went down, dragged his dog up and lashed him to the deck, he might not have time to secure himself too.

"Captain!" cried Lei. "I not know how do with this!"

The fair-haired girl was clumsily entangled in the sheets, and the ropes shook in her feverish hands.

"You see to Zeph!" Malva told Orpheus. "I learned to tie knots on the *Estafador*!"

She untied herself and ran to help Lei. Orpheus hesitated, but seeing that Malva was managing very well he clambered down the steps from the hatch. He found the big St. Bernard lying full length between two sea chests, with his tongue hanging out and breathing heavily.

"Come here!" he ordered. "And quick, by Holy Tranquillity!"

He grabbed Zeph by the back of the neck and began dragging him to the steps, but the animal began growling and bared his yellow teeth. A sharp sweat trickled down Orpheus's back. For several seconds he shouted, begged, hurled insults at his dog, with no result. The St. Bernard was rebelling, as usual.

"Well, you're on your own, then!" said Orpheus, letting go of his collar.

Frantic now, he took the steps to the deck four at a time. When he came out Malva and Babilas were on their knees beside the twins, busily tying the hawsers to the capstan. Behind them the wave rose like a blue wall. Though Babilas was lashed in place, nothing tied Malva to the ship.

"Get yourself secured!" Orpheus shouted, running to her.

He hardly had time to grab a rope and fling it round himself. Then he caught the girl by the waist and held her close. The wave raised the *Fabula*, sucked her in, unbalanced her. Orpheus rolled over the deck. His arms clutched Malva even more tightly. Cries of terror pierced his eardrums as the wave broke over the deck. It was like a deluge of cannonballs coming down on to the ship. The shrill cries of Lei and the twins were soon drowned out by the enormous crash of the wave breaking.

The *Fabula* lay on her port side, then on her starboard side, almost capsized. The shock was so violent that Orpheus felt himself being plucked from the deck. He was swept away by the water, lifted like a feather. Water rushed into his mouth and nostrils, buffeted him this way and that, whirled him round, swept over him, and finally knocked him right out.

When he came to he was lying on the fo'c'sle. There was absolute silence in his ears. He spat out water, coughed and retched. "Malva, Malva," murmured an insistent voice in his head. His arms closed on empty air. She had gone.

38

Malva's Island

Unlike Orpheus, Malva had not lost consciousness. When she felt him letting go of her, she had tried to cling to some part of the ship, but the current was too strong. The wave had taken her in its watery arms with a strange and almost gentle power, carrying her far from the *Fabula* at staggering speed.

For a moment Malva felt as if she were flying, riding the crest of foam as if it were a horse. She saw the sky above her race past. She saw the colours of the rising sun as the last morning mists dispersed around her like cotton wool. She didn't struggle. She was not really afraid at any point. Something in her told her that this supernatural wave had not appeared in order to kill her; she wasn't going to drown, she wasn't going to die. Or at least, not yet.

The foam carried her away, propelling her on for a long time. Then the wave seemed to die down, and its crest gradually moved lower. At last the wave washed Malva gently up on a beach, and left her there.

She lay on the sand, eyes closed, feeling dazed. The sun very quickly dried her clothes. She stopped trembling, stretched her limbs, and let the warmth of the beach penetrate her too. The sound of the ebbing waves lulled her. Now and then she heard the chirping of birds, the rustling of wings and branches. How serene and restful everything seemed here after all that fear and confusion! How good it was to let the sun make you drowsy, thinking of nothing but your own well-being. Malva told herself that the *Fabula* might have sunk, but she didn't really feel anxious. All that mattered to her just now was to feel the sand beneath her feet, her stomach, her cheeks, while a sweet breeze tickled her nostrils. Almost in spite of herself her heart was at peace.

Only after a long time did she open her eyes and stand up.

She was on a white, sandy beach that outlined the perfect curve of a bay. Trees with supple, arching branches on which red and brown fruits hung grew along the shore. A cone-shaped building rose in the middle of the trees.

The next moment Malva turned her back on the sea and, almost forgetting what had just happened, walked towards the building. Plants had grown on its dome, giving it a kind of undulating green hair. The ochre stone of the facade was decorated with a great many small carvings depicting people or animals, which seemed to tell the history of a nation now gone. Was it an ancient temple? A place of worship to the divinities of those people, or just a house, or a king's burial place? Red birds turned in the air, swooped above the treetops, and came down from time to time on the stone gables.

Malva stopped in front of the massive door marking the entrance to the building. She hesitated for a moment: should she go in? Did she risk disturbing the peace and quiet of this place?

She finally decided to walk round it. She would come back later, but just now it seemed more important to explore the rest of the island.

She left the beach and ventured into the undergrowth of the woods. The only sounds she heard were the calls of the red birds and the wind in the branches.

Malva was not afraid. She walked on without any anxiety. Although she had never set foot in this place, she felt as safe here as if she had known it all her life.

The forest soon opened into a clearing and in the middle of it, surrounded by trees with smooth trunks, Malva saw a lake of bubbling, steaming water. Her heart leaped. The words of old Bulo, the sailor on the *Estafador*, came back to her: hadn't he mentioned a lake like this one in Elgolia?

Malva went closer, knelt down on the banks of the lake and breathed in the steam. It smelled sweet, of fruits and honey. She dipped her hand in the warm water, and when she took it out she found that her skin had become softer, as fine as the skin of a very small child.

"Lake Barath-Thor," she murmured, marvelling.

She stood up, her heart palpitating. How could this miracle have happened? How could that wave have carried her to exactly where she dreamed of going? It was beyond understanding, but Malva was in no doubt: she really was in Elgolia!

Full of vigour and enthusiasm, she left the clearing and began running along the incline of the island. A path of soft grass appeared at her feet, and although the slope was steep she had no difficulty in climbing it. Soon the trees thinned out, giving way to more meadows with streams running through them. She raised her eyes. As she expected, on the summit of the island, growing on a flowery mound, a tree with a massive trunk spread its heavy branches. It was all exactly as old Bulo's story had said!

Malva crossed the streams with ease, brushed through the flowers, jumped over the rocks. When she reached the foot of the tree she was barely out of breath. She burst out laughing and danced in the grass until she felt dizzy. Then she leaned against the trunk of the tree and laid her cheek against its rough bark. "I'm on Mount Ur-Tha! I'm on Mount Ur-Tha!" she told herself. She had never felt such intoxicating happiness.

All around her, the island revealed its beauty. Majestic birds with red feathers soared above the trees, the rivers sang as they flowed between crystalline rocks, the surface of the sea crinkled in the bay, and everything seemed absolutely pure. So this was Elgolia: a place of peace and enchantment, a restful shelter, far from everything that had ever made Malva unhappy in the past. Here no one could make her marry anyone or become the kind of person she wasn't. Anything was possible here.

Remembering the promise she had made to herself, Malva began climbing the branches of the thousand-year-old tree. She scaled the trunk, clambered to the uppermost branch, and sat astride it to see the world. If old Bulo had been telling the truth, the magic of the tree was about to start working.

As soon as she was securely seated on the branch she felt a prickling in her eyes, and then a kind of burning sensation. She grimaced, but she did not close her eyes. She wanted to see . . .

"Galnicia!" she said, turning to look west.

The familiar outline of the Citadel appeared before her: its intimidating walls and towers on top of the cliff, like some great bird of prey, and lower down the silver waters of the River Gdavir winding its way along. It was such a shock that Malva had to clutch the branch to keep herself from falling off. Dizzy, nauseated, dazzled: she breathed slowly, but she did not close her eyes.

Next she saw the gardens of the Citadel, its south facade, and the first houses of the Lower Town standing in its shadow. The trees in the orchards had lost their leaves, as if it were the middle of winter. No fountains played in the basins, and no one was walking along the terraces. The whole place looked grey, dull, lifeless. The bells of the Campanile were ringing out at the top of the Upper Town.

Someone's dead, thought Malva, shivering. She turned her head slightly and saw a funeral procession going down to one of the bridges. A small, solemn crowd was following a cart covered with a pall. A Holy Diafron drove this jolting vehicle, and behind him, surrounded by armed soldiers, walked . . .

"The Coronador!"

As if her cry had scared it away, the vision blurred, and Galnicia dissolved into a kind of cold fog.

Malva felt a lump in her throat. If the Coronador was leading the mourners in this funeral procession, it must be someone dear to him under the pall . . . the Coronada?

"Is . . . is my mother dead?" cried Malva.

A peaceful silence was all the reply she had to this question. She put a hand over her eyes, caught her breath, and turned feverishly in another direction.

"I want to see Philomena!" she said in a voice that shook slightly.

The magic of the tree began again: the prickling, the brief burning sensation, then that strange feeling of being carried through space . . .

A vast plain of short, windswept grass sprinkled with snow appeared before Malva's eyes. She immediately recognised the Great Azizian Steppes where she had ridden so far in the company of the Baighurs. Her heart leaped again. When the vision became clearer, she saw a camp of oryak-skin tents with swirls of black smoke rising from its centre. Armed horsemen had gathered around a fire. They were rolling the handles of spears between their hands while the points glowed red in the embers. Malva recognised Uzmir in the middle of them. The Supreme Khansha's handsome face looked thin and hard.

Malva turned her head slightly. A young woman wrapped in a heavy oryak-skin cloak had just come out of one of the tents. For a few seconds Malva wasn't sure that she recognised her, and yet . . . yes, it was Philomena! Well, if the tree doesn't tell lies, she's *alive*, thought Malva with intense relief.

Philomena approached the circle of horsemen and took her place beside Uzmir. At that moment the men pulled their spears out of the fire and began to chant. Uzmir uttered a cry, and all his companions scattered. Only Philomena did not move. She stayed there looking at the flames with her head down.

She's crying, thought Malva, biting her lip.

The riders mounted their scrawny horses, and set off at the gallop in close formation, following the Khansha, who stood on the back of his mount. He was shaking his spear in one hand. Malva realised that the Baighurs were not off hunting. Philomena's tears told her so. Uzmir and his men were at war.

Malva closed her eyes. Her heart felt heavy. She didn't need to see who the Baighurs were fighting; she knew. The Amoyeds and the forces of Temir-Gai must have formed an alliance after the fire that destroyed the harem, and Uzmir's people must now be fighting on all fronts.

Malva shifted on the branch. All these visions left a bitter taste in her mouth. The happiness she had felt before had melted away, and her heart was drowning in grief. She set her jaw, opened her eyes again, raised her head to the sun and said, "The Archont! I want to see where the Archont is now!"

In a painful flash she saw a boat with slanting sails of woven bamboo, very different from any of the vessels she had seen before. Bleeding, lifeless bodies lay on its deck. She started as she heard cries. The last scene of a pitiless drama was being acted out at the stern of the boat.

The Archont stood on a chest, waving two swords at his opponents, two exhausted and bleeding sailors who were supporting each other in a final effort. Hatred distorted the Archont's face. He had a gash on his head, but he was not weakening. Indeed, with a great bound, he leaped on one of the two sailors, and Malva almost closed her eyes as he thrust his blade into the man's belly. The other sailor fell to the deck in his turn, and dropped his weapon. He was exhausted, but he managed to crawl behind the mast as the Archont retrieved the dagger of the man he had just killed. Horrified, Malva watched as the Archont slowly advanced, a dreadful grin on his face. The sailor trembled and begged for mercy, but Malva knew that all his pleas were useless. The Archont knew no pity.

He caught the man by the hair and plunged the dagger into his throat. Then he strode quickly over to the bows of the boat and searched under a heap of sails. He brought out something that Malva instantly recognised: a Nokros still containing several Stones of Life. With a victorious gesture he held his trophy up to the sun. Thanks to this stolen Nokros, he could cheat Catabea's deadline, and avoid the Immuration!

Malva burst into tears on her branch. The scenes she had just helplessly witnessed sickened her. She sobbed for a long time up there in the tree, overcome by anger and distress. She saw

Uzmir's face before her, grave and emaciated; she saw Philomena, abandoned on the frozen steppes in front of the dying fire. And then came the images of Galnicia, grey and wintry, the Citadel, the orchards, the streets, all of them a part of the childhood that she had wanted to forget, but that was still fixed in her heart. Clenching her fists, she pounded them on the branch until her hands were bleeding.

A long time later she found the strength to move. She sat back against the trunk, took a deep breath, and looked at the landscape around her. The sweet valleys and meadows, the calm forests, the cool streams of water, even the splendour of the Bay of Dao-Boa now seemed unreal to her. So much beauty almost made her feel ill. She no longer understood what had made her want to come here. How could she have left the beach without a thought for her companions who were still on board the *Fabula*?

She turned to the sea.

"I want . . . I want to see Orpheus," she murmured at last.

Her eyes widened, as the spell of Mount Ur-Tha began working again, showing her the mended sails of the *Fabula*.

The wave had struck the ship with such force that the rails were broken in several places. But all the passengers were there on deck, alive: Orpheus, Lei, Babilas, Hob, Finopico, Peppe, even Zeph, who was padding round in circles yapping hoarsely. They looked distraught and dazed. When she looked at their faces closely, Malva saw that they were crying. Orpheus was looking at the waves, clinging to the sagging rail. The distress in his face utterly overwhelmed Malva. Peppe and Hob, their faces streaming with tears, called her name: Malva, Malva, Malva.

"They think I'm dead!" she cried out loud.

The vision immediately disappeared, and Malva was alone in her tree again, unable to move.

"They think I'm dead," she repeated.

She felt like howling out loud, but she just didn't have the strength. She slid down to the foot of the tree, her legs trembling. Making contact with the ground reassured her a little. She knelt on the moss and looked at the sky. It was such fine weather, the air was so sweet . . . how could she feel so sad when she had finally reached Elgolia?

Feeling desperate, she retraced her steps to the bay where she had been washed up a few hours earlier. Her eyes no longer saw the rivers, her ears no longer heard the birds, her heart was caught in her breast like a frightened, frail little animal.

Once she was back on the beach, she made at once for the ochre stone temple. Although she had no idea what she would find there, her instinct told her to go in. She pushed at the heavy wooden door, which swung open with a groan. It was dark and cool inside. Rays of light fell through the cracks in the roof and insects buzzed around her as she walked in.

A stone slab covered with moss and cobwebs stood in the middle of the single room. Something was shining on top of the slab. Malva thought at first that a ray of light was lingering there, and looked up at the cracks in the dome, but no, it was not a sunbeam. She went closer, and then saw a long wand of pure crystal set in the stone. An intense, almost blinding light shone from its cut facets.

Malva looked at the crystal for a long time, fascinated by its perfect shape and mysterious brilliance. The light seemed to come from inside it. There was something alive about it, a kind of pulsing like a heartbeat. She put out her hand and touched its smooth surface.

No sooner had her fingers made contact with the crystal than

333

she felt warmed through by its light. Everything confused seemed to her suddenly clear. An intense sensation of well-being engulfed her; she felt she was herself, determined to live here for ever, to build her house here and make her dreams come true. The light acted on her like a revelation. Never mind Philomena and Uzmir! Never mind Galnicia, never mind the Coronada! Never mind Orpheus and his companions on the *Fabula*! She must live her life without them, far from them all. She must save herself by forgetting them.

Malva looked at her fingers on the crystal, and suddenly realised what it was.

"The Vuth-Nathor," she murmured.

She had known the name since old Bulo spoke of it on the *Estafador* just before the shipwreck. He had described its brilliance, he had warned his listeners against its lure. The Vuth-Nathor had haunted his nights and accompanied him through all his days. Yes, she remembered it all! The old man had wanted to take the treasure away, and that had brought disaster on him: he had been expelled from Elgolia, condemned to pursue a dream forever beyond his reach for the rest of his days, a dream that was now just a memory.

Suddenly she was afraid. She stepped back, her heart thudding, and moved away from the crystal.

Then she turned and ran out of the temple, her mind racing. When she was back in the sunlight looking at the white sand, the trees and the birds, she no longer knew what to do. The Vuth-Nathor had shown her, but it had not lasted long. She had only had to get away from the crystal for everything to become complicated again.

She sat down on the sand, drew her knees up to her chin and tried to think. If I stay here, what will happen? I'll build my house, perhaps I'll be able to live in freedom . . . but will I be alone forever?

Once again she felt like crying. Everything she had dreamed of until now was worthless without the people she loved. She had been wrong! She had thought that happiness awaited her in Elgolia, but in truth she had found only loneliness and regret.

She sighed and rubbed her face. On the other hand, what would happen if she gave up Elgolia? Could she join Orpheus, Lei and the others again? And once she was on board the *Fabula*, wouldn't they all be condemned to the Immuration?

What was the point of that?

Malva stretched out her legs and lay down in the sand, face turned to the sun. It seemed an impossible choice. She needed help, she wanted someone else to decide for her, or then again, why couldn't the wave that had brought her here take her away, even if it drowned her! She longed for Orpheus to appear on the beach, bend down and take her in his arms the way he had that very morning on the deck of the *Fabula* . . .

"Orpheus!" she called desperately.

But there was no reply, and her voice died away. The silence whispered its terrible murmuring in her ears. She ached all over.

After a while she got to her feet, dry-eyed. Swaying as she walked, she went back to the temple doorway. She had come to her decision as she cried and lay on the sand. And now, she entered the temple, went up to the Vuth-Nathor, and with both hands on it, pulled with all her strength. The light went through her again, illuminating her mind, but this time she resisted its call.

"Let me go back to my friends!" she asked. "My place is on board the *Fabula*!"

The Vuth-Nathor shone more brightly than ever. She felt a burning sensation on her palms, stinging worse and worse until she couldn't bear it. The burning made her cry out and suddenly take her hands off the crystal.

Nothing around her had changed. The temple was still there, damp and buzzing with insects.

"Let me go back to them!" she shouted again, for the benefit of the invisible Divinities. "I don't want to be here in Elgolia!"

The silence and the dim light made her heart sink. No divinity had lived here for a long time. There was no one to answer her request.

Devastated, Malva left the temple. Had old Bulo lied to her? Was the power of the Vuth-Nathor irreversible? Was she condemned to stay forever in the Bay of Dao-Boa, which no longer meant anything to her?

She went down to the sea. And suddenly, just as she was thinking of walking into the waves to end it all, she saw a sail on the horizon. A white sail, and the mainmast of a ship . . . it was the *Fabula*! Her heart leaped in her breast.

"Here I am!" she shouted, waving her arms. "Here I am! Come and pick me up, by Holy Harmony!"

She turned round. A ray of crystalline light was shining on top of the temple like the lantern of a lighthouse in the middle of the sea. Its radiance was guiding the *Fabula* in!

Malva jumped up and down and waved her arms until the ship was so close she could see the pale but beaming faces of Lei and the twins. They were laughing and crying at the same time, while Babilas and Orpheus handled the ship in the stern. She went into the water, first wading and then swimming, drawn to the *Fabula* as if by a magnet. At last Orpheus left the tiller and threw out the rope ladder so that she could climb back on board.

When she clambered over the rail her companions gathered around her. Zeph barked, but no one could say a word. Orpheus simply opened his arms, and Malva fell into them, unashamed, with unutterable relief and happiness.

"I'm back," she murmured. "Whatever happens I'll stay with you for always."

Then the *Fabula* turned and moved away from the shores of the deceptive land of Elgolia, whose promises Malva had turned down.

Another Stone of Life had crumbled inside the Nokros. The crew of the *Fabula* had only five days to find the way out of the Archipelago.

39

A Fishing Expedition

Malva said nothing about what had happened to her. During the next day the twins questioned her, begging her to tell them, but they got nowhere. The visions she had seen on Mount Ur-Tha haunted her memory. Every time she opened her eyes, she saw the beautiful shore of the Bay of Dao-Boa, and felt unspeakable pain. All she could do was shut herself in her cabin, pick up her pen and write down what she was feeling.

I have abandoned my dream, she wrote. *I fled from Elgolia. If Philomena knew, what would she think of me? I never stopped telling her about its beauties! Am I just a dreamer who's never satisfied? A spoilt child? An inconstant Princetta?*

Yet I don't regret my choice. I would have been so frightened alone on that island . . . and I'd never have forgiven myself for leaving the Fabula. I'd have felt like a criminal. So did I just act out of a sense of duty?

No.

I admit it . . . there was Orpheus too.

I can't tell the twins that. I've a feeling that they are very fond of me, and rather jealous. Poor things. But soon none of our little heartaches will matter much. When the Immuration opens up before the ship, we'll have nothing left but our tears.

Did I make the greatest mistake of my life when I decided to come back on board?

Sometimes Malva wondered if Catabea had intended to save her by calling up that wave and sending it towards Elgolia. Other times she thought the opposite, and suspected that the Guardian of the Archipelago had set a trap for her. What was the truth? It was impossible to know in this universe with its strange rules.

What I saw from the top of the tree preys on my mind, Malva wrote. *If my mother has died while I've been away, if Philomena is unhappy, if the Baighurs are at war and the Archont is murdering men on other ships to steal a Nokros from them, it's my fault. I am responsible for the whole disaster. How can I say so to the others? Even Orpheus might not want to listen. So I am confiding in my journal alone. Writing is all that's left to me . . . how angry my father would be to see me wasting ink and paper like this! But dear Coronador, do you still think that I write nothing but tall stories?*

When she had poured out her heart on paper long enough, Malva felt better. She looked at the Nokros. Acid was dripping on the second to last Stone of Life. Come on, she told herself severely. If we have only three days left to live, let's live them to the fullest!

She left her cabin and went up on deck. It was late in the morning now, and the sun was climbing to its highest point. The weather was hot, and the tides were still weak. As usual Finopico was fishing, with his feet wedged against the beak-head rail. Babilas was at the helm while Orpheus, Lei and the twins were repairing the damage to the sails.

"Let me help you," said Malva, going over to them.

Orpheus gave her a smile, and the twins were quick to make room for her. Malva was about to sit down when Finopico yelled out in pain. Leaning over the rail, he was tugging frantically at his line, but it was running out from its reel, and had cut the palm of his hand. With blood all over his jersey, the cook called Babilas to the rescue.

"It's a big one!" he cried. "A sparbot or a barraquin!"

His bamboo rod was bending under the weight of the fish, and the line was tense. Babilas lashed the tiller down, strode over and took hold of the rod. The two men tried hauling the line in, but the fish was thrashing about so strongly that they couldn't even get it above the water.

"We've hooked it!" cried Finopico. He turned the reel several times, while Babilas acted as counterweight.

The twins and Malva came over to the rail. Where the line disappeared into the water, they saw turbulence and huge bubbles. The fish struggling there must be an impressive size.

"Careful, I'm giving it some slack!" Finopico warned.

He let the line out a little, but at that moment it stretched taut so suddenly that it almost broke. Caught off balance, Finopico was carried away by his rod, and Babilas had to seize his belt to keep him from falling overboard.

"*Ganeg hosgid!*" swore the giant.

Finopico's distorted face had turned pale. His knuckles were white with effort and streams of sweat ran down his temples, but he wasn't giving up.

"Incredible!" he exclaimed. "I've never known such a strong fish! It may be . . . surely it is . . . a Ghoom!"

He and Babilas struggled for some time longer, shouting, grunting, cursing the waves and the sky, while the rest of the crew watched the struggle, fascinated. They could tell that the fish was leaping and diving below the frothing surface of the water, struggling fiercely for survival. Orpheus, who had joined the others, watched the scene uneasily.

"You'd better give up," he told the cook. "That fish is too strong for you."

Finopico turned a red and furious face on him. "Give up? Never! Someone find the harpoons! We must impale it and weaken it that way!"

Orpheus glanced unhappily at the surface of the water. "Oh, all right," he sighed. "Let's give it a try."

The twins hurried off to the galley and came back with the harpoons that Finopico had made on Jahalod-Rin's island. Meanwhile Babilas had rolled a hawser round Finopico's waist and tried its other end fast to the capstan, so that the cook wouldn't fall overboard.

"Harpoon it!" Finopico cried.

Hob and Peppe took aim and threw the harpoons into the churning water. The pointed wooden spearheads disappeared among the bubbles.

"Again!" shouted Finopico.

The twins took aim once more, and this time the harpoons hit their mark. For a moment they stood vertical in the water, and an enormous dorsal fin emerged, black and shining, serrated like a kitchen knife. Finopico let out a cry of victory, but his joy was short-lived.

In its pain, the monstrous fish bucked, lashed the surface violently with its tail, and shot straight ahead. Finopico's rod creaked but did not give way. A sudden movement shook the *Fabula*. Soon the ship gathered speed.

"It's dragging us away!" cried Orpheus, astonished.

Malva and Lei, both of them taken aback too, clung to the

341

rail. The enormous fish, wounded and furious, was hauling the *Fabula* along in its desperate course while Finopico, bending over his rod, shouted hysterically.

"Let go!" ordered Orpheus.

"No!" replied the cook. "It's the fish or me."

Babilas had stepped back. He seemed equally alarmed by the strength of the fish and Finopico's obstinacy.

The hull of the *Fabula* was now cutting through the water at an amazing speed. The fishing rod vibrated as the fin of the monster fish carved its way through the waves. Finopico was grimacing with pain or elation—it was hard to tell which—and the other passengers, pale with fear, felt the wind and the spray whipping into their faces.

Suddenly a mass of rocks appeared on the horizon, black and jagged. Orpheus felt his heart in his mouth. "It's dragging us towards the reefs!"

"*Bolbh kiglaeth yawz?*" asked Babilas in his husky voice.

"He ask if he should break rod?" Lei immediately translated.

"If the fish can't do it you won't be able to either!" said Orpheus desperately. As with all the strange things they had seen in the Archipelago, there was no explaining the power of Finopico's fishing rod to resist the strain.

"Leave it to me!" shouted Finopico. "I want this fish! It will exhaust itself. I know it will! By Holy Harmony, Captain, don't deny me this victory!"

Distraught, Orpheus looked in turn at Babilas standing ready to intervene, Lei and Malva watching wide-eyed, Finopico still clinging to his rod, the fish . . . and the reefs now rapidly approaching.

"If Babilas comes anywhere near me I won't answer for myself!" cried Finopico. With these words, he took one hand off the rod and unsheathed the knife he carried at his belt. Madness and passion seemed to double his usual strength. Without even flinching, he held the rod with one hand while he brandished his knife in the other. "I want this monster! No one's going to tell me what to do!"

Orpheus shuddered, and felt his hair stand on end. He took a deep breath to give himself a moment to think. Malva, Lei and the twins were already retreating towards the steps down into the hatch, dragging Zeph along by the collar to get him to safety. The angular, menacing shapes of the reefs stuck above the water. They were less than half a kilometre from the *Fabula* now.

"It's not a Ghoom of the Deeps!" Orpheus suddenly shouted to Finopico. "Your fish has only one tail, and its scales are black!"

The cook, still in control of his rod, turned an ironic glance on Orpheus. "Well spotted, Captain! But . . . but even if it's not a Ghoom, I . . . I'm not letting go!"

"We'll crash on the rocks!" replied Orpheus angrily. He made a move in Finopico's direction. The cook reacted at once, holding his blade in front of him. Insane laughter shook him from head to toe.

"The reefs! A fine death for sailors! We'll be torn to pieces! Crushed! Drowned! Well, that's much better . . . than ending up in the Immuration!"

He braced his legs a little more. Clinging to his rod and lashed to the capstan, his red hair blowing in the wind, he looked like a divinity riding astride his destiny. Near the hatch, the twins and the two girls were moaning in fear.

"Stop him, Captain!"

"We don't want to be torn apart!"

The reefs were quite close now. Given the speed that the *Fabula* was making, Orpheus wasn't even sure that he could still

343

avoid a collision. Thoughts came thick and fast in his mind: should he risk the life of Babilas? And his own? And the lives of all the crew? He was in a terrible dilemma. He would never forgive himself for what he was about to do . . . and yet do it he must!

In his own turn he took out his knife, raced to the capstan and began sawing through the rope that made the cook's body fast to the ship.

"What are you doing?" Finopico shouted.

"Let go of your rod!" Orpheus begged him again, seeing the hawser fray. "We can still save ourselves!"

The cook's mouth was twisted in fury. His gaze was fixed on the fin of the great fish and he seemed not to understand anything, as if he were obsessed by the creature to the point of losing his senses.

"No! I won't let g—."

He never had time to finish his sentence. The rope lashing him to the ship suddenly gave way, and the power of the monstrous fish met with no more resistance: Finopico tumbled over the rail, fell into the sea and was carried away by the fishing line. Lei and Malva cried out in distress.

The *Fabula* rocked on the waves, carried on by the impetus of its course, but finally slowed down and came to rest only a little way from the jagged rocks. A horrified and dismayed silence fell over the crew. The fish had disappeared into the depths, taking with it the rod, the line and the unfortunate cook.

Orpheus fell to his knees on deck, his knife in his hand, his face drawn. The others did not move. They stood there motionless, transfixed by the horror of the situation.

The waves lapping at the rocks made their perpetual murmur. Above the ship the sun was still shining, but down below, the crew was crushed by the weight of a terrible truth: in both the Known and the Unknown Worlds, living things could die, suffer, love, hate, struggle or surrender. Only nature itself never changed. Despite tragedy and torment, there would always be the waves, and the sun would always rise and set.

It was Lei and Malva who found the strength to move first. They went over to Orpheus, side by side, and put their hands on his shoulders.

"Thank you," they said in unison.

Orpheus raised his head. His eyes were full of tears. He looked at his hands and his knife. He felt he was a murderer.

"There was nothing else you could do," Malva tried to comfort him. "Finopico was out of control."

"He gone mad," Lei agreed.

Babilas had grasped the rail and was leaning over it to see if he could spot anything. But when he turned and his eyes met Orpheus's, everyone knew that there was no hope left. The cook had gone down with his monstrous catch.

Later, when Malva went down to her berth that evening, she was horrified to see that all but one Stone of Life had been entirely dissolved. It was as if the body of Finopico had disappeared for a second time. She began sobbing.

"I hate the Nokros!" she moaned. "I hate Catabea and this Archipelago! I hate the sea!"

She picked up the large hourglass and held it on her lap. There was only one Stone left in the upper part. One Stone, two days . . . and now only seven companions on board the *Fabula*.

"We'll never get out of here," breathed Malva, fascinated by the blood-red colour of the acid.

For a moment she felt like flinging the Nokros away, throwing it at the wall with all her might, to break to pieces there. She pulled herself together. She mustn't do that. Catabea had made it very clear that this wretched instrument must remain intact to the end.

"To the end," Malva repeated out loud. "But the end of what?"

Finopico's sudden death had devastated everyone; even Zeph, who refused to leave the deck, although night had fallen. At heart, every one of them felt that it was all over. The *Fabula* would never find her way out of the Archipelago, any more than all the other ships before her.

Malva rose to her feet with the Nokros in her hands, and left her berth. Stepping slowly, she crossed the space between-decks and knocked at Orpheus's door. When he opened it, showing a face ravaged by regret and sorrow, Malva held out the hourglass.

"Here, you take it," she said. "I don't want to watch time passing any more. The time held inside that thing looks like blood."

Orpheus put out his hands and took the Nokros. "You're right," he said. "It's for me to bear the burden of the countdown . . . since everything that's happened is my fault."

Malva stiffened, and shook her head. "It's all *my* fault, Captain. I was the one who started it. If I hadn't fled from the Citadel you'd never have set off after me. Not you, or Finopico, or all the others. I'm only a selfish, stupid little Princetta."

Her amber eyes misted over. Orpheus bit his lip.

"You mustn't think like that," he said. "In spite of everything that's happened, and even if we're all thrown into the Immuration, I shall never regret putting to sea and meeting

346

you. But for you I might well have died of despair back home in Galnicia."

Malva was looking at him so intently that he felt himself blushing.

"You're so . . . so alive!" he stammered. "So beautiful and so brave."

"Oh, don't," she said in a faltering voice. "It's very kind of you to say such things, but they're not true. I'm not brave; everything I've done was out of thoughtlessness or stupidity."

"I rather like thoughtlessness," retorted Orpheus. "I wasted so much time being wise and sensible and fearing consequences. Please don't regret being what you are."

He placed a clumsy hand on Malva's cheek. When she felt his large, warm palm against her face, she trembled. He took his hand away at once.

"Forgive me," he murmured.

"No, I . . ."

She wanted to keep him with her, but Orpheus closed his cabin door.

For a few long moments Malva stood there without moving. Her heart was beating fast in her chest, her wild emotions clashing like swords in a fight. That hand, so gentle, so large, so warm, placed on her cheek as softly as a butterfly—it felt so good! Had she any right to feel happy when the whole crew was in mourning?

Sobs mounted in her throat. She turned on her heel, and fled to her cabin.

Where can I begin this evening? Orpheus wrote in his logbook. *I don't seem to be able to put what's going on inside me into words. The worst and the best of it alike, the sweet and the harsh. I don't know who I am anymore.*

He turned his head to his cabin door, imagining Malva's distraught face there again. Then his eyes returned to the Nokros.

I feel so many contradictory things! I wish I could die, to punish myself for cutting the rope that secured Finopico, yet at the same time I so much want to go on living and stay with my companions. Have we any right to be sad and happy at the same time? I feel as if madness lies in wait for us in this Archipelago—even more so than the improbable-sounding Immuration.

I'm in the process of falling . . .

He suddenly stopped writing. The next few words were so overwhelming that he didn't know if he ought to go on. Writing them down would be painful . . . but it would give him such pleasure too! His hand was shaking.

. . . falling in love with the Princetta. Yes, that's what it is. I'm in love with her, with her eyes, her face, her mouth, her laughter and her tears, her doubts, her tempers, her rages and her dreams.

Now that he had confessed it, his pen ran across the paper without restraint; it was like a river flowing on.

She disturbs me to the core of my being. My heart leaps when I see her, my hands go moist, my thoughts are all confused, I smile stupidly. I'm not myself anymore. I'm not my father's son, or the orphaned child of my mother, or the Captain of the Fabula . . . I'm just a mass of tangled feelings, a man who . . .

He stopped again, and tried to see his reflection in his shaving mirror. He did indeed see a man there, with his cheeks hidden by a growth of beard and burn marks. A stronger, harder, more experienced man than he was when he looked at himself in the mirror of his house in the Lower Town. He frowned, and went on writing, but more slowly and hesitantly.

I am nineteen years old now. Malva is only sixteen. How could she love me as I love her? I'm an old man to her! I can't hope for anything but to keep her safe and take her out of the Archipelago, so that she can go on her way as she intends. I must hide what's in my heart, for fear of frightening her, for then she might take flight again. I must play the part of Captain, protector . . . and then, if I succeed in that, disappear from her life. Let her fly away. Like a bird . . . a magnificent bird.

He stopped for breath. The lines he had just put down on paper were growing larger and smaller by turn before his grief-stricken and exhausted eyes.

How could Malva ever love a man who sent a friend to his death?

Worn out, he closed the logbook.

40

The Last Stone of Life

During the night, the *Fabula* was caught in strong currents again. The water started growling like a ferocious animal and heaving under the hull, making any manoeuvres impossible. At dawn, the currents grew yet stronger, carrying the ship towards what seemed to be the heart of the Archipelago.

A network of islets had emerged from the water, like an endless necklace bordering the sea route along which the ship was now sailing. Most of them were desert islands, bleak and black as chunks of coal. Now and then less hostile islands appeared, covered with vegetation, or with birds that perched there motionless, but the current kept the *Fabula* from going ashore.

On board, the mood was one of anxiety and deep sadness. Stocks of food were running low. They had to scrape out the jars and divide the few dried fish they had left into seven portions. Their drinking water had taken on an unpleasant flavour of rotten wood.

The day passed dreadfully slowly. It was becoming clear to them all that the *Fabula* would never get out of the Archipelago.

That evening, when the crew assembled on the poop deck of the ship to share their last provisions, Peppe burst into sobs.

"It's all over!" he stammered through his tears. "We . . . we've failed! The Patrols will come looking for us tomorrow!"

The others exchanged glances of dismay. Catabea's words were present in all their minds, and no one could contradict Peppe.

"It's our fault," murmured Hob suddenly in a gloomy voice. "You've all faced tests . . . except for Peppe and me. We're not wanted on this ship. We're only stowaways."

Orpheus swallowed painfully.

"You mustn't think like that," he told the brothers. "If we fail it's no single person's fault. Zeph hasn't been put through a test either. And no one holds it against him. Well, it's the same with you two."

Lei, Malva and Babilas nodded in silence. But Peppe continued to weep and wail. He looked up at the sky and cried, "Send me a test too! Please! Anything! Send monsters, dragons, packs of wolves! I'll fight them, you just wait and see!"

Of course nothing happened. The sky was clear. A few stars began to come out.

"*Archim bawas*," sighed Babilas. "*Foadrom baidir.*"

"We must prepare die," Lei sadly translated. "Is fate."

A gloomy silence followed these words. The dregs of their soup grew cold in their bowls. Only Zeph went on lapping the yellowish liquid, unaware of the misfortune hanging over him.

Then Hob said, "The fortune-teller lied to us. We believed her because . . . because it was so nice to believe in it!" He took Peppe by the shoulders. "It doesn't matter," he whispered to him. "We've been on a splendid voyage all the same. Never mind the glory and riches, never mind . . ."

He raised his head with its dirty, tangled mop of hair, and looked at his companions. Then, in a small voice, he told them the secret that he and Peppe had kept so carefully until now.

"The cards foretold that we would do great things. They said we were destined to rescue the Princetta and save Galnicia from disaster. We stowed away on board the *Errabunda* to make sure the prediction came true. But best of all, the cards said that when we came home we . . . we'd become princes."

This time no one felt like laughing at the twins' gullibility.

"Princes? But . . . but of what country?" asked Orpheus gently.

Hob hugged his brother again and cleared his throat. "Princes of Galnicia," he murmured. "The fortune-teller said we . . . we could always marry the Princetta. That's our secret."

Taken aback, Malva raised her eyebrows. "I was supposed to marry you? Both of you?"

The expression on the two brothers' faces showed that they didn't know how it could be done either, but they hadn't thought too hard about the details.

"It was such an amazing thing to hear," said Hob apologetically. "Orphans like us, poor boys, thieves and vagabonds getting to be Princes! Now I know the fortune-teller was laughing at us. And even if we did manage to escape the Immuration, we know perfectly well that the Princetta wouldn't want us."

He said this so sadly that Malva felt a lump in her throat.

"I . . . I'm very fond of you," she murmured. "Don't think I'm not . . . but I—"

"Don't apologise," Hob interrupted. "People can't help how they feel."

Orpheus and Malva looked at each other sorrowfully. What the boys had said left them speechless. For a moment Hob had shared his dream with everyone, but now that vision of a bright future would never come true. He knew it, and admitting that there was nothing he could do about it had cost him dearly.

That evening, anyway, there was no future for any of them. Hardly any acid was left in the alembic on top of the Nokros. The last Stone of Life was being eaten away, full of holes, and broken in two. Like the hearts of the passengers on the *Fabula*.

When the wind rose on the morning of the last day, Orpheus had the sails taken in, hoping to slow the ship down slightly. But the winds blew so strongly that soon the *Fabula* seemed to be almost flying over the water. Gusts blew in under the cabin doors, making the timbers creak and raising sinister sounds like lamentations. It was cold. The crew had nothing to eat. Their hands closed on invisible things. They waited. There was no hope left in their wild eyes.

Eventually they shut themselves into their own berths, unable to meet each other's eyes or find a word of comfort to say. Even Orpheus and Malva, who dreamed only of spending this last day together, could not bring themselves to touch or speak to each other. Every time they found themselves alone together a fire flamed up inside them, and then they turned away.

Only Zeph had changed none of his habits: he stayed on deck, lying stretched out full length in the midst of disaster.

Towards midday, however, the winds died down and the current was not so strong. A sunbeam broke through the cloud cover. One by one the six passengers came out of their cabins. Up on deck, they turned their faces to the sun with the avidity of those who know they have little time left.

It was at this moment that they heard the growling.

It sounded like an animal and like stones grinding together, a growling that came from below, rising from the seabed or even beyond. It made the hull of the *Fabula* vibrate, and the mast shook. All the passengers felt a savage shock inside their heads.

Zeph had risen to his feet. He raised his wet nose and pricked up his ears, facing east. His stiff, arthritic hindquarters didn't prevent him from going over to the bulwarks, where he even managed to put his paws up on the rail.

Orpheus was going to see what scent he had picked up when the growling came again, even more powerful and deafening, leaving the Captain rooted to the spot. None of his companions seemed able to move a muscle either. The sea had begun swelling and pitching, while the noise grew ever louder.

Paws propped on the rail, Zeph was sniffing the air, uttering little yaps.

Suddenly the waves opened, and a huge creature emerged right in front of the *Fabula*. It was seated on a black rock, from which streams of sticky lava flowed.

Orpheus tried to speak, but his mouth, like the rest of his body, would not obey him. Powerless and terrified, all he could do was watch the monster that had just barred their way.

It was a gigantic dog with a bristling coat and powerful muscles. When it opened its mouth, its red fangs showed, and a trickle of molten rock ran down its chest. A dreadful smell of sulphur immediately rose to the travellers' noses, and Zeph began barking.

The monster turned its muzzle towards the St. Bernard, opened its fiery eyes and stared at Zeph. It towered above him from the top of its volcanic rock, but Zeph didn't back down. He went on barking defiantly, evidently unaware that he was the weaker party. The creature stretched itself in his direction, coming so close that its chops brushed the ship's rail.

Zeph growled again and arched his own neck forward. The two dogs were now nose to nose, ears back, ready to fight. From the monster's red jaws drops of lava fell steaming into the sea.

Zeph suddenly leaped aside. Miraculous as it might seem, he appeared almost to have recovered the vigour of his youth.

The monster immediately opened its jaws and tried to bite him. But Zeph was running up and down the deck of the *Fabula*, barking furiously. Up on its rock, the monster swayed its enormous head from side to side, tracking the St. Bernard's movements.

Orpheus and his companions watched this unlikely confrontation in stunned silence. Zeph seemed so weak by comparison! He might jump, leap, snap his jaws and raise a threatening paw, but he wouldn't last long against such a fiery adversary.

The black dog suddenly crouched on its rock and then leaped. It flew through the air and landed heavily on the deck of the ship.

Orpheus and the others turned pale. At close quarters the animal seemed even more enormous. Surely it would sweep Zeph away with a single blow of its paw.

Zeph, however, continued to dart about in front of the black dog's nose. He ran around the chests and empty barrels, brushed close to the rail, skirted the mainmast. But the creature was not impressed. It lunged at Zeph, once, twice, three times, digging its claws into the planks of the deck, biting crates until they broke—yet each time Zeph escaped. The lava dripping from the black dog's mouth left burn marks on deck, and there was the suffocating smell of sulphur and burnt flesh in the air.

At the seventh attempt the huge dog managed to bite the St. Bernard's tail. Zeph let out a howl, twisted and managed to free himself. He set off in panic, running in zigzags.

When the monster flung itself at Zeph again, the St. Bernard was driven back against the bulwarks. Orpheus thought Zeph's throat would be torn out before his eyes, but the old dog's reactions were amazing. He turned like lightning and leaped overboard. The big dog, carried away by its own weight, left the rail in splinters and followed Zeph as he fell.

From where they stood, the passengers on the *Fabula* could see nothing of what was going on below. They heard the water boil, and saw dense vapours rise in the air.

Suddenly Zeph came into view again; he had swum to the hot rock and clambered up on it, scorching his paws. Behind him, the black dog's dreadful jaws tried to seize their prey one last time, but its strength seemed to have left it. When Zeph reached the top of the rock, the black dog let out an anguished growl, and sank into the depths of the ocean. The St. Bernard had replaced the monster on its fiery throne.

At that moment Orpheus could feel his fingers, arms and legs again. Beside him, his companions recovered their voices and their power of movement. They ran to the rail, shouting the old St. Bernard's name.

On the rock, the flow of lava had dried up. Zeph, who had been yelping with pain, stopped bounding about. The rock had suddenly gone cold and was no longer burning his paws. He stood still, and turned his head towards the *Fabula*.

"Zeph!" shouted Orpheus. "Get off there, quick!"

"*Ilgad korf!*"

"Come back!" shouted the twins. "Hurry up!"

Zeph growled once more, and suddenly stopped moving. He

had bent his big head to one side, and was sitting on the hardened rock. He no longer barked or growled.

His eyes suddenly turned dull. The black rock was enveloping his paws, his legs and his tail. Before the horrified gaze of his companions on the *Fabula*, he was gradually consumed by the rock. Within a few moments, he had turned entirely into stone.

When even his muzzle disappeared under the black rock, Lei, Malva and the twins burst into tears.

"Oh, Zeph!" murmured Orpheus.

He raised his face to the sky to howl with grief and rage. But his cry was stifled in his throat. The metal silhouettes of the Patrols had just appeared, and they were making straight for the *Fabula*.

41

The Immuration

There was nothing but turbulent water as far as the eye could see, and the wind was still blowing the same way. Lightning flashed in the clouds as if the end of the world hung over this part of the Archipelago. From time to time, cries of despair seemed to resound in the clouds, distress calls from the depths of time that made the listeners shudder. This appeared to be a place where all human lamentations from the dawn of time came together.

Malva took Orpheus's hand. They did not exchange a word, but their intertwined fingers spoke of desperation, love and fear.

Lei, Babilas, Peppe and Hob grouped together at the prow, their faces marked with grief. When the Patrols flew over the *Fabula* they did not even tremble. They looked at them in silence, as a condemned man might watch a firing squad on its way.

There were grinding sounds, a turmoil of strident cries, and the human-headed birds came down on the battered deck of the ship.

"Welcome to the centre of the Archipelago," said the first bird ceremoniously, blinking its tiny eyes.

The others folded their wings and swayed their long necks.

"All the power of Catabea is manifest here!" announced another bird. "Here all converges and comes together! The sky and the sea join here! This is the axis on which our World turns!"

A third bird left the group and came over to Orpheus. "Captain, give us the Nokros!"

Orpheus felt his strength fail him. He would have liked to disobey, seize the bird's flabby neck and wring it, but his anger had run out. He withdrew his hand from Malva's, and with his back bowed went down to his cabin to find the Killer of Time.

When he came back with it, the others saw that there was almost nothing left of the last Stone of Life. The final drops of morbic acid would soon dissolve it. Orpheus put it down in front of the bird, which bent its neck to examine it.

"So you have failed, strangers! Just as we expected!" cackled the bird.

The assembled Patrols quivered with satisfaction.

"According to our information, you only just failed," remarked the bird who had spoken first. "You had only one test left to take, but your time has run out!"

"Not yet!" cried Orpheus, pointing to what was left in the hourglass. "Your Law says that we are not condemned until the last Stone has entirely disappeared!"

"What are you hoping for?" asked one of the Patrols, with derision. "When you passed the rock of the Black Dog you crossed the threshold. The currents are carrying you on. It's too late!"

Malva went up to the bird, her chin trembling. "Two of our companions are dead!" she said in a broken voice. "Was their sacrifice for nothing? You said yourselves that we nearly succeeded."

All the birds tilted their terrible little heads to one side—the same side—and looked scornfully at Malva.

"Sacrifice or no sacrifice, that's none of our business!" laughed one of them. "Nobody asked you to sacrifice yourselves. If two of you did, no doubt there was no other way open to them. There were eight of you, and you had eight Stones of Life. Only six of you were able to face the truth about yourselves. You have failed."

"It's my fault!" howled Peppe, burying his face in his hands. "Hob was honest! He dared to reveal our secret, and that counted as a test! But I'm not capable of anything. I'm the one responsible! Take me and let the others go!"

He flung himself on his knees and crawled towards the Patrols. But Hob caught him by the collar, and hauled him back with all his might.

"There's nothing to discuss!" one of the Patrols snapped. "Catabea doesn't decide piecemeal; the whole crew of a ship suffers the same fate. That is the Law."

At this moment another bird cried, "Tow her away!"

In perfect unison, the Patrols unfolded their metal wings and took off. Some closed their claws over the break-head rail, other clung to the poop taffrails, others again to the shrouds, the foretop, the capstan, the stays, the davits. They were everywhere. The ship bristled with the strange shapes of the Patrols like enemy arrows.

"All over now," murmured Lei. "We die in Immuration."

Babilas wrapped his arms round the twins, as if to protect them, but deep dismay could be read in his eyes. His astonishing strength had not helped him to save his fiancée in the past, and it

360

was still no use to him today. All he hoped for now was to help the two boys endure the shock and pass from the world of the living into the Immuration without too much pain.

Malva drew Lei towards her with her right hand, while her left hand held Orpheus's. She remembered the peaceful shores of the island of Elgolia, the soft meadows, the white sand . . . Orpheus bent his face over hers. She saw her own reflection in his blue eyes: the image of a young woman with inky black hair who had surely never been so beautiful before. Orpheus's lips touched her forehead. A thrill passed through her. And suddenly the *Fabula* took off.

Towing her with their wings, the Patrols carried the ship through the air, their long necks straining with the effort. They flew rhythmically, like machines. The ship flew through the sky, through the clouds, casting its shadow on the waves.

Down below, far beneath the hull, the passengers of the *Fabula* saw a huge whirlpool. It was the terrifying vastness of the Immuration: at the centre of the whirlpool, a black and gaping mouth opened on a void. The waters were pouring into it in a resounding cascade that seemed to flow on for ever. It was like seeing the real frontiers of the Worlds. That obscure, disturbing eye seemed to be swallowing up the sea with an ogre's greed. And in a moment it would swallow up the *Fabula* too.

"What's down there?" cried Malva to Orpheus, as the wind blew her hair back.

There was absolute terror in her wide, amber eyes. Orpheus felt his throat contract.

"I don't know! I've no idea what's down there! Stay with me!"

The condemned crew were huddling together, trying to overcome the fear flooding through them. They exchanged desperate glances, a few words came out, cries and moans, and

Babilas held the twins so tight that he almost choked them. Two tiny pieces of the Stone of Life were left in the Nokros, and a great deal of powder.

When the Patrols were right above the eye of the Immuration, and the dreadful noise of the whirlpool prevented anyone from speaking, they all knew that the final moment had come. The birds beat their wings in reverse to slow the flying ship.

"May the Law of the Archipelago be kept, may the sentence be carried out!" pronounced all the Patrols together.

They abruptly opened their claws and folded their legs. The *Fabula* instantly dropped into the eye of the Immuration.

The six passengers felt their stomachs rise to their throats. There was a deafening whistle and a great gust of wind.

At that moment Peppe escaped from Babilas's arms. The giant had no time even to move. Peppe rushed forward, leaped over the ship's rail—and jumped into the void before the *Fabula*'s hull had even touched its rim. His small, disjointed body plunged straight into the darkness, ahead of the *Fabula*, whose sails, spread in the wind, slowed her fall slightly.

He did not utter a single cry.

The others hardly had time to realise what was happening. Only Hob immediately sensed his brother's death in his own body. He thought his guts were tearing apart, his heart exploding, his soul was ablaze. And suddenly the Nokros broke to splinters, scattering the brown powder.

"Peppe!" shouted Hob, collapsing on deck.

The shock that followed almost threw him overboard, but the halyards tangling with the sheets caught him. The others clung as best they could to anything within reach as the *Fabula* was sucked into the Immuration like an insect being swallowed up by a toad.

362

Then there was nothing but a great black silence that was so dense that the ship seemed to float in it, weightless.

The sudden calm allowed Babilas, Lei, Malva and Orpheus to pluck up some courage. They crawled towards each other, feeling their way. Their gasping breath was misty in the dark. They felt empty, as if an explosion had blasted them apart. But when they realised that they were still alive their fingers intertwined again.

Now and then the darkness was illuminated by bright flashes which left temporary imprints on their eyes. Jolts threatened to throw them off balance. But they stayed there, lying on the ship's deck, their stomachs flat against its wooden planks, linking hands.

Suddenly, brighter lights lit up the dark. It was as if torches were flaring on the walls of a grotto. But when they looked more closely, the five survivors of the fall saw that these were no ordinary torches. Humans were being slowly consumed by fire as they hung from the sides of the Immuration.

The hair of some of them was in flames, the arms or feet of others were burning. There they hung in the middle of nowhere, twisting in pain, lighting the way for passers-by. It was such a terrible sight that Malva, on the verge of nausea, could not bear it and closed her eyes.

The *Fabula* went on falling, slowly and steadily now. She passed the successive levels of the Immuration, showing the terrified passengers the torments in store for them. Some prisoners were chained to pulleys, dying slowly of hunger and thirst. Others, buried in earthen cavities, were waiting to die of suffocation. They were in convulsions, opening their gap-toothed mouths like fish out of water. Others again were covered with insects, were being quartered, boiled alive, lacerated by daggers, were bleeding, contorting themselves, praying aloud for death.

At last, Orpheus rested his forehead on the deck of his ship, unable to take any more. So this was the Immuration: a prison to torture souls and bodies until Death came at last. A nightmare, an abomination, a horror.

The *Fabula*'s funereal progress went on for a long time, and no image was spared the travellers, who hardly dared breathe, nauseated and brimming over with pity as they were. They waited, still holding hands, for the fall to end and for the worst to be inflicted on them too.

But suddenly they saw daylight.

Orpheus, Malva, Lei and Babilas raised their heads. Above them, where the black hole of the Immuration should have been, the sky was bright blue. The ship's sails flew in the breeze and water lapped against the *Fabula*'s hull.

Orpheus stood up, supporting Malva as well as he could. He frowned, dazzled by the reflection of the sunlight on the water. Babilas and Lei rose too and turned, limping.

What had happened? Why this sudden bright light, this sunny day? Was it a hallucination? Yet they had all seen the same thing: the Immuration had suddenly disappeared. Not knowing what to think, they searched the sky for some sign, some kind of clue.

Then they saw Hob at the top of the mast, his legs caught in the rigging. The poor boy no longer even had the strength to call out or struggle free.

"*Yneb dawl!*" exclaimed Babilas, scrambling quickly to his rescue.

"He alive!" sighed Lei.

When Babilas had brought Hob down, and the two of them

had joined the others on deck their tears flowed, but they smiled too, and all their hearts were overflowing with emotion. The Immuration had obviously let them go at the last moment, and all they had done was pass through it from end to end.

"It was Peppe," said Hob in a shaking voice. "He . . . he so much wanted to show that he was brave." The boy gagged, stopped breathing for a moment, and went scarlet in the face. Then he burst into tears. "He thought it was his fault," he cried between painful sobs. "He couldn't bear the idea! So he threw himself . . . he jumped . . ."

Hob stammered, wept, stuttered out confused words for some time, while the others, mute and helpless, witnessed his grief and couldn't comfort him.

Finally Hob sat down on the capstan, exhausted.

"He did that . . . he did that . . ." he kept repeating, his cheeks stained with dirt and tears.

At last Babilas knelt down in front of him and hugged him. "*Yvn Peppe oiraim an bardan,*" he whispered. "*Alch islu gwelchan mabeut. Cosgoaim danrh pobaim.*"

Lei, who had come closer to them, translated, though she was shaking all over. "Your brother Peppe save life of you and us. He jump when last drop of acid reach Stone in Nokros. Now we must live to thank him."

Hob let the giant rock him in his arms, still murmuring words in his incomprehensible language, and gradually his tears dried up.

When they were all calm again, Orpheus went over to the battered rail and looked at the ocean stretching out ahead. Malva joined him. She was in a state of shock, but her eyes shone again when they rested on Orpheus. He felt his heart beating violently.

"I think we've left the Archipelago," he said in a neutral voice, still numbed by too much grief. "Peppe did a terrible thing, but thanks to him we're back in the Known World." He bent his eyes on Malva's, and took a deep breath before he ventured to go on. "What do you want to do, Princetta? Now that we've survived so many trials, I suppose anything is possible."

"Anything?" repeated Malva. She sighed. No doubt Orpheus was right. After seeing some of their friends die and others suffer, after feeling such fear and urgency, the travellers' natures had probably become harder. Their priorities were not the same as before. Some things that had seemed important now didn't matter. Etiquette, politeness, the demands of a comfortable life—none of it seemed to have any point now. So yes, anything really was possible.

Malva put her hands to her temples. The blood was beating in her skull. At that moment her decision seemed to her obvious. She raised her head.

"I would like," she said, looking steadily at Orpheus, "I would like to go back to Galnicia with you, Captain."

PART THREE

Coming Home

42

The Twin Stars

When night fell, Orpheus stood on deck to observe the sky. The stars were back in their familiar places: Proximedes shone in the east, Aldebagol in the west, and at the zenith Orpheus saw the constellation of Oriopaea.

"Come and look," he told Hob, who was still looking helplessly at the bowl of food that Babilas had brought him. It had gone cold ages ago. However, he raised his head, hesitated briefly, and then joined the Captain. He lay down on deck beside him, looking up at the vast night sky.

"See that?" said Orpheus, indicating a luminous point in the heavens. "That's Alphius, the brightest of them all. And there's the constellation of the Allicaitor. You can see the stars Betelrig and Vegeb beside it."

Hob followed Orpheus's finger, more interested than he had expected by the beauty of the heavens. Each star was like a flower. And to Hob, who had never been taught anything at all, knowing their names was like possessing a treasure. Orpheus told him all he knew: the names of Altares, Ichab, Tolimuk, Hyperades. It was as if he were singing a lullaby. Finally he pointed to two stars, very close to each other and shining brightly.

"Those are twin stars," he explained. "Their names are Astor and Olux."

Hob shivered. Twin stars? Were they really identical?

"From Earth," Orpheus went on, "they look almost stuck to each other, but they're really thousands of kilometres apart."

"Like Peppe and me, then," the boy murmured. "We're thousands of kilometres apart, yet we'll always be together."

Orpheus nodded, and there was silence. Hob's eyes were fixed on that part of the sky where the twin stars shone.

"Every time I want to think about my brother," he said, "every time I miss him badly, every time I need to talk to him, I'll talk to those stars. It will be as if Peppe were there looking down on me."

A faint smile touched his lips, and at that moment Orpheus knew that sooner or later, Hob would manage to live his own life, and Peppe's absence would not be too much of a burden on him.

"Do you really think the fortune-teller was making fun of us?" Hob suddenly asked. "Peppe believed that story of being princes so much. He really thought one of us would marry Mal—I mean the Princetta."

"What about you?" asked Orpheus gently. "Did you believe it too?"

The boy's mouth drooped slightly with disappointment. "You're the one she loves, though, aren't you?" he sighed. "You're the one she'll marry."

Orpheus could not repress a wild leap of his heart. He didn't know exactly what Malva felt about him, but she had flung herself into his arms, had let him kiss her several times without objection, and then there was that intensity between them when they looked at each other. He didn't know anything about women, but intuition told him that they had forged a very strong bond. He skilfully dodged Hob's question.

"Malva hasn't been through all those trials and ordeals just to find herself going into the Sanctuary with a husband on her arm yet again, has she?"

"She's free," admitted Hob gravely.

"Free as air," Orpheus repeated thoughtfully.

Another silence settled between them. In the sky above, more stars were coming out all the time: constellations, nebulas, galaxies. Compared to those distant powers, the problems of the human heart seemed unimportant. A thousand things could happen on Earth: there could be storms and tempests, war and famine could ravage nations, love could be born and die, but none of that would prevent the stars from following their course across the sky. Observing it, Hob and Orpheus felt soothed.

"Those stars will guide us back to Galnicia," murmured Orpheus. "And once we're home we shall only have to look at them to remind ourselves of what we all went through together."

Two days later the *Fabula* crossed paths with a vessel from the kingdom of Norj on its way to the Orniant. Its captain, a tall, fair-haired young man, offered to take the survivors of the Archipelago on board his ship, but with his companions' consent Orpheus declined the offer. They all wanted to make for Galnicia as fast as possible. The captain of the other ship did not try to make them change their minds. He gave them food, two barrels of drinking water, a fishing net, and a few elementary navigational instruments: a map, a compass and a sextant. He couldn't help asking the exhausted travellers what had happened to them, but Lei, acting as interpreter, was very evasive. She told him about the storm and their shipwreck on an island, but she didn't mention the existence of the Archipelago or the Immuration. Everyone on board the *Fabula* knew it wouldn't be easy to explain their passage beyond the boundaries of the Known World. For the time being, it seemed best to say as little as possible about it.

During the last dinner they ate on board the Norjian vessel, they asked their host for news of Galnicia. He didn't seem to know anything about the disappearance of the Princetta, how her marriage had been called off, or the diplomatic consequences. Galnicia, he said, was a country that kept to itself. It was secretive, and so unwelcoming, that no stranger had set foot in it for a long time.

These remarks troubled Orpheus a great deal. It had been about a hundred days since he had set off aboard the *Errabunda* as quartermaster, not a remarkable length of time for such a dangerous expedition. Had the Coronador lost hope as he waited? Had he been deposed by conspiracies and intrigues? If not, what accounted for the way Galnicia had so suddenly shut itself and its misfortunes off from the rest of the world? The Norjian captain, who had been at sea for several weeks himself, was unable to answer these questions.

Malva also felt deeply uneasy when she heard the news. The vision she had seen of her country as she sat astride the thousand-year-old tree on Mount Ur-Tha came back to her: the funeral procession, the bare trees, the disturbing silence reigning over the Citadel . . . it looked very much as if there had been some disaster.

And yet when the *Fabula* put to sea again the next day, the five members of the crew found themselves in a cheerful mood. Well fed, wearing clean clothes and provided with sea charts, they enjoyed sailing over familiar seas. They could find their bearings again, and any dangers lying in wait seemed insignificant compared to those they had already overcome. So when the sails were hoisted and Orpheus took the helm, crying, "On course for Galnicia!" his companions' faces lit up. Orpheus smiled at them. He was happy to be going home too, although at heart he thought how odd that was. He had hated Galnicia, and dreamed only of leaving it—how could he be impatient to set foot in the country again? When he saw the Upper Town once more, wouldn't his ghosts come back to haunt and torment him? Wouldn't he immediately regret leaving the sea and his adventures there?

From the stern of the ship, he watched Malva clambering nimbly around in the sails. He banished his gloomy thoughts. With Malva beside him he felt strong, able to face down any ghost.

It was several weeks before they saw the coastline of Sperta. Malva stood on the fo'c'sle, one hand shielding her eyes. She seemed nervous and melancholy. Lei noticed, and joined her.

"Do you see that line of white rocks over there?" Malva asked her.

"They like skeleton bones," said Lei, shuddering.

"They're reefs, and very dangerous. That's where Philomena and I were shipwrecked on board the *Estafador*."

The Princetta's eyes had darkened. She gazed at the shapes of the reefs, and remembered it all: the prow crashing into the sharp rocks, she and Philomena plunging deep beneath the water, and then drifting on rafts made from the covers of the hatches until the terrible moment when the nameless creature . . .

"It was here that I was attacked," Malva added. "We were swimming, hoping to get close to shore, and suddenly . . ."

She grimaced and jumped; it was like a reflex action. Then she turned pale, her breath came fast and she had to sit down.

"You very sensitive," remarked Lei, unbuttoning the collar of Malva's jersey to help her breathe more easily. "Wound cured now. Nothing to fear."

As if to reassure herself, Malva rolled up her trouser leg to expose her calf. There was still a long white scar on her skin.

"If Finopico alive, he tell you what beast live in this sea," said Lei sadly. "Then at last you know name of nameless creature!"

Malva stared gloomily at her scar for some time. Then she said, "Finopico left us his books. Why don't I look at them?"

It suddenly seemed a very good idea. She went down to the galley, and behind a jumble of fallen shelves and empty jars she found the books that had once been Finopico's. She shut herself in her cabin for the rest of the day.

At nightfall, as the *Fabula* was slowly entering the channel linking Tildesia to the marshlands of Eastern Armunia, Orpheus began to feel anxious about the Princetta's prolonged absence. He handed the helm over to Babilas and went to knock on her cabin door.

Malva was sitting on her bunk surrounded by a mountain of open books. Frowning with concentration, she was studying the engravings and descriptions by the light of a candle.

"You ought to come up and get some fresh air," suggested Orpheus. "It's pleasant up there, and you'll ruin your eyes reading all that small print."

Malva gave him a vague look. It was obvious that she hadn't heard a word he had just said.

"I didn't know there were so many species of fish in the world. Do you think Finopico knew about them all?"

"He knew much more than I'd have ever thought," replied Orpheus, remembering their conversation just before Finopico's death. "He was mainly interested in rare species. He dreamed of being admitted to the Maritime Institute with the other specialists."

"Poor Finopico," sighed Malva. "I still can't quite believe that he'll never come back. I sometimes think I hear him scolding the twins . . . or Zeph."

Her voice shook. Orpheus went over to her, and when he sat down on the edge of the bunk he saw the tears that threatened to brim over and fall down her cheeks.

"We've lost so many friends," she said. "I feel . . . I feel it's not right for us to be still alive, while they . . ."

And now her tears flowed. Orpheus took Malva in his arms to comfort her. Until now they had all carefully avoided calculating the cost of their voyage to the Archipelago. Finopico, Peppe and Zeph were lost—and the survivors missed them terribly. But the days went by, full of work and anxieties. They had to hold their course, hoist the sails, repair damaged parts of the ship and feed themselves, all of which helped them to keep sadness at bay. But when she opened Finopico's books, Malva was opening old wounds too. Every page, every word made her think of Finopico, and those who had been lost.

"When we're back in Galnicia we'll pay tribute to them," said Orpheus, stroking Malva's black hair. "Every Galnician must know who and what they were."

Malva was sobbing, her tears falling on Orpheus's hands.

"I don't know," she said brokenly, "I don't know what I'll do when we arrive. It just seems so . . . so far off, so . . . impossible."

Orpheus held her close.

"I'm here, I'm here," he repeated, letting her abandon herself to her grief.

They stayed in each other's arms for a long time, their hearts beating fast and their fingers intertwining. Orpheus kissed Malva's forehead, her cheeks, her hair. He wasn't afraid of feeling as he did any more. Gradually Malva calmed down.

"I was looking for the name of a sea creature," she finally explained, suddenly moving away from Orpheus. She told him about Vincenzo's treachery, the wreck of the *Estafador*, and showed him the scar on her leg.

"Lei healed it when we were in Temir-Gai, but I shall bear the scar for the rest of my days."

Orpheus picked up the candle and brought the flame close to Malva's bare leg. He looked at it for a long time, placed a finger on it lightly and traced the white mark.

"The creature had fearsome jaws," he murmured. "Those parallel marks suggest that it had two rows of teeth."

He touched her skin again.

"There . . . and there," he said. "Two rows of pointed teeth."

He raised his head, met Malva's eyes, and blushed.

"I think I have an idea," he said to cover up his embarassment. "If I'm right, it would be . . ."

He quickly put down the candle and searched the works spread out on the bunk. Finally he found the book he was looking for. It was the one Finopico had been reading on the evening when they confided in each other. He leafed feverishly through it.

"Look," he said.

He pointed to the engraving of the Ghoom of the Deeps, and read its description out loud. Then he handed the book to Malva, who looked at the illustration.

"Well, if that's the creature that bit me, I was lucky. It could have dragged me down to the bottom of the sea."

"And if it is," Orpheus went on, "then Finopico was right, and the Ghoom isn't just a legend. It really exists."

Malva looked at the engraving closely again, and then at her scar.

"He so much wanted to prove that he wasn't wrong," sighed Orpheus. "Poor man, finding that fish had become an obsession with him. And if we're right, he had the proof of it before his eyes!"

He put his hand on the Princetta's leg once again. She had goosebumps. Orpheus slowly closed the books and piled them up on the floor.

"You're cold," he told Malva. "You must rest now."

He picked up a blanket and made her get under it. When her head was lying on the pillow, her long, inky black hair was spread round her face like a halo.

Orpheus went very close to her. There was a silence. Malva closed her eyes, and with infinite gentleness Orpheus placed his lips on hers.

At that moment their hearts were like the twin stars shining in the sky: two bright little points amidst the vast darkness of the universe.

43

Galnicia Ahoy!

Hob was asleep in the maintop when a seagull dropping fell on his face. He woke with a start. The bird flew away screeching, as if to mock him.

"Filthy bird!" said the boy crossly, wiping his face on his sleeve.

Only then did he realise that this was the first gull he had seen in months. He sat up at once and leaned forward. Far away, he could make out the shape of land . . . and of a large building on top of a hill. Hob widened his eyes, opened his mouth, and shouted, "Galnicia! Galnicia, ahoy! Land ahead!"

Malva, Babilas, Lei and Orpheus rushed up from the central hatch and crowded to the fo'c'sle.

It was a grey, still, cloudy day, but there was no mist; the coast of Galnicia could clearly be seen, and so could the mouth of the River Gdavir.

"*Melfed liagh twyll!*" exclaimed Babilas.

His suntanned face suddenly softened, and Lei saw a tear of

joy in the corner of the giant's eyes. Her own feelings, of course, were not as strong; Galnicia was not her own country, and yet again she would be a foreigner. All the same, she felt glad to have arrived, and the idea of setting foot on dry land was pleasant. Most of all, she was impatient to mount a horse; Malva had promised to give her the best in her father's stables and an escort of soldiers to take her home across the Orniant.

Hob, in great excitement, clambered down from the sails and dropped heavily to the deck.

"We're coming home!" he cried. "Bringing the Princetta! The Coronador won't believe his eyes! We're heroes!"

And bursting into laughter, he began a little dance, whirling Lei away with him in circles and pirouettes until they were both breathless.

"We are heroes, aren't we, Captain?" he asked, stopping to get his breath back.

"That's not for me to decide," said Orpheus, smiling modestly. "And you ought to wipe your nose better than that before asking a girl to dance with you. Anyone would think a bird had been doing its business on you!"

Hob went red as a beetroot.

"Well, at least we'll get a reward, won't we?" he grumbled. "I seem to remember the Coronador talking about mountains of galniks."

Standing by the beak-head rail, Malva was in melancholy mood. It was she who had decided to go back, no one had made her, but hearing Hob talk she couldn't help feeling like a trophy being brought home from the hunt. Orpheus went over to her and put his hands on her shoulders.

"Don't listen to Hob!" he murmured in her ear. "If you want to change your mind you still can. We'll come ashore further away, somewhere close to the frontier, and you can disappear. No one will know you were here, no one will know where you're going. Not even me if you like. All you'll have to do is disappear again."

The more visible the coast became, the harder Malva's heart was beating. The Citadel, the river, the Campanile at the top of the Upper Town . . .

"No," she said firmly. "We'll put into port here, and I won't run away. As for the reward, do what you like about it. If my father is still alive, then—"

"But what makes you think the Coronador might be dead?" Orpheus interrupted her. "He's still young! You've been away for less than a year, Malva. Things can't have changed that much."

She shrugged her shoulders.

"It's just a feeling I have."

As they approached the entrance to the port, the five passengers on the *Fabula* were surprised to see a heavy bronze chain slung between the harbour walls to keep ships out. Orpheus told Babilas to cast anchor, and when the ship was at rest he turned to his companions.

"It was one of the Archont's edicts from when the Coronador had given him authority. The port was in quarantine . . . but the edict was rescinded to let us leave. I don't understand why the chain's still there now."

From where the *Fabula* lay they could see the masts of ships at their moorings. Hob counted only a dozen. So where was the rest of the fleet?

"And the fishing boats?" asked Malva, worried. "And where are the seagulls too?"

She was right. The sky was empty above the harbour, and however hard they strained their ears they couldn't hear voices, or the sound of barrels rolling, dogs barking or pulleys creaking. The port was silent.

Babilas and Orpheus looked at each other, and came to an agreement. Without a word, the giant leaped up on the rail and dived into the cold water. The others watched him swim to the harbour wall, and shouted encouragement to him when he reached it.

Once he had hauled himself up on the wall, breathless and dripping wet, Babilas pulled on the enormous bronze chain. Seaweed and shells clung to it. He grimaced, stepped back and managed to detach it. Orpheus raised the anchor, and the *Fabula* finally came into harbour.

Assembled in the bows of the ship, the passengers saw a depressing sight: the ships, dusty and rusty, were rotting after lying so long in the mud. Their masts were bent over like old men. Gutted barrels, empty chests and debris were scattered over the deserted landing stages, and the tavern doors all along the quaysides swung in the draughts of air.

"What's happened here?" wondered Orpheus, as the stem of the *Fabula* cut through the muddy, stagnant water.

"The place smells like dead fish," Hob said.

At the end of the quay Orpheus threw Babilas a hawser so that he could make the ship fast. Malva was very pale, but she indicated that she was all right: they must disembark and go into the city to find out what had happened. At Orpheus's command, Hob put a gangplank out from the catwalk to the quay, and when they were all on land the little procession set out towards the streets of the Lower Town.

Everywhere they went, they saw houses with their doors closed. There was no sound, no smell, no human presence. It was cold. An unpleasant draught of air made Orpheus sneeze several times.

"Perhaps they've all gone to a party?" suggested Hob. "Perhaps they're waiting to surprise us?"

He said this to encourage himself without believing it, and the further he went the fainter he felt. Memories came into his mind at every step, memories of the time when he was living rough on the streets with Peppe. They had stolen an orange from an orange-girl here, they had fought a rival gang there, and they had shared the takings from a day of begging under that porch . . .

"There aren't even any stray cats around," murmured Orpheus, feeling more and more uneasy.

When they came close to the River Gdavir the five companions were even more baffled. Even at the lowest point of the city's mourning, when it was believed that the Princetta had drowned, the Lower Town had never seemed as gloomy as this.

"Hey, look at that!" Hob suddenly exclaimed, pointing to the piers of the bridge. Strange, grey, supple plants were swaying in the wind on the banks of the river. "Do you remember, Captain? Those seeds I stole from the cook in the Citadel! The seeds the messenger brought as a present! They've come up!"

Hob dragged the others down to the riverside.

"They look like . . ." said Malva hesitantly, going over to the plants, "oh, they look like . . ." She touched the grey stems and then pulled at their seed heads. Little seeds fell into the palm of her hand. Malva's face lit up. "Yes, they're paghul!"

"You know this plant?" asked Hob in surprise.

"I certainly do! Uzmir and the Baighurs were always chewing it when I rode over the Great Azizian Steppes with them!"

"Uzmir! That was it!" cried Hob. "That's the funny name of the messenger who came to tell the Coronador you weren't dead!"

Delighted, Malva smiled and riffled through the grey leaves to harvest the seeds.

"It's a miracle that the seeds came up, Hob. Paghul usually grows only in stunted little groups in the harsh climate of the steppes! Try this!"

She offered seeds to Babilas, Orpheus and Lei. "You chew them," she explained, stuffing a handful into her own mouth.

"*Hadsin tlu!*" said Babilas, making a face.

"He say paghul taste of nothing," Lei translated.

"He's right," agreed Orpheus.

They stayed there for a little while, watching the currents of the river. Once, the Gdavir flowed through the whole country, shining silver, and the Galnicians were proud of its splendour. Now its waters were murky and yellow, mingled with mud and dead branches.

Orpheus looked up at the Campanile that dominated the Upper Town on the other bank. Birds were wheeling slowly around it like vultures. He swallowed a few more paghul seeds, and took a deep breath.

"Come on," he told his companions. "Maybe there's someone at home in the fashionable parts of town."

But they found no one in the wider, cleaner streets of the Upper Town either. The fountains in the middle of the squares were clogged with moss. Cobwebs quivered in the wind at the doors of the big houses. Orpheus sneezed again.

When they reached the Campanile they called for the Holy Diafron. No reply. Orpheus knocked on the door of the house where he had been born, but Berthilde didn't open it, as he had half-hoped she might.

"This place freezing," said Lei. "Many bad vibrations! I want leave!"

"Wait," Malva begged her. "I'm sure there's some good reason for all this."

But Lei shook her head. "Terrible things happen here. Disease, poverty, war. Everyone dead!"

Hob started trembling. He cast a distraught glance at Babilas, who was standing there motionless in the wind, not sure what to do with his big hands.

"Everyone dead!" repeated Lei, wide-eyed. "We die too! I want leave!"

Orpheus took the fair-haired girl by her shoulders.

"It's only been five months since I left the City!" he exclaimed. "People were going about their business then! They were walking around, playing, arguing! They were alive. They couldn't possibly have all died in such a short time. It's just not possible!" He let go of Lei. "Let's go up to the Citadel. Something must have happened to make everyone take shelter there!"

They went swiftly down the empty streets again, but when they reached the gates of the Citadel they were closed too.

"That makes sense," Orpheus reassured himself. "The people have locked themselves inside."

He went over to the bell-pull hanging from the pilaster by the gates and tugged it hard. The rusty chain gave way and came off in his hands.

"*Pertort gwener dorim a ustwig,*" said Babilas.

Lei didn't have the strength left to translate his words, but the others understood what he had been saying when they saw the giant climb the wall, hauling himself up by his arms. He managed to jump down on the other side. Soon after that they heard creaking, and the gates opened wide.

Malva was the first to enter the precincts of the Citadel. She immediately noticed that weeds had grown in the middle of the gravel all along the avenue. Further away, under the shade of the sycamores, the rain had dug ruts in it, and no one had taken the trouble to fill them in. If a carriage tried driving this way it would be thrown into the ditch! Malva had never seen the gardens in such a state. Wherever she looked she saw only tangled grass, rusty tools, abandoned carts, broken branches and dead trees. She felt she had come back in a nightmare to haunt her own childhood.

Malva was overcome with emotion when she saw the West Wing of the Citadel. Its roof had fallen in. Further on, level with the cliff, you could just see that the walls were pitted with the marks of cannonballs. There could be no more doubt that the Citadel had been attacked . . . and had not resisted. Malva hid her face in her hands. She had never expected to see her country in this state. Galnicia was obviously abandoned and deserted now.

Behind her, Hob, Babilas, Lei and Orpheus were walking slowly on, with increasing reluctance. When they saw that Malva was crying they stopped.

At that moment someone appeared at the end of the avenue: an old man with tousled hair, limping towards them and muttering. Orpheus quickly joined Malva.

"Who's that?" he asked, pointing to the man.

Malva wiped away her tears, and, as the man approached, she narrowed her eyes, trying to recognise his wrinkled face and unsteady gait. As far as she could recall, none of the servants, chamberlains, gardeners or cooks limped like that. It wasn't until the last moment, when the man looked at her, that Malva recognised him. She uttered a stifled cry.

"Father!"

The Coronador was no longer the man Malva had known. He had little in common with the stern, intimidating monarch who had humiliated her in public. She saw before her a sick old man who inspired nothing but pity. And she had feared this moment so much—if only she had known!

The Coronador stopped beside her, his eyes full of tears. He spoke her name. "Malva, Malva," he repeated hoarsely. Then he put out his trembling, brown-freckled hands to her and spoke her name again. When he moved to take her in his arms, she let him.

For as far back as Malva could remember, her father had never allowed himself to show her such affection. Never.

44

Ten Years

The Coronador was living in seclusion in the East Wing of the Citadel, with a handful of faithful servants who tried to keep up the appearance of the old days. Rats scurried amidst gilding and silk hangings, and dead leaves whirled in the draughts. On rainy days puddles formed under ornamental tables and dressing tables, and water ran down rust-spotted mirrors, leaving black marks. The ruined mattresses were leaking sawdust, the clocks had lost their hands, the shaky chests of drawers accumulated dust, and the curtains were hanging in tatters at the windows.

When Malva followed her father into the kitchens and the ballroom, when she climbed the stairs and walked along the galleries, she felt dizzy. This was the way she had gone on the night of her escape. There had been such bustling about in the Citadel then! Where were the maids who polished the floors? And the menservants who lit the candles in the chandeliers? Walking over the threadbare carpets, Malva wondered what turmoil had changed her home while she was away.

Exhausted, she stopped to look out of a window facing south to the terraces. She saw an old gardener standing on a stepladder trying to trim a hedge. He was swaying on his feet, and his white hair was blowing in the wind. Not far from the great basin, the bandstand had fallen in. The last time Malva saw it, a small ensemble had been there, rehearsing the serenades for her wedding. She even remembered the tune they played, and the warm scent of jasmine wafting in the evening air.

She turned to her father. "Tell me what happened," she said.

The Coronador nodded his head, and led the newcomers to the Hall of Delicacies. They passed two maids who recognised Malva and burst into tears.

The Coronador invited his guests to sit at the high table, and he himself removed the sheet covering it. Underneath, the ajouca wood was still smooth and shining.

"I've always made sure this table was ready to receive visitors," said the Coronador, with a touch of pride. "It is all that remains of our past glory."

He sat down with his guests and thought for some time, no doubt wondering how to begin his story. In the silence, the draughts chilling the room made Orpheus sneeze. Hob, in awe to find himself there, was sitting close to Babilas, while Lei waited patiently for the old monarch to offer an explanation. Malva had taken Orpheus's hand and was holding it tightly under the table.

"We so hoped that you would return, Malva!" the old man began. "Your mother . . ." His voice broke, and he cleared his throat. "Your mother wore out her knees praying at the Altar of the Divinities. She left so many offerings to them . . . by Holy Harmony, I wish she could have lived to see you come back!"

Malva heard these dreadful words without really understanding them. All this time, far from the Citadel, she had never supposed that her absence would really make anyone suffer. She had imagined her parents' anger and disappointment; she hadn't thought of them actually grieving for her. And yet . . .

The Coronador wiped away a tear and went on, "The Coronada died three years ago."

"Three years?" gasped Malva.

"That's impossible!" cried Orpheus. "Your Alteza . . . the Princetta left Galnicia a year ago. And I've been gone only four or five months. You must remember the *Errabunda* and the *Mary-Belle*!"

The Coronador drew his white brows together and looked carefully at Orpheus. "The *Errabunda* . . . yes. Were you her Captain?"

"Only her quartermaster," replied Orpheus modestly. "I'm Hannibal McBott's son."

The Coronador waved his hand vaguely as if shooing a fly.

"It's all so long ago," he said. "But I think I remember old Captain Hannibal. He was a great credit to our fleet in the past."

"I must set you right there!" replied Orpheus forcefully. "My father was not a credit to the Galnician fleet, or his country, or his Coronador. He betrayed you. He was only a pirate, a robber who never believed in the precepts of Tranquillity and Harmony."

"Really?" said the Coronador.

He was silent for a moment, his face working as he tried to collect his thoughts.

"You were saying that my mother the Coronada died three years ago," Malva went on, faintly. "That can't be right! Your memory must be playing tricks on you."

The Coronador placed his hands flat on the table. "Look at these hands, Malva!" he said. "They're useless, they shake, but see: they still have ten fingers. And those ten fingers allowed me to count the years that have passed since you went away. Ten fingers. Ten years. And . . . well, many things have happened here in those ten years."

Silence met this statement. How could they believe anything so absurd? How could time be so distorted that it passed more quickly in Galnicia than anywhere else? It was impossible! Yet at the same time, it did explain certain oddities: the rundown state of the city, the Coronador's lined face and white hair . . . and after all, so many inexplicable things had happened in the Archipelago. Perhaps the Nokros had eaten up more time than they realized.

"Go on," said Malva. "I want to know everything."

"After more than a year without any news of the *Errabunda*," said the Coronador, "I gave orders for a second expedition to set out. I don't remember the names of the ships that left any more. They never came back either. Then, giving up all hope of expeditions by sea, I sent out troops of armed horsemen. They set off for the Orniant to liberate you from the Emperor Temir-Gai. Only one of my men came back, two years later. He brought bad news: a pitiless war was laying waste the steppes. My soldiers found themselves caught up in the fighting, and were all killed. The worst news of all was that Temir-Gai no longer held my daughter prisoner. No one knew if she was alive or dead."

Malva sighed as she heard this story. One by one, her visions on Mount Ur-Tha were being confirmed. Her mother was dead, the Baighurs and Philomena had known the horrors of war. She shuddered. Had they survived?

Darkness was gradually invading the Hall of Delicacies, but no servant came to light the chandeliers. No one around the table dared move.

"So we had sent out three expeditions to no avail," the Coronador went on. "We had no heir to the throne. Little by little, despair took hold of our hearts. The Coronada fell ill. People were plotting all over the country. The Archont had sown discord everywhere. Only a spark was needed to light the smouldering fire."

"The Archont is dead," said Orpheus. "He pursued us over seas and oceans, but he won't be coming back again."

"Did you kill him?" asked the Coronador.

"No," said Orpheus, "but he was left a prisoner in a certain place, an Archipelago that—"

Under the table, Malva squeezed Orpheus's hand a little tighter to make him stop talking.

"We didn't see him die, Father," she said, "but I don't think he'll be coming back either."

"Good," sighed the Coronador sadly, "although it's too late anyway. Galnicia was attacked on all sides. Terrible battles were fought here too, until the final collapse. That was two years ago. Cannons and hordes of soldiers from Dunbraven and Andemark—it was carnage. The inhabitants of the Upper Town were the first to flee to the mountains. Then the people, starving and suffering from disease, were decimated. The survivors left the Lower Town to take refuge further west, near the frontier. I don't know what's become of them. I am not Coronador now, and Galnicia no longer exists. It has been divided up amongst our conquerors. All that remains is this ruined Citadel, where I am granted permission to end my days."

His voice died away. He was out of breath, bowed down by grief and fatigue. He looked at Malva.

"All these years I have never stopped thinking of the dreadful day when you disappeared. At first I thought you had been abducted. Then I held the Archont responsible. I was angry, and I wanted to find you to restore order to my country. I wanted my property back! At last, one day a maid brought me a letter she had found while doing housework in a little alcove in the South wing. It was just after the Coronada's death."

Malva gave a start. Her farewell letter! How much time had passed before it reached its destination? Years and years!

"When I read the letter," the Coronador went on, "I realised the truth. I suddenly understood why my daughter had . . . had run away. It was because of me."

The Coronador sounded like a broken man.

"I know that letter by heart. I have read and reread it until my eyes were worn out. You are right, Malva. From that day on, remorse has kept me from sleeping. Every night I thought of what I had done. I saw myself through your eyes . . . a cruel, heartless man. And so I was: a Coronador obsessed by power and duty. A father unable to understand his daughter."

Hob, Lei, Babilas and Orpheus looked at the old man's face in amazement. They turned to Malva. She was very pale, and didn't know what to do or what to think. The revelations had stunned her.

"But you have come back," murmured the Coronador. "That's all I hoped for: to see you again and ask you to forgive me."

The tears that the Princetta had been trying to hold back suddenly rolled down her cheeks. Her mouth opened, but only a sigh came out. And at that moment, Orpheus knew that Malva would be able to make peace with her father.

45

Reparations

The five survivors of the *Fabula* settled into the Citadel with the Coronador. Hob, who had dreamed of being admitted to the place for so long, was beside himself. He strode along the corridors and galleries, ignoring the general dilapidation and exploring every nook and cranny with an excitement that he couldn't contain. He got lost in secret passages several times, and Malva had to go and find him. In the evenings he walked in the now wild gardens, his eyes riveted to a particular place in the sky. Orpheus guessed that he was talking to Peppe.

Babilas and Lei found what quarters they could in rooms that the bad weather had spared. Malva refused to go back to the room that had been hers as a child. She asked Orpheus to help her move a bed to the alcove of her bedchamber in the South wing. The little room was damp and the window panes were broken, but apart from that nothing had changed.

"This is where I want to sleep," said Malva, looking at her reflection in the dressing table mirror.

She lifted her long black hair and then let it fall over her shoulders again, remembering the night when she had given herself a hedgehog haircut . . . she smiled as she recalled Philomena's cries of horror, and then sighed. Where was her chambermaid now? Would she ever see her again? She banished these gloomy thoughts, and looked at Orpheus.

"I'd like it," she said, blushing, "if you were to stay in the Citadel near me."

Orpheus gave a start. He placed his hands on Malva's waist.

"Stay in the same wing as the Princetta?" he said, smiling. "Isn't that against all protocol?"

"There isn't any protocol now," replied Malva.

Orpheus nodded. His heart was thudding wildly.

"In that case, I'm happy to say yes," he told her.

The days and weeks went by. There was so much to do in the Citadel. Babilas set about repairing the leaking roof in the East wing. Lei and Hob took over the horses; they spent whole days in the stables caring for the old nags there. Once again, Lei's medicine had to work a great many miracles.

Malva and Orpheus put the Coronador's affairs in order. They installed themselves in the Council Chamber and classified, arranged and copied the official records, so that the memory of the country would be preserved. It was tedious work.

Now and then Malva raised her head from the account books, looked at the Galnician flag hanging above the hearth, and remembered the day when her father had made her burn her notebooks. She no longer felt the humiliation that had gnawed at her heart for so long.

"One day I'll write our story," she said thoughtfully. "The Galnicians must know what happened to us in the Archipelago."

"And there must be new maps too," added Orpheus. "The limits of the Known World should be pushed further south. The scientists at the Maritime Institute would be astonished if they were still here!"

He picked up a pen and sketched the outlines of the islands, adding their names: Catabea, Jahalod-Rin, the island of the Unseen . . .

"Here's the rock where Zeph was trapped, there are the reefs on which the toothless men ran aground, here are Finopico's reefs. And there's the site of the Immuration, where Peppe sacrificed himself for us . . ."

Malva shivered. The friends they had lost were sadly missed. To banish her melancholy, she went back to work with determination.

The Coronador was growing weaker every day. He spent his time sitting in a rickety armchair, looking at his gardens as they began to emerge from their neglected state. Malva often went to see him, though they did not talk to each other much. What could you say after so many years of silence?

As the weeks went on, news of Malva's return spread to the old provinces. The boldest of the Galnicians decided to come and see for themselves if the rumour was true. They arrived by the road from the north, bringing their possessions, and came to the gates of the Citadel. Malva was glad to welcome them, and they in turn raised their eyes to heaven to thank Holy Tranquillity for preserving their Princetta's life.

Referring to the city maps and the records she had restored, Malva gave all the new arrivals a place to live. A dozen families set up house in the Lower Town, and before long children could be heard playing in the streets again.

Further off, in the port, Babilas and several of the new townspeople had begun repairing the ships. They caulked the hulls, stood the masts erect and repainted the landing-stages. Some fishermen came back, and on certain mornings set up their stalls on the quayside and sold their catch. It was all on a very small scale, but Malva could feel her country's soul slowly reviving.

"Do you ever feel any regrets?" Orpheus asked her from time to time.

"For coming back?"

"Yes. For not staying in your ideal country."

"I wouldn't have liked it in Elgolia without you," Malva replied. "No, I have no regrets."

One morning Lei and Hob called Malva to come outside, where the weather was fine. The trees in the orchards were coming into bud. Lei and Hob were sitting proudly astride two chestnut mares who were pawing the ground outside the stables.

"Look!" cried Lei.

She dug her heels into her horse's side, and set off for the sycamore avenue at a gallop, followed by Hob, who was laughing whole-heartedly. At the other end of the avenue they turned and rode back to Malva.

"Those were the last two!" Hob told her.

"Horses all healthy now," Lei added. "Thirteen in good condition."

"See what this one can do, Princetta!" cried Hob. He shorted the reins, dug his heels into the mare a few times, and she reared and turned round on her back legs before doing a little dance, which delighted Malva.

"I didn't know you rode so well! You could almost compete with the Baighur horsemen!"

"Exactly!" said the boy. "Lei's promised me we'll go by way of the steppes!"

Malva looked at him, unable to believe her ears. Hob at once looked downcast, realising that he had given away a secret.

"What's this all about?" asked Malva in concern, looking at Lei.

Lei sighed, and then decided to tell Malva her plan. She missed her country and its customs, and above all her family. Her heart felt a little heavier every day. So now that the horses were healthy, she wanted to go home to the kingdom of Balmun.

"My place there," she added. "And Hob . . ."

The boy blushed, and went closer to her. He had grown a great deal recently, and riding and looking after the horses had made him sturdier.

"I've decided to go with Lei," he said. "I feel too sad here in Galnicia without my brother. I must go away again. A long way away. I'm going to escort Lei. What do you think, Princetta?"

Malva opened her mouth, and found she had nothing to say. She had not marked the passage of time since their return. Day had followed day, and she hadn't noticed Lei's sadness.

"You're going by way of the Great Azizian Steppes, then?" was all she said.

Lei nodded.

"Good," sighed Malva. "When are you going to leave?"

46

Farewells and Meetings

It was still dark when all the inhabitants of the Citadel met outside the stables. The air was chilly. The maids clutched mended shawls around them, the menservants were stamping their feet to keep warm. They stood in a circle around the Coronador, who, in spite of having a cough, had wanted to get up early to see Hob and Lei off. Nearby, Malva, Orpheus and Babilas were watching the last preparations.

Once the two chestnut mares were saddled and loaded up, the two travellers mounted. Their faces were drawn from lack of sleep, but it was obvious that they were impatient to be off.

"Are you sure you have enough food and water?" asked Malva, going over to Lei. "And what about musketoons? The roads aren't safe! Suppose you meet the Amoyeds . . ."

The daughter of Balmun pointed to a blade hanging from her saddle.

"And blankets?" asked Malva. "You'll need them when

you go over the snowbound passes on the borders of Gurkistan."

"We've thought of everything," Hob reassured her. "The cook's even given us some jars of herrings with myrtle berries to take to Lei's parents."

"Excellent!" smiled the Coronador. "There's nothing better than herrings preserved in the Galnician style."

The sun rose above the horizon. It was a sign for the travellers to leave. Hob raised one hand and signalled to Orpheus.

"I shall take our bearings from the stars," he told him, with a lump in his throat. "I shall always remember the night you showed me the stars on the deck of the *Fabula*."

"Peppe will be watching over you," said Orpheus. "So don't do anything foolish!"

"I never do anything foolish these days," the boy told him.

Lei stifled laughter. Her pearl-like eyes passed over the faces of her friends, and lingered on Malva. She held out her hand.

"Look after yourself," Malva begged her, holding it tightly. "I don't want to lose any more of my friends."

"We take great care, I promise."

Malva patted the horse's glossy coat. "You do realise that when you get home everything will have changed there? The time that's passed in Galnicia will have passed in Balmun too. Ten years, nearly eleven now."

"I get used to that idea. My parents perhaps dead, not my brothers and sisters. They grown up is all."

"If you'd like to come back here and visit now and then, you'll always be welcome."

"You too, Malva. If you want see kingdom where Lei live, you very welcome too. Always."

"I don't feel like going away again just now," sighed Malva. "I need to rest, and . . ." She cast her father a brief glance. He was coughing again. "And the Coronador isn't well, so I must stay with him."

"And Orpheus!" added Lei, winking.

Malva nodded. Then she put a hand under her jacket and brought out a scroll of paper, which she handed to Lei.

"It's a message for Philomena. Give it to her if you meet her on the steppes."

Lei took the letter and promised she would. Then Babilas and Orpheus went to say their own goodbyes to the two riders.

Then Hob and Lei turned their horses towards the road out of the Citadel, following the same path as the cart in which Malva and Philomena had escaped, hidden in barrels of Rioro wine. They waved one last time, and gradually moved away.

Malva and Orpheus, red-eyed, stood for some time outside the stables without moving or speaking. Then they climbed to the northern side of the ramparts of the Citadel. There was a wide view from up there, and they could watch the two chestnut mares on their way.

"They're already far off," sighed Malva.

At that moment she saw silhouettes moving along the same road, but in the opposite direction.

"Who are they?"

Orpheus narrowed his eyes. It looked like a long procession of peasants on foot. They made a moving ribbon going along the road, like a troop of ants.

"Galnicians," he murmured. "At least a hundred of them. It looks as if they're on their way home."

From their observation post, Malva and Orpheus watched the progress of the column. Gradually they could make out women and children, soldiers carrying old carabins under their arms, beggars, merchants, sailors, noble Donias, even a Venerable Monje, and two or three Holy Diafrons, who could be recognised by their yellow caps worn at a slight angle.

"We must welcome them!" said Malva, shaking off her melancholy mood. "These people must have walked for days and days! Let's open the doors of the Hall of Delicacies to them!"

Orpheus followed her as she climbed downstairs. He helped her to put the Hall in order and prepare the registers listing inhabitants of Galnicia, and then went to ask the Coronador to join them for the event. It was the first time since the fall of the country that so many Galnicians had made for the Citadel at the same time!

A few hours later there was a great line of people waiting in the gardens. It stretched from the middle of the Hall of Delicacies to the first streets of the Lower Town. Everyone was shouting, talking, calling out, exchanging news, and making such a noise that the Coronador could hardly make himself heard. Old men sat down on the grass, groaning, to rest their sore feet, tradesmen dumped their handcarts anywhere they could find and tried to sell fruit now overripe from the journey, while soldiers uncorked bottles of Rioro found by some miracle in the cellars. Malva had ordered the wine to be distributed along with food. It was like a carnival.

However, when the people entered the Hall, they all suddenly fell silent and removed their hats. They made their way towards their Princetta, eyes wide as if they couldn't believe what they were seeing. They had to touch Malva's hand before they were convinced that she was real. Not only was she alive, she looked almost the same as she did when her portrait was painted. Just a little thinner, perhaps, and with a more serious look, but her amber eyes still enchanted all who saw her.

She had taken her place on a chair hastily mended by Babilas; its seat was still rather unsteady. Beside her, on his faded throne, the Coronador sometimes started when he heard people speak to him. As for Orpheus, he stood back in the shadows, slightly removed from the others, watching the scene with growing emotion. He had always dreamed of seeing the Princetta reunited with her people. And this time, he knew, it was for good.

"We've missed you!" the women told her.

"We thought you'd died among the barbarians," said the men.

"You can't think how we've suffered!" wailed the noble Donias. "Just imagine—we had to eat roots and wild pigs' tails!"

They all crowded around her, weeping, and thanked her. Malva accepted their affection humbly. In exchange, she distributed houses, workshops and responsibilities among them, and they all set off, reassured that a new life awaited them in either the Upper Town or the Lower Town, whichever they preferred.

The soldiers laid their rusty carabins and musketoons at the Princetta's feet and swore to be faithful to her. The Holy Diafrons murmured blessings into her ears. The tradesmen promised her presents, and when Malva gave the peasants plots of land they shed tears of gratitude. At the back of the room, three menservants wrote down everything she had given in the official registers.

At last an old woman in a black cape, carrying a big bundle, knelt before Malva. "I came back in spite of my great age," she said to her, "hoping you could give me news of someone who set out in search of you. A young man I raised—he was on the first expedition, the one that set out ten years ago . . ."

Hearing her voice, Orpheus emerged from the shadow, his heart beating fast. "Berthilde?" he asked hesitantly.

The old woman looked up, recognised him and burst out sobbing. "He's alive! By Holy Tranquillity, he's alive!"

After the shock of seeing Orpheus, Berthilde was taken to an antechamber to rest. Malva cast an enquiring glance at Orpheus, who briefly explained who the old woman in black was before going to sit with her. Berthilde was in a state of great excitement, wringing her hands and repeating, "Thanks be, thanks be, thanks be!"

While Berthilde had always seemed old to Orpheus, he saw her so worn out by age and suffering that he thought she might fall to dust before his eyes.

When she was over her initial shock, Berthilde was able to sit up, and found the strength to tell Orpheus all that had happened to her: her despair, her lonely and interminable wait in Hannibal's icy house, then war with the invading hordes from the north.

"One morning I heard riders coming, shouting in the next road. I took fright, collected a few things together and left. I wasn't the only one. The Upper Town emptied all at once, and we found ourselves on the road like beggars."

"Going where?" asked Orpheus.

"Far away to the frontiers. That's where I found shelter, in a village built by cave-dwellers and abandoned long ago."

"You . . . you lived in the caves?" asked Orpheus in amazement.

The old woman nodded. She had stayed there for more than two years with other Galnician refugees. But cold, hunger, and the fear of being discovered, attacked or killed could not overcome her determination.

"I always looked after what was yours," she told Orpheus proudly. "I never gave up hope of seeing you again some day, and giving back what you left me when you went away."

She bent down, opened the bundle she had brought with her, and took out some knick-knacks that Orpheus recognised: objects of no great value, but part of his childhood. Then she opened a small box. Orpheus went pale. It contained Hannibal's jewels and gold.

"This is only a small part of your fortune," said Berthilde apologetically. "I couldn't carry it all, and I suppose the rest was stolen. I am so sorry."

Amazed, Orpheus was staring at the casket.

"I know you didn't want to accept anything from your father," Berthilde murmured. "But this gold is all that's left of him. Please take it."

Feeling very awkward, Orpheus didn't dare refuse it.

"Hannibal loved you," the old woman added. "I watched him with you over the years, and I know how much he thought of you. He loved you more than anything in the world."

Orpheus looked into the depths of Berthilde's eyes, and thought of all that had happened to him since the two of them last saw each other.

"I will take it," he said.

Berthilde smiled.

"And now you must rest," added Orpheus. "We'll find you a room."

The old woman shook her head. "It's kind of you, but no. If you will allow me," she said, taking a bunch of keys from her pocket, "I'll sleep at home in the McBott house."

She had kept the keys too! Orpheus couldn't get over it, but he was quick to grant her request. He called some servants and told them to take the old lady to the big white house at the foot of the Campanile.

"And I'll come and see you tomorrow," he promised, kissing Berthilde's lined forehead.

47

A Last-Minute Visitor

The procession through the Hall of Delicacies went on for a week. Galnicians came to the Citadel from everywhere, and the constant crowd tired the Coronador so much that after three days he said he wasn't going to leave his bed again; his daughter could cope with everything very well by herself.

The crowd came and went in a state of great excitement, thronging the streets and squares, the banks of the River Gdavir, and going all the way to the harbour, where ships from every point of the compass were loading and unloading cargo.

One evening when Orpheus was out, Malva was about to rise from her chair and go back to her own room when a final visitor turned up. She heard one of the menservants sigh, and almost sent the late-comer away, but she sat down when she saw the state he was in. He entered the Hall of Delicacies with a crutch under each arm, back bent and breathless with the effort. His bare feet were dirty and bleeding under the folds of a monje's robe. He must have suffered a thousand torments before reaching the Citadel, and although she was exhausted, Malva didn't have the heart to turn him away.

"Come here," she said, "and tell me your name."

The man dragged himself over to where Malva was sitting. His face was hidden under the wide hood of his robe, and only some locks of grey hair escaped from it. This must be a very old monje, she thought to herself.

"My name," said a trembling voice, "my name is Miguel. I have come from so far away to see you, Princetta."

"I'm listening," smiled Malva, leaning forward in an attempt to see the monje's face.

"May I speak without fear in this place?" the voice asked again. "I have something to tell you in confidence, and . . ."

Malva assured him that the servants wouldn't hear anything.

"I have come from so far away," the man repeated.

"From the frontier?" asked Malva.

"Much further than that! I have crossed a sea, I have passed through unknown lands . . ."

"What kind of lands?"

"Lands from which no one ever returns," replied the shaking voice.

Malva felt a shudder run down her back.

"That," said the man from under his hood, "is why I want to speak to you. I know you will understand. Your intelligence and wisdom are famous. But what about these servants?"

Malva turned to the three poor fellows half-asleep over the registers, and felt sorry for them. "That's all for today," she told them. "You can leave us now."

The three servants didn't wait to be asked twice. They put their pens down and left the Hall of Delicacies. Malva was alone with the monje.

"There's no one else here now," she said.

"No one else here!" breathed the monje. "You and I, alone. How glad I am!"

"So what lands did you want to tell me about?" asked Malva, her curiosity aroused.

The monje straightened up. He dropped his crutches, which made a dull sound as they fell to the polished floor. Malva was going to lean down and pick them up, but she suddenly stopped. She leaped to her feet as the monje flung back his hood to reveal his face.

In spite of his long hair, Malva recognised him at once. Those piercing eyes, as grey as metal, that triumphant smile . . .

"The Archont!" she murmured, with a sinking feeling in the pit of her stomach.

He immediately drew a sword that had been hidden under his robes. She screamed.

"Let me tell you, then, about the Archipelago," snarled the Archont, moving forward with the sword held in front of him.

Malva knocked her chair over as she retreated, shouting, "Orpheus!"

"He won't hear you," snapped the Archont. "We have all the time in the world to talk, like the old friends we are! Let me tell you what I have endured to reach the end of our story at last, Princetta."

He slashed the air with his sword and it whistled in Malva's ears. She was shaking, the terror flooding through her making her breathless. But suddenly she remembered the secret passage. Its entrance was in the back wall of the room just a few steps behind her.

"Let me tell you about the sailors whose Nokros I stole so that I could hold out . . . they lost their heads, all of them, as you, Princetta, are about to lose yours now!"

Malva retreated further and further until her hands were touching the wall. Her fingertips felt for the way into the passage.

"I thought you'd died in the Immuration," she said, trying to gain time. "I was so happy to think of you undergoing Catabea's tortures!"

The Archont, smiling, advanced on her. "As you see, Catabea let me go! I followed the Law of the Archipelago, I explored my true self. All my hatred, and even beyond it . . ."

Malva felt the slight recess marking the entrance to the secret passage beneath her fingers. She pushed with all her might. The door gave way, and Malva fell backwards. Taking advantage of the Archont's surprise, she rose, turned, and began running down the narrow passage. It was bathed in darkness.

Behind her, she heard the Archont shout, "You won't escape that way a second time, Princetta! This isn't Temir-Gai's harem. I know these secret passages as well as you do!"

And he set off in pursuit of her, uttering demented cries.

48

The End of the Passage

Orpheus felt a need to walk in the Citadel gardens for a little while. It was not warm, for a north wind had risen, but the sky was clear, and fountains played cheerfully in the basins. He turned up his collar and was wandering along the garden paths at random, hands in his pockets. As he walked he thought of his father. He no longer felt revulsion or anger towards him. He even planned to ask Malva to go to the graveyard with him that evening, where they would place flowers on the graves of the Coronada and Hannibal together.

He was at this point in his reflections when he began to feel cold. He sneezed once, then a second time, and decided to go in.

When he was within sight of the sycamore avenue he met the servants who had been at work with the Princetta in the Hall of Delicacies all day. "Is the audience over?" he asked them.

One of them explained that there was a single visitor left, a poor cripple, but Malva was talking to him alone and had told them to go. Orpheus frowned. He didn't much like the idea of Malva alone with the stranger. He turned back to the terrace and entered the great hall through its glazed door.

There was no one at all there. A vague fear seized him.

"Princetta?" he called.

There was no reply. He took a step forward, saw the over-turned chair . . . and the pair of crutches lying on the floor. His heart leaped in his chest.

"Malva!" he shouted.

At that moment he saw the open door to the secret passage in the back wall. This final clue convinced him that something had happened. He stepped inside the entrance to the passage and called again. Holding his breath, he listened. There was no reply, only silence.

Panic took hold of him. He raced back into the Hall of Delicacies, snatched up a musketoon, and made his way into the secret passage.

It was dark, but he had only to follow the narrow passage, guiding himself by its walls. Malva had already taken him there to show him the way she had escaped the night before her ill-fated wedding. Orpheus remembered the turns in it, the flights of stairs, the marks she had mentioned to him. Musketoon held before him, he began to run.

The further he went, the more he feared that something terrible had happened. Who was this cripple who could chase someone without his crutches? An impostor, of course!

"The Archont?" Orpheus asked himself out loud.

The possibility chilled him to the bone. He had so much wanted to believe that the man had died in the Archipelago. Was it possible that he too had escaped?

Orpheus reached a place where the passage branched,

and stopped. To his right, it went up to the apartments. To his left it skirted the kitchens. He hesitated, listening carefully to the sounds that came to him, but none resembled cries or running footsteps. He opted for the passage on the left, remembering that it was the one along which Malva had guided him.

He ran on into the darkness, his throat dry, his eyes strained until he thought he saw light at the end of the passage. Yes, a door was open to the air outside! That was the way Malva had gone!

Orpheus cocked the musketoon. As he reached the open door he slowed down. He heard horses pawing the ground with their hooves; this was the way to the stables. A gust of cold wind blew back his hair. The smell of the horses filled his nostrils, and he felt like sneezing. He pinched his nose very hard with his free hand to stop the sneeze.

At last he put his head through the opening. There was Malva, hiding behind bales of straw. She was breathing fast, and perspiration ran down her face.

Orpheus took another step. He saw the Archont, sword in hand, prowling round the bales of straw and snarling.

Orpheus's vision blurred slightly, the result of fear and strain. His hands were sweating on the butt of the musketoon. And his nose was itching so badly!

Holding his breath, he raised the barrel of his firearm to eye level and tried to take aim at the Archont. But the man kept moving, bending down, straightening up. He drove his sword blade into the straw with a hideous smile on his face. At last Orpheus made up his mind to push the door further open; otherwise he couldn't do anything. The draught was stronger. Orpheus pinched his nose even more tightly. He raised the musketoon again, and suddenly the Archont was in his line of fire.

He crooked his forefinger on the trigger of the weapon. There was a little click.

The Archont turned to look at the door, and saw Orpheus aiming at him. A flash of surprise showed in his grey eyes. But just as Orpheus pulled the trigger, he sneezed so hard that the bullet went astray.

He sneezed again, twice, losing control of the situation. And suddenly he felt the sword blade pass through his chest, and heard the Archont's exultant voice.

"I've run you through once before! This time it's for good!"

Orpheus opened his eyes. The Archont was standing over him. He had taken advantage of the sneezing fit to leap in and disarm him. Orpheus felt such pain that he thought he was exploding inside. He fell to the ground without even uttering a cry.

Then he heard nothing but the beating of his heart. He saw a bale of straw fly through the air and come down on the Archont. He saw Malva pass in front of him and straighten up with the musketoon in her hands. He saw the Archont retreat, open-mouthed.

He didn't hear the shot, but he realised that Malva had fired.

The Archont staggered and fell back, his chest covered with blood, and then disappeared from Orpheus's field of vision.

Head back on the straw, Orpheus smiled at Malva as she leaned over him. How beautiful she was! Her face, her amber eyes, her black hair . . . but why was she crying? Why was her mouth moving like that? What was she saying?

She's saying my name, Orpheus told himself. She loves me.

Those were his last thoughts.

414

They buried Orpheus three days later.

At the head of the funeral procession, the Coronador, Berthilde and Babilas supported Malva. The young Princetta could not take her eyes off the coffin. Behind them came a crowd of silent Galnicians.

A hole had been dug in the graveyard, not far from the two graves where Hannibal and Merixel McBott lay at rest. In spite of her deep distress, Malva had wanted to arrange everything herself. She had ordered a gravestone from a craftsman in the city—not a stone, but a slab of mesua wood, the hard timber found in the Orniant—and she had had an inscription carved on it:

Orpheus McBott. Captain of the ship Fabula, *which crossed the seas south of the Known World for the first time. Loyal to his country, the friend of all, the first love of one.*

49

A Gift From Far Away

A month passed. Then another. And then another.

Summer was beginning.

In the languid afternoons, Malva often sat on a stone bench in the graveyard. She spent hours there with a bunch of wild flowers in her hands. Sometimes she fell asleep.

The memory of Orpheus haunted her: his eyes, his hands, his voice. Her heart was laid waste, a desert, a wilderness.

Yet she was only seventeen. Her legs carried her about almost despite herself. So she went on living day by day, or at least appeared to go on living. She talked, she listened, she received ambassadors, soldiers and simple washerwomen; the Hall of Delicacies remained open until late in the evening.

One day Malva found a delegation waiting there for her when she got back from the graveyard. Amidst the gilding and silk hangings stood several men with lined faces and slanting eyes. They wore dusty clothing and big leather boots.

In the middle of the group Malva saw a tall, strong man, and a woman with cheeks as smooth and shining as apples. When she saw Malva come in, the woman flung her arms wide and began crying.

It was Philomena!

Uzmir the Supreme Khansha stood beside her, and they were accompanied by several Baighur horsemen.

Malva thought her heart would explode with joy. She flung herself into Philomena's arms, crying her name aloud. Their embraces, tears of joy and trills of laughter went on for a long time, before the astonished eyes of the servants, who had never seen anything so out of keeping with protocol in the Hall of Delicacies.

"Malva! Malva!" repeated Philomena, hugging her. "I feared for you so much! I thought you were dead. I looked for you everywhere, everywhere! All over the Orniant!"

"I feared for you too," said Malva, gulping. "Oh, if only you knew!"

After a while Uzmir came over and embraced Malva in his own turn. "I always told Philomena that you were still alive somewhere," he said in his guttural voice.

"You speak Galnician!" said Malva in surprise.

"Philomena taught me your language," smiled the Khansha. "The first time I came here I didn't know a word of it. That was long ago, very long ago. How is the Coronador?"

Malva sighed, and explained that he was losing his memory, and soon his legs would not carry him any more.

"I heard that the Coronada was dead," murmured Philomena. "Your friends told us the whole story."

"Hob and Lei? You've seen them?"

Uzmir and Philomena nodded their heads at the same time. "They spent a long time looking for us in the great steppes,"

Philomena explained. "They gave us your letter, and when I knew where you were I asked Uzmir to saddle the horses. Your friends have gone on their way to Balmun now."

So much good news all at once, so many things to say, such strong emotions . . . Malva turned her amber eyes on her former chambermaid.

"I want to know all about it!" she demanded. "Everything!"

"Very well," replied Philomena, laughing, "but first I want to show you something. Come with me."

She led Malva outside. A dozen Baighur horses were tied up behind the West Wing, grazing on the lush grass of the orchards. Three carts stood in the shade of the plum trees.

A boy of about five or six was sitting on one of the horses. He was handling the reins of his horse, watched closely by a fat woman who was giving him advice in Baighur. Malva observed him for a moment in silence. Under his cap of oryak skin embroidered with gold thread, his face was paler than those of the other Baighurs, but his slanting eyes certainly resembled Uzmir's.

"Let me introduce you to Hainur," said Philomena. "My son."

"And my son too," added Uzmir proudly, going towards Hainur. On seeing his father, the boy pulled at his reins and dismounted. Uzmir took his hand and leaned down to whisper something in his ear. The child happily clapped his hands, ran to one of the carts, searched a chest in it and took out something wrapped in fabric. He looked at his mother, asked her a question in Baighur, and then turned to Malva, smiling. He gave her the package.

"Here is a present for the Princetta of Galnicia," he said in Galnician.

Malva had tears in her eyes. Hainur's beauty, movements and

voice, all he represented, touched her heart. She bent down to take the package, trembling.

"Open it," Philomena encouraged her.

Malva undid the wrappings. Inside she found a long-stemmed pipe made of precious metal.

"A chibuk?" she said in surprise. "Why, I thought the chibuk was only for married women!"

Philomena gave her a mischievous glance. "Lei and Hob told us that you were in love, Princetta. They mentioned a certain Captain Orpheus . . . even if you aren't married, that deserves a chibuk, I think!"

Malva smiled, but there was a sudden lump in her throat. Her heart fell, her smile disappeared, and before Philomena's distressed eyes she burst into sobs.

"What's the matter, mama?" asked Hainur anxiously. "Doesn't your friend like our present?"

Malva had knelt down in the grass. She was weeping and weeping and weeping, holding the chibuk in her clutching hands. Of course, Lei and Hob didn't know what had happened. They had left several days before the tragedy! Malva raised her head and put her hand out to the little boy.

"I like this . . . this chibuk very much," she reassured him, between sobs. "But I'm . . . I'm crying because . . . the man I love isn't here any more."

"Has he gone hunting oryak?"

Malva smiled through her tears. "You could say so, yes . . . but we don't have any oryak here in Galnicia. So he's gone far away . . . very far away. I don't think he will ever come back."

Hainur had moved close to Malva, and was looking at her gravely.

"I know what you ought to do," he said. "You ought to keep

the chibuk and wait until you find another man to love. Then you may light it."

Malva bit her lip and wiped her eyes. "Do you think there will be someone else who will love me in the Known World?"

Hainur knelt down in front of her. He leaned forward and kissed Malva's wet cheeks.

"I love you already," he said.

Malva was feeling better now. She looked at Philomena, whose face was full of concern.

"You have a wonderful son," Malva told her. "He has a real gift for comforting people." She stood up and took the chibuk under her arm. "There," she sighed, "enough sadness! You are here, and I want to give you a fitting welcome. Come with me!"

She went into the Citadel, followed by her guests, and went first to the kitchen, where she gave orders for a banquet to be prepared.

The cooks immediately set to work. Pans were scoured, and strainers, graters, casseroles and spits went into action. It had been many years since there had been such festivities in the Citadel!

Malva called on the maids next, asking them to polish the silver, get out the china, beat the carpets and light the Hall. She summoned gardeners and musicians and arranged for lanterns in the trees, fountains and serenades. Little Hainur ran up and down the staircases and along the corridors laughing.

Then they all separated to rest before the dinner.

Malva withdrew to her room with her precious chibuk. She placed it in her alcove. The gift moved her deeply. It represented both her lost love and the promise of other loves and other joys to come. It was the perfect link between the past and the future.

*   *   *

That evening, seated around the huge ajouca wood table and under the sparkling chandeliers, the guests talked until very late. They included Babilas in his new ambassadorial robes, Uzmir, Philomena, Hainur and the rest of the Baighur delegation, the Coronador, slightly inclined to fall asleep over his plate, Berthilde, who had made the effort of coming up to the Citadel for the occasion, the Holy Diafron, several scientists from the Maritime Institute, foreign travellers, elegant Donias in low-cut silken gowns, sailors who laughed loudly and told stories of storms and tempests, and a dozen children recruited by Malva to keep Hainur company. Of course there were many absent from the table whom the Princetta would have wished to see there: Orpheus, Peppe, Finopico, Lei, Hob . . . even the Coronada. Malva wished she could have shown her mother all this.

But she had made up her mind that grief and regret would not reign in the city that evening.

Squid stuffed with grasshoppers slipped down the guests' throats, with many a good draught of Rioro, and fig ragoût tickled their palates. So did paghul cakes. As for Philomena, she devoured herrings in the Galnician style, since she hadn't tasted them in years!

When everyone's appetite was satisfied, Malva rose to her feet and for the first time told her story: her flight, the treachery of the Archont and Vincenzo, the wise woman of Sperta, the Amoyed attack, Uzmir's intervention, their journey east until she was abducted, Temir-Gai's harem, the ordeal in the Baths of Purity, the Cage of Torments, the unexpected arrival of Orpheus, the twins and Babilas, and then their impossible return voyage to Galnicia.

The guests listened to her tale with bated breath. Their eyes opened wide as she spoke of the Archipelago, Catabea and her Patrols, and the hazards lying in wait for the *Fabula* on the islands they came to. They wiped away tears when she told them how Peppe had sacrificed himself so that his companions would escape the Immuration.

Finally Malva raised her glass, and everyone drank to the memory of those who had paid with their lives during that venture beyond the frontiers of the Known World.

Then Philomena and Uzmir took up the tale. They described the expedition to Temir-Gai's harem that they had mounted trying to rescue the Princetta. They spoke of the fire, the terrible battle that followed it, and then the Emperor's declaration of war against all the free peoples of the steppes. The war had gone on for over six years before the Amoyeds and the Cispazians, their numbers severely depleted, gave up their wish for vengeance.

"Hainur was born just as peace was made," said Philomena, hugging her son. "He stands for peace itself."

"*Bodgmain Hainur tellin ar tuilder!*" said Babilas. And as no one understood the language of Dunbraven, he grimaced and translated for himself, rather in Lei's style. "I drink to Hainur! He the son of love and peace!"

The company applauded, and bottles were quickly emptied. It was very late when they all parted to go to their beds. Before she did so, Philomena put a hand on Malva's arm.

"You said nothing about Elgolia," she whispered. "Have you given up your dreams?"

Malva's head was spinning. She felt happy and tired. She looked her friend straight in the eye.

"You were right," she told her. "Elgolia doesn't exist. Or not the way I thought it did. But I haven't given up anything. I intend to make Galnicia a kind of Elgolia. What do you think?"

"Knowing you," said Philomena with a wide smile, "I think you're perfectly capable of doing it, Princetta!"

Epilogue

Every morning Malva dressed like a peasant girl: a plain dress, a cotton scarf over her hair and rope-soled shoes, and then she slipped out of her bedroom. She looked discreetly in at the kitchens and put a few delicacies into her pockets: marzipan cakes, swallow and aniseed pies, or liquorice shortbread. Once out of the Citadel she set off along the avenue of sycamores, passed through the gates in the wall, and made her way along the alleys of the Lower Town.

The place had been teeming with activity like an anthill since the early hours of the day. Pedlars pushed their handcarts along the newly paved roads, bricklayers and carpenters climbed scaffolding, groups of children made their way to the schools that had just reopened, blacksmiths worked at their forges, water-carriers swayed along between the stalls, bakers set out batches of rolls, and old people put chairs in their doorways. They were all greeting each other, calling out and chattering.

Malva particularly liked to watch the washerwomen perched

on the flat roofs of adjoining houses where they spread out sheets and shirts, arguing with each other the whole time about one thing or another. Both young and old had opinions on everything. Their gossip told Malva a great deal about the people of Galnicia and their present state of mind.

"They say the Coronador is senile!"

"That's right—my cousin says she saw him standing in front of an olive tree for hours, talking to himself."

"Never mind, the old fellow has nothing to worry about. Even if the Princetta isn't married, she's well up to governing the country!"

"You're right there! We can all be grateful to her. But for her, we'd still be living on the road like beggars!"

"Poor thing, though. They say she wept for days over the body of Captain Orpheus."

"I'm not surprised. He was so brave and handsome! You don't find a man like that around every street corner!"

"Meaning your husband isn't like that?"

"You want to know what my husband would say about you?"

"All the same, I'm sorry for our Princetta. Her so young, and so unhappy in love!"

"It was all the Archont's fault. That man . . ."

"I remember the days when the country was in mourning . . . just seeing him go down the street with his soldiers gave me nightmares!"

"It's a pity he died instantly. A toad like that deserved to suffer!"

"Well, he ended like the dog he was—thrown into a mass grave, no Holy Diafron, no Ritual."

"Oh, do stop saying such things, it turns my stomach."

"Here, speaking of stomachs, who's going to the fish

auction in a little while? They say there's been a miraculous catch."

And the washerwomen continued in this vein, laughing and chuckling, paying no attention to the young peasant girl listening to them in the street below. They spread their white sheets out in the sun, and their plump pink arms dipped from one laundry basket to another in a complex, fascinating dance. It was the same every morning. When she had heard enough, Malva sighed and walked on.

She went down to the River Gdavir to watch the paddle boats coming up from the harbour with their cargoes of fish or barrels of Rioro. They went upstream towards the northern provinces. A treaty had recently been signed between Galnicia and its neighbours. Babilas, now an ambassador, had undertaken negotiations with Dunbraven, and had worked diplomatic miracles. The country had certainly lost a good deal of territory, but the main thing was the restoration of peace. The people in the provinces had food again, famine no longer threatened them, and they were beginning to live as prosperously as they had once before.

As she crossed the bridge, Malva always glanced at the paghul crops that now grew all along the river banks. She thought wistfully of Hob and Lei. She hadn't had news of them for months.

At last she began the climb to the Upper Town. The shutters of the shops were open, there was hustle and bustle on the terraces outside the taverns. Noble Dons shared tables with tattooed sailors, Donias in silk skirts sat beside old fortune-tellers from Tildesia. Small children played around the fountains, and sometimes foreign visitors arrived with exotic animals on leashes: allicaitors, Aremican carcayotes or kangustis from

426

Frigia. Malva wondered if a tourist might arrive some day mounted on a nuba-nuba or a celestial-charioteer . . . or even an enlil, the creature domesticated and ridden by the Amoyeds! She shuddered at the memory. She had seen so many strange things during her journey.

Arriving at the Campanile, Malva knocked on the door of the McBott house three times. Berthilde walked with difficulty now. It took her a little while to come and open the door.

"Ah, it's you, Princetta!" she smiled.

Once inside, Malva took off her scarf and shook her hair free. Then she let Berthilde lead her to the sitting room.

"I've brought you some rhubarb macaroons today," she said, sitting on the sofa.

Berthilde gave her lemonade, and they spent several hours together talking quietly. Their favourite subject was Orpheus. Malva wanted to know everything about him as a child and a young man, about Merixel and Hannibal, and Galnicia in the old days.

Berthilde told stories, repeated herself, and scratched her head as she sought her memories. What fascinated Malva most was the story of the last meeting between Orpheus and his father. She trembled every time Berthilde told her the details of their conversation, but she never tired of living through the scene.

"But I wonder what good it does for me to tell you all this," sighed Berthilde. "You're so young—it troubles me to see you always looking back at the past. What are you going to do with these details?"

Malva smiled mysteriously. She knew exactly what she was going to do with them.

Around midday she left Berthilde and went back to the

427

Citadel. The throne needed her presence: she had people to receive, ambassadors to send into the provinces, and many important decisions to make.

One of those decisions concerned Finopico.

Malva summoned the new directors of the Maritime Institute and told them to dispatch a scientific expedition to prove that the Ghoom of the Deeps really existed.

The scientists protested: the creature was only a mythical being, they said.

"I like mythical beings," retorted the Princetta. "Without them we'd have no dreams to pursue."

She spread the sea chart out on the large table in the Hall of Delicacies, picked up a pen and drew a line round the place where the *Estafador* had sunk. Then she showed the scar on her leg. Much impressed, the scientists stopped objecting. It was decided that the expedition would set out a month later.

Another decision Malva made involved the map-makers. She summoned them too, and showed them the piece of paper on which Orpheus had drawn his map of the Archipelago.

"You must throw away the old maps and sea charts," she said. "I want you to make new ones including the islands to the south of the Known World."

The map-makers turned pale. Pushing back the limits of the Known World was impossible! But Malva would not take no for an answer. Above the drawing, she wrote in large letters *The Archipelago of Orpheus*.

"That will be the official name of the region from this day on. Now get to work!"

The map-makers nodded and went away with the drawing. Malva sighed. She had wondered for a moment whether to ask for Elgolia to be added to the new maps. In the end, she decided that Elgolia should remain secret, hidden. A dream, in fact.

Some time later the Coronador died.

The next was Berthilde.

Malva founded an orphanage for street children in the old McBott house: The Peppe Institute. There would be no dark cells or harsh treatment in the orphanage; she would see to that in person.

Later still, the scientific expedition came back from the Sea of Ypree. After months of research, the holds of the ships were full of strange and unknown fish. None of them looked anything like the Ghoom of the Deeps.

To the despair of the Institute scientists, Malva sent out a second expedition. She would continue to send them until the *Finopicuum de profundis* took its place in the official books.

Winter came again. Philomena and Uzmir had their horses saddled and set off for the steppes. It was time for them to rejoin their people. Philomena cried and Hainur, standing on his horse's back, did a farewell dance for Malva.

They promised to come back next summer to see her.

At last Malva received a letter from the kingdom of Balmun. It was signed by Lei and Hob.

They told her about their many adventures, the welcome they had found in Lei's family, and the days of festivities that followed. Both were very well, they said.

The twin stars shine every night here too, Hob wrote, *and I believe the fortune-teller was right . . . for here I am as happy as a prince!*

They ended their letter by asking Malva to give Babilas and

Orpheus a hug from them. Malva decided to write and tell them how Orpheus, in trying to save her life, had lost his own.

That day she went to the graveyard again. Standing in front of Orpheus's grave, she talked and wept for a long time. Then she knelt and kissed the ground.

After that she went back to the Citadel. Babilas was receiving dignitaries from Polvakia and Sperta in the Hall of Delicacies, so Malva discreetly disappeared.

She went to shut herself in the alcove, drew the curtains, lit a candle, opened a notebook and sat down at her dressing table. As she gazed at her own reflection, she remembered again the day she had decided to run away. The words of the letter she had hidden here behind the mirror came back to her. But her rebellion, her anger and disgust no longer tormented her. She had shaken off that painful past. So the time had come . . .

She dipped her pen in the ink.

On the first page she wrote the title of the story she was going to tell. It was called *The Princetta and the Captain*.

Then, writing feverishly, she began: *To the north, the walls of the Citadel dropped straight to a sheer precipice. Perched there on its rock, it looked like a watchful bird of prey, unfolding its towers and wings above the valley and casting its imposing shadow on the calm waters of the River Gdavir.*

She wrote all night, her words reviving the distant days when she still knew nothing of the joys and sorrows of the world, and bringing back to life all who had accompanied her on her fabulous journey.

THE END

430

Anne-Laure Bondoux has written many books for children and adults in her native France, including *The Killer's Tears*, a Mildred L. Batchelder Honor Book; the Linus Hoppe books; and the People of the Rats trilogy. About writing *The Princetta* she says: "When I was ten, I devoured stories about explorers. I asked my parents for a world map and hung it above my bed. On it, in pencil, I traced the itineraries of Marco Polo, Phileas Fogg, Ulysses, Magellan and Michael Strogoff. Real or make-believe, these characters fascinated me, and I swore that one day I, too, would circumnavigate the world." A former educator and journalist, Anne-Laure lives in Paris with her husband and two children.

Anthea Bell has translated numerous children's books, including *Dragon Rider* by Cornelia Funke and *The Story of Anne Frank* by Mirjam Pressler. She lives in London.

DISCOVER MORE ENCHANTING STORIES BY

● *The Books*

★ "A magical retelling of the Grimms' fairy tale. . . . Hale's retelling is a wonderfully rich one, full of eloquent description and lovely imagery. . . . Fans of high fantasy will be delighted with this novel."
—*SLJ*, starred review

"Enchanting. . . . A beautiful coming-of-age story."
—*The New York Times Book Review*

"Powerful and romantic."
—*Kirkus Reviews*

"This novel's pulsing heart lies in rich writing and sharply drawn characters, elements that will be devoured by genre fans just like kindling beneath flames."
—*Booklist*

AWARD-WINNING AUTHOR SHANNON HALE

of Bayern ✴

★ "Hale makes profound statements about war and peace, friends and strangers, men and women and all the different kinds of battle. Her language glimmers like firelight, like sunshine on water as she propels readers along a river of wonderful writing to the tumultuous and heart-tugging climax." —*Kirkus Reviews*, starred review

★ "[A] stirring, stand-alone adventure. . . . Suspenseful, magical, and heartfelt, this is a story that will wholly envelop its readers." —*Booklist*, starred review

★ "This novel will be a special treat for readers of Hale's other two companion books, but it also stands on its own as a unique and tender coming-of-age story." —*Publishers Weekly*, starred review

★ "This high fantasy is rich in detail and lyrical in writing. While it helps to have read the two previous books, *River Secrets* stands on its own. But fans of the genre will no doubt rejoice in immersing themselves in this magical world by reading all three." —*SLJ*, starred review

Look for Shannon Hale's new novel

In this little-known fairy tale from the Brothers Grimm, Shannon Hale brings fans another heartrending tale of mistaken identity and love gone awry.